VISANTHE
IN
RUIN

First Edition

3 5 7 9 10 8 6 4 2

Saint John's, Antigua
West Indies

Copyright © 2023 L. M. Sanguinette
All rights reserved.

ISBN: 979-8-9868910-3-3

Visit the author's website at
https://lmsanguinette.wordpress.com

DEDICATION

To those who find themselves on unexpected journeys, and
those who are still searching.

VISANTHE
IN
RUIN

L. M. SANGUINETTE

CONTENTS

Yozora
Osiir
Mid
Camp Saar
Araldin Fields
Red Desert

HAIZEA
ILISO
DLE ISLE
SOLIA
IDUNE

PROLOGUE

THE TALLEST TOWER in the Ur kingdom sat on a desolate rock in the middle of the ocean. It commanded a view of the other islands in the archipelago, the most dominant of which were the mainland of Solia, and the crescent-shaped wall of ice and mountains known as Iliso. The tower was guarded by a shifting mist that, if inhaled, could cause disorientation and memory loss. The price of trespass was great, but the contents of the tower were priceless—vital to the survival of the Ur—and their safety was not to be taken lightly.

The only unhindered glimpse of the outside world came from a small balcony that wrapped around the top of the tower like a lighthouse. There, a woman with hair bleached white by the sun and skin as dark as volcanic soil paced back and forth, scanning the dawn sky for a cloud.

Her task, although tedious, was vital to her people's survival. The outer island of Iliso and its icy terrain was guarded by the infamous General Kyara and her winter soldiers, but the inner islands were her domain. No one had ever breached the inner islands of the Ur nation, much less the forbidden tower she protected. Even if an enemy army managed to cross that first threshold into Solia, they would still face an insurmountable challenge in her.

As she waited, a stray cloud appeared on the horizon. She watched as it drifted closer until she could feel the entirety of it, even down to the raindrops that comprised it, with her outstretched hand. She inhaled deeply, gathering her strength for the task she had been performing for over forty years. Her fingers twisted and turned, seizing the droplets in the cloud as though they were right in front of her, and not miles out to sea. Few could manipulate water from such a distance. She had been specially trained for this task, handpicked by her predecessor. She had learned to sense the moisture in the air. Her control extended even up to as far as a few miles. She was taught to think of all the water in her reach as a tapestry. To move a single cloud, all she had to do was pull a thread.

With a deep exhale, she made a graceful circular motion with her palms, drawing the cloud closer before releasing it into the sea of them that shielded their archipelago from the outside world. Day in and day out, she moved the clouds into formation, creating an army of overstuffed soldiers, barricading their kingdom against any threat. As one of the smaller nations in Visanthe, the Ur had to be cunning and resourceful to maintain their independence. If ever attacked,

General Kyara and her soldiers could transform the droplets in the cloud army into icy weapons. But few, if any, could navigate the sea of clouds to even reach Solia. In the three hundred years since its creation, no enemy had succeeded.

CHAPTER 1

UNWELCOME WATERS

THE SHIP ROCKED GENTLY with the twilight currents, a sensation that had lulled most of its occupants into a pleasant, dreamless sleep, but the young human aboard this galleon of magical beings was too agitated for even the most nightmarish sleep. As a result, Griffin found himself at the receiving end of the agitated lecture. Thankfully, he hadn't been able to sleep either; otherwise, he would've contemplated murder.

A headache had been brewing in him ever since they'd left port. No amount of meditation or water had yet been able to quell it. To make matters worse, the human came in with a fury.

"You promised you would find her!" Jasper yelled, sending resting gulls flapping from their perches atop the crow's nest into the night skies. The starlight danced across their feathered backs as they circled and settled once more into their nests.

Griffin rubbed his temples. "I know what I said," he hissed, trying not to wake the whole ship or whatever sea monsters he'd been told lived in these dark waters. "But the situation required a different approach."

"What about your friend in the army?" Jasper prodded. "He must know something."

"General Isaac is unavailable for conversation," Griffin sighed, remembering the conversation they'd had after the battle. Jasper didn't need to know of the mess they'd left behind or the threats mounting against them. He'd only insist on them turning back and searching for Savara themselves. But there were bigger problems at hand that demanded their attention.

Griffin downed another glass of water and an awful-tasting syrup that Brass had made for him once he'd told him they would be embarking on their journey by way of water. It had the double effect of soothing his stomach from the swaying of the ship and taking away any stress-induced migraines that reared their ugly heads.

"We can't just sit on our hands and wait. We've got to do something," Jasper scoffed.

"What makes you think I haven't?" Griffin growled as he crossed his arms over his chest. The move had the unintentional effect of reminding Jasper what had happened during their time in the Harri territories, though he knew Jasper was the last person who needed reminding of anything. Griffin's burns from the battle in Idune had all but disappeared, leaving only light patches of scarring on his forearms. It had been a gruelling fight, but in the end, they had all made it out relatively unscathed. The physical scars would fade eventually. The mental ones concerned him.

It had only been a fortnight since the battle and the group was still worse for wear. Storm was bound to using her right arm for the time being, but she'd be better soon enough. She was too stubborn to let the injury stop her. Sebastian had been spared from any great injury, though he spent most of his mental energy worrying about Storm's condition and annoyed at her refusals of his help. There was Lance, his childhood best friend whom he'd once thought…

No. Griffin forbade himself from finishing the thought. *No more wishful thinking.* Eventually, they'd have to speak. Maybe not of their shared past, but at the very least of what future lay ahead. Right now, the thought of him would only bring on the desire for a drink, and that would do no one any good.

And then there was Jasper, the painful human whose voice was, at present, only adding to the throbbing in his head. Jasper kept himself up most of the night worrying about *her.* Griffin wouldn't admit it aloud, but this was something they had in common.

"Yes, but—"

"Your feelings for Savara apart, we do have other matters to take care of. Do we not?" Griffin reminded him.

They'd made a deal. First, they would find a way to restore her memories, then they'd save her from whatever mess she found herself in. If the information in the bloodthirsty book was to be believed, they needed Savara to remember the time before her divination. Until then, she was relatively useless, which also meant she was safe.

Jasper pressed his glasses to his nose and stared at the ground, the anger in him subsiding, replaced by something of a more sober nature.

"Yes," he mumbled, the word barely a whisper. He tugged at his sleeve, holding back words Griffin knew he'd never speak without help, but with another heavy exhale, he instead turned for the door.

"How is it?" Griffin asked, tone softening to put Jasper at ease. "Your… condition?" His eyes hitched on the black veins tracing the length of Jasper's arm, the ones he'd tried to hide under his long-sleeved tunic. Griffin had seen those marks before, though it hadn't occurred to him when he began seeing them on Jasper that they were of the same origin. His father's arms were riddled with them in his lifetime.

It was those books. Whatever knowledge they contained came at a deadly price. If Griffin had put the two together sooner, he might have worked harder at dissuading Jasper of their charm.

Jasper tucked his arm behind his back guiltily. "I've had better days."

"If it becomes too much…"

"I'm fine, Griffin," Jasper hissed. "Don't forget, I'm not doing it for you."

"I haven't forgotten anything, but you will not be able to protect her if you cannot protect yourself," Griffin replied.

Jasper avoided his gaze, but Griffin knew his words had landed. Jasper's dedication to his friend was admirable. A small pang of guilt appeared in his chest. If he were in Jasper's position, nothing and no one would sway him. He knew that his words, and what little guidance they might offer, would not be enough to convince Jasper otherwise, but they might give him pause for the time being.

"I left Brass in Idune to see what he can find out about her disappearance," Griffin added, hoping to lift his spirits, even if only slightly. "If there's something to be found, he'll be the one to find it." Jasper nodded, his frown lifting as he headed for the door. "It's probably best to leave that book alone for now. It's already taken enough of you…" Griffin called out to him. All he saw was the back of Jasper's head, but Griffin sensed his apprehension at the words. Jasper's pause lasted only a moment. In the next, the door closed heavily behind him, leaving Griffin alone to his thoughts.

The slivers of moonlight danced across the wooden floor, shifting with the soft currents beneath the ship. Griffin strode over to the porthole at the far end of his room, opened the latch, and poked his head out. He took a deep breath, letting the sea breeze fill his lungs. Its salty scent brought him back to the shores of Yozora where he'd spent the better part of his winters training to be the soldier his father would be proud of.

The royal guards had never been known for their compassionate training methods, but compared to the time spent with his father, even the days in which he'd been stretched out and pushed to his breaking point seemed like bliss. Now, many years later, he was thankful for their strict and torturous methods of training. At least he was prepared. There was a war coming, and not everyone was going to make it through, but Griffin would be damned if he didn't do everything in his power to keep his friends safe.

Jasper cared about Savara the way he cared about his friends. Griffin knew that, if it came to it, Jasper would lay down his life for her. It was admirable of him, endearing even. Jasper was a curious creature; so very human, and yet, so readily adapted to Visanthian life, as if he'd been bred for it from the beginning. Griffin shook his head, entertaining himself with the idea that he'd even begun to care for that powerless lump of skin and bone.

As he stared up at the night sky, his mind wandered back to their final night in Idune and the grave conversation he'd had with General Isaac, the one he neglected to share, knowing it would only make Jasper worry more.

* * *

"They are elevating General Dhoot to the Council," said General Isaac. He'd schooled his features into indifference, but the tension in his voice said otherwise.

General Dhoot, the commander of one of the largest divisions of the Harri army, was nothing but trouble. Griffin had sensed as much from their previous encounter. Bloodlust and a desire for power lingered beneath his polished exterior.

"They can't be serious," growled Griffin. "Have they skimmed over the other possible successors? Lady Amaia couldn't have agreed—"

"Lady Amaia has less sway with the council now that Lord Ori, may he rest in peace, is no longer at its head."

Griffin narrowed his eyes at his friend. "And who is?"

"The leader of all Harri armed forces himself, Lord Andor." General Isaac admitted. "Considering that the world may very well be at war, the council, and the people, thought it best to have a more… militaristic leadership going forward."

"They can't possibly believe that General Dhoot has the best interests of the nation in mind," Griffin scoffed.

"That, my friend, is exactly what they believe." General Isaac bit his lip. "He has more sway than anyone because of his popularity with the aristocrats—and plebeians, I might add."

"I'm sure there's someone else who could serve as a military figurehead…" Griffin thought aloud, continuing his incessant pacing across the floors of the darkened war room. "What about you? Couldn't you—"

General Isaac raised a hand to interrupt. "Thanks for the vote of confidence, my friend, but I am being reassigned."

"Reassigned?"

"To head up the troops on the western front and keep the peace on the border with the Argia. After the attack on Idune, people fear there are more fires to come and think it's best to keep relations with the Argia *contained*."

"They're moving you from the capital?"

General Isaac frowned, no longer able to meet his eyes. "I'm afraid so…"

"I'm at no loss as to who might have suggested such a thing," Griffin growled, halting his steps as he processed the gravity of General Isaac's words. "That means they are taking you out of negotiations?"

"Correct." The pair exchanged a nervous glance before General Isaac added, "If news gets out to General Kyara of the Ur that we have lost Lord Ori, we might have a full-scale invasion along the entire eastern border."

"She wouldn't risk her army for a tiny plot of land. Not when she knows of the Harri nation's strength."

"She would, knowing how that might favour her in trade, and if the only person who was able to reason with her is now dead." General Isaac stiffened. "If word gets out of Lord Ori's death—"

"I am afraid, my friend, it is no longer a matter of if but when."

General Isaac blanched. "Well, then… when word gets out," he corrected, "there will be nothing and no one to stop her."

Ever since Griffin took Savara to the palace at Osiir, he'd known that her memories had been tampered with. His own, too, if the lapsus at her divination was anything to go by. He had already planned to make a trip to the Ur islands. Somewhere in Solia, there was an old Ur woman who had been long branded a witch for her ability to turn a potion. Maybe it was worth it to pay a visit to Iliso, and hope, for everyone's sake, that General Kyara was in the mood to listen to reason.

"Thank you, my friend," said Griffin with a heavy sigh. "You have given me much to think about." He turned for the door, readying his mind for the journey ahead of them, when General Isaac called him back.

"I know that look, Griffin," said General Isaac, his voice serious. "Do not get yourself involved in this war."

A smile tugged at Griffin's lips as he cocked an eyebrow. "I have no idea what you are talking about."

"You forget, we were sparring partners for over two years. I know your planning look intimately," General Isaac reminded him, a wry smile tugging at the corner of his mouth. He pulled a piece of parchment from a pile on the war table and began to scribble. When he finished, he clapped his hand on Griffin's back and handed him the note. "If you do somehow manage to get yourself into trouble, I'll be positioned at this station."

"Should I take offence to your surety at me landing myself in trouble?"

General Isaac laughed. "You also forget, it seems, the many times we spent cleaning the floors of the kitchens because of your landing us in trouble."

"How could I forget? I'm still picking the grime out of my fingernails." The two shared another laugh before Griffin added, "Thank you, my friend."

"No, thank you. It is twice now that you have saved my life, and I am not sure how much of these debts I will be able to settle."

"If all goes well, you will take them to a distant grave."

General Isaac nodded.

Griffin slipped out of the room without so much as a goodbye. He pocketed the piece of parchment and made off to find his friends. A war between the Harri and the Ur would be a problem, but if the final goal of the Arima lay in collecting legends, no nation would be spared from the bloodshed.

CHAPTER 2

COCOA AND CONVERSATIONS

JASPER COULDN'T SLEEP, and his conversation with Griffin left him feeling uneasy. He paced the length of the deck, contemplating all that was said, with only the stars for company. The sound of waves gently knocking against the ship's hull reminded him of his childhood days when his parents urged him to learn sailing, thinking it was a useful skill for an island boy. He never thought he would find himself on a galleon like the ones he read about in historical articles, the kind adventurers and explorers used to traverse the globe before it was determined to be a globe and not a plane.

The child in him still marvelled at the fact that there was an entirely new world, inhabited by all the creatures that filled his fairy tales and mythology books. The adult in him even wondered if those ancient adventurers he admired had also stumbled across this world. But the rest of him focused on the trouble at hand, not to be distracted by the things that reminded him of home and the island he'd left behind—the one that sat waiting, in another world, with the promise of expeditions to already known places and the studies of things that would have little bearing over his personal life.

The black veins tracing his arm acted as a constant reminder of how this world differed from the one he'd grown up in. Jasper regretted not heeding Griffin's warning that nothing good was traded in blood. He was so determined to get Savara home that he would have paid whatever price he had to—and did. But Savara was nowhere to be seen, and to add insult to injury, the book had syphoned out part of his life. Now, staring down at the wiry outlines beneath his skin, he regretted his stubbornness.

Jasper removed his glasses and proceeded to clean the lenses with his sleeve as he pondered his actions. He had never been this stubborn before, and he always thought things through. Why now did he feel this way? Maybe part of it was the need to prove to himself that he wasn't useless, to show he could hold his own in the face of men like Griffin. Deep down he knew that the other part was to prove his love for her. Either way, his every emotion had been heightened since he crossed. This world seemed to corrupt all that it touched, and not even knowing this made him immune to its charm.

None of that mattered now, he realised as he replaced his glasses. His best friend was missing in a world he knew very little about, and what little he did know terrified him. There was nothing that he or anyone else could do but hope. When his feet grew numb from the constant pacing, Jasper leaned himself up against the railing and stared out into the grand expanse of darkened sea.

For all of Griffin's moaning about not awakening things that shouldn't be woken, he found it surprisingly peaceful. *This world wasn't all bad,* he thought to himself, watching the shimmering reflection of the bright moon on the black water.

Jasper had been enchanted by this world the moment he touched its soil, as anyone else who was fascinated by old mythology would have been. If his old professor could see him now, living among the cultures they had only briefly covered because of their "most likely fictitious" origins, he would probably have a heart attack on the spot. But Jasper realised that this world, like all worlds, contained dark secrets that would keep anyone, regardless of their origin, up at night.

It wasn't so much the fact that some of the people in this world had powers—the magic of the elements running through their veins to conjure on a whim—or the fact that he had been roped into a war between nations and barely survived. No. What terrified him was something that could affect not only this world but his world as well. It was something he had learned from the same book that had caused the spider's web of blackened veins beneath his skin. A prophecy, a warning, and one they couldn't escape. For now, all they could do was wait and see how the events unfolded.

Jasper stared down at his darkened veins, the weight of his secret resting heavily on his heart. Only Griffin knew the truth of his condition, though he figured Storm suspected something by the way she'd always narrowed her eyes at his arms before addressing him. At least, now that he'd survived, she addressed him by his name. Since then, Griffin had started to warm up to him as well, to the point where Jasper wondered if it wasn't just pity on Griffin's part.

Griffin had made him swear to keep the secret from the rest of the group, saying there was no use in scaring anyone. It was a terrible secret, but one that must be kept, nonetheless. Jasper agreed though he knew it was only a matter of time before the elements of the legend were set in motion. Soon, Savara would find out—if she hadn't already. Soon, they all would.

Jasper thought of her now, wondering where she was and hoping it wasn't already too late. After all, she was the reason he'd gone searching for the information and allowed the book to infiltrate his mind. She might just be the reason the book was created in the first place. A sad smile graced his face as he thought back on his motives. He'd rightfully assumed the book contained information that would help Savara understand her past, but the truth within the pages was something darker than he'd ever imagined. She, his best friend, and the person he most admired in the whole wide world, was an instrument of darkness, the likes of which the world hasn't seen for centuries. A Harbinger of Death. The sinister legend had cost him part of his soul to attain, and whatever remained was at the mercy of fate, an entity to which, until now, Jasper hadn't given a second thought.

"Legend of the stones?" He mused to himself. "More like a tale of blood and bonds."

Suddenly, thunder cracked loudly above him. Jasper fixed the spectacles that Griffin had given him on his nose and gazed up at the sky. Grey clouds had swept over the stars, snuffing them out one by one. The scent of rain filled his nose as he sucked in and released a deep, steadying breath.

"You'd better get inside," called the captain. "A storm through the night brings one hell of a bite," she added melodically.

Jasper quickly rolled down the length of sleeve to cover his arms and grinned at the busty, self-assured woman strutting down the deck towards him with two cups of steaming cocoa. Her boots clopped heavily on the old pine flooring, punctuated by the jangling of her many gold bangles. She swished her tight, sun-bleached, white curls from her face and batted her sparkling blue eyes at him. "I've never heard that one before."

"That's because you've never sailed from Yozora to Haizea in the winter," she laughed, handing him a mug. "And trust me, you wouldn't want to, either." She leaned next to him and stared up at the clouds. "We're in for a long night."

"You can tell that just by looking at a cloud?" Jasper asked.

"When you've been a sailor as long as I have, you can hear it in the wind, taste it on your tongue, feel it in your bones…" She took a deep, warming sip and sighed in delight. "Time is one hell of a teacher."

"Please, you don't look that old."

"You're cute," she replied, patting his cheek with a hand that the cocoa had warmed. "You better get inside before you catch a cold. I'm not a healer, and I don't do sick people."

"I'm not that bad at sea," Jasper replied.

"No…" she smirked, "I've seen worse. But there's no denying the rain is coming."

Jasper propped himself up against the railing again as he sipped his cocoa. *Sav always could tell when there was a storm coming,* he thought with a soft smile, imagining it was her standing beside him. He nodded and gazed out at the danger lurking on the horizon rather than seeking out warmer lodgings.

The captain imitated his posture as she spoke over the lingering echo of another loud clap of thunder. "You don't seem like Griffin's usual brand of troublemaking playmate."

Jasper laughed under his breath as he turned to her with a warmer smile. "Should I be offended?"

A streak of sheet lightning lit up the bow of the ship, causing her curls and toothy smile to glow. "I'd say it's an improvement on his part."

"You sound like you've got a fair bit of dirt on him. Care to share?"

"We sea captains don't do dirt. We do gems; lock 'em away in chests, and only bring them out when it's in our interest to do so," she chuckled. "And we definitely don't share."

"Wouldn't that, and the fact that we're on your ship at his request, imply that you yourself are or were at least once his 'usual brand of troublemaking playmate'?" Jasper mused.

"Hmm… Clever…" She raised a coquettish eyebrow. "I like clever. Not enough to share details, but I will admit he and I have a history…"

"Ah."

"Not the romantic kind. That kid hasn't a romantic bone in his body—or at least none that he's consciously aware of," she said, glancing at the floor. Jasper knew Griffin was somewhere below deck in one of the rooms beneath them.

"Charm, though, he's got shipfuls of that… He may not be on his own now, but something tells me he's still the lost kid I met all those years ago, and still very much alone…" The captain smiled a melancholic smile. "But then, I've said too much already."

They finished their cocoa just in time for the rain. It started as a light shower, giving them the chance to head indoors before the real downpour began.

Jasper's image of Griffin differed vastly from the captain's. Where he saw fierce calculation, she saw a fearful child. Which was he? And what did that mean for the rest of them? Jasper followed the corridor towards his cabin. Before retiring, he turned back to her and waved goodnight, finding her eyes had never once left his person.

"You know, people believe the sharpest cuts are made by blades," she began as her eyes fell to his arm. "They're wrong. The sharpest cuts are made by secrets." The captain donned a sad smile before entering her room, leaving Jasper alone with her words and his secrets.

CHAPTER 3

FIVE TO GO

THE APPRENTICE SKULKED around the chamber, anxiously awaiting his master. The Prince of Shadows only summoned him on the rarest and most unpleasant of occasions, but there was no telling as to why he'd been summoned this time.

The ordeal in Idune was over.

Five gemstoned slits remained etched into the skin of his back, each one the promise of a stone. Five of seven. Four of which whose locations were known, and one yet to be seen. Five of seven scars, and, as collateral, five of seven bits of his soul.

He'd memorised the exact conditions of the soul bonds and had repeated their terms in his sleep for the better part of fifteen years. Even in his youth, he'd known of the legends surrounding the Prince of Shadows, and of his trouble. He especially knew not to make deals with spirits; it was the one decent thing his mother had taught him. But anything, even a spirit darker than any known to man, was preferable to the life he'd led before. Every so often, the city of stars would call to him, luring him home with the promise of star falls and midnight feasts and a chamber in a castle lined with books and a single grand piano. But he learned from a young age that a city bathed in starlight held more shadows, more unpleasant secrets than anyone would care to admit. That's why, he supposed, the hollow halls and darkened corridors of the empty shadow palace seemed more welcoming. At least here, he was the thing in the dark.

The Apprentice pulled a small metal trinket from an inner coat pocket and flipped open its lid. To anyone who didn't know, the ornate object looked somewhat like a pocket watch. But a trained eye would see through the clever disguise of the casing, notice the polished obsidian disk sitting within, and name it for what it was, a scrying mirror. For those moments when he couldn't read the stars, he'd resolved to seek visions within the darkness. Two sides to the same power—one heralded, the other frowned upon. But such prejudice was yet another reason to leave home.

Tonight, however, neither the darkness nor the stars had anything to say. No explanation regarding his current summoning to the palace of spirits. The Apprentice closed the lid and replaced the scrying mirror in his pocket. Times were dark indeed if not even the shadows wished to speak. He continued his pacing up and down the corridor, when a tingling sensation ran through his scarred palm, stopping him dead in his tracks. He frowned as he contemplated the jagged star-shaped mark.

She's afraid, he realised. A feeling he'd come to recognise as shame formed in the pit of his stomach. He'd already done too much as it was to protect her, and still it felt… insufficient, somehow. At first, he'd believed it was only the effect of the stones, these sudden twinges of feeling, but he'd since figured out that each moment spent with her brought back some of what he'd lost, even if just for a little while. The stars had asked him to keep her alive, nothing more. He didn't have to care about her state of being or her emotions. Quite frankly, he didn't have to care about her at all. And yet, every sensation that rattled through his scar gave him pause.

If he was honest with himself, this concern for her was beginning to get on his nerves. Each memory he had of her haunted his every waking moment. Where his mind had once been uniquely consumed by his task, he now found thoughts of her slipping in. And nightmares. Before her, he didn't have nightmares—granted, his sleep wasn't exactly peaceful either. He'd replayed their last encounter in his mind many times to the point where the resentment marring her face as he disappeared—as he left her to other captors—was ingrained in his skull.

It was supposed to happen this way. The stars had told him so, though, after having put the current crusade in his head, he never did like listening to the wretched things. They never seemed to tell him anything good. This however was important. Painful, but important—apparently. There was more she had to learn, and she wouldn't learn it holed up with her little friends in that camp of theirs.

His hand trembled again.

Part of him wished he could run to her now, even against the stars' wishes, but his master was waiting. Instead, he stared down at his palm, wondering just what kind of horrors she was facing.

Souls like yours attract the broken, he'd said. Before her, such a phrase would never have graced his lips, but meeting her changed everything.

The thing inside him made a mistake when it broke the capsule in his palm. Part of her remained embedded in the scar tissue, tingling every time she felt strongly. He'd taken to staring at it frequently, more so since she returned to Visanthe. The connection strengthened with proximity. As he looked at it now—the violent remains of glass burrowing itself into flesh—he almost smiled. If the thing inside him had only known what would come of this act, it might not have been so adamant.

But that was always the problem with these kinds of monsters; they were short-sighted.

The rumble of oak against black marble startled him back to reality. The Apprentice ran his fingers through the raven-coloured locks on his head, letting out a heavy sigh as he prepared himself for what lay beyond the doors. He smoothed out his coat and allowed his feet to carry him, as they had many times before, into the chamber.

The Prince of Shadows sat haughtily on the gilded, wiry throne that had been fashioned into the shape of a star. Thin, veiny streams of something akin to stardust floated near the ceiling above him, seeping through the cracks in the palace walls and spilling out into the stagnant world beyond. In his fingers, The Prince of Shadows turned over two stones identical in shape and size: one glowed bright orange like the dawn sun, and the other a jade green. His beady, plum-coloured eyes sought out his apprentice through the shifting darkness of the various sconces and soul matter. A smile curled on his lips.

"You have done well, my child," The Prince of Shadows said, breaking the silence of the room. The Apprentice replied with only a ceremoniously low bow. He usually held his tongue with his master unless explicitly spoken to. As careful as he was with his words, he was hardly better than a new-born when compared to his master, and even the tiniest slip up could have dire consequences. "And yet, I sense I have been too lenient with you." With a twist of his wrist, the two stones disappeared from his hand. "Our work is not yet finished," added The Prince of Shadows, abandoning his chair and stalking towards him. "Are you up to the task?" the Prince of Shadows asked.

From out of nowhere, a creature—a terrifying, winged panther with eyes as red as blood and fur as black as night—appeared. It stretched and fluttered its wings, making a graceful round of the floor before coming to rest at his master's side. He'd seen this fearsome beast before. It was an ageless creature, as unique as its master, born of the night and bred to ferry souls from this world to the one beyond.

"Yes, my prince," The Apprentice replied, cautious of the threats mounting against him.

The Prince of Shadows bent down before him and lifted his chin, glaring deep into his eyes. The Apprentice pushed whatever doubts he had into the darkest corner of his mind, hoping they remained just out of reach. "I will not accept failure," his master added.

"I will not fail," he replied.

The panther stalked behind him, a low growl emanating from its heavy chest.

"No, you will not," The Prince of Shadows agreed, turning back to his throne, when an echoing whistle sounded from his lips.

Suddenly, The Apprentice felt the sharp sting of claws streaking across his back, each one corresponding to the remaining slits, renewing the bonds left many years prior. He clenched his jaw, forcing himself to remain steady despite the pain. His doubts remained, as did his feelings, but the renewed urgency of the fresh bonds drowned out even the sharpest of cries from within.

No, he realised. The masters of spirits themselves watched over him closely now. No, he could not fail.

CHAPTER 4

CONVERSATIONS WITH NO ONE

"SHE MUST BE REMOVED, Anissa. There's no other way," said the youthful-looking leader with floating white hair and ageless caramel skin. The clarity and decisiveness of her voice betrayed her advanced age. She spoke softly, but there was no remorse in her words—no comfort either.

"She's just a child!" roared her mother, though their eyes hadn't met since she'd slipped those accursed rings on her finger.

Savara had known it was a bad idea to go through with the Divination. She'd felt it in her bones, that feeling of wrongness, of something unnatural in the nature of her mark. She had never told anyone of her feelings. How could she? Her mother had been on her case about receiving said mark and the importance of their powerline for as long as she could remember. Savara almost wondered if it wasn't her mother's overly wishful thinking that brought the mark into existence last minute. She wished she had managed to burn the stupid thing off. That way, she wouldn't have to sit through any more of this conversation that decided her fate—the one to which she was not allowed to object or intervene. Savara did what she always had in such situations; hold her tongue, retreat, and act as if the rest of the world didn't exist. It didn't bring her any comfort this time, but then… it never truly did.

As the adults spoke around her, Savara's mind retreated to the last conversation she'd had with the entity in the palace—a non-corporeal spirit that roamed the halls and gardens—watching over it and her… or so he said. A spirit who called himself *No One*.

No One had told her that the ceremonies were nothing to be feared, that he'd seen countless children of the sun pass through them without fear. She could tell that even he had been concerned about her mark, especially the ominous timing of it.

No One claimed to be from a time before divinations. A time when children were born with their powers. A time that both praised and feared the elemental magic of the world. The divinations took away that fear. *No One* claimed they took away a lot more, but he refused to elaborate. *No One* had once even let slip that he was surprised she could hear him, for there had not been anyone with such a talent since his lifetime. It was sometime around their first encounter, an offhanded, wary compliment that he assumed she would've forgotten. But, in a palace where she blended into the shadows, the words of acknowledgement had stuck with her despite their caution.

"A child who will grow up to be a problem, Anissa," added the Harri lord, rousing Savara from her memories. The Harri lord hadn't paid much attention to her during the ceremony, but the moment the star-shaped platform deposited her on the empty sixth point, he hadn't taken his cautious, two-toned eyes from her. "*Their* kind are—"

"I don't care about *their* kind!" her mother yelled, the anger fraying at the delicate edges of her usually sweet voice. "She is *my* kind, *my* child. What do you know about having a child?"

The Harri lord looked close to speaking, but held his tongue instead, knowing better than to challenge a queen of fire.

"Anissa, my dear, be reasonable," whispered the Zerua king from behind his cloud-ridden beard. "We must think of what is best for our people."

The Zerua king's eyes were apologetic as they contemplated her. Savara had fonder memories of him. He was the only ruler she had ever come to know at any length, and therefore the only one who showed any sympathy towards her situation.

On one of the many occasions her mother had "requested" she join a political trip to Haizea, Savara had managed to get lost in the palace gardens as a heavy fog set in. Rather than crying out for her mother, she lay on the ground and began drawing shapes in the mist. The old man, who she later found out was the king of all Zerua territories, caught a glimpse of her strange act and, instead of admonishing her like her mother later did, joined in her play. He summoned light breezes to shape the mist into figures—birds, butterflies, even a dragon. Savara was ecstatic. Her mother, not so much.

It was later revealed that her mother had threatened to burn the entire place down in search of her. This had all happened right around the time Lance disappeared, and if she had put the two together sooner, she might have realised her mother was being overprotective of her *because* of Lance. But when they arrived home, her mother went about ignoring her again as if nothing had happened.

"Anissa, this child will not replace the boy you lost," the Izar leader added.

Her mother's rage exploded at the mention of Lance, consuming the space around her in blinding white flames. All the leaders shielded their eyes. At that very moment, she could've outshone the sun. But her flames fizzled out quickly under the weight of heavy tears as she dropped to her knees.

Savara had never seen her mother cry. Seeing her now, broken and brought low by the only heir she had left, Savara forgot every harsh and unforgiving comment she'd ever made, every unkind memory of her mother. All of it was replaced by the deep desire to apologise for her very existence.

"If I may..." said the unfriendly voice of the sturdy woman who looked more ice than person. The bright blue of her eyes bore into Savara's skin, piercing her flesh like the sceptre at the woman's side. If Savara could have cried, she would've, but the woman's gaze held her captive, frozen in place like the prisoners that supposedly lined the path to her icy domain. "There might be a way around any… overly dramatic measures."

Savara recoiled, an eerie sensation creeping into her veins. The other adults in the room might not have been able to feel it, but she could. There was more to the ice queen than meets the eye. There was bloodlust in her heart.

* * *

Savara had no idea how long she'd been screaming before the sound of it startled her awake, only that it took her a while to steady herself. It especially didn't help that she'd woken up to the biting cold of a strange room, bound to yet another uncomfortable chair.

Savara furrowed her brow, hoping to alleviate the throbbing in her head. Was that a memory? Clarity of thought was elusive through the pain. Perhaps the whole thing had been a strangely vivid dream. It would not be the first time. But the layers of it were unlike any dream she'd ever had. Memories upon memories. She couldn't shake the sinister feeling taking root in the pit of her stomach. Why now?

She groaned into the emptiness of the room. The last thing she remembered was a hard knock to her head from behind. Could it be that the hit had jogged some of her memories? What if they had been hidden and suppressed all along, and now they were resurfacing? A part of her didn't want to remember, didn't want to confront the darkness that had taken them from her. Dream or not, she had seen the fear in the eyes of world leaders as they contemplated her fate; they looked at her as though she was evil incarnate. But did evil powers make one evil? No, she couldn't be. She wouldn't be.

Still, part of her was left to wonder.

Savara's mind drifted back to her conversation with the Prince of Shadows before her evident capture. Her powers, he'd said, had something to do with spirit, with blood— neither of which sounded good. And then there was the matter of her title, the one he'd called her as though praising a deity. Three little words had never instilled such fear in her before, and she doubted any others would ever come close. She was the Harbinger of Death.

One thing was for certain; Death followed her. She could feel him lingering nearby. He'd taken all the members of her bloodline so far and was watching her next. If she survived, he would doubtless reach out for those she held near and dear. Death was waiting, and she intended to keep him that way.

For now, she pushed those thoughts aside and focused on the present. She needed to figure out a way to make sense of her situation, and fast. As the migraine in her head subsided, a single word roared in a guttural fashion from her throat, consumed by the darkness of her cell.

"Fuck!"

CHAPTER 5

BURNING SKIN

JASPER WOKE TO THAT DREADFUL feeling of fire beneath his skin. The night terrors were in full swing ever since he'd started feeding that book. He shot up in his cot, whipped off the blankets, and ran his nervous fingers through his hair, reminding himself that he was awake—that he was alive. He focused on the breath in his chest as he waited for the remnants of the nightmare to fade. The jumbled mess of cries for help from unknown voices and faces that time forgot had plagued him for the past few nights, and tonight turned out to be no different.

"Not again," he mumbled to himself.

The boat rocked beneath him in the stronger currents of the storm. On a better night, the sensation might have lulled him to sleep. Not tonight. Tears stung the rims of the eyes he wished not to close again, knowing he'd only return to the same scene.

Outside, lightning streaked across the cloudy night sky. The twilight hour stretched on. There was still a ways to go before morning, but Jasper couldn't steady himself. His laboured breath echoed in the emptiness of his cabin. He was exhausted, but there would be no more sleeping. Of this, he was sure. He stared down at his trembling hands, where the blackened veins at his wrists bulged. A world away, he might have believed it to be the result of a disease. Here, he knew better.

The book was syphoning out parts of his life, parts of his soul, trading it for whatever malice laced its pages. With each prick of his fingers, Jasper noticed the streaks of black swirling in each drop of blood, like streaks of oil on water, tingeing it darker and darker as time went on. Had this darkness been a simple question of appearance, he might not have minded as much. But nothing in this world was ever so simple. The knowledge he'd gained from the book had come at a price, and not of blood alone. It cost him his sleep, the breath from his lungs, the warmth from his bones…

Jasper rose from the bed, dragging his feet across the floor towards the cracked mirror hanging on his wall. The dream had left him pale and shivering. His eyes fell on the web of blackened veins trailing from his wrists to his elbows. The sight of them was nauseating.

Yet, nothing—not the nightmares, the veins, the sickness—would deter him.

At this point, the knowledge he'd gained, let alone the act itself, was addictive. When Griffin had first come to him with the task of researching this book and similar ones in his library, Jasper had expected to find catalogues of historical events. The contents of this book alone, however, were a surprise to them both. As was the manner of attaining the information. Myths, legends, rituals—all available to him at the prick of his fingers. A drop of blood—a sliver of his soul—for the truths hidden from the world.

Jasper had already uncovered more secrets than he'd cared to admit. He'd shared many of these with Griffin in their research on the legendary Arima race—the Blood Daemons, as they were colloquially known. However, there were other secrets, darker ones, that he didn't dare share. Secrets he couldn't share. Secrets that not even Griffin would accept.

The first of which was that the god of this world, the thing they called *Iturri*, was actually an entity. A spirit of sorts. One that had more say in the ruling of these lands than it should've, or at least once upon a time. A few centuries ago, it disappeared without explanation. But the voice in the book told him that there was a reason and one he could learn… if only he'd pay the price such information demanded.

More than once he'd been tempted. But he'd yet held strong in his endeavours. His mind was on Savara and her condition, and for the moment, he'd successfully kept any other urges at bay. He could not waste a single drop of blood on knowledge that had no bearing over his task.

The next—and considerably darker—secret that he'd learned from the book terrified him. This one he couldn't share with Griffin, or anyone for that matter, not even should he wish it. He didn't know at what point he'd realised it, between the first drop of blood and the start of the nightmares, but he'd come to know without a doubt that the book held not only malice but a soul. One it intended on using.

Jasper hadn't noticed the effects of it at first, but now, they were as clear to him as his reflection in the mirror. Something inside him was changing. Growing. He could feel it taking root inside him. Whatever soul had been instilled in the book was being merged with his own. The voice that called to him from beyond the leather binding rang through his nightmares. Strength that was not his own flowed through his body, as did knowledge from a life he'd never led. Perhaps that was how he became so adept at sparring in so little time. Perhaps the muscle memory had been there all along, only it hadn't belonged to him. As his own life dimmed, another's grew, one that belonged to something— or someone—else.

A noise from the hallway caught his attention. Jasper stepped away from the door, in case whoever was beyond could hear his breathing. He didn't want any of them to know of his true condition. They had more important things to worry about. He waited at the foot of his cot until the footsteps beyond the door faded down the hall. Once he was sure no one was awake to hear, he reached over for the cane and unsheathed the hidden blade.

In the dim light of the stormy twilight hour, Jasper danced around his room executing a flourish of parries and feints against his shadow. He'd become lighter on his feet, moving around the small cabin with ease, even in spite of the rocking of the ship. The practise was the only thing that truly kept his mind from the book and its secrets. The focus it required lulled him into a state of flow that drowned out any other voices that bounced around between his ears.

Yet, tonight, not even the swordplay could take the words from his mind. The final secret. The legend of the stones.

Only when the end is nigh…

The next streak of lightning brought with it a boom overhead, but not even it could drown out the words.

Seven stones… Seven bonds…

Jasper turned on his heels and slashed at the air. He'd only ever let Griffin in on the first bit of the legend, but he was sure Griffin assumed worse of it still. Rightfully so.

That which no blood may currency…

He pointed the blade downwards as if to block an opponent's strike. The final line remained unspoken but ever present on his tongue. It would not pass. It could not pass.

And so it is as once begun…

Jasper turned to the mirror once more, finding a new glowing amber hue to his usually plain brown eyes. He blinked, watching it come in and out of focus. His lungs burned. He drew short, shallow breaths. Sweat beaded on his bare chest, catching the occasional glints of light streaking across the heavens.

To splintered worlds, a setting sun.

CHAPTER 6

SOBERING STORMS

ANIKA STORM HATED STORMS. Ever since she was a little girl, she'd feared the sky-splitting forks of lightning and earth-shattering cracks of thunder. She wasn't too fond of ships either, yet somehow, she currently found herself suffering through both at the same time.

The roar of thunder startled her from her nightmare-ridden sleep. The lightning that split the sky sent shivers down her spine. Her glittering silver eyes remained fixed on the heavens from behind the porthole in her room as she waited for the tossing of the ship to stop. Another violent crack sent her cowering beneath the sheets. Storm had begun to count the clicks between the next flash of lightning and its subsequent boom of thunder when she heard a knock at the door.

"What!" she yelled, letting her nerves get the best of her.

"Looks like I'm not the only one who can't sleep," replied Sebastian softly as he poked his head through the doorway. He'd pulled his golden trellises back into a bun and shaved his beard. There was something almost romantic about his face, but Storm refused to linger on the thought. Her mind was fixed on when the next strike would occur.

Sebas had become irritatingly present since Idune, always looking for ways in which to assist her, as if she were incapable of doing anything anymore. When they were off the damned boat, she'd show him otherwise, maybe give him an injury of his own to nurse. For now, it was all she could do to keep food down and her mind from spiralling about all the things that could sink a ship.

"Sebas, I'm not in the mood for—" she began, when the thunder sounded above. Storm dove her head under the covers again, long before the trailing roar finished.

"I'm not a fan of the thunder either," he smirked as he stalked over to the bed. The flashes of light filtering in through the porthole highlighted the various scars and scrapes along his bare torso and arms.

Storm moaned from under the sheet, though the muffling of the cloth made it sound more like a whimper. "Why are you even here?"

"As I said, I couldn't sleep, and I was looking for company."

"You were looking for someone to warm your bed," she hissed through the sheets. "Have you tried one of the sailors? Or even the captain? I'm sure she'd be happy to oblige."

"No warm beds, just company tonight. And by the looks of things," he added, pulling at the covers to reveal her scowl and smirking as she clung fast to her pillow with the next strike of lightning, "you could use some."

Storm cast a furtive glance out the porthole once more as she tried to decide which she feared more: the storm or him.

"Don't try anything funny," she grumbled, expecting another boom anytime soon.

"I swear on Iturri."

"Don't swear on sacred things, Sebas. They have a way of biting you in the ass…"

"As inviting as that second part sounds, I promise to be on my best behaviour," he said, a coy grin spreading across his face.

With another tentative scowl, she slid to one side of the bed, allowing him to glide into the little patch she'd left open. "Know this; I have a knife and I am not afraid to use it."

"You say that like we aren't old friends."

"How confidently you use that word for someone who does nothing but get on my nerves."

"I'd like to think that, as I'm currently sitting in your bed, that little statement of yours isn't entirely true."

"I—" The next crack of thunder sounded like it was right above their heads. Rattled, Storm cowered against Sebastian's chest, covering her head with the pillow. The move was unintentional. Under better circumstances, she'd never let him this close. But, comforted by the heavy beat of his heart, she couldn't find the strength to pull away.

Storm focused her hearing on it, timing the thunder with each thump, the even pulses helping to steady her own. She'd counted up to five when she felt his hand rest across her back. Beneath it, her muscles tightened, but she made no move to be rid of it. His touch had a soothing warmth to it that she remembered from the way he'd cleaned her wounds in Idune. It was the kind of warmth that made her fearfully weak and left her longing for his touch even after he disappeared. Despite her many denials, she hadn't forgotten it and doubted she ever would.

"When Simon and I were little, we used to take our blankets and pillows and hide out under our beds when the storms came," Sebastian offered. She knew he was trying to distract her from the one outside. "We would play 'who could fall asleep before the next crack of thunder,' that way we wouldn't have to hear it." His voice was riddled with a yearning she'd scarcely heard from him before.

Pressed against his chest, Storm focused on the low, rumbling echo of each word he spoke. The sincerity coupled with the depth of his voice took her mind off the grumbling skies beyond. She imagined the two little boys camping out under tiny beds, dreamy-eyed and warmed by a log fire as the cacophony in the clouds raged on above them like a deadly lullaby.

"And then, one day, a real storm hit…" His heart pounded; his inner fire dimmed. "The day started as clear as any other in the Araldin fields. My father had us working with him in the stables, showing us how to pick woodlice out of the moss-elk, or something else that seemed important at the time but…" Sebastian sighed, the sound swelling in his chest like the rustle of the wanton breeze through the trees of the home she'd long since abandoned. "We must have been just shy of twelve, I didn't have my fire yet, and I didn't think I was going to get it… But I wasn't put out by it. I didn't need it. Simon and I liked working on the farm with our parents. Anyway, I think the rain came first. It was as if someone had turned on a tap in the sky. My father thought it was a blessing. He even said that some of the creatures would've died without that storm, but I would've given up all the creatures to stop what happened next."

Storm noticed his chest tighten beneath her. She didn't understand why Sebastian had decided to speak so candidly about his past but, needless to say, she'd forgotten the storm.

"We didn't hear the scream from the house over the thunder. By the time we decided to head back, the house was already ablaze, the rain doing little to quell it. I remember men in burgundy tunics coming out from behind it. The mafia. My father turned back to us and told us to run into the stables and hide in the twig rabbit burrows as soon as we saw the next flash of lightning. I'll never forget the look in his eyes… I didn't realise it at the time, but that look was 'goodbye too soon' and 'I love you' wrapped into one. We did what we were told. We ran as fast as we could and didn't look back until we reached the cover of the trees. Simon jumped into the first burrow he saw, but I turned back just in time to see it…

"They were quick. The sword slid in and out of him faster than the next flash of lightning. I screamed, but the thunder overhead brought me cover, thankfully, or they might have turned back for the two of us. I ran after them, filled to the brim with rage, but they were on horseback and long gone by the time I got there. My father's body had bled out, staining the soil beneath him. As I held him, lifeless in my arms, the symbol appeared on my wrist. I like to think it was because of my rage that I got my fire—because I swore to whichever god was listening that I would not rest until the mafia goons that took my family from me were dead…"

Storm hadn't moved throughout his entire story. She feared what would happen if she spoke, so she pretended to sleep, all the while wishing she knew how to be of comfort to someone she admittedly didn't hate and had secretly begun to like.

Sebastian stroked the hair back from her face, checking to see if she was still awake. "Hmm," he smirked softly, "I guess all you needed was a bedtime story." She felt him flinch, as though considering getting up. Instead, he snuggled closer and assured she was properly covered by the blankets. "Rest. You'll need it," he added, gently caressing her hair until he finally drifted off to sleep.

Storm played at sleeping as best she could, but her mind was wide awake. She almost regretted how she'd treated him over the years. She'd wrongly assumed his type of arrogance and self-importance came with an over-indulgent family, not a dead one. Storm even began to wonder whether those traits had become his defence mechanism, but then, who was she to judge anyone else's methods of coping?

In the deeper hours of twilight, the thunder and lightning had died down, leaving only a mild shower in their wake. Sebastian had made no other moves to leave. Storm felt his chest rise and fall profoundly beneath her head and his hand settle on her back. He'd drifted off and she wasn't going to wake him.

"I'm sorry," she replied, in a whisper so soft not even Death could hear. Storm spent the last moments of the rainy night pressed against his chest, savouring the beat of his lonely heart. Once she was sure he wouldn't stir, she gently picked herself up from on top of him and made for the door, realizing she'd get no sleep tonight.

CHAPTER 7

THE LAND OF SHIMMERING ICE

"MAKE HASTE, YOU SLUMBERING seals! We're entering the clouds," shouted the captain to her crew. Men and women scurried across the deck, readying themselves for the misty wall that separated them from the land of shimmering ice. The sails were adjusted, the treasures secured, along with several dozen bottles of expensive wines. The flag was lowered and replaced with one that belonged to the Ur, appearing slightly less "pirate-like".

The captain slipped into a long white coat lined with polar bear fur that accentuated her curvaceous figure. The jingling sound of her boots rose above the commotion as she strode over to relieve the young woman at the helm. Another crewmate scurried up the crow's nest, calling out directions to avoid the floating ice chunks around them. Frost crept slowly over the bannisters and spread in crystal lattices over anything that was still wet from the storm. Everyone scrambled to find coats and blankets as they drew nearer to the blinding white wall of clouds.

"Here, put this on," the captain said, tossing an oversized hat to Jasper, swerving just in time to avoid an iceberg. "Cover your eyes. And if anyone speaks to you, keep them covered."

Jasper gaped. "What?"

"Stare at their feet for all I care. Don't look up."

"Why?"

She sighed. "Eyes like yours, sweetness, pretty as they are, attract attention, and I'm trying to avoid any unwanted scrutiny. Folks here are not as accepting as they may be in the Harri territories." She winked a heavily lashed blue eye at him and swerved again in the opposite direction.

"Lucinda!" Griffin called as he rose from below deck, looking green in his pale winter coat. "Was there not a less turbulent path?"

"Griffin, darling, bane of my existence, if you had wanted an easy ride, you should've boarded a diplomat's ship. I told you I'd get you in unseen, I never promised anything about what condition you'd arrive in." She waved a lackadaisical hand in the air and added, "but, please, if you do decide to upchuck your insides, do it overboard. I just had the pine redone and I'd hate for the bile in your stomach to ruin it."

Jasper struggled to keep a straight face as Griffin shot him a murderous glare before moving towards the railing. "Have you two sailed together before?" Jasper asked, watching the captain yank at the helm, partly to dodge the ice, but mostly to annoy Griffin.

"What a curious creature you are. Not falling for his charm, are we?" the captain responded with a narrowed gaze and a chuckle.

"More like trying to figure out his character," Jasper clarified.

"Not all games should be played or puzzles solved," the captain said with a cryptic smile, between various shouts to her crew. "Once upon a time, when we were acquaintances in a time neither of us wishes to remember in detail."

"It seems Griffin has a lot of those," Jasper sighed.

"And be lucky he does…" The captain lowered her voice. "Griffin views the world in black and white, good and evil, just and unjust, and deep down, he wants nothing more than to be a hero. This drive of his has him rubbing shoulders with all sorts of characters, both on the elite and fringe ends of society who all, in one way or another, fall for that same charm. He's saved countless souls—even some who, in my opinion, weren't worth saving. But then, who am I to talk?" She smiled. "He saw the good in them, even when they couldn't see it in themselves. Because of this, he's got a network of people who may not align with his cause but will support him in any way they can."

"Hence the ship?"

"Hence the ship. He's seen the darkest of dark nights and the brightest of days, and not one of them has ever made him stray from his goal. If I were to guess, I'd say he needs to prove something to himself. But he's not content with improving one life, he must save them all. As annoying as he is, that part of him is endearing, and sooner or later, we all fall for it. At our core, we all wish for a better world and to, in some way, be a part of it."

"Does that mean you're an idealist like him?" Jasper asked.

"Not in the slightest. I'm here for a good time, not a long one. I'm a lover of fine wines and finer things—especially when they come at a bargain I can't refuse," she added with a wink. "Griffin believes people should strive to always do good. I believe in filling my coffers first." She sighed. "That being said, if he occasionally asks me to turn a blind eye as he boards one of my rumrunners, I'm happy to do so. Although, I won't say I wasn't curious as to why he wanted to get into Iliso..."

"You would think that the islands would be the most sought-after tourist destinations," Jasper remarked.

"Solia, yes. It's all palm trees and pineapples, though getting approval to enter is no simple feat. But Iliso?" She laughed. "Tourists there are drawn and quartered. Whatever he's planning must be worthwhile, or else the alternative dire. Now, quiet. I need to focus," Captain Lucinda said as she squinted towards the approaching barricade of clouds.

Captain Lucinda scanned the black water for something that Jasper knew only she could see, making a hard starboard turn when she finally caught sight of it. Two chunks of ice shaped like rum bottles were spread just far enough apart for the ship to fit through and into the clouds—a secret way into Iliso. After what the captain had said of their treatment of trespassers, he hoped it was truly secret.

Captain Lucinda cleared her throat and began to yell. "All hands, on deck! Brace for cloud impact!"

The wave of cloud consumed them whole in a matter of seconds. A frigid wind swirled through the white haze, sticking snowflakes to eyelashes and chattering teeth. Jasper turned towards the stern of the ship where, sure enough, he saw that they had made their way between two fjords that he was sure could not be seen from beyond the clouds. The frozen walls towered imposingly over the sides of the ship until they mixed in with the clouds above their heads.

"Kanala be ready," Captain Lucinda growled to the women whose arms were coated in the curious turquoise marks—which were only visible thanks to his spectacles— that branded them divine. They took their places along various points of the deck. "I'd hold onto something if I were you, sweetness, we're headed for the Longya," she called to Jasper. "And somebody, bring Griffin a bucket before he ruins my deck!"

The wind intensified, causing the water beneath them to churn violently. The Ur kanala aboard had the daunting task of steadying the ship and keeping it on course through the rapids of the Longya. The vessel bounced and rocked, jolting through jagged icebergs and sudden sharp turns. Jasper couldn't help but notice Captain Lucinda seemed unfazed, even a little entertained by their perilous passage. Griffin, on the other hand, had gone from green to white, and Jasper found himself chuckling at the sight of the man he'd thought invincible brought low by some rough water.

The ship made another sharp turn to portside, finally steering towards calmer waters. They arrived in the middle of a frozen bay, tacking off onto a small dock made of reflective ice and pine bark for grip. Three soldiers waited for them, alongside several crates of rum. Their skin, like Lucinda's, was as dark as the water and their hair as white as the snow. Jasper imagined that if they ever decided to go swimming in the icy water, they'd blend right in with their surroundings.

Captain Lucinda made an impressive jump from the deck to the dock, landing gracefully before rising to shake hands with a burly, polar bear-like man with two large, icy cornrows trailing across his head and down his back. Jasper watched from above, heeding her words of warning. When the time was right, Griffin would lead him and the rest to their end destination. There was no reason to tempt fate now by mingling with a difficult crowd.

"Lucy, what took you so long?" the man growled.

"Storm weather caused a delay," she replied, unfazed by his menacing demeanour.

"I've never known you to be afraid of a storm," he said as he flared impressively large nostrils. Two little clouds appeared from his nostrils as he huffed before adding, "You are growing soft in your later years."

"The only one soft here is you." Captain Lucinda drew her sword and pointed it at the man's throat. The two women behind him raised their arms and lifted icicles from the depths of the ocean, aiming them at her. After a few tense seconds, punctuated by chattering teeth and cloudy breaths, the man laughed in an unpleasant way that sounded too cold to be welcoming.

"My Lucy," he grinned, revealing razor-like teeth. "It's good to have you back."

"It seems, brother, your wife is overfeeding you," she laughed as she withdrew her sword and patted him on the hefty stomach he seemed to have attained since their last meeting.

"And I wouldn't have it any other way. What have you brought me this time?"

"Sixty bottles of sweet wine from Yozora and four barrels of port from the bay of Voleur," she said, counting them as her crew offloaded the ship. "Make that fifty-nine," she laughed as she plucked a bottle out of the crate, ripped the cork off with her teeth, and took a swig.

The man clapped his hand over her shoulder. "Come sister, we have a meal ready for you and your crew before your next launch." The pair were about to stroll off when the man noticed a swish of white feathers aboard the ship. "You!" he called. Jasper looked around but found he was the only one still on deck. "Quit standing around and help offload."

"Aye, sir," Jasper replied quickly, scrambling to pick up a crate of wine. Captain Lucinda gritted her teeth and shot him a warning look before turning to her brother.

"Where do you find these people, sister?" her brother laughed. He stalked over to where Jasper had just rested a crate of wine down with great difficulty. "It would be easier, sailor, if you removed your hat."

"Can't sir," Jasper replied nervously.

"Can't? Sister, I hope you keep this one around for the comedy, for he is of little use otherwise. Isn't that right, sailor?" Jasper kept his eyes beneath the brim of his hat like the captain had warned and nodded, but the man would not be swayed. He ripped the hat from Jasper's head and tossed it to the floor. "You will do as you are told."

"Yes, sir," Jasper said, squinting his eyes shut quickly.

"Brother, leave my crew alone," Captain Lucida called with a nervous edge to her voice.

"Sister, you must be firm with them, or else they will not respect you," the man replied. "Look at me when I am talking to you, sailor."

Jasper cast a glance towards the captain, whose eyes were wide with alarm. Feeling pressured by the man's heavy breath on his neck, Jasper slowly raised his head to meet the eyes of the towering man in polar bear skin.

The man took a step back, frightened by what he saw, and quickly proceeded to draw his sword. "But wait. Sister, what kind of joke is this?" he demanded, but Captain Lucinda was already beside him with a sword to his neck.

"You try my patience, brother, and you forget my ferocity," she hissed. "I am not the child you shipped off as a common slave, nor am I above spilling familial blood for my own well-being. Drop your weapon."

His guards raised daggers of ice from the ground beneath them and aimed them at her.

"Let not the gods hear of your blasphemy, sister," he replied, cautious of the blade at his throat.

"Let them speak of my resolve, brother."

"And mine," Griffin replied from behind them all. The women with the icy daggers were flanked by Storm and Sebastian, and Griffin stood, whips of light in his hands, ready to shatter the very ice on which they stood in the worst of cases. "Now, do as she said. Drop the sword."

"You," the man growled to Griffin. "Why am I not surprised."

"It's nice to see you again too, Kaito."

"I always had a sinking feeling the gods would bring you back to me."

"If it's any consolation, I'm not too keen on seeing your face again either," Griffin said dryly. "But there are worse things on the horizon than run-ins with unfriendly acquaintances. So, how about we all drop our weapons and head somewhere warm before we freeze to death? I will explain everything then."

Kaito huffed, contemplating what he clearly considered to be two bad options before nodding to his girls. They relented, turning the icy daggers back into streams of water and casting them to the endless sea. Jasper didn't know whether to feel relieved at being spared a skewering or worried that this bear of a man had agreed to lead them back to his den.

Griffin ordered Storm and Sebastian to stay aboard the ship with the captain. His excuse was for them to help her maintain a watch over their new cargo, but Jasper knew his concern lay in their old one, the strange man they'd picked up in Idune. If Griffin was tense before, it was nothing compared to how he was with that man around.

When Jasper had asked after the identity of the man with the strawberry blonde hair and eyes that looked like two balls of magma, Griffin had practically threatened to rip his throat out. All he knew was that, thanks to the spectacles Griffin had given him, he could see the glowing yellow marks beneath the man's skin, and knew he was a well of untapped power. His inner light matched Sebastian's, but his marks were more numerous, and his disposition guarded, reserved, too cold for someone who hailed from the lands of fire.

They arrived at a small cabin, concealed behind heaps of snow, and were hastily ushered inside. The cramped room was further constricted by the piles of what Jasper assumed were illicit goods stacked high around them. A round table and a collection of chairs, neglected and dusty, filled whatever space remained.

"We are men of civility," began Griffin as he took a seat.

"Bold of you to make that claim," retorted Kaito, settling into the chair opposite him with a scowl.

Jasper remained uncomfortably close to Griffin. Something about the situation didn't sit right with him, and not just because he was seated facing the man who nearly decapitated him. He scanned the room, taking in as much as possible, hoping not to involve himself in more trouble. Griffin continued to converse with the man, but Jasper sensed that even he was uneasy.

"Why have you come crawling back to Iliso? And what mess have you tangled my sister in?" Kaito demanded.

Ignoring his irritation, Griffin replied, "Your sister can hold her own in any mess and knows how to make her own decisions."

"You think I don't know that?" Kaito glowered at him. "Griffin, you already know that I am not one of your fans, and still, you taunt me?"

"I know you're more interested in what I have to say than in killing me," Griffin retorted.

Kaito leaned back in his chair with a coy grin. "At least some lessons stick with you. I'll ask once more. What exactly is this mess you have involved my sister in? Why risk your neck coming back into Iliso?" Then, with a wicked frown and a crease in his brow, Kaito looked over at Jasper and asked, "And what in the name of Iturri is that?"

Griffin glanced over at Jasper and said, "That last one is a slightly complicated topic. As for your other questions, to make a long story short, we are looking for someone who can manipulate the effects that water has on a person. We are looking for a witch."

"A witch?" Kaito let out a warm laugh, his breath turning to fog in the cold of the cabin. "Chasing ghost stories, are we?"

Griffin smirked. "You and I both know they are anything but."

Kaito huffed, crossing his meaty arms over his torso. "And where do you expect to find a witch?"

"Solia, the original home of witches."

"You have always been bold… Even if you do happen to find a witch, you will know they do not work for free."

"I am well aware of the cost of a witch's assistance, and I am ready to pay," Griffin replied.

Jasper noticed Kaito drop the façade of disinterest he'd been playing at for the better part of the conversation. He and Griffin had never spoken about a price, though, by now, Jasper knew he should have expected something in exchange for the return of Savara's memories. He made a mental note to prod Griffin for the details later, knowing that somehow pulling teeth would be an easier task.

The mention of witches had piqued Kaito's interest. Judging by the look in his eyes, Griffin's knowledge of what appeared to be ancient Ur lore—and the truths behind it— were apparently cause for concern. What's more, his readiness to pay for whatever help the witch could offer seemed to add weight to his statement. Again, considering Jasper had never heard Griffin mention a price before, if this detail was the one that finally loosened Kaito's tongue, he worried the price might be steep indeed.

"Aside from the ridiculous idea you have of finding these legendary beings," Kaito began, carefully navigating their conversation to not give any information away freely. "Why in Iturri's name do you need a witch?"

As Griffin formulated a response, Jasper's eyes drifted over to the guard biting her nails beside the door. She seemed tense for someone working with the upper hand. Every so often, her eyes would flit over to the frame as though waiting for something. Jasper furrowed his brow and glanced about the room. He could've sworn there had been two girls escorting them, but now, only one remained.

"You should know by now the curious properties of water," he heard Griffin reply.

There was a slim chance Griffin was going to tell Kaito more than that, but Jasper knew his interruption would be welcomed, especially if there was trouble to be had. If he was correct and there were two women originally, trouble would arrive soon enough. "Griffin," he whispered, tapping him on the shoulder.

"What?" Griffin growled.

"We were escorted by two guards."

"Jasper, I don't have time for—"

"Well, now, there's only one. I'm almost certain the other didn't enter the cabin with us either…"

Griffin furrowed his brow. "This was a trap," he realised all too late.

The door flew open with a sudden crash, extinguishing half the candles as a new, unfriendly cold entered the room. Jasper retreated, inching himself behind Griffin, the sound of his racing heart ringing loudly in his ears. Griffin clenched his jaw and summoned a slither of light to his palm beneath the table. They had been tricked, led like lambs to slaughter. But they were not the only ones subjected to this fear. Even Kaito tensed as his attention shifted to the new arrival. The world stilled as the statuesque woman with the intimidating aura marched through the door.

CHAPTER 8

COPPER AND STEEL

BRASS HAD ALWAYS BEEN good at "snooping" as Griffin called it. It was one of the many things that had bonded them all those years before. Brass didn't like to think of it in such crude terms. After all, the wind didn't snoop, it was simply there to catch whatever stray bits of information might cross its path, and bluster along on its merry way. Yet even he was forced to admit that his current act was too intentional to be happenstance.

The day had been long and filled with mourning, the funeral lasting from early in the dawn well into the night. The Harri's tradition of turning death into a final fete came as a surprise to someone who had once willingly caused so much of it. He had always been taught to pray, before and after a strike, for the safe ferry of the souls he stripped from their bodies. Death was a sombre matter, or so he'd believed. The longer he lingered in the town's festivities, the more he began to suppose this tradition of turning soils against the backdrop of merriment was a form of prayer, a communal wish for safe passage from this lifetime. Besides, under the circumstances, they would need to enjoy all the merriment they could find. There was no certainty of it in the coming future.

As the night descended on Idune, it brought with it the promise of mystery and a chance at the truth. Brass had spent the day keeping an eye on people Griffin had said played an influential role in their battle against the possessed Argia. By nightfall, he'd eliminated all but one suspect in Savara's disappearance, the now-councilman Dhoot. Now, Brass played shadow to him as he shuffled through the crowds of patrons dancing through the streets. The more time Brass spent around the councilman, the more he realised that Griffin was right to be wary of him.

The councilman was a shifty character that malice had taken a liking to, and one who was quite adept at keeping himself to the shadows. Brass had witnessed him engage in underhanded dealings amidst the festivities, trades in illegal wares, bet making, and more, lost on all eyes but his own. And when it was time to be a public figure, he would dawn a mask of virtue that left the crowds in raptures. But that was all it was, a mask.

Brass climbed up the tallest building he could find with a view of the ceremony and watched as the councilman navigated the rest of the festivities. As he waited, he contemplated the length of time that had passed since he'd last undertaken a similar mission. The feeling of once again playing companion to the wind came back to him as though it were only yesterday, and not a distant memory. He could almost hear the cold, detachment of the king's voice commanding his network of spies. Brass was raised by the monks of the guard, taught to be stealthy and swift, to appear as inconsequential and forgettable as the air in a room. He knew how to use the echoes of the breeze to mask his breath, how to trap voices as whispers in the wind, he even knew how to avoid footfall altogether. He was—in his king's own words—as perfect as air itself.

A solitary, heavy thump from inside his chest snapped him out of his reminiscence. There was no use lingering in the memory of the life he'd left behind.

The full moon above reflected on the white of his tattoos—sun, moon, and star—and he felt as though Iturri was watching over him. Brass waited until the last stumbling drunk had made it back into his wood and paper townhouse and ousted his last lantern before stepping over to the precipice of the roof. He inhaled deeply, relishing the way it filled his lungs. On the exhale, he jumped, freefalling from the tall trellises of the imperial court building and into the night sky. There was an art to it, to the surrender of one's body to the whims of the wind, and Brass was an expert.

The feeling of flying with purpose again made his heart flutter, but Brass knew better than to let his emotions get ahead of him. He steadied his breath and waited. When he sensed the nearing of the earth below, he raised a steady hand out in front of himself. A pocket of air formed beneath him, scooping him from his freefall and righting him before resting his feet on the ground. The orchestra of the night—

rustling branches, howling winds, distant coos of owls—reminded him of the life he once lived. Back then, these were the sounds that made his bed and the graves of those he'd killed. Back then, he hadn't questioned the ways of his people or the blood that quenched the thirst of their lands.

But the death of his friend forced him to open his eyes.

With the thrill of his old life present, Brass shook away the thoughts until his mind was, once again, as clear as the breeze that accompanied him. His feet guided him through the cobblestone streets, keeping to the shadows of the flickering streetlamps, towards the house at the edge of the city belonging to councilman Dhoot, unaware that he too was being watched.

Given the modesty of such a house, Brass was surprised to find more than a handful of guards patrolling the grounds. He wondered why this new councilman had at least twice the guards of the other members of the council.

A cloud drifted slowly over the moon, providing cover for the night's task. Each light-footed step he took remained in the shadow of the night's perfect moon. None of the guards patrolling the grounds took notice as he slid inches behind them, making his way up to the stone walls of the house. He slid two small daggers out from his tunic and prepared himself to scale the wall, when he felt the familiar prickle of approaching life on the back of his neck. He turned, finding himself face to face with the ends of two thin swords.

"Brass?" said a voice he hadn't heard in almost a lifetime.

His eyes travelled up the blades, glossing over the two different metal hilts and the hands that held them. Two sets of cloudy grey eyes stared back at him, the faces looking almost as surprised as his own. They were something out of a dream, phantoms of the life he once led. If they hadn't spoken first, he might have believed they were figments of his imagination.

Brass blinked, still questioning the sight before him as he cleared his throat. "Copper? Steel?"

CHAPTER 9

A CAPTIVE

SAVARA STRUGGLED AGAINST the bindings for so long that bloody rings had formed at her wrists. Since the memory had startled her awake, the seconds had ticked by tediously. The air around her smelled of moss and mud, something she wouldn't have minded so much if she knew where she was or why she was tied to a chair in the middle of the dimly lit room.

No one had come to check on her, and there were no windows in the room to signal any passage of time by way of charting the sun. The bump on her head throbbed impatiently, though she was sure it had been hours since she'd been dragged unconscious from the forest floor. For all she knew, she'd been here for days.

Her mind had grown too tired to think, which thankfully meant it was too tired to replay the events of the battle that had been so fresh before her capture. Prior to her run-in with The Apprentice, it didn't require much concentration for the images of her friends facing off against the flames of the possessed Argia to appear in her mind. She had relived the sights of crumbling buildings, charred corpses, and fountains of blood more times than she'd wished to count. And then, there were the shadows. Gruesome spectres made of ashes that bent to the whims of their prince and his apprentice. They'd taken up permanent residence in her mind ever since they attacked her outside of Osiir.

Before her capture, Savara could recall them all. Now, the storms in her mind had quieted, and numbness was beginning to settle in.

Her stomach growled, the sound echoing in the empty room, a painful reminder of her hunger. Even worse, now that she was awake, her powers had awakened too.

Savara, the sole heir to the Argia throne, was exiled for a divination that she had no control over, and it left her with bloodthirsty powers that were named after the things that gave nightmares to the dark. Trapped in this room, there was nothing to distract her from their luring calls. Her powers gave her the ability to sense souls around her, finding the echoes of heartbeats and fear in others, and sometimes even feeling them herself. But the worst part was that her powers had a mind of their own, and since she'd reached Visanthe, they had been vying for control, preying on her mind and begging her to do terrible things. She had even relented once, but it was a mistake she'd never make again.

Another growl sounded from her stomach. Hunger may have weakened her powers, but she could still sense someone had appeared and was waiting on the other side of the wall. She tried to wriggle free, but the rope bindings sliced deeper into her skin, causing her to wince in pain.

"Face me, you coward!" she yelled, hoping whoever was on the other side of the wall could hear her. Fresh blood rushed to her cheeks, swirling around her gemstone scar. It felt heavier in her weakened state, and Savara knew she was running a fever. She couldn't believe how quickly it had come on, leaving her wondering if there was more to it than just hunger. In the back of her mind, she heard Big Tog's voice remind her of the deadly nature of their bond. Could this be what he meant? The click of the door unlocking at the other end of the room sent a cold sweat beading on her forehead.

"So…" began a sly and menacing voice she'd heard only once before, at the dinner party she could barely remember under the current, bleak circumstances. The man strode through the door, his pointed nose high in the air as if enjoying the scent of her pain. "I gather that you are somewhat of a rare commodity, my dear," said General Dhoot, his envious green eyes piercing the dimly lit room like homing beacons. "I must say, I was expecting more of the heir to the Argia throne… given the facts."

Savara glared at him, defiance shining in her eyes despite her weakened state. "I have no idea what you're talking about," she lied. Though withered in her hunger, she could sense the man's plotting through her powers. She felt the craving in his soul for strength and control, the need to dominate at any cost. It reminded her of what Griffin had told her over dinner about the different kinds of power.

General Dhoot shook his head. "Don't play dumb with me, girl," he said, gripping her jaw between crushing fingers and glowering at her. "I know what you are, I know what power runs through your veins."

Savara eyed him cautiously as the colour drained from her cheeks. The only people in Idune who knew were those in her inner circle, and they would never betray her… But then, that wasn't entirely true, was it? There were others who knew. The Prince of Shadows and The Apprentice… and Big Tog. He'd claimed to have made a deal with the devil and that was why he'd known. Perhaps General Dhoot had made a similar deal.

Weak as she was in her current state, Savara knew she had to press him for information. Pride burned in him. Perhaps she could use that hubris to her advantage. If she could get him talking, he might reveal how he knew of her powers and what plans he had for her.

"Then shouldn't you be afraid like everyone else?" she retorted, raising her chin to give him a better view of the fire in her eyes. If he had any sense, he'd back away now. Even she feared her powers and what they were capable of. The title alone, bestowed upon her by The Prince of Shadows, stilled her heart. "If you're so sure of the facts, then you must know what they call me."

The general grinned, accepting her challenge. "The Harbinger of Death," he replied. "Our dark master certainly knows how to turn a title." A low sinister laugh crept from his throat. "Such spirit you have. You may have the others fooled, girl, but, unlike everyone else, I also know that you do not use your powers. If you did, you might have prevented the attack. As it stands, you are worthless."

Savara balled her bound hands into fists. "Are you sure about that?" she hissed. She needed to prove him wrong and keep him afraid of potential retribution. In his eyes, she spied a flicker of doubt.

That, she could use.

She steadied herself, focusing on the part of her powers that already fed her his emotions and ignoring the part that wished for blood. It was no easy task, made harder by the fact that she was nursing both illness and hunger, but she managed to find in him a sliver of fear. If she could twist the ability to feel emotions into the ability to inflict them, then she might be able to mimic the sensation of harm without actually having to use that side of her powers. There was no guarantee it would work. She'd never done something similar before, but her survival was on the line and now was as good a time as any to try.

Using threads of her power, Savara reached out, creeping a cold sensation into his heart as she pictured fractals of fear digging into his chest. When nothing happened, she willed more force into it, and suddenly, the general dropped his hand from her jaw. The exercise used up whatever ounce of energy she had left, but it seemed to have worked.

For a split second, General Dhoot's severe brow quivered, but he corrected it quickly. "Parlour trick," he growled.

"Was it?" she countered.

He flared his nostrils at her as he contemplated his next move. It may not have been much, but she'd successfully pulled at the frays in his pride. "Regardless, you won't be using those powers on me if you ever want to see your friends again," he growled, incisors on full display. Suddenly his hand was at her throat. She was at a loss as to why he'd lashed out until she caught a glimpse of the rubies on her cheek reflected in his eyes. General Dhoot forced her face to one side, having only then noticed the brilliant red gash. He ran his spindly fingers over the gems in disgust. "To whom did you bind your soul?" he whispered at first, but when she didn't answer, he yelled, "Tell me!"

Savara winced as the harsh sounds of his voice hit her ears. "Big Tog," she breathed, the rubies humming on her cheek at the sound of his name.

"What did you promise?" he demanded.

Savara thought back to the night she'd gotten the scar. In her mind, she could still smell the heavy stench of black coffee on Big Tog's breath as he'd carved the line on her cheek. Back then, she had never heard of a soul bond. She hadn't known that it was a promise attached to the very fibres of one's soul, or that the incompletion of said promise had dire consequences. He hadn't specified his terms at the time, and he'd taken advantage of her ignorance. Later, when he explained that she would have to complete two impossible tasks, finding his son amongst the possessed Argia and killing The Prince of Shadows, she realised how foolish she'd been. Griffin had often harped on about the importance of secrets, keeping things to yourself until it was in your favour not to. With this in mind, she considered her response carefully.

There was one word that perfectly encapsulated everything that Big Tog had asked for, and the emotions he'd asked with. One word, one goal.

"Revenge," she hissed.

General Dhoot released his chokehold and glowered at her, his fear flickering in his gaze. "What do you know?"

"I know that you had a role to play in the Argia's attack," she lied, but in his eyes, she found all the confirmation she'd needed. She'd been right from the beginning. He must have something to do with the abduction of Big Tog's son, which is why he now feared that he would become a target for said revenge. She smiled, letting him believe in his false assumption.

"Get comfortable, princess. You're not going anywhere. If I have to, I'll wring that mafioso's neck myself," he declared, throwing a roll of bread to the floor. "You should eat," he added, a sly grin spreading across his face, knowing very well she couldn't pick it up in her weakened state. "You looked famished. Besides, I see big things in our future."

"I thought I was worthless?"

"Today, yes, but tomorrow is a new day." With that, he clasped his hands behind his back and retreated to the other room, locking the door behind him.

Savara screamed after him, though she knew what little good it would do. She'd traded one beast for another, and her fever was on the rise. Her stomach groaned at the sight of the roll on the ground. Soul bond induced fever or not, if she didn't eat, she would die down here. Tears flowed over the stones on her cheeks and down her chin in frustration. Her situation felt hopeless. Her strength waned. In these dark times, she thought of her friends, wondering where they were and whether they were safe. She hoped to be reunited with them soon but, given the circumstances, the thought itself seemed impossible.

CHAPTER 10

GENERAL KYARA

A COLD BREEZE FLOODED through the room, extinguishing half of the candles and sending shivers down their spines. The missing woman had returned accompanied by at least ten others, who now surrounded the cabin, standing at attention. Another woman, with a mohawk of frosty white dreadlocks and a ferocity unmatched by even the most wicked of seas, entered the room.

Her feet clomped heavily on the wooden floor, and the force of her steps rustled the snow on the roof above them. The gossips of neighbouring armies had many names for her—the Snow Beast, the Ice Queen, the Warrior of the Frozen Wild. And though some may have been said in jest, no one dared cross General Kyara aloud. Word of her ruthlessness carried far beyond the borders of the warring Ur and Harri provinces. She was known to all for her icy-fisted control of the Ur army—and anything within 100 nautical miles of their seas.

Griffin cursed under his breath as he flexed his fingers, conjuring a faded blue mask in front of Jasper's lighter brown eyes. He should have thought of it sooner, but he had been nursing his seasickness and hadn't believed Kaito to pose as big a threat as the towering woman before him. He knew General Kyara wouldn't be so easily swayed by his smooth talk and would become incensed at any mention of crossings or gates. That story wasn't for her ears. There weren't many people in Visanthe who frightened him, but the bead of sweat forming on his brow despite the chill in the room reminded him that she, the woman who could wrestle a polar bear with her bare hands and come back unscathed, was an exception. Her glare alone felt like an attack. He had to control his fear if he didn't want her to dig too deep. The only advantage he had was that she didn't play mind games; she was blunt, brutally so. The question now was whether she'd believe the truth.

Kaito dropped all airs of power and pretence he had shown before, blanching as he got to his feet. "General Kyara," he said, crossing his hand over his heart and dipping into a low bow.

She flared her nostrils as she gazed upon them all. "What is the meaning of this?" she asked in a grumble that could have stilled oceans. She glared at Kaito first, furious at one of her own who looked as though he had been keeping secrets. Then she cast her icy gaze towards Griffin who met the challenge in her gaze with equal immovability. Finally to

Jasper, who kept his head down. She didn't seem to notice the shroud placed on him, thankfully.

"You," she barked at Griffin, whipping out a sharpened spear and aiming it at his throat. Her cold eyes scanned him slowly from head to toe before meeting his. "Izar. Have you come to spy on us?" She pressed the point into his Adam's apple.

Griffin stifled a shudder and took a deep breath, careful not to unintentionally stab himself on the point of her spear. He should have remembered the animosity between the Ur and the Izar over having interfered in land disputes. Of course she would see him as a threat. "No, ma'am."

"Funny I should catch you sneaking into my domain, then."

"I swear on Iturri, my business here is my own," Griffin added, hesitating as he considered the gravity of the information he was about to share. It was time to come clean, but he worried what repercussions such news might have. "I am no longer associated with them."

Griffin felt a flicker of Jasper's confused glare on the back of his neck but, to his credit, Jasper kept his lips sealed. He may have been smart enough not to make his confusion known to the rest of the world, but Griffin knew there would be questions later.

She pressed the spear deeper into his neck, drawing a sliver of blood. "Your kind are liars, and I know better than to believe any of your manicured words. Before I kill you, I demand you tell me how you managed to get into the kingdom."

He stole a glance at Kaito, who looked mortified at the question. In his eyes was the silent plea not to mention his sister, knowing General Kyara's wrath would extend to them as well.

He must think very little of me if he's worried that such a thing would cross my mind.

"I am kanala, ma'am," Griffin replied, raising his hand slowly as little orbs of blue light appeared around the room. "I was guided by the light of the stars to this place."

General Kyara was not moved. Her scowl deepened as she contemplated him with murder in her eyes. "A kanala *not* attached to the Izarian guard? Ha! Do you think me gullible?"

"No," he replied, dimming the lights once more. "And I wouldn't dare disrespect a person of your standing with a mistruth. I parted ways with my nation over... a severe difference in opinion."

"Why then, risking your neck on the well-known chopping block of my wrath, are you here?" she growled.

As he expected, his truth had not lessened her distrust. If anything, she looked warier than before. An untethered agent was just as bad as a tethered one.

Before Griffin could respond, Kaito chimed in, as though wanting to seem useful. "He spoke of witches, General. But that's ridiculous... There hasn't been a witch for—"

"Quiet!" she barked. Unlike Kaito before her, she did not play at being amused. She took the allegation as seriously as a declaration of war. "What do you know of our witches?"

Griffin considered his words carefully, wondering what he should say—what he could say—that wouldn't sound like an execution petition. The truth was as good as any place to start, but he knew better than most that some truths shouldn't be spoken aloud. "With all due respect, ma'am, I'm not sure it is something you want spoken of in such open circumstances."

"I'm waiting, Izar," she retorted.

"It concerns the divination of the Argia princess…"

General Kyara's face went livid, dark as the deepest oceans and twice as cold. A muscle twitched in her mouth as she contemplated his words. In the cold of the room, little spouts of hot air shot from her nose. "Everyone out," she growled, her words falling as thick as fog from her lips.

Kaito's curious eyes shifted from Griffin to General Kyara, wondering what secret the two of them shared and how it connected with the strange lore of his land. "But—"

"Out!" she yelled, stabbing her spear into the damp wood. On that violent command, they all bowed out, except for Griffin, who knew he had some serious explaining to do.

He nodded to Jasper, assuring him that everything would be fine. Kaito might try to pry, but Jasper was too smart to reveal anything. Besides, Griffin was now confident that Jasper could hold his own. Standing alone under the weight of General Kyara's gaze, he wondered if he could say the same about himself.

"What does a peasant like you know about such a divination?" General Kyara hissed as she narrowed her eyes at him.

Despite the coldness of the room, her gaze burned on his skin. Intimidation was her strong suit. "I know that memories were altered," Griffin began. Her glower deepened, her anger rising despite his attempt at neutrality.

Unlike the previous short-lived outbursts made for the quick instilling of fear, this anger swelled the way the tides withdrew in preparation for shoreline-altering waves. "And that the only ones capable of such a feat are amongst the most gifted of your people," he added.

General Kyara's inhale echoed like the sound of a retreating wake. Her eyes were as cold as the snow around them. The pressure of her glare was matched only by that of the ocean. "My people, and whatever gifts they possess, are my jurisdiction and mine alone," she declared. She lifted her spear from the floor, leaving a gash that time would only widen, and aimed it at the hollows of his throat again. "Spy or not, you know too much. I might ask how you came about this information, but I find I don't care as long as you do not live to breathe such words again."

General Kyara pulled her spear back, ready to impale him where he stood, but Griffin was quick to react, redirecting her force and causing the spear to clang against the wall. Intrigue creased her forehead as she stumbled to regain her balance.

"I see you are familiar with Ilisoan fighting techniques," she said, her eyes narrowing. "Using your opponent's force as a means to their downfall."

"I was trained in all styles of fighting hailing from Osiir to Iliso," Griffin replied, deftly sweeping a chair out of the way to create more space in the cramped room.

General Kyara positioned herself for hand-to-hand combat. "Impressive," she said. "But it won't help you against me."

They circled each other, exchanging loaded words instead of blows, fists at the ready. "Tell me, what were you trained for, Izar?" General Kyara asked, a coy smile on her lips. "Do you fear an attack in your old age, little star?" she added to herself, referring to the leader of the Izar.

"I have already told you, I am no longer associated with the Izarian guard," Griffin replied, ducking and dodging as General Kyara swiped at him.

"Then why are you looking for my assets?" she demanded.

"I need to speak with the witch who took everyone's memories after the divination," Griffin said, lunging forward confidently. General Kyara swerved and turned, fists still high, but Griffin regained his footing with ease.

General Kyara charged at him at full force, ramming him up against the wall with her forearm. The little cottage shook from the impact, dislodging snow from the roof above. "How do you know such a thing occurred?" she prodded, keeping his throat pinned just enough to speak but not enough to escape.

"I remember the rain…" he choked.

"What does it matter?" she continued, pressing down harder.

"She needs them back…"

It took a moment for her to realise what Griffin meant, by which time his vision had grown fuzzy. "She's back… The Argia princess?"

Griffin nodded as best he could under her force.

"Are you insane?" General Kyara snarled in anger, looking as though she was ready to take a bite out of him. "She will bring destruction upon our lands!"

Maintaining her gaze cautiously, Griffin freed a blade from inside his coat. He pressed it to her chest, just enough so she could feel its point. Startled, she stared down at his hand. "Tricky Izars," she scoffed as she released him. "I should have expected nothing less."

"I mean you no harm, but you must listen to me," Griffin pleaded. "She is back because *they* are back."

Fear flashed across General Kyara's eyes as she paced back and forth on the damp wooden floors, her mood growing increasingly manic. "They cannot be back," she protested.

"But they are," Griffin countered firmly.

"No, you don't understand…"

"With all due respect, it is you who does not understand. I've faced them. They are back," he replied, emphasizing each word. And if his confession wasn't heavy enough already, he added, "They are working with your enemies."

General Kyara's hand darted to her spear and flung it with a force that embedded it deep in the wall just above Griffin's head. He didn't flinch, knowing he needed to show strength if he was going to get anywhere with her.

"She remembers nothing, not even the mother who bore her. I need to know why. What in her past was so dangerous that she had to be stripped of everything?" Griffin placed a hand over his heart and bowed as Kaito had before her. "I mean no harm to you or your people. I only wish to understand."

General Kyara contemplated him with narrowed eyes. "I see your resolve. Clearly, I do not frighten you. I wonder whether you will feel the same if you are given the information you seek. The truth is a dangerous thing, young Izar, as is the past."

"More danger will come from not knowing," Griffin replied firmly.

"Hmm… Your arrival just so happens to be a fortuitous event. Fate, or else Iturri, must be on my side. I'll give you the witch that took your friend's memories, on one condition."

Griffin knew better than to blindly agree to unspoken deals, he'd told Savara as much the last time they were in a compromising situation. "Name it. Neither of us is foolish enough to agree to unknowns."

General Kyara smiled. "Not here, but I shall take you to my domain and explain my request. Should you agree, you will get what you seek. Should you not, I may not feel as inclined to lenience at your unwanted arrival on my shores."

"Well, then, I see no need for us to freeze here any longer."

"If you hadn't wished to freeze, young Izar, you should've remained on your own shores."

Griffin nodded. Having reached a shaky agreement, the two of them strode out of the cabin. Jasper looked to him for some sort of signal, but he simply pursed his lips. They left Kaito and his band of thieves and followed General Kyara and her soldiers deeper into the surrounding fog. Her troubling words played over in his mind, and he couldn't help but wonder what kind of danger they were walking into.

Jasper kept close, looking for some sort of consolation from him. Griffin knew he would need to explain everything once they were alone. He had been tentatively cultivating trust between them for months now, and that trust was about to be tested in ways he couldn't even imagine.

CHAPTER 11

SWEET WINES AND BITTER SORROWS

"TELL ME, PRETTY BOY, what is a clearly well-bred Argia like yourself doing with this lot of ragamuffins? And why is it you've locked yourself in the hold of my ship?" Captain Lucinda asked, punctuating her sentence with the many jangling bangles and other noisy trinkets on her curvaceous person.

Lance lifted his head from his hands and sighed. "You'll forgive me, madam. I'm not much in the mood for talking."

"Madam? Well, that is a first. You'll forgive me, sir, if I rather don't care," the captain replied in her best mocking-royalty accent. "Besides," she added as she ripped away the cork of a bottle, took a swig, and offered him the rest. "Those who claim they wish not to talk are the ones in most need of it."

He stared at it for a moment, contemplating it thoroughly before bobbing his head and relenting to a swig. "I suppose you are right."

"Always," she said, flashing a brilliant smile that revealed a row of pearly white teeth.

"Why don't you start by giving me your name? I don't like nameless entities on my ship… Even had to give a few spirits the heave-ho," she said in jest, but Lance remained silent. "No? Fine, we'll round that iceberg again eventually." She chuckled. "What about where you're from? You got a family?"

Lance hesitated before answering. "It's… complicated," he said, taking another swig of wine before passing the bottle to her. The sweetness of it was beginning to loosen his lips.

"Family generally is." She grinned mischievously before her next sip. "You sound like you've got a lot on your mind. Good thing I have plenty of bottles," she joked, but Lance couldn't bring himself to laugh. As they perched on opposite crates, the captain uncorked a new bottle of wine and handed it over. "Talk. We've got nothing but time."

The ship rocked gently beneath them as they settled in for a long conversation.

Realizing Captain Lucinda wasn't about to give up anytime soon, Lance righted himself, ran his fingers through his hair and cleared his throat. "I was young and foolish once. I hadn't been content with my place in life or seen the importance of my role. I suppose it was boredom more than anything—all I wanted was a friend."

"Doesn't sound like a reason to drink," the captain replied.

"Not yet," he mused. "I eventually found that friend. Someone to sit with me through the monotony of my life. For a while I was happy. But as easily as he'd come into my life, he left, and I was alone again. I had a family and responsibilities—I was constantly surrounded by people… But I was all alone." Lance sighed. It sounded worse out loud than it did in his head. Before the captain could comment, he added, "I'm not proud of what I did. I was weak and undeserving of my position. I fled, escaping the only life I'd ever known in search of the only friend I'd ever had. But, as luck would have it, people like me weren't meant for the streets."

"Why didn't you turn back?" she asked.

"I was kidnapped not long after leaving. I cannot say whether it was out of fear or necessity that I forgot, but eventually, I gave up any hopes of returning to my former life. In the end, I chose to forget, to let it all fade from my mind until I was a shell prime for filling. Eventually, there was nothing to remember. I was too far gone. I found safety and kindness in the arms of someone cruel, someone whom I would've otherwise avoided. Someone whom I treated as a father, and followed without question…" He let his words trail, unwilling to admit all the terrible things he'd done during his time with the mafia. "And now, I've been forced to dive back into the world I'd fled, with all my bad decisions walking beside me aboard your ship. Memories of the mother I lost and the sister I abandoned, the face of the only friend I've ever had, all a constant reminder of my failure…" He bit his lip again, the daring red fluster of shame creeping across his cheeks and nose, helped on by the generous amounts of wine.

By now, the empty bottle dangled from his hand like a forgotten prop. Lance contemplated it, his mind hazy from the sweet wine and the weight of his own story. He couldn't remember if he had finished this one by himself or if the overly perky captain had passed along the dregs. He rested it at his side and buried his face in his hands, letting his locks of strawberry blonde hair fall in rippling curls over them.

Captain Lucinda had coaxed the whole story out of him with nothing more than a few bottles in the dimly lit hold of her ship, which swayed unsteadily in the choppy waters. The story had been festering inside him ever since he woke up in those cells, ready to burst like the many champagne bottles he used to pop for his radiant queen mother and her house of wealthy guests.

"I see…" she said, heaving a heavy sigh. "I understand the need to drink."

Lance nodded. "I had no recollection of any of it before Idune. I wonder if it isn't best to let dead things lie."

"You were one of the possessed that Griffin told me about…" Captain Lucinda realised, placing a pensive finger at her lips.

Lance held his tongue. Of all the things he'd done, that was the worst. He'd been handed off by the man who treated him like a son to a literal devil. His body was used as a vessel for shadows, a weapon of war. Luckily, the battle in Idune hadn't lasted too long. He already had enough blood on his hands. But the damage was done, lives were upended, and he was to blame.

"Fate has an interesting way of docking us at our correct ports, whether they were our intended or not," she added once it was clear he would not speak again. "Perhaps you are being given the chance to make amends."

Lance lifted his head to meet her severe gaze. "I wouldn't know where to start."

The captain smiled. "Talking tends to be a good place, so I'd say you're making decent headway. My next suggestion would be to spin this yarn to the person it concerns."

"Easier said than done," he replied.

"Something tells me you might be surprised," she mused. "Not that it is of any interest, but Griffin and I go back quite some time now. Not as much as you two, but enough to know he's got a regrettably good heart. Even if his mind is a calculating hellhole."

Lance bit down on the smile growing on his lips. It was nice to hear that Griffin hadn't changed since they were boys. That part of him had always been endearing.

"When I first met him, I was a fair bit younger than you are now, traded off to make the beds of men whose pockets were full but heads empty. I too fled my situation, boarded a ship with no desire of turning back. I'd 'persuaded' the captain at the time into letting me work in exchange for passage." She winked. "Sure enough, we'd docked at the Bay of Voleur and the captain had me lifting the sacks on my own, trying to convince me that I wasn't cut out for the job, that being a woman meant I hadn't the strength for all the manual labour required to make the crew." She laughed, popped the cork of another bottle with her teeth, and swallowed an excessive amount. "I sure showed his ass."

"You made crew? Is that how you got this ship?"

"Well, not exactly…" She grinned. "I was a weakling back then. Couldn't lift a single sack. But when I was down in the hold, I found a certain stowaway-turned-do-gooder who promised to help if I didn't rat him out. We got all those bags off the ship before the captain got back from the house of whichever Argia woman he was tangling sheets with. When we were halfway back to Iliso, I told the captain in no uncertain terms that I was taking over. I slit the throats of five men before the crew turned in my favour. The captain jumped ship. Not willingly of course, but I'm sure he made better fish food than man. Anyway, I walked into my new quarters only to discover that Griffin had left with the only lifeboat and half the old captain's questionably procured treasures. To this day he owes me a decent amount of coin— not that he will ever pay it back, but I like to remind him I have something over him. Take back a bit of that control he seems to have over everyone else."

"Sounds like Griffin," Lance said with a laugh.

"I'd like to think I know him well enough to know he's not the type to let things go easily. If you meant something to him, I'll bet my ship you're still bouncing around in that pretty little head of his."

Lance had wondered the very same thing ever since they'd left Idune, but he'd been too afraid to ask. "I don't know where we stand right now," he replied.

"Then you're the only one, sugarcane." Captain Lucinda raised a mocking eyebrow. "I may be exceptionally in tune when it comes to affairs of the heart, but I can't be the only one who has noticed him pause at your door, hand poised to knock, only to talk himself out of it."

The blush deepened on Lance's cheeks, but a frown grew on his lips. "That's… inconvenient." Lance took another excessively long drink, looking to drown out the many questions bouncing around in his mind. One regrettably escaped his lips before he could seal it away. "Have you ever had to decide between doing what you know is right and doing what you want?"

"Unlike Griffin, *right* has never been my guiding star. I tend to believe *right for you* makes for a better life. Have you ever stopped to think whose book of rules you're living by?"

No, he hadn't. Lance had always followed—his mother, his surrogate father, and then the shadows. He'd done as he was told without question. Before he ran away, he was considered the perfect son, the perfect prince. Even after running away, he'd fallen back into a similar role. "Society? Tradition?" he supposed, both plausible but neither satisfying.

"Fancy scapegoats," she countered. "Love—*real* love—always finds a way."

"Love is… messy. Terrifying."

"Sometimes, the things that terrify us the most are the ones we must look forward to. The best kind of love happens where there is the most fear, the most to lose, because oftentimes, there is also the most to gain… But what do I know?" she mused, rising from her perch and flinging another empty bottle to where someone other than her would find and dispose of it. "You think on it, and while you're at it, think of a name. As I said, I don't do nameless things on my ship. They're bad luck."

He smiled. "Lance. My name is Lance."

"Well, Lance, if you ever need to talk—or drink—you know where to find me." She replaced the hat on her head and started back towards her cabin, but before leaving she added, "Oh… and if I'm right—which we both know I am—and your ass is nobility, best believe you'll be paying double for each bottle we've consumed once you're happily seated on whichever golden throne you came from."

Lance chuckled and sat on her words a while longer. She made a good argument, but she had no idea what it meant to one of the last heirs to the House of Orrin. He had always dreamed of seeing himself on the throne. He pictured himself, a dazzling, sun-shaped crown atop his brow, strolling through the halls of the whistling palace. But, if he *did* take up the mantle, he and Griffin could never be together. He'd known as much before, yet, after everything that had happened, remembering it hurt more.

CHAPTER 12

SHADES OF GREY

THE ROOM WAS DEATHLY quiet, except for the growling of her stomach which seemed to fill the space. Her lips were dry and cracked, causing her pain with every movement. Cold shivers ran down her body, accentuating her weakness and leaving her alone with the demons in her head that tormented her day and night.

You killed him, they sang when she thought of Ori. *You pushed your friends away,* they harped when she missed Jasper, Griffin, and the others. Sometimes she imagined she could hear the menacing hiss of Big Tog, reminding her of their deal. But at least he couldn't kill her from here, wherever "here" was. She had screamed until her voice grew hoarse, but she knew she had to keep trying. Someone had to come eventually. Someone had to hear her cries for help.

"That looks like quite the bind, princess," his charming, roguish voice echoed in the shadows.

"Why you?" she moaned, the words coming out as little more than a crackling breath. "You can't be serious…"

The Apprentice stalked towards her, his features schooled into his usual brand of nonchalance, but what little strength her powers could steal told her he was trying extraordinarily hard to look effortlessly uninterested. "Serious as death itself, princess." His midnight blue eyes seemed to glow brighter in the dim light of the room, more so when they met hers. "You look… rough."

If she'd had the strength, she would've cursed his very existence. She would've mocked his lack of descriptors for someone who placed great importance on wording. Sadly, "No shit," was all she could manage.

The veins at his wrists bulged as he clenched his fists, contemplating her sorry state. "It's going to be impossible to talk to you like this," he scoffed, disappearing the way he had come: in a cloud of sparkling black dust.

"Wait!" Savara yelled hoarsely after him, but before she could pull together the strength to curse every drop of blood in his body, he returned seconds later with a pitcher of water.

"Drink," he said, slowly inching it towards her lips.

She was tempted—yearning for an end to her maddening dehydration—but she no longer trusted him. She figured he might still be working with General Dhoot, and this could be a destructive new tactic. Savara pursed her lips and stared back at him, unable to hold his gaze with her waning strength.

"Don't be stubborn. If I were out to make you suffer, I'd leave the pitcher out of reach and you here to rot."

His curious scent of night flowers swirled around them, lulling her muscles into relaxation even as she struggled to draw breath. Her heart was uneasy at the thought of him, but the sandpaper roughness of her throat spoke louder than any doubts she had. She exhaled briefly, allowing him to bring the pitcher closer to her parched lips. Savara drank deeply, feeling the tension and dehydration in her body slowly ebb away. The throbbing pressure in her head built to a crescendo before receding. Her next exhale was cold and tinged with the water that soothed her aching throat. There might have been something else in it, a medicinal herb perhaps, for she felt a new strength spreading from her toes to her fingertips. It grew gradually like a small sapling reaching for the sun, and she knew that, without his help, she might not have felt such a thing again.

"Why are you helping me?" she whispered, relenting to tiredness rather than disdain.

"You don't say 'thank you,' do you?" Despite the cold of his tone, she spied the relief in his eyes.

In response, Savara narrowed hers and replied, "You're the reason I'm in here. Remember?"

"I remember you saying you didn't need my help…" He ran his fingers through tendrils of inky black hair, looking as though if he didn't put them to use, they might jump free of his palms and sprint off. "Ready to admit you were wrong?"

"No," she said flatly, her voice laced with irritation. His arrogance always seemed to push her buttons. Once upon a time, she had trusted his voice to guide her from inner torment, but now she despised every utterance that spilt from his lips. Savara had been foolish before, following blindly after the promise of adventure in his mysterious ways. But she would not be so foolish again.

"You're not seriously choosing this damp, mouldy cell over my help, are you?" he asked, his voice now laced with frustration. But Savara remained silent, not willing to engage in another round of their argument. "Iturri be damned, why are you so stubborn?" He paced in front of her, his agitation growing. "They'll come back for you…" he added, dropping his facade of charm as he knelt before her. "They'll torture you again."

Savara looked away, refusing to meet his gaze. She couldn't forget how he had betrayed her trust. "You're not innocent either," she hissed. "You led me to the Prince of Shadows, killed my friend, and left me with these goons."

"I wouldn't hurt you," he confessed, his tone softened by genuine concern. The vibrant energy that used to ripple off him retreated. He almost reached out to rest a hand on her knee, but his hand lingered between them before dropping as if he thought better of it. Instead, he rested it in his lap and stared down at his open palm and the star-shaped scar covering it.

Savara held her reservations about him, but she accepted that he wasn't here to harm her now. In any case, he wouldn't be any worse than General Dhoot—who was probably on his way back with some new kind of torture.

"Why did you come?" she asked, noticing the furrow of his brow as he contemplated his palm.

The Apprentice thought about it for a moment, closing his fingers over his scar. "Nothing you should concern yourself with," he said as he pulled a knife from his coat pocket.

Savara's heart raced as he stalked behind her. She braced herself for the worst when she suddenly felt the cords around her wrists and ankles loosen. Confusion struck first, but soon, relief washed over her as she realised what he'd done.

He'd set her free.

As she stretched her limbs, Savara felt a rush of gratitude towards The Apprentice, despite the reservations she held about him. She imagined the sweet release she would feel once the stones were removed from her face, but for now, being able to move her arms and legs freely felt like a small victory.

Savara struggled to stand, her weakened state causing her to stumble towards The Apprentice. But he was quick to react, catching her in his arms with a gracefulness that made her heart skip a beat. As she looked up at him, their eyes locked in a moment of unspoken uncertainty. The Apprentice's deep gaze held a flicker of concern. Savara felt her breath catch in her throat. For a moment, she forgot about her current condition and the danger that still lurked beyond the walls.

Their eyes remained locked for a beat longer, before he slowly turned away, breaking the spell that had been woven between them.

"You need food, and not whatever that is," he said, nudging at the cold roll with his foot. He tried his best to steady her, but the combination of hunger and illness had her swaying back into his arms as soon as he'd let go. The Apprentice sighed. "If you come with me, I'll see to it you are cared for."

Savara frowned. There was something in his eyes that made her want to believe him, but she wasn't about to get hurt again. She wasn't about to fall for another trap. "How do you expect me to trust you?"

As he met the challenge in her gaze, his own expression humbled. "I don't," he replied curtly. "But I'm also not whatever horrible creature you think me to be… The world isn't black and white, Savara. Nor are my motives."

His statement caught her entirely off-guard. Never had he before shown any emotion other than apathy—at least on his surface. This statement sounded injured somehow, and on top of that, it was the first time she could recall that he'd addressed her by her name. "I don't understand why you care."

The Apprentice shook his head. "Only you would question the person throwing you a lifeline."

"You think I don't have reason to?" Savara hissed, thinking of all the ways he'd let her down before. She tried to push herself off him but winced as a wave of pins and needles rushed over her ankles. The Apprentice's strong arms held her steady and guided her down. As she slumped back into the chair, she couldn't help but notice a soreness on the backs of her thighs from sitting uncomfortably for so long. But even pain was preferable to being in the arms of an enemy.

"My intention was never to hurt you. I figured you would've seen that by now…" He said his last words in hushed tones, not necessarily for her ears, but she heard them regardless.

Savara looked at him, her expression a mix of confusion and suspicion as she considered the sincerity in his words. As if in a final attempt to sway her, he reached into his pocket again and pulled out the box he'd given her before her kidnap, the one she'd dropped as she was knocked unconscious, the one which contained the Arima stone. He'd gone back for it, she realised. He'd come back for her. But why? Why did he insist on helping her, even though he worked with the Prince of Shadows?

She still didn't fully trust him, but she couldn't deny that he had just saved her life—again. As she stared at the box, she remembered why she'd come to Visanthe in the first place. There was still more to her past that she needed answers to, and her uncle's killer was still out there, somewhere. His small gesture of goodwill reminded her why she couldn't rot in a cell, and why there was still more to live for.

"Okay," she said finally, her voice barely a whisper.

"Okay?" he repeated.

Savara nodded hesitantly, unsure if she was making the right choice. "I'll go with you."

His eyes widened as he contemplated her again, the product of shock and relief blooming on his face for an instant before he caught hold of his emotions. "…okay."

With a gentle but firm embrace, The Apprentice lifted her into his arms, cradling her close to his chest. She could feel the steady rhythm of his breathing and found herself unconsciously searching for his heartbeat. When she heard nothing for an extended period, she began to fear that they were somehow already dead. But then, from the depths of his chest, she heard a faint thump—so soft she almost missed it. She waited, and two dilated seconds later, heard it again. Low and distant as it was, he had a heart.

He held her tightly with one hand and reached into his pocket with the other, producing the same sparkling dust as before. As the shimmering cloud enveloped them, Savara couldn't help but feel a twinge of hope. He was right, she'd never been able to pinpoint his motives, but without his help, she knew she wouldn't have stood a chance against her captors. Her powers were weak, and her feet could barely support her weight. Despite her reservations, she knew he was still the better option. At least, since she didn't trust him, he wouldn't be able to deceive her. But that was a battle for another day. For now, she had other things to focus on, like surviving in a world that seemed determined to destroy her. Besides, wherever they were headed was surely better than this cell.

CHAPTER 13

THE CURSE OF TWO WORLDS

THE CENTRE OF ILISO was not the frozen wasteland of myth that had been spread throughout Visanthe. Instead, the path leading from the misty outpost to the heart of the merchant city was a marvel of natural beauty.

Pools of turquoise waters illuminated by stolen bioluminescent fish weaved through paths of fanciful ice sculptures depicting narwhals, sirens, and polar bears. A riot of pink and lavender flowers grew in well-tended gardens, covering any bare ground amidst the snow on the main crescent-shaped landmass. Along the walkways, these plants found homes on windowsills and stone basins. Bridges of ice, adorned with moss to prevent slipping, connected the smaller landmasses, allowing canoes to glide beneath them on the pristine waters. This was a city of wonder, a testament to the ingenuity and beauty of those who had created it.

Bridges of ice lined with moss connected each of the smaller landmasses, leaving enough room underneath for canoes to glide through the pristine waters. Each landmass pertained to a different industry. Some were for growing food, marked by greenhouses made of ice that allowed peeks into botanical wonders of all colours. Others were for markets, lined with vendors in stalls, cottage-like shops, inns, and pubs. Some were left blank for training or simply meditative contemplation. But of course, all were guarded by the great tower off in the distance that kept their lands, and those of Solia, hidden from the outside world.

People hurried about their day as normal, haggling with fish vendors over arctic char and cod, commenting the weights of these were not as they were last week, stopping by the tailors for the newest polar bear skin coat or arctic fox fur scarf, or simply watching the whales on their migratory passage. The on-duty soldiers in their blue and white, fur-lined uniforms patrolled the streets, chattering amongst themselves jovially about the results of the last swim race or the rigorous training they'd undergone that week, whilst the off-duty ones roamed the pubs, seeking out bitter ales and cards.

Jasper gazed in awe at the ingenuity of the civilization. He'd been just as fascinated by the modes of transport in Idune and how people hinged on their powers to find their way in life. Here, it seemed, people had done the same. Coming from an island, water had always interested him, but not nearly to the creative extent of the people around him now. For him, water was a part of life. For them, water was a *way* of life. Transport, energy, food, entertainment—it connected them in ways he'd been too comfortable back home to consider.

Many things reminded him of his small island home, but so many others were new, foreign, exciting—or would've been if they didn't also make him think of Savara.

She would've loved this, he thought, as he stared into the canals at the shifting shadows beneath the surface. He'd come to think of Visanthe as a waking dream—sometimes it would scare him more than his nightmares of being eaten by dinosaurs, but other times, it would surprise him with beautiful depictions of life being fully lived. Maybe this was the adventure Savara had talked about. *She always loved fantastical things*, he remembered with a sad smile. But he doubted either of them could've imagined anything so grand as this.

When the curiosity wore off, he began to notice the strange way that people treated them in their procession toward a well-guarded snow fort. The crowds parted like the tides, not because of his eyes as Griffin and Captain Lucinda had warned before, but because of General Kyara and the two soldiers that flanked them. She strode through the city with him and Griffin in tow, her heavy feet on the bridges making even the water below them ripple. Soldiers whose paths they crossed, regardless of their current state, snapped to attention, placing fists over their hearts, and bowing their heads as she passed. Griffin nodded curtly to each one while he waved awkwardly to the friendlier-looking ones, receiving mostly raised eyebrows and scowls in return.

"Not like I was asking to be friends with you either," Jasper mumbled after passing a particularly grumpy-looking woman.

As they continued through the maze of bridges and isles, he wondered how his companions were doing back on the ship. Storm and Sebastian had both been in a mood this morning, and he hoped they wouldn't kill each other if left alone together too long. And then there was that man they'd picked up in Idune, Lance. Jasper had a sinking feeling he was more than just a common war prisoner, but Griffin had refused to speak on the subject, leaving him to wonder what purpose the man served. Curiously, the button of his nose, the protrusion of his collarbones, and the gentleness of his lips reminded Jasper of Savara. Perhaps if he'd lingered on the thought a little longer, he might have drawn some interesting conclusions, but all his thoughts were dashed as they reached the snow fort.

The structure before them loomed tall and formidable, built entirely of ice and compacted snow. Its walls rose high and proud, not as grand as the walls of Idune, but still impressive enough to deter any would-be attackers. As they approached, the kanala beside them got to work, their power turning the three-foot-thick door of solid ice to water in a matter of seconds. The waves parted with a soft hiss, allowing them enough time to pass through before the kanala reverted them to ice.

Stepping inside, Jasper's eyes widened in surprise at the scene before him. Fully harnessed and equipped bears roamed the interior of the ice fortress, serving as the main mode of transportation for its inhabitants. Some were fitted with armour, while others pulled carts loaded with supplies. The sight was both surreal and awe-inspiring, and Jasper couldn't help but feel a tinge of fear as one of the bears came close, its wide black eyes penetrating his soul.

"Nice bear," Jasper remarked, raising his hand to touch its snout. The bear recoiled, and huffed its foul, fish-scented breath over him.

"No time for making friends, Jasper," Griffin mumbled low enough so only he could hear. "Stay alert. We have eyes on us everywhere."

"I gathered," Jasper replied, watching the many dark faces glowering back at them as they left the open courtyard in favour of a private war room. "Remind me how I always get saddled with you?" he added as his eyes hitched on a line of guards holding silver-tipped spears. "I'm sure Storm and Sebastian need a babysitter."

"What do you think Lucinda is there for? Besides, if I'd left you with them, I might return to find you headless," Griffin said dryly, but there was a glint of amusement in his eyes. "We don't want that, do we? Although, given your apparent liking for dangerous creatures…"

"I think you're beginning to warm up to me," Jasper teased. At least their whispered conversation would take the edge off their grave encounter with one of the most fearsome leaders in all Visanthe.

Griffin raised an eyebrow at him. "Don't get your hopes up," he countered, a small smile playing at the corners of his lips as he entered the room.

Jasper rolled his eyes and followed him inside before the doors slammed closed behind him.

General Kyara's war room was a large, dimly lit chamber carved entirely out of ice and compacted snow. Along the walls were various weapons racks, displaying a range of deadly implements such as ice spears and javelins. The centre of the room held a massive, oval-shaped table made of polished ice, with a ridged map of Visanthe spread across it. Miniature figurines of soldiers, each with a unique insignia, were placed in battalions along various edges of the Ur territories, indicating the movement of troops and battle plans. A war was being waged, and Jasper hoped they wouldn't find themselves in the middle of it—again.

"Tell me, Izar child," General Kyara said as she plopped herself heavily into a chair at the opposite end of the room. "Where is our young Argia princess now?"

"Safe from the hands of those who would wish to exploit her," Griffin replied, narrowing his eyes at her.

Even though Jasper knew Griffin had no idea where Savara was, he hoped that his words rang true.

"I notice your pawns are poised for war," Griffin continued. "I must warn—advise you," he corrected himself, noticing her prickle at the word, "that war with the Harri would be futile. Their leadership has taken a more militaristic stance in recent months."

"Contrary to what you must have heard on the outside, Izar child, I have no interest—*yet*—in taking back my lands from the Harri. There is something much more pressing on my agenda. And it is this something that will earn you speaking time with the witch that took the princess's memories."

Jasper struggled to mask the surprise growing on his face. Had they finally found the person responsible for stealing Savara's memories? At first, the prospect of finding them excited him. For as long as he'd known her, Savara couldn't recall anything before coming to the island. The mystery surrounding her intrigued him, the lack of a past was one of the first things that stood out about her, but after getting to know her, he realised that her personality alone was enough to pique his interest. There were the countless hours spent at Skully's watching people, and inventing life stories for each passerby, the many times she'd recount to him her strange dreams that seemed to have been lifted out of fairy tales, the ones in which she'd dragged him out to the cove to snorkel around the sunken ships, leading him through jellyfish-infested waters to watch as the sea turtles fed. They spent many nights on the beach staring at the stars, talking about everything and nothing at all, as she was unable to sleep in her house, fearing all sorts of ghosts and things he didn't believe in. For years, he longed to know about the life she had before coming to the island, and now, he might finally get that chance.

But then, he remembered how defeated she looked after saving him from the shadows, after Camp Saar burned down, after the battle. At that moment, he wondered if it was selfish to want her memories back, as they might hurt her more.

General Kyara's heavy sigh at the other end of the room startled them. "Should you ever breathe a word of this to the outside world, you will be found and dragged to whatever ocean finds you closest and fed to the cruellest creatures of the deep."

General Kyara's words sent a chill down Jasper's spine. He swallowed hard and exchanged a worried glance with Griffin. The gravity of the situation was not lost on them. They both knew that the consequences of revealing what they had just learned could be dire. The threat of being fed to sea creatures was a stark reminder of the danger they were in. Jasper couldn't help but feel a twinge of fear and wondered if they had made a mistake by coming here.

Griffin's response was more measured, and he maintained a calm demeanour, nodding in agreement with the general's warning. Jasper admired his ability to stay composed in such situations. He tried to follow Griffin's lead and nodded in agreement, hoping to avoid any suspicion. Despite his fear, Jasper was determined to do whatever it took to help Savara, even if it meant risking his own life.

"Here in the Ur kingdoms, we have somewhat of a split ruling," General Kyara explained, her tone shifting slightly. "Regarding world politics, I am, of course, the face of the kingdom. However…" Jasper could feel the tension in the air as she trailed off, "my younger sister controls Solia, and was technically given the crown by our father upon his passing. She sits in the palace, guarding the more important artefacts of the Ur, one of which I am somewhat desperate to have in my possession. Especially if what you say is true of those Blood Daemons," she finished, her eyes flickering between Jasper and Griffin.

"What exactly are you asking of us, then?" Griffin asked, concern lacing his voice.

"In our culture, if there is a challenge to the rule of law, it must be overseen by outsiders, parties that harbour no feelings towards either the existing ruler or the challenger," General Kyara explained, her tone solemn. She paused for a moment before a sly smile curled on her face. "We do this to ensure the legality of transition and prevent accusations of foul play. That is where you come in. You will bear witness to and legitimise my taking of the crown."

CHAPTER 14

MASTER OF HERBS AND POISONS

"SAVARA, YOU'RE ALIVE!" Simon exclaimed as he entered the room, his voice laced with relief and disbelief.

Savara struggled to open her sleep-ridden eyes, trying to make out the contours of the man standing in the brightened doorway. The light behind him made his outline hazy, but she recognised his voice and the gleam of his glasses.

"Simon? Is that you?" she asked, her voice hoarse.

Simon rushed to her side, dropping a basket of produce, which sent apples and potatoes rolling across the floor. "It is you!" He rested a gentle hand on her forehead. "And you have a serious fever…" Simon hurried to a series of cabinets, almost tripping over the spilt produce in his haste, and began fiddling with vials. "Where in the world have you been? And what happened to you?"

Her head throbbed with each word he spoke. The Apprentice had abandoned her yet again, but this time, she seemed to be in better hands. "I was captured," Savara moaned as she struggled to sit up on the hay-filled mattress. This was the sixth time she had woken up to less-than-ideal conditions. She had stopped hoping that it would be an isolated incident after the third time, realizing that she would have no such luck. A vicious chill rushed over her shoulders as the slit on her cheek began to itch. "I don't feel well," she added weakly.

"I can tell," he said as he returned with a mug of some hot, dark liquid. "Drink this, let's try to bring that fever down." Simon handed the steaming mug to Savara and pulled a thick woollen blanket from one of the other cabinets in the small cottage. He draped it over her shoulders, tucking it in around her body to keep her warm.

Savara sipped the liquid, which tasted of peppermint, wood, and something sharp she couldn't quite place, but it helped with the shivers. As the warmth spread through her body, the fog in her mind dissipated slowly. The world around her began to take on proper shapes through her bleary eyes: a small wooden table and chairs, rough stone walls, and a simple kitchenette. It appeared to be the modest makings of a small cottage, and by the chill and faint scent of woodsmoke and herbs in the air, Savara guessed they were still in Idune.

"Simon," Savara began when the throbbing in her head died down, "where is everyone?"

Simon took hold of her wrist, and with it, started to count the pulsations of her heart. The purse of his lips told her that he expected better. He fixed his glasses on the bridge of his nose and replied, "They're headed to Iliso."

"They left us?" Savara shot to her feet with all her might, but her strange illness had other plans.

Her head throbbed with the effort of sitting up, her body heavy with exhaustion. She dropped back to the mattress and leaned back against the pillows.

Simon knelt before her and rested a warm and reassuring hand against her back. The ringing in her ears had subsided somewhat, but she still felt dizzy and disoriented.

"They went looking for the person who took your memories," Simon explained, his voice low and soothing. "Brass stayed behind to search for you, and I…" He trailed off, scratching the back of his neck with a guilty expression. "I'm no good in a fight. Sebas wouldn't have gotten into half the scraps he did if it weren't for me."

Savara shook her head. "Simon, that's not true."

"It's alright, Savara," he replied with a sad smile. "I figured the best thing for me to do was stay out of their way. I got a job at the university and promised him I'd keep my head down."

Savara's mind was racing, trying to make sense of everything. "I still can't believe they left without us."

"It's not like they wanted to," Simon reassured her. "They couldn't find you, and the council forced them to leave after its newest member took charge."

Savara's heart sank at the mention of the council. Ori's death had changed everything, and she knew that the new council member was likely to be less sympathetic to their cause. "Who took on his role?" she asked, her voice barely above a whisper.

"Lord Andor now sits at the head of the table," Simon began, his voice laced with concern. "But their newest member is also a military man by the name of General Dhoot. He's looking to persecute anyone who had anything to do with the attack, which is why Griffin had everyone leave as soon as possible. The council doesn't know me, or Brass for that matter, so we were able to stay and search for you… Though I haven't seen Brass for the past two nights."

Savara winced at the mention of the general. She had hoped to never hear of that slimeball again after he had kidnapped her, but it appeared she was wrong. Griffin's words echoed in the back of her mind.

There are two kinds of power in this world, Savara. Respect, which comes at a price to you, and fear, whose price is paid by others. Respect is earned only through your own suffering and humility, but fear is gained through deception, manipulation, and—on occasion—blood. Sometimes, the difference between them is so fine that they can be mistaken for each other, but if you look closely, you can see where the past leaves its mark.

Savara hadn't understood then what he had meant, but after spending time in the cell, strapped to the uncomfortable wooden chair, she found the truth in his words. She realised what Griffin had seen at dinner, that the general's past lingered on him like the foul stench of rotting eggs. His power came from blood.

"He's the one who held me captive," she finally replied, her voice barely above a whisper. The memory of her time in captivity sent shivers down her spine. She felt the need to wrap her arms around herself as if that could protect her from the general's wrath.

"That's not good. We need to get you out of here as soon as possible, but with your fever and malnourishment, it will be challenging to leave Idune," Simon said with a sad smile. "However, I can at least address the second problem."

Simon moved to the kitchenette and began to prepare a hearty stew using carrots, potatoes, green and purple tubers, and a slab of meat. He sparked two rocks together to start a small flame under the pot and added a pinch of salt and some ground spices to enhance the flavour. In no time, two steaming bowls of stew were placed on the small multipurpose table.

"Here you go, this should make you feel better," Simon said, offering a bowl to Savara.

Savara inhaled the aroma of the stew, which alone seemed to warm her insides. She replied with a weak smile, "Thank you," before tucking in. She closed her eyes and savoured the taste of the food on her tongue, letting out a soft hum of delight as it slid down her throat. "Simon, this is incredible! Has anyone ever told you that you're an amazing cook?" she exclaimed.

Simon blushed, "You're just hungry," he said, taking another spoonful of the stew. "I do have one question, if you don't mind me asking."

"Of course not," she said, resting the spoon in the bowl.

"You were captured, right?" he asked. Savara nodded. "Then how did you get here?"

A frown spread across her face. "I'm not entirely sure. A man came for me in the cell, and the next thing I knew, I was waking up on this bed." She decided it best to leave out *who* the man was, for now. After all, despite the various times he'd saved her life, The Apprentice couldn't be trusted. He worked with The Prince of Shadows, a man whose very nature was marked by blood, and whose fate seemed regrettably intertwined with her own. "It was all a blur."

"Well, the good thing is you're safe now, but we do need to see about getting you to the rest as soon as possible. If this new councilman finds out you're missing, he'll turn the entire city inside out looking for you."

Savara nodded before taking another spoonful. As grateful as she was to The Apprentice for bringing her to Simon's doorstep, she couldn't ignore the fact that his intentions were often shrouded in mystery. She almost wanted to believe that he had her best interests at heart, but the truth was that she couldn't trust him completely. It was yet another reminder that this world was layered with secrets and hidden motives, always watching and waiting for the right moment to strike.

Savara took a deep breath and exhaled slowly, trying to calm her racing thoughts. She stared down at her bowl, pushing the contents around with her spoon. She forced her thoughts away from The Apprentice and asked about Jasper's well-being instead.

Simon paused between bites before responding. "He was worried. Refused to leave. Griffin convinced him it wasn't safe, and they would be of more use elsewhere. Must have meant something to him. Left without a fuss after that."

Savara couldn't help but feel guilty for pushing Jasper away after Ori's death. She thought about how Ms Short used to say Jasper had always been by her side through everything, and how foolish she had been to cast him out just because he was human. The thought made her stomach churn with regret. At that point, between the guilt-ridden memories creeping back in and the sickness she knew had something to do with the gash on her cheek, she'd entirely lost her appetite. Savara set the bowl down on the table.

"Griffin always has an agenda…" she said with a heavy sigh.

Simon's compassionate eyes rested on her face. "He has for as long as I've known him, but he's a good guy." He reached out and placed a hand on her shoulder, offering her a small measure of comfort. "Jasper will be fine."

Savara didn't meet his gaze, instead turning her attention towards the main door and wondering what kind of trouble was lurking beyond it. "I hope so."

CHAPTER 15

FEVER DREAMS

SAVARA TOSSED AND TURNED, battling against the grooves of the uncomfortable hay mattress beneath her. The nightmares were back in full force. Even as she woke, strangled by the blanket that should've been protecting her, she could feel the flames licking her skin and the smoke clogging her lungs.

By now, she knew better than to say it was only a dream. The people she'd seen, the things she'd done… this was no dream. This was a warning. She pulled the blanket over her shoulders and made for the kitchenette, looking for something to make tea with. Something strong like peppermint would surely take away the chills—or at least leave her with more pleasant ones.

Savara plucked one of the small iron pots from one of the wooden shelves and filled it with water from a pitcher. She stared out at the night sky through the kitchen window. The lights of Idune glittered below, blotting out some of the smaller stars. She sighed. A younger her loved the stars. That younger her hadn't lost friends and loved ones in a war for a world she knew very little about. Now that she'd seen what troubles this world housed—the troubles she did—she cursed the very stars for their mocking glares.

She thought back on the conversation she'd had with Ori, staring out at the same stars under better circumstances. If people were descended from stars, did it mean that their actions and emotions were too? And their cruelty? Savara wondered what kind of hatred the stars must contain to breed evil like the Prince of Shadows and Big Tog… and The Apprentice.

She pulled her gaze from the stars and began searching for the spark rocks Simon had used to light the stove, knowing that their gaze would continue to haunt her well past the break of dawn.

"Looking for these?" called a voice from the shadows.

Having grown accustomed to his insistence in appearing out of nowhere—and where he wasn't wanted—Savara suppressed what should've been a scream and rested her hands on the counter. Her head slumped between her shoulders as she let out an exasperated sigh.

"You could give someone a heart attack like that," she hissed.

The Apprentice smirked as he strode over and leaned himself up against the counter beside her. "Don't worry, princess. The day I make your heart stop, you can believe it won't be out of fear."

Savara ignored him and snatched the two rocks from his hands, sparking them together with more force than required to set the house on fire, but the woodchips refused to light. "Will you ever leave me alone?"

There was a vibrance to him that hadn't been there on the other occasions they'd met, though the last time, she'd been too weak to notice anything other than the aching in her bones. Now, with her powers back in relative working order, she noted that even the air around him seemed lighter—his heart less void of feeling.

"That fire in you attracts me like a moth to a flame. Life can be dreary without it, that fervour, that yearning. A body is, after all, only a shell. It needs a fire to keep moving… So, in short, no," he said as he held his hand out towards her. Her eyes hitched on his scar as they had before, but the expectant wiggle of his fingers snapped her out of her daze.

Savara plonked the rocks in his palm and crossed her arms. "You and your colourful words…"

"Wording is everything."

"Then, try these ones… You killed my friend."

"We're doing this again?" The Apprentice asked casually as he sparked the two rocks together. In a single clink of the two stones, the flames roared to life, munching merrily on the woodchips beneath the pot. "One of these days, princess, even those hands of yours will be marred with blood, and then you'll have to accept that no one is fully righteous." He leaned in a little closer, the light of the flames highlighting his roguish grin. "But for now, let's just enjoy this moment, hmm?" Savara lowered her brow at him but couldn't help but feel a flutter in her chest. "You're welcome," he added, the twinkle in his eyes making it clear that he was enjoying their banter.

"That was luck," she growled.

"That was experience," he countered with a wink. His eyes traced over her form, taking in the way the firelight danced across her features.

Savara found herself hugging the blanket tighter over her shoulders, a new heat rising in her. "Why are you here?" she hissed.

The Apprentice rested the rocks on the counter and closed the gap between them with another step. "I felt I was needed," he said, his eyes glinting mischievously.

Savara grimaced at him. "Because you somehow sensed I needed help starting a fire?"

"Because that slice on your cheek is giving you a fever, and if your dreams are anything to go by, you won't last much longer unless we break that soul bond."

Savara took a bashful step backwards, pressing herself as far as she could into the countertop. "You can see my dreams?"

The Apprentice raised a pointed brow and smirked, letting the light of the moon catch the apples of his cheeks. "Ashamed?" he asked, his voice littered with coquettish delight.

She whacked him on the shoulder. "My dreams are private. For my eyes only," she hissed again. She feared if she raised her voice she'd wake up Simon, and she didn't quite know how to explain the appearance of The Apprentice to him, especially as she couldn't explain it to herself.

"Relax, princess. I can't see anything. I just know when you feel strongly about things. Fear, worry, joy, passion…"

Savara hoped his list of emotions stopped there, but judging by the grin plastered across his face, she guessed he sensed quite a few more that she would've rather kept private. Still, in all her time in Visanthe, she'd never encountered anyone with that particular power. It was almost like her own reading of other people's souls, though she needed to be close to the subject. He was always miles away when he read hers. But how?

She narrowed her eyes at him. "You plan on sharing how you're privy to my innermost feelings?"

"Depends," he said, lacing his arms across his torso and staring down at the pot of water that had just reached a boil. "You plan on sharing that tea?"

Part of her wanted to strangle him, but she knew it would be best to keep her emotions in check. If he could truly sense the stronger ones as he claimed, who knew what he might do with that information? There was a chance he'd pass it on to The Prince of Shadows at the earliest opportunity, and if so, he'd know precisely how to hurt her most. Savara shut her eyes and took a deep breath, visualizing constructing a wall within herself to suppress her feelings. When she opened her eyes again, she met his eager gaze and groaned. "Fine."

They strode out into the night, two cups of tea in hand. The blanket draped over her shoulders helped to ward off the cold mountain night. The Apprentice looked unfazed by the chill in an elegant long-sleeved tunic so black that it seemed to absorb light. He looked more relaxed than ever. The only other times she'd seen him, he'd been dressed in a finely tailored black suit. *Dressed to kill,* she thought with a frown. She couldn't tell whether the shivers that crawled up her spine came from a stray gust of mountain air or the thought, but as she turned to face him, she noticed another grin creeping across his face.

"Are you going to tell me now? Or are we going to freeze out here?" Savara asked, teeth chattering.

"That simmering anger of yours is enough to keep us both warm," he teased, but as she narrowed her eyes at him, he held out his scarred palm. "If you must know… This," he confessed.

Savara gazed down at it sceptically, the strange star-shaped mark that seemed recently healed and yet not entirely gone. "What is it?" she asked, reaching out to graze her fingers over it, but he pulled his hand away.

"I might have been the one to find your inner light, the part of your soul which controls your powers, and let's just say I might not have been as careful with it as I should've…" he explained, taking another sip of his tea.

"I don't see what that has to do with us being connected," she said.

"At the time, I didn't realise it, but a piece of you became stuck inside me," he replied, his expression turning serious as he gazed down at his palm.

Savara tensed. The truth made her uneasy, and the fact that he seemed to enjoy making her uncomfortable didn't help. "What do you mean a piece of me is stuck inside you?"

"Don't tell me you don't feel it too. A connection," he began as he inched closer, "a bond..." The Apprentice hovered over her, the sweetness of his warm breath clouding over her head as she stared up into his eyes. Tonight, those midnight eyes of his glowed with the vibrant hue of blue lightning. The scent of night flowers rippled from him, along with an air of mischief that only her powers could make palpable. Something had changed since they'd last met in Idune, an added playfulness and fervour for life that made her more wary of him.

"Forgive me if that isn't the most comfortable thought," she growled.

"You've been after the truth so long, I thought you might take more pleasure in finally hearing it," he replied, taking amusement in her discomfort.

"What made you decide to open up?" Savara said as she rolled her eyes.

"Maybe one of the locks on my mouth has broken..." The Apprentice raised a coquettish eyebrow. "Maybe the light of the moon is as magical as they say..." He reached out and brushed a strand of hair from her face, his touch sending shivers down her spine. "Or maybe the tea loosened my lips." He grinned as he took another steaming sip. With an easy sigh of delight, he added, "Definitely the tea." He leaned in closer, his breath warm against her cheek. "You might want to drink some before your lips turn blue."

Savara felt her cheeks heating up, and she was suddenly acutely aware of the moonlight highlighting her face. She hastily pulled away from him, avoiding his gaze, and focused on the mug in her hands, hoping to conceal her blush. "What are you doing here? And why do you insist on getting on my nerves?"

The Apprentice laughed at her apparent nervousness. "As I said, we need to break that soul bond if you're ever going to feel better."

"There is no *we*," Savara corrected him as she rested the mug down on the windowsill and hugged the blanket tighter around her body. "Simon's taking care of my fever, and I'll find some way to break the soul bond myself... without killing anyone."

"Easier said than done, princess."

"I don't need your help."

"Something tells me that's not how you really feel," he teased.

"So, you're an expert on my feelings now?"

He rested his mug beside hers. "No, but I do know a lot more than you give me credit for... For instance, I know that when you're mad at me, the pain ebbs. Or that you don't hate me as much as you think you should," he smirked as she narrowed her eyes at him. "Besides, your fever is torturing me as much as it is you. I'd sooner have you rid of it, for my sake."

"How thoughtful," Savara replied, her voice laced with sarcasm.

The Apprentice shrugged. "You don't tend to respond well to my thoughtfulness, so I thought I'd try being a little selfish."

"And here I thought that all you were was selfish, but by all means, start now," Savara said as she glowered at him. "It's not like you haven't already done enough damage..."

Suddenly, The Apprentice lifted her chin, bringing her under the full glow of the moon. Savara's breath caught in her throat as he stared intensely into her rainbow-flecked eyes. She tensed, intimately aware of his proximity, sensing the heat of his body radiating onto hers.

"Oh, princess," he said, his voice low and husky. "I can do a lot more damage."

Savara felt a different set of shivers tracing her spine, and this time, she couldn't suppress the emotions they carried. The blanket now seemed useless, even in the chill of the twilight air. Her breaths grew shallow, and her heart pounded in her chest. She wondered if he could hear it, standing as close as he was. But then she heard his own heart echoing in her ears and realised that part of this new fluster belonged to him as well. The heat of their bodies cocooned them against the cold as her powers drew them closer together. Where her breast met his chest, she felt their hearts beating in perfect synchronization, and a blush crept onto her cheeks.

The Apprentice grazed his thumb over the rubies marring her face, unfazed by their malicious sheen. "Tell me," he whispered. "Tell me you don't feel this connection between us. This magnetism…"

"I…" she began, but her brain fogged like the warm breaths they shared. She let the sound trail, filling what little space remained between them. She closed her eyes, trying to clear her thoughts as her heart raced at his touch. She knew she needed to resist him, but it was becoming increasingly difficult to do so. Her throat went dry. As she opened her eyes, she spied a similar pang of desire and uncertainty in his.

"Savara," he began. "I—"

Suddenly a light flickered on from inside the house. "Savara, is that you outside?" Simon called.

The Apprentice dropped his hand from her cheek as she turned towards the door. Simon leaned up against the doorframe, rubbing his sleepy eyes with one hand and holding a lantern in the other.

"Yes," she called back reluctantly. When she turned back, she found herself standing alone in the chilly twilight air, flecks of sparkling dust falling around her. Her heart sank.

"What were you doing out here?" Simon asked, his sleepy eyes hitching on the two mugs that rested on the windowsill.

"I had a nightmare and needed some air," she said with a heavy sigh. She picked up the two mugs and strode past him, depositing them in the washing basin before returning to her room.

Savara slumped back down onto the uncomfortable mattress and wrapped herself in the blanket once again, her mind racing from the encounter. She couldn't shake the unsettling feeling that there was more to The Apprentice than meets the eye.

That strange scar of his and the ability it gave him to sense her feelings was troubling, but more so was the fact that he'd only relayed part of the story. How had he gotten it? And why did he insist on appearing when she was in distress? Savara stared at the little box opposite her, the one that contained the Arima stone. His insistence that she have this stone bothered her. It felt as though he were trying to tell her something, but she couldn't understand what. The lack of clarity surrounding the subject of the stones bothered her. And his entanglement in the hunt for them more so. Every time they parted ways, she was left with more questions than answers. She was determined to find out what other secrets he was hiding.

Her finger danced lazily over her lips as she replayed the scene in her mind, trying to wrap her head around what had happened. She knew she was supposed to hate him. He'd done terrible things to countless people. And yet, each time they met, she couldn't help but find new layers to his façade. Perhaps this was his latest ploy to turn her world upside down, his latest form of torture. His mannerisms always had coquettish undertones, but never had he been so bold, so open in his teasing. Why now?

She couldn't deny the pull between them, no matter how much she wanted to. It was as if they were two opposing forces, drawn inexorably towards each other. The thought of his proximity made her heart race and her cheeks flush. If they hadn't been interrupted, what might have happened? Had she wanted more to happen? If he had planned to confuse her, judging by the way her heartbeat echoed in her ears, he'd more than succeeded.

CHAPTER 16

MOMENTS OF WEAKNESS

AS THEY RETRACED THEIR steps through the labyrinth of bridges and floating structures, Jasper couldn't shake off the unease that had settled in his stomach. The thought of legitimizing General Kyara's rule had him on edge, especially considering the potential consequences. After everything they'd been through, he'd built up a tentative trust with Griffin, but that didn't mean he agreed with him or his way of handling things.

The twists and turns of the pathways seemed to reflect Jasper's inner turmoil. He stole a glance at Griffin, who had an unwavering look of determination on his face. He knew Griffin well enough to know that once his mind was made up, he wouldn't back down, but Jasper couldn't help but worry about the consequences.

"Griffin, are you sure about this?" Jasper asked.

Griffin didn't answer immediately, his attention seemingly focused on the path ahead. Jasper could sense the weight of his thoughts as they continued walking.

"Legitimizing General Kyara's throne is a risk," Griffin finally spoke, acknowledging Jasper's concerns. "But it's a risk we have to take. The witch who erased Savara's memories is out there, and we need to find her. I'm certain General Kyara knows something about it, and we can't risk her not cooperating with us."

Jasper nodded, understanding the urgency of their mission. However, he couldn't shake off the feeling that they were walking into a trap. "But at what cost?" Jasper asked again, his voice heavy with concern. "What if we end up starting a war?"

"We'll do everything in our power to prevent that from happening," Griffin replied.

Jasper wanted to believe him, but he couldn't shake off the feeling that they were treading on dangerous ground and might be in over their heads. They made their way back to the ship, where Storm and Sebastian were waiting for news of their encounter with General Kyara.

"What did you mean when you spoke about witches demanding payment?"

"You of all people should've realised by now what I meant."

"Blood…"

Griffin nodded. "Like most things in this world. If everything goes smoothly, we will enter Solia as guests of the queen, alert her of the danger to the Ur stone, and find the witch who altered Savara's memories without any swords being drawn," Griffin explained. "And whatever price must be paid, I will pay it."

"Griffin, you can't—"

"The book has already taken too much from you. I've seen the way your hands shake; I've heard your screams. I will not let you put yourself through any more of this torture. Let's just hope that a steep price is our only worry."

Jasper nodded, finding a new appreciation for Griffin in his declaration. "Should we not find Sav first? After all, she is the one who needs her memories back."

"No," Griffin replied abruptly. "If my hunch is correct, she is safer wherever she is now."

Jasper narrowed his eyes at him. "You lied."

Griffin paused his stride and glowered at him. "What do you mean?"

"You told General Kyara the same thing, that Sav was safe. But you don't know that…" Jasper prodded, but Griffin held his tongue. "Why would you make that claim?"

Griffin took a deep breath. "Savara has powers that the world has not seen in many lifetimes, ones that give her an intimate connection with blood. You already know how dangerous blood can be…" Griffin's eyes fell on his arm, reminding him of the web beneath his sleeves. With a bashful nod, Jasper tucked it behind his back. "Such powers instil fear, warranted or not. I wouldn't put it past General Kyara to remove someone she considered a threat to her nation."

Jasper had seen the murderous vein in General Kyara for himself. He knew that Griffin was right, but he wasn't content with how everything had turned out.

As he went over the plan in his mind again, Jasper almost laughed at the thought of no swords being drawn. Storm and Sebastian drew swords the way they drew breaths, and, whether he sought them out or not, fights followed Griffin like moths to a flame. Even more troubling still were the many unanswered questions bouncing around in the back of his mind. Why did they need Savara's memories? What good would come from finding them without her present?

"You remembered her from before, right?" Jasper said, beginning his new line of questioning.

Griffin raised an eyebrow at him. "Where are you going with this?"

"You knew Sav before all this. Before her divination…"

"Jasper, you have a way of dancing around the things you wish to say that irritates me."

"You could've filled in the gaps in her memory yourself with whatever you remember, but you didn't. You chose to keep what you knew a secret and convince her she needed someone else to return them. Why? What more do you need to find?" Jasper was determined to get to the bottom of things this time.

Griffin lowered his voice as he spoke, keeping an eye out for the occasional canoes that crossed beneath the bridge they'd stopped on. "I know you're not fond of my methods—"

"It's not your methods that bother me. It's the fact that you shut us all out while playing with our lives. I don't know what happened to you in the past to make you this way, and I don't care. I just need to know what you want with her because, unlike with you, she isn't a pawn to me."

Griffin's features softened. "I may not feel the way you do, but I do still care about her."

"Prove it."

"I don't know everything. I only remember snippets. She was still just a child when I was sent away. I do remember she had a way with creatures, as though she could understand them on a different level. I doubt I'm the only one who'd noticed."

Jasper considered Griffin's words for a moment before nodding. "There were a few times back home where I'd noticed things as well. But how does that relate to her memories?"

"Savara's powers are steeped in blood and spirits, remember? I'm sure that book of yours told you that children aren't supposed to manifest powers before their divination." Griffin paused as a pair of on-duty soldiers passed by. The soldiers shot them a dirty look but kept walking, a reminder that they weren't exactly welcome here. "Well, I believe she did," Griffin continued when they were out of earshot. "And if that's the case, and Savara manifested her powers outside of her divination, then she is unbound by Iturri."

"Meaning she would be able to wield the stones together…" Jasper realised, remembering the prophecy he'd read about in the book. The prophecy, the legend involving the seven stones of Cartha, foretold the end of Visanthe. It included a ritual that involved the uniting of the seven stones, and which could only be completed by a soul unbound by Iturri. Jasper hadn't given much thought as to the meaning of that last part, but Griffin must have understood it immediately.

Griffin gave a small nod. "It would seem so."

"So, the legend is true?" Jasper asked as a chill not caused by the air around them settled over his shoulders.

"*All* legends are true if you go back far enough," Griffin replied. "If this prophecy is to be believed, then the fate of Visanthe rests on finding the seventh stone and the person who can wield it…"

Unease settled in Jasper's stomach. "And if Savara is that person, then General Kyara isn't the only one who would consider her a threat…"

Griffin's expression was grim. "No, she's not. That's why we need to find her before anyone else does. There is a chance that Savara's past might hold a clue to finding this seventh stone, but until we get her memories back, we will never know for certain."

Jasper frowned, fixing his glasses on the bridge of his nose before nodding. Nothing about their plan sat right with him, but it was the only one they had. "It feels like we are going around in circles," he said. "Like nothing we do gets us any closer to saving Sav or stopping the Arima."

"Perhaps fate has other plans for us," Griffin replied as he gazed up at the clouds overhead. Jasper had seen him do this very thing before, as though he were looking for answers in the skies. The scowl on his face seemed to say he didn't find any, or at least none that pleased him. "Fate is, after all, a curious thing," he added. "Each action, as trivial as it may seem, has its consequences, and each one is determined by powers much greater than ourselves." His voice sounded as though he were reciting scripture rather than engaging in casual conversation.

"Do you really believe that nonsense?" Jasper asked.

"I have to," he replied without further elaboration. "Now, swear to me you won't breathe a word of this to anyone," Griffin added as they neared the ship. "Not even to her."

Jasper let out a heavy sigh. He wasn't too fond of the idea of fate, of something dictating his every move, robbing him of his free will. But he couldn't deny the nagging feeling that maybe there was some truth to it. Still, he hoped that if fate were real, it was on their side. "I swear."

* * *

Storm sat on the edge of her seat, sharpening her favourite blade with meditative precision. The metallic ring of steel against stone echoed in her ears, soothing her mind and bringing her to a place of safety. It had been nearly five years since she had abandoned her family's home, the house where the winds never died. Yet, she could still hear the melancholic song of the house in the back of her mind.

As she made another sweep of stone across steel, she imagined herself sitting in the misty gazebo, sharpening the blades her father would never have allowed her to use if he had known. Even now, she feared that she would see the grey clouds of his rage sweeping across the floor the moment she opened her eyes. After all, he was the reason she had learned to fear storms.

"It's almost terrifying to think that you look more peaceful holding a weapon," Sebastian called from the doorway. The light sea breeze that drifted through the open door carried his scent deeper into her room. He always smelled of ash, the good kind that reminded her of a warm hearth on a cold winter's day, and not of the corpses they'd left behind in Idune.

"What do you want?" Storm grumbled, keeping her eyes closed and head down.

"The pleasure of your company, Stormy my dear," Sebastian smirked as he stalked over to her.

"I can't imagine why."

"Really? I can't imagine why I'd wake up to an empty bed this morning, especially as I thought…"

"You thought wrong."

Sebastian furrowed his brow. "Anika, you're not seriously—"

"Whatever happened last night was a mistake. A moment of weakness," she said, but she couldn't meet his gaze. "We were lonely or scared or both… but it was just that. A moment."

Storm was usually good at suppressing her feelings for him. Until recently, she hadn't realised they existed. Between the fire, the battle, and now, the thundery night they'd spent together below deck, suppressing them became a challenge almost too great for even her. But she had to remain strong. She needed to remember that whatever moments they'd shared had been just that. Moments. She knew of his reputation. His heart was as fleeting as a candle flame, and she wasn't going to be another conquest. She ignored the tension that settled between them as best she could, keeping her eyes fixed on the blade, rather than the scowl she could sense he donned.

"You're something else, you know that?" Sebastian groaned as he crossed his arms over his chest. "You wouldn't know a good thing if it stabbed you in the side with a broadsword."

"What's that supposed to mean?"

"You plan on ignoring what happened?"

"Sebas, nothing happened."

"We spent the night, or part of it at least, in each other's arms. Would you call that nothing?"

"Yes. Get over yourself, Sebas. I'm sure you've spent countless nights the same way." The words tasted bitter on her tongue, but she knew it was the truth. She'd heard as much from his own lips on many an occasion.

"And what? That's reason enough for you to pretend there isn't something between us?"

"I'm not another conquest, Sebas. Not another name you can scratch off a list. Not another log for your fire," she growled. She could feel an angry fluster blooming on her cheeks.

"You're a coward, Anika. You keep yourself distant because you're afraid of losing people."

Her grip on the sword tightened as Sebastian's words pierced through her. "What would you know?" she retorted, her voice laced with bitterness.

Sebastian's gaze remained unwavering as he spoke. "Don't think I haven't seen through you, Anika. We may share trauma, but we deal with it in very different ways."

"I'm not talking about this with you, Sebas."

"You can't keep it bottled up, either."

"I can do whatever I please! Now, get out or else—"

"Or else what?" he hissed as little flames shot out of his nostrils in exasperation. "You see, I'm afraid of losing the ones I love, so I hold them closer. But you? You push them away all on your own." In her silence, his anger subsided. "Why do you insist on fighting me, Anika?"

"I'm not doing this, Sebas." Tears stung Storm's eyes as she clutched the sword tighter, but she would not be so weak as to let him see them fall. "Leave," she mumbled.

Sebastian's expression softened. He took a tentative step towards her, wanting to reach out, but seemingly thinking better of it. "Is that really what you want?"

"Leave!" she yelled, thrusting the sword towards him. She met his eyes, her own filled with defiance.

The fire in Sebastian's beautiful citrine eyes dimmed, mirroring the pain she'd struck in him. He took a step back as if recoiling from a physical blow. She could see in his face that he was searching for a sign of her relenting, hoping that she would change her mind, but she kept her expression guarded and impenetrable. Storm buried whatever part of herself that held such emotions deep down, determined not to let anyone get too close. She didn't know how much longer she could hold back the tears, but she'd be damned if she let them fall in front of him now.

"Fine," Sebastian replied. He retreated slowly, turning his back to her. "You were never a conquest," he added in a whisper so soft it could've been mistaken for a prayer on the wind. The door slammed shut behind him, echoing through the empty room.

And then, she was alone, left with only her thoughts and tears. Storm leaned up against the wall, her body shaking with suppressed sobs, her sword clattering to the ground. All the emotions she had long ignored came rushing to the surface, and she couldn't hold them back any longer. If he hadn't already decided to be rid of her, she knew this would do it. He could walk free and she could be spared the future of pain that would come with falling in love again.

CHAPTER 17

THE PRIEST

THE SUN STRETCHED ITS rays over the tops of the mountains, rousing the villagers below. Savara waited for Simon to depart for work before she slipped out into town. The Apprentice was right, whether she wanted to admit it or not. She had to get rid of the soul bond before it killed her.

As she dressed, she considered the box with the stone. If, for whatever reason, Simon came looking for her and found it instead, she worried it might put him in danger. She removed it from the box, ignoring the luring calls for blood, and placed it into a small satchel which she tucked into one of her pockets. Better to keep such a dangerous thing on-person than have it fall into the wrong hands. She draped a traveller's cloak over her shoulders, fixed the hood so it covered the part of her face containing the bond, and set off into town, hoping there might still be a chance of finding Big Tog's son. If she could somehow manage to return him to Osiir, the first part of the bond would be complete, possibly buying her some time to find a solution to the second part— one that didn't involve murder.

Traversing Idune unchaperoned was a stark reminder of how much the city had changed since the attack. Scorch marks now marred the once-pristine stone buildings, and remnants of charred wood served as a painful reminder of the flames that had once engulfed the city. The air was thick with tension, and fear seemed to permeate the very fabric of the city. Parents clung tightly to their children, and everyone walked with a wariness that was absent before. Terra Soldiers loomed on every street corner, their watchful eyes scanning the crowds for any sign of trouble. Savara knew she had to be extra vigilant, lest she be reported to the council. If General Dhoot was indeed in charge, being caught could mean a return to the dark, cold cell where he had kept her before.

Savara stuck to the darkened lanes and smaller streets, knowing they would lead to the shadier side of the city. Each city had one, a place where the rule of the shadows became the rule of law, a place that normal citizens tended to avoid, and those who lacked the means to be anywhere else called home. If Big Tog's son was hiding out anywhere in Idune, she reasoned it would be here, away from prying eyes.

This side of the city was vastly different from the manicured streets of before. The buildings were almost a half-size larger on top than they were at ground level, and pressed tightly together in a way that made it seem as though if one fell, so would they all. The streets were a mix of dirt, cobblestone, and weeds. Most of the people wore travelling cloaks, possibly to avoid being associated with the slums or because, like her, they too had something to hide.

As she rounded another corner, Savara found herself in the heart of the slums, a small square bustling with a market and rimmed by various shops. Blacksmiths, tailors, a bookshop, a stationery shop, a bakery, and a small chapel surrounded the market. Patrons shuffled around the wooden stalls in haste, making it hard for her to manoeuvre through the centre. Instead, Savara chose to watch from the sidelines, trying to spot any out-of-place people who might look like Big Tog's son. She scanned the crowd, looking for anyone with red hair, fair skin, yellowish eyes, or a lingering hint of malice, but no one quite fit the profile. She did, however, notice a fair amount of people dressed in the colours of other nations, who haggled in foreign accents, and whose mannerisms, if nothing else, were a dead giveaway that they were not from Idune. At least, in that way, she would not be entirely obvious in her pursuits. She knew she had to keep searching, even if it meant risking her safety.

Savara lingered near the bakery, lured by the scents of cinnamon and anise that lulled her into a waking dream of sorts. The world took on a distorted quality, slowing as a different scene took place in her mind. Additional patrons strolled through the market, their phantom forms shifting in and out of view. A little girl tugged at her mother's flowing gown, begging for a cinnamon roll.

Savara blinked, startled by the new visions and unsure if to believe her eyes, but they only grew clearer. She could almost feel the warmth of a different sun on her shoulders, despite the heavy fabric of her travelling cloak. It wasn't until she heard the words *"Savara, behave,"* from the woman's mouth did she realise it wasn't just a vision but a memory. Another one.

The two ethereal figures rounded one of the stalls and faded from sight. Hesitant to let them slip away, Savara followed, weaving through the many market patrons, avoiding both those before her and those who existed only in her mind. She trailed them to the stationer's first, watching as the woman—her mother—picked out a quill whose feather extended an arm's length into the air, and then to the blacksmiths for a dagger whose handle was filigreed in gold, and finally to the chapel.

The building looked more run down at present than in her memory, the white paint chipped, the wood of the roof bleached by the mountain sun, but the feeling of danger that emanated from its interior was palpable in both. The marks on her cheeks tingled, resonating with something within. Her younger self hesitated at the door, looking as tense as she felt now, but her mother marched in, beckoning her inside.

Savara held her breath as she entered, following the visions into the dark.

The gilded pulpit shone under the lights of the various candles rimming the walls. They cast tendril-like shadows across the ceiling and floor that turned the relatively bare inside of the chapel into a cage. The pews followed the lines created by the shadows, whereby in standing the worshippers were bathed in light and in kneeling they were blanketed by darkness. Savara shivered at the thought.

The noises beyond the chapel doors died upon entry, leaving only the hollow sound of the wind filtering in from wooden slats high above her head, and something that sounded like whispers in her ears. Savara removed the hood of her travelling cloak to better locate the sound, but to her dismay, the room was empty. She followed the lingering voices to the pulpit, where an old, leatherbound book that looked to weigh more than she did sat open and catching dust. A flickering flame at the edge of the book bathed the open pages in an eerie green light. Beside her, the visions reappeared, along with that of an elderly priest whose eyes were white with blindness.

His voice was as soft as the rustling of pages as he said, *"Have you come to steal our secrets?"*

Her mother's melodious reply, *'Only death may hide, only time may steal, only blood bears witness to the truths we conceal,"* brought a gentle smile to his wrinkled face.

"Your Majesty." The priest bowed his head. *"What can I do for The Queen of White Fire?"*

"I wish to consult the oracle, but I must ask that this remain a heavily guarded secret." She pulled the dagger from within her cloak. *"I offer this tribute, Father, as a token of my faith."*

The priest nodded. Despite his blindness, he collected the dagger and held it up in the flickering candlelight. *"What is it you wish to know, Your Majesty?"*

"I need to know about my child..." her mother whispered.

The old priest furrowed his brow but nodded, ignoring whatever troubling thoughts he might have been thinking. The priest gazed into the eyes of her younger self, the all-seeing whites of his own causing her to recoil.

Savara could sense his worries even now, even in the darkness of the chapel, as though they lingered in the air, caught in the same web of time that held her memories hostage. But before the priest could speak, the vision faded from view. The beating of her heart echoed in her ears. She hadn't realised she'd held her breath.

"Is that it?" Savara whispered into the dark. A tingling feeling had crept into her palms. It felt like hunger for the missing part of herself and came from the depth of her soul. "That can't be it!" she yelled, her voice echoing through the empty chapel, dislodging pebbles from somewhere in the rafters.

"Are you lost, child?" a faint voice said from behind.

Savara turned to find an older version of the priest from her memories standing before her expectantly. His eyes were as white as she remembered, a tangled grey beard dangled at his gut. His presence felt heavier somehow, as though an invisible weight clung to him.

"I'm sorry, Father. I didn't mean to trespass."

"You have an air about you, child, that I find familiar." He stepped towards her; his unblinking eyes hitched on her face. "Have you come to steal our secrets?"

"No, I…" she began but caught herself. The vision she'd seen gave her an idea of how to get more answers. She cleared her throat, reciting the words her mother had used. "Only death may hide, only time may steal, only blood bears witness to the truths we conceal."

The priest tilted his head in contemplation. Savara spied a stream of blood-red gems peeking out from under his robes that trailed down his neck and likely further. She unconsciously raised her fingers to her cheek, running them over the gemstones carved into her skin. They were the same… Whomever this man was, he'd made more than one soul bond. Maybe that was the cause of the heaviness she sensed around him. Savara gulped, the thought alone sending shivers down her spine.

"I have not heard those words for quite a time." Despite the density of the air surrounding him, the priest moved with great agility. He brandished a gleaming dagger, aiming it at the hollows of her neck—the same dagger from her vision, unchanged by time. "Which tongue have you stolen them from, thief? And what is it you wish?"

"I'm sorry," Savara stuttered. "I'm not a thief. I remembered my mother saying it to you the last time we were here, and I wanted to know what it means."

The priest narrowed his eyes at her as his fingers held tighter to the hilt of the dagger. "The last person to speak the ancient greeting of priests was the late Queen of White Fire. It is true, she came with a child, but that child has long since perished. So, I ask again. Who are you?"

"I swear I am she, daughter of the Queen of White Fire, the last queen of Osiir," Savara replied.

He twirled the dagger between his fingers and retracted his attack. "Give me your hand, child," he said, extending his other hand towards her.

The nerves in her body tensed. The priest had an energy about him not unlike that of other powerful souls she'd encountered on her journey. Savara figured it was best to do as he said. Besides, he looked plenty capable with that knife of his. Should she decline, he might let it find a new home in her.

She rested her hand tentatively in his palm. In an instant, the dagger slit her palm, sending blood pooling in the wrinkles that lined it.

"I call upon thee, Iturri, one and only spirit, deity of our lands." A cold wind swirled around them, blowing out all but the one above the grimoire. "Let blood see truth for blinded eyes, let tainted words be marked as lies." He pushed her bleeding hand into the flame. Savara squirmed under the force of his grip. The flames flashed from green to white as they seared her skin. She tried to pull away, but he held her tighter. The scent of singed hair and skin filled the air. Beads of sweat formed at her brow and upper lip.

"Stop!" she screamed, but it was too late.

The thing inside her woke, summoned by her pain.

Rays of darkness launched themselves at the priest, tossing him to the other end of the room and ousting the final flame. Savara clutched her burned and still-bleeding hand close to her heart and rushed over to where he lay crumpled on the floor. His robes had lifted to reveal limbs covered entirely by blood-red gemstones.

"I'm sorry, I didn't mean to hurt you," she pleaded, but the priest waved her away.

"Your hand still bleeds?"

Savara looked down at her chest where the blood had begun to seep into her clothes and nodded. "Yes," she whispered.

The priest frowned as he rubbed a sore spot on his head. "No mark… Then it is true. You are she, the young princess of darkness. But how are you still alive?"

Savara offered her good hand to him and helped him up from the floor. "I cannot say, Father. I know nothing of my past. I was guided here by a vision—a memory, possibly—and was hoping you might be able to help." As she spoke, she willed her skin shut. The sickness of the soul bond on her cheek slowed her progress, but soon, there was nothing more than a faint red line in her palm where steel had met skin. "I want to know what you told my mother the last time we were here."

The priest hobbled over to the pulpit, lit the green flame once more, and began to flick through the pages of the old grimoire. "The phrase you spoke before was a greeting used by scholars of old, from the days before divinations. Those who know it are few, and those who use it seek out knowledge that has long been forbidden in our world."

"Then why would my mother use it?"

The priest sighed as he turned to face her. The flames cast sinister shadows across his wrinkled face. The whites of his eyes burned bright in the eerie light. "She was troubled by your lack of a mark. As I understand, a vision came to her one night in which the gates of Middle Isle crumbled into the sea, and a child was consumed by black flames. That child was you."

CHAPTER 18

UNANSWERED PRAYERS

THE WHISPERING OF THE chapel began anew, the sound still unintelligible in her ears, but she felt as though the voices were mocking.

"What did that dream mean?" Savara asked.

"Dreams are fickle things. Sometimes they are simply a manifestation of our worries. But Her Majesty's dream was something of a different nature." The priest took up the dagger once more, pricked his finger on the point, and pressed it to the page. The small droplet of blood seeped into the parchment, causing the letters to rearrange themselves.

Savara's eyes widened as she watched the new words form before her.

"Hers was a prophecy. The awakening of the one destined to change this world as we know it, the Harbinger of Death."

The words had come to her even before he spoke them. They rang through her mind in the voice of the one who'd first told them to her, the Prince of Shadows. Goosebumps danced along her shoulders, making their way from the nape of her neck down to the base of her spine.

"Can you tell me more about what that means?"

The priest's hollow eyes fixed blankly on her. "Your divination signalled to all that a change is coming to Visanthe, one that had been prophesized before even the exile of the sixth race," he said, his voice swelling as he spoke. "The divisions of power will crumble, divinations will cease to exist, the evil of the realm will roam free once more."

Savara looked down at her palms, the weight of her malevolent powers bearing down on her. She couldn't imagine how all these prophesized events would come to pass. Finally, she let out a defeated sigh. *Griffin was wrong,* she thought. *I am a monster…*

"Is there any way to prevent these events from happening?" she prodded.

"The knowledge I share pertains to the past. I can only provide insight into the immovable, the concrete, that which has already come to pass. This prophecy was written long ago, and I have no records that speak to the prevention of such events. Therefore, I must conclude that these ill-fated events are indeed fated." The priest lifted his gaping sleeve, revealing an arm covered in stones. The only skin visible was that from his fingertips to his wrists, as though he wore a suit made entirely of rubies. His blinded eyes fell on a wine-coloured, hexagonal stone in the centre of his forearm as he continued. "I told Her Majesty as much the last time we spoke."

Thinking it might be her only chance, Savara seized the opportunity to speak about her mother. "What was she like, and why can't I remember her?"

"Her Majesty was fierce and cunning. She ruled the Argia lands with calculated charm and a whip of flames. There was peace in her kingdom, though she herself was at war. Losses piled up for the ruler who gained her crown at only sixteen: parents, a son, a husband, and supposedly a daughter. How you stand before me remains a mystery, young princess, but it suggests Her Majesty was at least successful in preventing that loss." The priest bowed his head solemnly. "It is a shame she would meet her own end but half a decade later." He dropped the sleeve of his robe and set out to relight the sconces on the walls. Despite his blindness, he dodged each bench and every unsteady stone, intimately aware of his surroundings. Savara wondered if it was familiarity or some other power that gave him such an ability. "But Her Majesty was a cursed woman who, in seeking out power, brought about her ruin. Once set in motion, ruin cannot be stopped. As for why you cannot remember, all I can offer is a stone reading."

The priest tapped his foot on the floor, raising the stone and warping it into the shape of a large chalice. He waved his hand in the air and summoned a variety of pebbles from around the chapel. They swirled in the air overhead, rounding themselves out and carving symbols into their faces, before falling gently into the basin. The priest then took up the knife once more, summoning the spirits around them for another request.

"Reveal to me, oh great Iturri, the truth behind this child's past and the reason for her memory loss." One by one, he slit the tips of his fingers, letting the blood fall to the basin below, each droplet sizzling as it touched the stones. "Give me your hand again," he said to her, his expression grave and determined.

Savara consented, extending her palm, and wincing at each prick of her fingers. As her blood hit the basin, she felt a strange new connection to the powerful force buzzing about the stones. The priest's voice grew distant as he chanted an incantation. Her eyes glazed over, as though she were falling into a deep slumber.

"It will all be okay, Savara, my sweet."

Savara opened her eyes to find her mother's tear-streaked face hovering just above her own. She looked down at a dripping wet yellow tulle gown that looked sickly green in the sad blue hues of the stormy morning. Her black hair hung in loose knots that the rain had ripped away and dragged down from their manicured forms atop her head. She felt droplets pooling at her chin, unable to tell whether they were the result of the rain or the tears she'd been crying.

Her mother's amber eyes sparkled even brighter in the storm. Raindrops sizzled as they met her skin, refusing even to ruin the shoulder-length blonde curls that framed her mother's face. "You will be safer there," she whispered. "And you will forget this turmoil." Her mother planted a warm kiss on her forehead. The scent of peaches, cinnamon and cream emanated from her as though it were baked into her skin. Savara savoured that scent, feeling closer to home than she had in a long time. Her mother's scent warmed her better than any fire ever could. But then, her mother pulled away.

The woman before her had eyes that shimmered like the turquoise waters of a tranquil sea on a sunny day. Her dark face was framed by two perfectly knotted white braids that cascaded down to her hips. She wore a dress that flowed over her body like a waterfall, but her disposition was anything but calm. She briefly frowned at the young princess before closing her eyes and summoning a myriad of raindrops to her fingertips. She pressed her hands gently to Savara's temples…

Savara opened her eyes once more to find three stones hovering above the basin. The priest plucked them one by one from the air and turned them over in his palm.

"The double chalice, the sign of interference," he said as he stared at the first one. "Your memory loss is not a natural phenomenon. Someone has tampered with your mind."

Savara nodded. And now, not only did she know when but who as well. The woman she'd seen in those brief seconds of hazy recollection had controlled the water around her. Whoever she was, she must've been from the Ur nation, and by the way she dressed, there was a good chance she was royal too. The experience had left her with a throbbing headache and a stream of tears that cascaded down her cheeks.

"The wilted rose, the sign of loss," the priest continued. "Of which there has been much. With regards to your mind, it appears what was done cannot be undone…"

Savara's heart echoed in her head as the priest spoke. She looked down at her hands, clasping them tightly in her lap, and tried to calm her racing thoughts. But the unease lingered, like the shifting shadows cast by the sconces.

"That can't be right."

"This troubles you," the priest said. "Why?"

Savara bit her lip as she contemplated how to explain herself. "I am starting to regain some of my memories… at least, I think I am. How would such a thing be possible?"

The priest frowned. "If so, my assumptions were correct. You are dying."

"What?" Her lungs constricted. She felt as though her world had collapsed in that very moment.

"The bond on your cheek is laced with malice. Your soul might be replaying the events of this lifetime in preparation for the next."

"But I can't…" she stuttered, struggling for breath. "I need to know…"

The priest rested a hand on her chest. "Be still, your life is yet your own."

Something in his touch quelled the swelling anxiety. Savara took a moment to compose herself before her next question. The last thing she'd expected from her journey was to be working under such a limited time frame. Now, it was imperative she get all her answers as fast as possible. Maybe then, she could reverse the damage that had been done before it was too late.

"Iturri chooses its host and form, right?" she asked, remembering what Griffin had told her in his tent upon her return to Visanthe. The priest furrowed his brow and nodded. "Well, I need to know if I was a good person before or if…" She'd never spoken this fear aloud, not even to

Jasper, but it haunted her ever since she found out about her powers. She wondered if she was somehow flawed, broken, cursed even. Destined for only destruction. She wondered if it had always been that way. "Or if I have these powers because I wasn't."

"Not even your memories, young princess, will show you such a thing. That knowledge resides in your heart, and there alone. You should know better than any that a heart is a powerful thing," he said as he stared down at his arm. "It controls things more powerful than memory."

"Forgive me," Savara began. "Are those stones on your body…"

"Soul bonds? Indeed, but not malignant like yours. The holy men of our lands are bound by blood. Our teachings, our secrets, and those of others. These are the marks I will take to my grave. Blood is intimately entwined with spirit, and the heart is the organ of blood," he added. His tone of voice hinted at knowing more, but his explanation ended there. Instead, he turned back to the final hovering stone.

Savara could feel the apprehension in the air between them. His movements were slow, heavier than she'd seen them before. She almost thought she'd heard him sigh as his fingers closed over the stone. As he brought it close to his chest, a twitch in his lips betrayed his sorrow.

"What's wrong?" Savara asked.

"It was the same stone I pulled for Her Majesty all those years ago." He unfurled his fingers and brandished the little stone towards her. "The pierced circle…" The priest hesitated. "Sign of death."

His words lingered in the stillness of the chapel, raising goosebumps on the back of her neck. "What does that mean?"

"Whatever you may be, young princess, you cannot escape the darkness. It follows you, clinging to the very blood beneath your skin. Darkness with a history much longer than your own." The priest dropped the stone in the basin once more and muttered under his breath, "Dark attracts dark…" He turned his clouded eyes to the doors of the chapel. "Even now, as we speak, a spirit with vengeance in its heart has arrived in Idune."

"Please, I need to know more," Savara begged, but the priest shook his head.

"You are in danger, child. The owner of that soul bond on your cheek draws near, impatient and hungry."

"If you know of my bond, please, at least tell me where I can find what I am looking for."

Reluctantly, the priest reached into the basin, plucked a final stone, and brandished it towards her. "The wave, the sign of travel and movement on water. Now please, young princess, leave this place. Seek out other lands, and, if you can, live."

"But—"

The priest stomped his heavy foot and thrust a palm out in her direction, shifting the stone floor beneath her. It carried her out of the chapel as the wooden doors closed behind. The loud thud sent birds flapping from the roof and turned the heads of a few market patrons.

Savara fumbled the hood of her travelling cloak back on and tugged the sides in close to hide the smear of blood on her chest left by the priest's test. She sought refuge in the shadows of the buildings that lined the market square. She already stood out like a single white rose in a field of red ones, and if this danger was as close as he'd made it seem, she needed to leave, and fast.

Her mind kept going back to the stones covering the priest's body, wondering how he could move with such swiftness despite being almost entirely covered. With her powers, even standing near him was enough to sense the heaviness that comes with a lifetime of soul bonds. Having felt the weight of a single soul bond on her skin, she wondered how he was standing at all. But she didn't have time to think too hard about it. A familiar tingle of malice swept over her, emanating from the centre of the market.

He was here. Big Tog. As if reading her mind, the ram-horned figure appeared amidst the crowd, gazing up at the chapel she'd just fled.

Savara weaved through curious patrons, dodging glares, and unfriendly faces. She needed a hiding place, or at least a better vantage point. She ducked into one of the small crevices between shops that held only tall tubes and discarded crates. It didn't offer much in the way of visibility and nothing in the way of escape, but it did have a decent view of the entrance to the square. If she could plan out an unsuspecting route, she could make her escape.

Suddenly, a pair of hands grabbed her, cupping her mouth and tugging her further into the crevice.

Savara squirmed beneath her travelling cloak, cursing her decision to don it. The thing she'd used to keep herself hidden was now the thing that made her blind. If the person behind her was working with Big Tog, she knew the only way out would be through a fight using the very thing she'd been taught to use by the mafioso himself, her powers.

"I don't want to hurt you," she mumbled from beneath the hold as she closed her eyes, homing in on the person's soul. Something about the almost-emptiness of it seemed familiar. Her suspicions were confirmed the instant the person spoke.

"One day, princess, I'd like to see you try."

Savara let out an exasperated sigh. Only one person ever called her princess. He pulled back her hood and spun her around to meet his eyes.

Of course, when things go bad, he appears… Savara glowered at The Prince of Shadows' lapdog. If she'd been more focused on her surroundings than planning an escape, she might have noticed the scent of night flowers had replaced that of waste.

"You," she hissed.

Slivers of sunlight glistened on his inky black tunic making him stand out even against the shadows of the alley. Mischief glinted in his eyes. "It's nice to see you too, princess," The Apprentice replied, looking more self-assured than usual.

Savara rolled her eyes. "What are you doing here?" She wriggled herself free of his grip.

"Have you already forgotten?" he smirked as he leaned up against the wall. He contemplated the scar in his palm fondly as he spoke. "We're connected. I feel all those worries and fears of yours."

She palmed her forehead. "Fine, but what are you doing here now?"

"Good question. Better question. What are you?"

"I don't have time for your nonsense."

"Nonsense? I'm offended."

"Good, so go!" Savara peered around the corner once more, searching for the characteristic copper hair curled into ram horns. "You're nothing but trouble."

"You didn't seem to think that last night," he said, a coy grin spreading across his face.

In truth, she'd thought she'd imagined last night's events. Hearing them acknowledged and from his lips no less, sent shivers down her spine. She was ashamed to even consider the part of her that had wanted something to happen between them. He was no good, the worst of bad omens, yet… he still insisted on being there for her in moments of difficulty. "Last night I was half asleep and sick. I wasn't in a position to be making good choices. There was nothing else between us."

"Sounds like a denial of passion, princess. Enjoy it. I hope it'll keep you warm in the winter."

"In case no one ever told you, passion does not equal trust."

"So, you admit it?"

"Besides," she continued, ignoring his comment as she turned back to him with a stare that could've pierced flesh, "I don't have time for this. I'm trying to get out of here, find Big Tog's son so he doesn't kill me, be free of this," she pointed to the stones on her cheek, "and get back to my friends. Your constant inconvenient appearances are not helping."

"Hmm…" He pretended to pick dirt from his nails. "Inconvenient appearances? So, I take it you aren't ready to accept my help then?"

"I wouldn't call what you do *help*."

The Apprentice raised a heavy black eyebrow. "The man you're looking for is waiting for you just beyond the northern entrance. He has two goons positioned on either side of the square, one leaning up beside the church and smoking a cigarette, the other in the baker's pretending to eat a hot cake that has long since gone cold."

"Shit…" she mumbled as she stomped her foot on the ground.

"The way I see it, princess, you're not getting out of here alive *without* my help."

Savara peered around the corner again, looking for the two men he'd described. Sure enough, she spotted them both, and the route she'd planned would've taken her past them and into the hands of a furious Big Tog. Once again, she was stuck with him as her only chance for survival. It wasn't a position she was fond of, but it wasn't worth dying over either. Savara slouched her shoulders, letting the weight of the cloak hang heavy over them.

"This doesn't mean I trust you."

"We'll get there eventually. I'm patient." The smirk on his face turned into a full grin. Mischief burned in his eyes as he spoke. "Brace yourself," he added as he reached into his pocket and pulled out a handful of that awful travelling dust.

So, that's how you keep appearing, she realised, the frown on her face growing deeper with each passing moment spent with him.

Reluctantly, Savara stepped towards him and took hold of his outstretched arm. *Wherever we're going is better than here.* She repeated the words over in her mind like a mantra of protection. All she had to go on was the shaky word of a man who'd just as soon leave her for dead if his master so wished it. But then, there was something to his constant saving her that made her wonder where his true intentions lay. This thought and her mantra occupied her mind as the sparkling black dust consumed their bodies.

CHAPTER 19

SHOP AT THE EDGE OF THE WORLD

THEY LANDED ON THE wooden floor: The Apprentice gracefully and with a soft thud, Savara with three consecutive thuds—a shelf, a table, and a hard fall that made her intimately aware of the bones in her backside.

Savara rubbed it as she looked around at the towering walls of rolled fabric around them. She'd knocked into one on her shaky landing. Out of the corner of her eye, she spied a large wooden table, whose edge had dug into her side as she'd looked for something with which to stabilise herself. A cold breeze trickled in from the slats in the floor beneath her, shifting the stray threads, clippings, and random buttons scattered about it.

"Where are we?" she asked, rubbing her sore backside.

The Apprentice offered her his hand and helped her up. "The tailors. I'm not walking around this city with you covered in blood." He strode over to a curtain at the opposite end of the cramped room, ripping it open to expose the main sala of a small dressmaker's shoppe, lined with mannequins in draping gowns of mostly silvers and whites, with other colours lining the racks between. "For one thing, it'll make us stick out more."

Savara stared down at the second-hand tunic and pants that Simon had found for her and frowned. The ill-fitting clothes alone would make her stand out beside The Apprentice; the blood smeared across her chest wouldn't help either. It hadn't been hard to convince her that she needed to change, but she would've been content with any old thing. Most of the clothes in the shoppe looked made for royalty. They reminded her of her trip to Osiir and how she'd tried on her mother's dresses. She walked out of the drafting room and towards a mannequin with a white dress with slits on either side of the legs and draping sleeves that looked eerily similar to one she'd seen before. Possibly in a dream.

"I don't have money for anything, especially not things like these," she said, admiring the delicate gold embroidery at the bust and hips.

"I do," he replied as he flipped through the racks of clothes himself. "Find something pretty. We need you looking presentable."

"Why?"

He pulled out an emerald velvet dress with a plunging neckline. "This one is nice. Reminds me of that night we danced. Green is your colour," he said with a wink.

"I'm not wearing that."

"You're right, too heavy."

"It's not that—"

"Is it the green? I know it's a vibrant colour, but it brings out your eyes."

"No, I like the green, but that's not what I meant."

"The colour will stick out here too. Let's find something a little more muted…"

"I don't need your charity."

The Apprentice raised a brow at her as a grin spread across his face. He laughed softly. "Who said anything about charity? I fully expect to be reimbursed. And at the rate you're going, between saving your ass and getting rid of the stones on your cheek, you're in deep." He strode over to the mirror and fixed the collar of his tunic.

"So, you're taking advantage of me." She crossed her arms over her chest and scowled at him.

"You know, princess, one day it would be nice to hear the words 'thank you' come out of that stubborn mouth of yours," he said as he stalked over to her.

"It would be nice if you ever did something worthy of being thanked."

"Saving your life isn't enough?"

"Not when you're also working with the person trying to take it."

"Have you ever considered the fact that I…" he began, but the words froze on his tongue. His mouth continued to move for a second as though he were chastising her, but his voice made no sounds. The Apprentice shook his fists at his side before taking a calming breath. He ran his fingers through his hair and scoffed. "Has anyone ever told you how frustrating you are?"

"Then why do you insist on *saving* me?" Savara demanded.

The Apprentice took a turn about the sala, letting the soft click of his boots against the wood fill the silence between them. "You've got a lot of questions," he replied finally.

"And you, very few answers."

"I have a lot more than you think."

"Then why can't you ever give a straight one?" Savara hissed as she watched him fiddle again with the dresses.

The Apprentice gazed up from the racks of clothing and narrowed his eyes at her as he contemplated the question. "Maybe not all questions are meant to be answered…" He toyed with some of the mannequin's dresses, still searching for the one that would best suit her. "Maybe you wouldn't like the answers I'd give…" He doubled back, more composed than before. His elegant stride planted him before her, close enough that she was pinned between a rack of clothes and his chest. "Or maybe…" he added, a grin spreading across his face as he looked down. "I just like doing your head in."

Savara scowled at the mischief growing in his eyes. "And you call *me* frustrating?"

"Good, so we're even." The Apprentice brandished a coy smile as he pulled a dress from one of the hangers behind her. "Try this one on."

The dress was simple, airy, the colour of morning fog with covered sleeves and a corseted waist that bled into a thick satin skirt.

"No way. I'm not a court monkey. Plus, I won't be able to move quickly. If you insist on me changing, find me some pants… please."

"Fair… But you still must look somewhat presentable." The Apprentice scoured the room once more, this time returning with an elegant, off-the-shoulder blouse, a small corset, and pants. "Alright, how about this, my little *court monkey?*"

"Still not a court monkey, and definitely not yours." Savara rolled her eyes at him. "Why the corset?"

"Here, the boning is made of light steel and the lining is weaved with thin metal strands. A tad heavier than traditional cloth, yes, but a must for anyone who gets into as much trouble as you do."

"Hmm…" She narrowed her eyes at him before snatching the clothes and stomping into the back room.

"Careful, princess," he called to her. "You keep glowering at me like that and one day your face will freeze that way."

Savara made a crude gesture towards him before drawing the curtain. She slipped into the new clothes, hid her old ones in the corner of the drafting room, and admired herself in the mirror. These seemed to fit her nicely, accentuating what little curve she did have in her waist and shifting up her bust.

What worried her now was his insinuation of needing to blend in. She had no idea how far they'd travelled or what was in store for her. Savara sighed deeply. She lifted her hand and stared at her open palm. The marks from the priest's test had vanished, but she could still feel the tingle of her powers in the lines on her skin. She may not like her powers, but she couldn't deny their utility. If she ever encountered more people like the priest and The Apprentice, swordplay would never be enough to protect her.

Savara closed her fingers over her palm and sighed. It was time she redefined her relationship with her powers. Murderous as they may be, they might also be the only thing protecting her in the end. She re-tied her travelling cloak and, noticing something hard at her side, reached into the inner folds of fabric. *The stone…* she remembered. It pulsed in her hand, finding synergy with the stones on her cheek, lightening their weight ever so slightly. She didn't have time to wonder at the strange effect it had on her, only that she sensed it prodding, sending strange slivers of feeling through her bones. It was best to keep it tucked away for now, The Apprentice was waiting for her just beyond the curtain and she didn't need her powers making an appearance. Savara shoved it between the fabric and boning of her corset and strolled back out onto the main floor.

She cleared her throat to get his attention. "Good?" she asked.

The Apprentice finished scrawling a note and placed it on the counter under a sack of what she imagined were coins before looking up at her. He blinked as if trying not to gawk. "Well," he began, a grin spreading across his face. "It's certainly better than those hand-me-down tunics you were wearing, but…" he paused as he stalked towards her.

Savara narrowed her eyes at him as he neared. She tried to take a step backwards, but her feet were bolted to the ground. His proximity raised the hairs on her neck.

The Apprentice dropped his face to the side of her cheek. "I still can't get the image of you in that green dress out of my head." Savara recoiled and made to swat his face, but he caught her hand easily. "Calm down, princess," he said with a laugh. "I just like to rile you up."

"Keep it up and one of these days you won't catch my hand," she scoffed.

"I look forward to that day," he replied. His free hand made to part her hair from her face, hovering in place until she allowed him. As he brushed the strands from her eyes, his own lingered on the scar across her cheek. His grin faded into something more melancholic in nature. "Let's go. We don't have all day." The Apprentice pulled against the attraction between them and made for the door.

Savara furrowed her brow as she contemplated him. Between the new clothes and the outbursts, she was beginning to feel more like her old self again. The fever and pain of the soulbond lingered, but less so when she was around him. Whatever claims he'd made the night before about distracting her from the pain might have some weight to them after all. It wasn't quite safety that she felt around him, but it was no longer fear either. She raised her hand to the gems on her face, thinking about the connection he'd forged between them, wondering too if her symptoms had lessened because they were plaguing him too.

"Do you plan on telling me what we're doing?" Savara called as she followed him onto the street. A heavy fog had set in wherever they were, making it hard to see more than a few feet in front of her. What little street she did see beneath her feet wasn't cobblestone, like in Idune, or sandstone, like in Osiir. It was a mixture of wood and marble. Lightheadedness swept over her as she breathed in the thinness of this foreign air. "We aren't in the Harri provinces, are we?"

"Very astute of you, princess," The Apprentice replied.

"Where in the world are we?"

The fog at the end of the street began to clear. The Apprentice slowed his step, waiting for her to catch up. "The high lands of Haizea…" he said, tilting his head upward towards the tall spires of the cloud palace.

"You've got to be kidding me," she hissed. Savara removed her hood to get a better view of the structure. Columns of white marble loomed over them, rising from the mist like apostles reaching for the heavens. Behind them, a grand staircase led to a chapel-esque structure boasting a domed roof with gold and silver detailing that glowed under the nearness of the sun. "Why are we here? I need to get back to my friends and find some way to get rid of this soul bond. We need to go to the Ur nation."

"You don't want to be involved in that one, princess. Things are about to get crazy in Iliso."

"How do you know that?"

He tapped a finger to the bow of his lips, reminding her of whatever lock he had on them that prevented him from speaking openly. "Trust me."

"The more you say it, the less I feel inclined to," she mumbled to herself.

It was true, something about him was different, more vibrant, more open. He'd saved her from Big Tog and the shadows. He'd rescued her from the cell. But that didn't take away the fact that he worked with the Prince of Shadows, that he killed Ori—and probably countless others. Her trust was a luxury, and one she wasn't ready to give. So long as he kept his promise and didn't hurt her, she'd go along with his plans. Savara stared down at her palm, imagining the scar in his. It was a good thing he couldn't read her thoughts, that way, he wouldn't know how lost she was when it came to him.

CHAPTER 20

SWORD TO SWORD

STORM HADN'T WISHED TO remain on that cursed boat. The rocking, even as they were docked, was driving her insane. It reminded her of the kite gliders they used to ride on back home but with one subtle yet important difference. When she was ready to get off, there was always firm ground awaiting her. Not on a boat. On a boat, she was surrounded by those same sickening currents, only magnified.

After her argument with Sebastian, her emotions had run wild, getting the better of her as she'd been told many a time not to allow. Storm sheathed her sword and strapped it to her belt. She'd be damned if she stayed on this floating wine barrel any longer.

"Mind that cold fury of yours doesn't wreck my ship," the captain called from the other end of the hall, standing between her and freedom.

"Why don't you mind your own business?" Storm growled, maintaining the urgency in her strides.

The captain laughed, her infectious sound only amplified by the jingling of her many bangles and necklaces. "Funny you bring that up," she began as she crossed her arms over her bust. "This just so happens to be my ship, and everything that goes on in my ship is my business, ergo, you and that cold fury of yours…" She blocked Storm's path with her arms and whispered. "My business."

Storm huffed. "What do you want?"

"Lucy," the captain said, extending a hand out towards her. "I'd take it if I were you," she added with a vicious smile. "I'm just as proficient as I've heard you are with a sword, but I'm also conveniently lacking in all the morals that allow you to hold your nose up so high."

Storm cocked her eyebrow at the fierce captain, sizing up the threat. "Anika," she replied finally. "Though everyone calls me Storm."

"Good," Lucy said with a menacingly bright smile. "I have a thing about nameless entities on my ship, but now that that's out of the way, you look like you could use a sparring partner."

"What I need is to get off this ship," Storm replied, unrelenting in her anger.

"As much as I am offended by that comment, this ship being the pinnacle of sleek aquatic ingenuity and aerodynamics—and my own, personal design, of course—I do understand that you people of the air are not as well-versed or appreciative of the somewhat temperamental nature of water. As such, I have arranged an alternative."

"Fine, so long as it will get me off this ship faster."

Lucy clapped her hands together, the sound of the bangles filling the hallway. "Excellent, follow me."

* * *

Lucy and Storm wandered the maze of frostbitten wooden docks in the small, seaside village. Around them, children played with snowballs and tried their hands at spearing shimmering fish from the comfort of the docks.

Though Storm was grateful for the extra coat Lucy had provided, the cold didn't bite into her as much as she'd believed it would. Her own home in the land of a thousand storms was always being hit with some new frigid current of air from one of the surrounding mountains, whether her father's mood had any hand in it or not. Despite the overall chill in the air, the people around the village seemed friendly, jovial in spite of the harsh climate. A group of little ones brushed past them, racing towards one of the newest canoes. One accidentally bumped into Storm in her haste as she tried to keep up with the others. A small girl with eyes as bright and blue as the ice beneath the surface of the sea stared up at her.

"I'm sorry," the little girl offered as she dusted the snow from them both.

Storm sighed, the heaviness in her chest releasing slightly. "Be careful, and watch where you're going," she replied softly, unwilling to acknowledge the many ways in which the little girl chasing after the friends she couldn't keep up with reminded Storm of herself. Storm gave her a pat on the icy white braids lining her head and smiled. The little girl in turn beamed up at her and hugged the outside of her leg before racing off to find her friends.

"You are a tortured one, aren't you?" Lucy asked after having witnessed the scene play out.

"What's that supposed to mean?" Storm growled.

"Exactly what I said it does. I may flatter and exaggerate when it suits my needs, but I don't mince words. I am not as measured as you and your people are with the ones that come out of your mouths, though I hesitate to call what you do measuring… more like bottling, compacting, and trying to forget things that wish not to be forgotten."

"Lucy, I never agreed to personal interrogation."

"No, but I figure being surrounded by people on a daily basis who aren't quite as in-tune with the ways of the feminine might play a hand in your detrimental behaviour," she said as she led Storm out of the village and to a makeshift arena of dirt and frost. Around them, various glaciers glinted in the midmorning sun.

"You're purposely trying to ignite me, aren't you?"

"Guilty as charged," Lucy said with a mischievous grin. "I'd hate to spar with someone who lets their baggage consume them. Makes for an uninteresting victory. I'd never truly know if it was my skill or their detriment that caused it, and I am a prideful being. Can you see how that might not sit well with me?"

Before she could restrain herself, a cackle fell from Storm's lips. She clapped a hand over her mouth quickly, but the damage had been done.

Lucy shook her head. "Don't fight it," she laughed. "If we're going to have a chance at healing…" she waved her hand in the air, gesturing to Storm's body, "any of that, we're going to need you to allow things to flow. Won't that feel better?"

Storm bit down on the grin forming on her face. "What will feel better is me wiping that smug look off your face when I beat you in combat."

Something bright and wild sparkled in Lucy's eyes, contrasting against the blinding white of the tundra around them. She marched to the centre of the arena and drew her sword. "I like a challenge."

Storm discarded her coat and drew her sword in response. She cocked her eyebrow and allowed the smile to spread, knowing she'd wipe that grin off Lucy's face in no time.

The two women circled each other warily, swords at the ready, silently assessing each other's stance and grip. The only sounds in the arena came from the crunch of their boots in the gravelly snow-dusted dirt. Storm's breathing was steady, even despite the chill. She was focused, her eyes homed in on Lucy's, never once lifting for even a second. She had trained for years back home to be at least half as able as anyone with powers, and eventually, she'd surpassed even them with her abilities. She was confident she could hold her own, but Lucy was no slouch either. Storm could tell by the unrelenting sparkle in her eyes that this would not be an easy fight.

Suddenly, Lucy lunged, her sword a mere flash in the sunlight. Storm parried the strike, but Lucy had other tactics in mind. She spun around and aimed a kick at Storm's side. "Here in Iliso, we tend to use our opponent's weight and force against them," she called out.

Storm dodged just in time and countered with a quick jab of her sword. Lucy deflected it easily. The two women stalked back to the edges of the arena, re-evaluating their next moves.

"You plan on giving up all your tricks so easily?" Storm barked.

"Oh, it won't matter if I give you a play-by-play of my moves. I'll still beat you in the end," Lucy mused.

"Is that so?" Storm grinned before lunging into a direct attack. Each swift strike of hers sang in the wind. Her speed was something to be rivalled but, to her credit, Lucy put up a good fight.

For what seemed like hours, the two women clashed swords, each trying to gain the upper hand. They were evenly matched, and it was impossible to tell who would come out on top. Sweat trickled down their foreheads, and their breathing grew laboured.

"You ready to talk about what had you so fired up earlier?" Lucy asked in their next clash of steel.

"You ready to stop holding back and fight me properly?" Storm replied.

Lucy wiped the sweat from her brow and smirked as she said, "Just remember, you asked for it." Lucy charged again, her strike another feint for Storm to rush into a defensive pose that would only throw her off balance. Lucy curved at the last second, aiming for the soft bit of skin between her shoulder blades. Storm jumped, launching herself into the air and rolling over Lucy's back in an impressive feat of aerial acrobatics.

"And I was wondering when you were going to show me the real strength of the infamous Zerua fighting style."

Storm shook her hair out of her face as she stuck the landing and frowned. "If you must know, I wasn't divined. I don't have any air-related powers."

"Impressive." Lucy stuck her sword in the ground momentarily and took a bow. "And if you must know, neither was I." She snatched up her sword again and stood at the ready.

"It seems, then, that we are a decent match."

"A perfect one, I'd say," Lucy replied as she wagged the tip of her sword in jest.

Storm consented to her request for an attack, another hour easily going by between clashes of will and metal. Finally, after what felt like an eternity, Lucy made a mistake. She overextended herself, and Storm saw her chance. She swept forward like a strong gust of wind and scored a hit on Lucy's arm.

Lucy stumbled back, clutching the slit on her arm. The fight was over.

For a moment, there was stillness, utter silence apart from the sounds of their laboured breaths. Then, in a move that surprised even Storm herself, Lucy burst out laughing. "I haven't had that much fun in years," she said, grinning through the pain. "I can't believe you landed a hit. I was almost beginning to doubt you."

Storm sheathed her sword, retrieved her jacket, and walked over to Lucy. "Are you alright?" she asked, her voice lined with genuine concern.

"It'll take more than a scratch to sink my ship," Lucy beamed. "I will admit, though, you're a hell of a fighter."

Storm smiled. "You're not too bad yourself."

She dropped to Lucy's side and, for a moment, both women lay against the chilly ground, catching their breath and basking in the afterglow of the fight. Around them, the glaciers continued to glint in the sunlight. Above them, a light snow began to fall.

Finally, Lucy spoke up. "You know, I think we make a pretty good team."

Storm turned her head towards Lucy and raised an eyebrow. "Really? I just beat you in combat."

Lucy grinned. "It takes a strong person to beat me, and I wouldn't trust anyone who couldn't at least land a scratch on me to watch my back. Friends?"

Storm considered for a moment. She had always been a solitary person, but there was something about Lucy that she found intriguing. Maybe it was her bold and brazen nature, or her mischievous grin. Or maybe it was just the fact that she had put up a good fight. Whatever it was, Storm found herself nodding.

"Good! Then as your friend," Lucy began, propping herself up with the energy of someone who hadn't just endured hours of sparring. "Tell me, what had you so ruffled this morning?" Before Storm could reply, Lucy clapped her hands and jumped up onto the balls of her feet. "Hold that thought. Better yet, let's do this over drinks. I know the best pub in town, and sorrows always go down better with spirits."

Storm pushed herself to stand. "I hate to break it to you, Lucy, but I think that's called alcoholism."

"It is for anyone who isn't lucky enough to have me as their best friend. Besides, I'm buying this time, so I suggest you take advantage of it. Believe me when I say it won't happen again."

Storm shook her head and laughed. "Iturri help me. Alright, Lucy, lead the way."

CHAPTER 21

INTERRUPTIONS

GRIFFIN WAITED OUTSIDE the shabby wooden door as he had many times since they boarded the ship. Hand poised to knock. Intestines bunched in knots. Yet, he let it hover. The time he spent there was beginning to make him feel sick, and not because of the swaying of the ship beneath his feet.

It had been many years since Griffin had seen his friend. He'd almost forgotten their shared past. But then Savara appeared, and with her, long-forgotten memories surfaced. He was almost content believing his friend was dead. At least that way, he could mourn and move on. But fate was a fickle mistress, having brought them together once more.

Griffin had always prided himself on being able to separate himself from his emotions. That was his strength, the log he clung to when the world wished to drown him. But now? He couldn't even work up the nerve to knock. Instead, he sighed and dropped his hand yet again.

"Griffin?"

Startled, he turned to find Lance standing at the other end of the cramped hallway. "Lance…"

"You look troubled," he said from a distance. "Is everything okay?"

Griffin tried to relax his shoulders as he spoke. "Fine. I was just coming to tell you that Jasper and I will be heading into Solia alone tomorrow. Fewer bodies draw less attention…"

"You two certainly are close," Lance commented as he crossed his arms over his chest. For an instant, Griffin spied the beginnings of a small frown forming at the edges of his mouth, but Lance quickly schooled his features back into neutrality. It seemed the princeling was still good at masking his emotions.

"We share a common goal," Griffin replied, tension lining his voice. Lance's comment had struck a nerve. He couldn't understand why, but he suddenly felt a wall building inside him, guarding his intentions—his emotions.

"Is that all you came to say?" Lance asked, a twinge of hurt flickering in his eyes.

"Yes," he replied, biting down on the rest of his words. His shoulders tensed. His jaw tightened. Their brief conversation felt like an exercise in walking on thin ice. One false step, one wrong word, and the whole thing would shatter, leaving him to drown in the cold and sorrow.

Lance let the frown bloom across his face. "Lying doesn't suit you, Griffin. It never has."

"You've been away too long to remember what suits me and what doesn't," Griffin said as he moved away from the door. Anger bubbled inside him, but he couldn't understand why. Wasn't this what he'd wanted? To be back with his friend? How many times had he dreamt of this very moment? Yet, standing here, no more than two feet from him, Griffin felt that gurgling of anger in the pit of his stomach. He dipped his scarred chin as he strode past his friend in the corridor. He wasn't ready for the truth to be spoken aloud. Not yet. He didn't want Lance to see how much he cared, how much he wanted things to be like they used to be before their friendship had been tested by distance and time.

Lance shot a hand out and grabbed him by the forearm. "Some things can't be forgotten." When he didn't reply, Lance added, "Can we talk?"

"What about?" Griffin asked, scared of the answer. They had many things to talk about, air that needed to be cleared between them. Savara, for one. Griffin had yet to share with him his side of the events leading up to Idune. The reason he'd run away when they were kids was another topic of interest. But somehow, what Lance said next surprised him most of all, considering what he'd known of his friend in childhood.

Lance released his arm and cleared his throat. "I'm ready… I wish to regain my throne."

* * *

Savara followed The Apprentice up the misty staircase, cautious of the lack of visibility. The feeling of familiarity that had tortured her throughout her time in Visanthe gnawed at her again, and more so the closer they got to the entrance of the palace. As they passed through the first threshold of clouds, the mists parted around them, revealing the top of a sprawling hedge maze on either side of the stairs—right where she'd expected it to be. Savara quickly realised she'd been here before. The only question now was why.

The Apprentice paused at the door, watching her curiously as she climbed the last flight of stairs. She arrived at the landing slightly out of breath due to the combined thinness of the air and added weight of the corset. A gentle cloud rose around them, obscuring the stairs and the gardens once more.

"What are we waiting for?" she breathed, irritated at how silent he'd been since they started their ascent. "After all that chatter, you're ignoring me?"

Suddenly, Savara felt the prick of a sharp object at her side, one that could easily pierce flesh if only with enough weight behind it. She turned to find sparkling silver eyes glowering at her from the other end of a spear. The figure they belonged to was still shrouded by the haze.

"That," he smirked as he raised his chin. "You're getting slow in your old age, Bismuth."

"Don't forget that I'm the one that trained you, Amon."

The clouds parted to reveal two soldiers clad in shining metal armour that blended in easily with the surrounding haze. The one who'd spoken was a middle-aged bald man with dark skin and grey eyes. He lifted his spear from beneath

The Apprentice's chin. The one at Savara's side was a youth, a girl with no more than fifteen years to her name. Her recently shaven head was lined with the marks of an inexperienced hand.

"How can I forget when you use every opportunity to remind me, you oversized tuning fork?" The Apprentice replied.

"Still a nuisance, I see. At least the king will be pleased to know the conditions of your match have not changed. Whom have you brought with you?" Bismuth added, glancing at Savara. The Apprentice whispered something too low for her to hear in the man's ears, after which he nodded and called to his ward. "Mercury, child, you can put that away now."

The young girl reluctantly lowered her spear on his command, but her sceptical eyes were fixed on them.

"I shall let the king know of your arrival. I believe you're just in time for lunch," Bismuth said as he tapped the door with his spear. The wooden panel lurched open with a loud groan.

"Is he still on a diet of broth and bamboo shoots?" asked The Apprentice.

Bismuth winked at him before leaping several feet into the air and disappearing into the clouds. Savara was surprised at how someone of his age and stature moved with such swiftness until she remembered they were now in the Zerua territories. The only other Zerua she'd met was Brass, and to call him light-footed was an understatement. What had he told her when she'd first seen him float? He'd called it a habit;

one he was trying to kick. Was that a habit of being Zerua? Or something else entirely?

The young guard, Mercury, followed suit moments later, leaving Savara to stare at the space she'd occupied. Maybe it was time for her to admit that there was still more to learn about these lands—and not just the Zerua lands, but all of Visanthe.

The Apprentice started through the entrance. The sound of his footfall on the marble floors echoed in the cavernous hall. Savara hesitated, waiting on the balls of her feet as she gazed inside. The chamber beyond was bare, wilfully undecorated, and spacious. A draft had taken up occupancy in the room, and not even the heavy door could cut its path. Pillars and platforms circled the rotunda, giving way to glimpses of other rooms. A light mist wandered across the floors, as though the entire palace were bathed in a dream.

"You coming, princess?"

The echoing call of his voice snapped Savara out of her daze. She eyed him curiously, noticing the ease with which he glided across these halls. Familiarity. A softness had settled into the harder contours of his face. The makings of a smile sat at the corners of his lips, beneath the sharp tendrils of onyx coloured hair. There was something almost regal in his stance as he waited, shoulders high and chin higher, but not so much as to forget the world around him. No. His eyes saw all, carried suffering and strength—and would continue to do so. It was a side of him she might have only glimpsed before in passing. Here, it was on full display. Another side, a playful side. And then, of course, there was the matter of the new label attached to him.

"Did he call you Amon?" Savara played the name over in her head again. Amon. It was a powerful name, to be sure. She couldn't decide if knowing his name made her fear him less or more.

The smile unfurled across his face. "That is how names work."

"Funny that you of all people should make such a comment," she hissed.

"I know your name, princess, but I also know how much it irritates you that I don't use it." He winked.

She made to smack the grin off his face when the sound of her own name startled her. "Savara?"

"Brass?" she replied, spinning round to find her favourite of Griffin's friends standing before her. The initial smile his presence brought on was quickly dashed, replaced by a furrow in her brow. "Aren't you supposed to be in Idune?" she asked, staring at the thin plates of shining armour covering his usual grey tunic. His silvery eyes glittered in the midday sunlight, matching the colour of the clouds around them.

"I could ask the same of you," he said, mimicking her furrowed brow. "How have you come—" His eyes hitched on the shady figure of The Apprentice hovering in the doorway behind her.

"Is there a problem?" Amon asked.

"You." Brass withheld the gentleness in his voice. "You have returned."

"As have you," Amon replied with an equal distance in his tone.

Savara watched the rest of their conversation play out through a series of cold stares, flared nostrils, and a final, mutual bob of the head, though it seemed to be shared out of courtesy alone.

"The king is expecting us," Amon urged. "It would be rude to keep him waiting."

Brass nodded but, as Amon strode deeper into the palace, cast a gust of wind in front of Savara to keep her from walking away. "Be careful whom you trust, Savara," he whispered, his voice riddled with concern. "I have told you this before."

"Brass, I have to ask you—" she began, but he placed a finger to his lips.

"I will find you." He cast another glance at Amon's lingering shadow. "He cannot hurt you here." Before she could reply, he leapt into the air, disappearing into the clouds as the others had before him.

Once again, Brass's few words had rattled her. Brass had never spoken volumes, but he also never minced words. He knew something, and she'd be damned if she wasn't going to find out what it was. Savara hurried inside after Amon, hoping he hadn't noticed her lingering.

CHAPTER 22

THE LAND OF A THOUSAND STORMS

THE BREEZES THAT MOANED through the palace of winds sounded like voices of the past, calling out for their stories to be heard. Savara tried her best to tiptoe, feeling that her presence here—or anyone's, for that matter—was a form of sacrilege, but, somehow, even her lightest steps seemed to echo. She stuck close to The Apprentice—Amon—as they traversed the various halls. Her nerves had tensed to the point of snapping, yet he looked entirely at ease.

"How do you two know each other?" she asked softly.

Amon laughed. "You don't need to whisper," he replied, his voice at a normal volume, echoing like his footsteps as he strode to a raised platform. He scanned the floor beneath them, swatting the mists away as he searched.

"What are you looking for?"

Suddenly she heard a soft click. Part of the platform gave way, revealing a set of rungs leading upwards. "That. This palace was built for people who don't need stairs, but you and I…" He looked down at her. "Ladies first."

She interlaced her arms across her chest. "Are you going to ignore my question?"

When Savara didn't move, he added, "When we get there, I'll be sure to tell the king that you were the one who made us late." Amon bit down on the grin forming on his lips as he contemplated her. "Fine, you win, princess. How about we make it a game?"

"Why is it always a game with you?"

"Why not a game, princess? You take life too seriously," he replied, ushering her to the rungs. "I'll give you three questions, but after each, I get to ask one of equal value."

Savara considered his suggestion. It was the first time he was willingly offering to answer questions, though she feared what might come of his curiosity. Still, she figured it was an offer she couldn't refuse. "Alright," she said as she began to climb. "But I won't answer anything intimate, so don't even try."

"You brought up intimacy all on your own, princess," he smirked.

Savara scoffed. "I— Ugh! Has anyone ever told you how frustrating you are?" she looked down to find him staring, having not set foot on the ladder yet.

"I'd hoped you'd do better with your questions, seeing as you practically beg me for answers every time we meet."

"It was a rhetorical question, you ass," she hissed as she hoisted herself onto the platform.

Amon arrived swiftly behind her, winking as he reached the landing. "Sure," he mocked, gesturing her towards a darkened hall.

Savara rolled her eyes and followed him. "Fine, first question. Why do you work with The Prince of Shadows?"

Amon cocked an eyebrow. "You know I can't say."

Savara narrowed her eyes at him. "Figures…"

"Try asking better questions if you want better answers."

She groaned at him, regretting having agreed to this mind game. "Fine, how come we're here?"

"You're not very good at this game. You did hear me say the king has invited us to dine, right?"

"Don't play coy. You know what I mean."

Amon's expression turned serious as he halted in his tracks, causing Savara to nearly bump into him. "If you must know… The king and I are old friends. I have a standing invitation which I haven't used in over a decade. I thought it would be nice to pay him a visit. Besides, you needed a place to hide out, and what better place than a palace in the sky, known to few outsiders, that can only be accessed by a single staircase?"

"But you're an Izar. Why would you ever come here?"

"Ah, ah, ah, princess. My turn," he said, a grin curling at his lips as he resumed his stride. She hadn't heard his question yet, but Savara already sensed trouble. "Why are you so against my helping you?"

"Because you're a killer?" she hissed. "Because you always land me in more trouble? Because even though I can sense your soul, I'll never feel like I understand you… Take your pick."

"I've never harmed you," he said, his voice lowered as he spoke. "Nor do I intend to." For a moment, she wondered if he'd overheard the whispers she exchanged with Brass. "On the contrary, saving you has gotten me into more trouble than you're worth."

"What do you mean?" she asked, but again he pointed to his sealed lips. "Ugh, fine. Same question as before. Why would you, an Izar, come to the Zerua kingdom for safety?"

Amon prickled, strolling in silence for a moment as he considered his words carefully. "My mother is somewhat important in the Izar territories. People expect things of her, and in turn, she expects them of me. But I was never a welcome addition to her life. She'd made that perfectly clear to me in my youth." A muscle twitched in his jaw, but he didn't seem to linger on the thought. "I'd been here before with her, and the king had treated me with respect and kindness. When I had found myself without a home, he gladly took me in—whether for political leverage or otherwise—and we soon became friends. He's like a father to me... though, as you might have seen, not all his guards consider it wise."

Savara felt a sadness creep into her chest upon hearing his story. She had already imagined there was more to him than meets the eye, but she'd never considered what traumas he might have that led him to become what he is now. Yet, when she searched his soul for a similar sadness, she found nothing, no regret or remorse, only indifference.

They rounded a corner and followed the hall towards another set of stairs.

"Is that the reason for the standoff between you and Brass?" she asked.

"Brass and I are not on bad terms, per se. He was good to me during my time here. But he left, and since then, we've been on shaky ground. He thinks I wronged someone close to him, and I've allowed him to believe that. I'd rather his contempt than his thinking I can be helped."

"Is that how you treat everyone?"

"Sorry, princess. That was your three used up."

"I didn't want to ask that last one!"

"And I didn't want to be late. Things don't always go the way we want," he said. Savara grumbled, but Amon shook his head. "My turn." He grinned as he helped her up to another platform. Savara narrowed her eyes at him but allowed him his next question. "Are you happy here in Visanthe?"

She raised a brow. "Is that how you plan to use your question?"

"As a matter of fact, yes."

"Well…"

Savara thought back on her time in Visanthe. Between captures, killers, and her powers, she knew the sensible answer would be no. Yet, the memories that came to mind weren't of these things. She thought of her training sessions with Sebastian, her tea times with Brass, dancing with Griffin, learning about the animals from Simon, even her times with Storm were arguably not as bad as she'd once believed. She admired them; cared for them. There was a chance, she realised, that she'd even grown to love them like the family she'd lost.

And Jasper? Their relationship had changed much since they jumped worlds, but she'd seen him grow, more so than he ever would have back home. The thought of his lackadaisical smile, that mess of brown hair, and of course the gleam in his eyes, brought tears to her own.

Then, Savara remembered the wonder that filled her each time she sensed the magic of the lands. The songs in the wind, the vibration in the ground, even the light of the distant stars felt different here. She didn't understand it, she feared she might never, but knowing it existed filled a void in her that she'd all but given up on filling. There were days when she'd have to fight for her life, but there would always be others in which she could just *be*. Like it or not, she realised, this truly was her home.

"I was scared at first," she began, biting down on her lip as she pulled together her thoughts. "I still am. But I don't think I could go back. The world I came from felt… stifled? This one feels wild—free. It may very well kill me one day—*you* may very well kill me one day—and even still, I know I'm supposed to be here."

"Hmm," was all he said, accompanied by a slight smirk. The small sound betrayed more interest than perhaps he'd cared to admit.

The pair strolled to what looked to be a final door at the end of the maze of corridors. The scent of food escaped through the gap between the wood and the floor. Savara's stomach grumbled. The last time she'd eaten properly was Simon's tossed-together soup, and whatever feast lay behind the door smelled substantially more filling. Between her fear of the various events of the morning and her curiosity at their change in nations, she'd hardly noticed her hunger. But now, standing a mere panel of wood away, she felt weak to it.

Amon reached for the doorknob. His hand hovered just above it, trembling. Before she could ask about it, he snapped it back and smiled. "I have one more question to use, don't I?"

"Is that your question?" Savara asked, noticing a crack in his façade of perfection. The sudden trembling in his hand worried her. She knew something was wrong.

"No," he smirked. "But I think I'll hold onto my question a little longer. I have a feeling the debate's still out on the answer." Amon reached for the doorknob again and turned it. "And, if it means anything, I have no intention of killing you, nor of seeing you dead."

The door swung open, leading to one of the strangest dining room Savara had ever seen. There were no other walls on the opposite side of the room, only a sea of grey clouds, swirling around the edge of a cliff. Thunder rolled around them, sending chills down her spine. Guards in polished metal armour stood on either side of them, holding spears like the one the young girl had pointed at her upon arrival. At the end of the long table, she spied their host, an elderly man with a dangling white beard that made up for the lack of hair on his shiny brown head, and eyes that shone the silvery colour of the moon.

Noticing their entrance, the man pushed himself to stand, wiping his lips lightly with a cloth before speaking. "I was wondering when the winds would return you to me."

CHAPTER 23

REACQUAINTED

SAVARA LOOKED TO AMON for guidance on how to proceed, trembling in the presence of the king and his guards. Amon dropped easily into a low bow. Savara mimicked his movements, fearing the strange quiet that had settled in the room. A ripple of energy tugged at her soul. It had all the characteristics of a swollen storm cloud that, when burst, would level houses. Curious as to its source, she took a steadying breath and focused on summoning that strange searching energy. As much as she disliked using her powers, she knew how useful this *one* aspect of them could be.

The king's eyes met hers, as though he'd been seeking her out. It was him, she realised. His energy was something born of storms, deep-rooted and destructive, and yet…

The king dipped his head, a sign the guards took to withdraw their spears. "We have much to catch up on," he said in dulcet tones as he gestured to the other seats at the table. Amon strolled over to him, allowing the king to take hold of his head and press it to his own. The corners of his mouth tilted upwards as he spoke. "What has kept you, my boy?"

"Other engagements," Amon replied with a guilty smile.

The king released his hold and nodded knowingly before turning to Savara. Now knowing what lurked beneath his skin, the clarity of his gaze made her uneasy. It reminded her of the way Ori had looked at her during their first encounter, as though he could read her every thought and see all her faults. Other than her uneasiness, and Amon's strange twinge of guilt, she couldn't feel any other emotions in the room. With the number of people around, she knew she should've at least felt *something*. Savara pursed her lips. This room had a vague emotional dullness to it that only added to her concern about their situation, especially given the depths of the king's power.

"Please take a seat. You are just in time to eat. My chefs are the best in Haizea," he beamed. "I must inform you, though, in my home we do not eat meat. I do hope this is not an inconvenience to you." Savara shook her head and held her tongue. "You never did like my storms," he added, as if attributing her distance to the lack of warmth in the room. Her curiosity prompted an airy laugh that, in his youth, might have been charming, but was now coupled with a wheezing that raised the hairs on her neck. Before she could deny it, the king clapped his hands. On cue, a fire on the only other wall in the room was lit. "I seem to recall, the last time you were here, you said my room looked gloomy without a fire."

Savara blushed as she took her place next to Amon. "I always did like sitting by the fire," she replied, dropping her guard as the comforting warmth grew. "But I can't say I remember having told you that..." *Or having been here, or having met you,* she thought as a servant rested bowls of broth and noodles before them. Side dishes followed, with sauteed tofu and leafy green steamed cabbage. Savara's stomach growled as the scent hit her nose. She picked up the chopsticks at her side with the proficiency of someone who'd been using them all her life, but she knew this skill couldn't have come from her time in the other world—and especially not from anything Ms Short had cooked. She stared at the silver-tipped wooden sticks between her fingers, trying to grasp onto phantom memories from a forgotten life. After a moment, she considered the possibility that it wasn't worth remembering.

The king nodded. "I know. I will not pretend I was not present at the ceremony when they stripped you of your memories, Princess Savara of the Argia. Though, I believe those powers of yours belong to other lands. Would you care to tell me how it is you have returned?"

Savara's breath caught in her chest. *He knew.* What's more, he hadn't flinched as he spoke. He knew of her nature, and he wasn't afraid. The only other person who spoke of her nature with such ease sat beside her, unmoved by the conversation. She turned to Amon, who continued eating his cabbage and tofu. Amon ignored her gaze as he said, "The winds are changing, and it was time she returned home."

"I'm sorry for intruding on you like this," Savara quickly added, fearing the king's reaction. "I know my powers aren't natural—"

But the king's laugh stopped her. "Not natural? I would wager yours are the most natural of all. Free yourself of worry, young princess. There's darkness in all of us. That is why your young friend here is a favourite guest of mine. We share this opinion… among others."

"I believe you taught me that on one of my many field trips," Amon replied, gently tapping a napkin to his lips.

For some reason, he continued to ignore her. Only moments before their entry, he couldn't keep his eyes off her, and now? It was as though she were a painting on the wall. She watched him reach for another dish, willing him to look her way but to no avail. His attention remained fixed on his food. Each unhurried, graceful bite he took revealed yet another side to him. One that, contrary to what she'd believed, could enjoy life—or at least part of it.

"And a fast learner you were. Curiously, those visits are something the two of you have in common," the king offered. "Among other things, I'm sure."

Savara furrowed her brow as she swallowed another mouthful. "What visits?"

"Amon, dear boy, you haven't told her?" he laughed. "One would think you'd relish in the thought of having a kindred spirit."

"Kindred spirit?" Savara prodded, her noodles slipping from her chopsticks and back into her bowl with a soft plopping sound. She almost choked on the words alone.

For the first time since they'd entered, Amon turned to her and smiled. A glimmer appeared in his eyes; a mischievous spark coupled with the dull glow of longing. "I'd appreciate it, Uncle, if you didn't divulge all my secrets with acquaintances." With that one look, he consumed her, taking in every line on her face, every hair on her head, every stone in her scar, as though he'd never get the chance again. A fluster grew on her cheeks.

"I know you better than even your mother, Amon. Our games of Go have taught me to not underestimate your long-term strategy."

"Your flattery will not guarantee you a win in this evening's game, Uncle," Amon smirked as he returned his gaze to the king.

"You have not been here for years, my boy. It is possible I have improved in my age."

"I'll believe it when I see it," Amon laughed.

Savara's stomach twisted. She'd never heard him laugh like that; a genuine, innocent, almost child-like laugh, with no hints of malice or sarcasm. It was a beautifully rich, full-bodied laugh that raised the hairs on her arms. Outside of this palace he'd been guarded. Here, he looked so relaxed, so at home. For a moment, she almost forgot he was a killer.

"Before we play, you might like to show the young princess around the gardens. I have a feeling she might find them soothing, especially after a long journey."

"After a journey like hers, what she needs is a good night's sleep," Amon countered.

"I can speak for myself, thanks," Savara retorted. Amon raised his brows, brandishing a coy smile as he ushered noodles into his mouth. She knew she'd caught him off guard with her outburst, but he looked more pleasantly surprised than anything. "And I think the gardens would be nice," she added, further challenging his resolve. She wasn't going to miss the opportunity to uncover more of his secrets.

The king patted his lips with a napkin and snapped his fingers. At the sound, another servant breezed in with a trolley carrying a fine porcelain tea set and soft sweets. "Now that that's settled, I wanted to ask, my dear," he began, pouring three steaming cups of jasmine tea. "And I know it is a personal, rather intimate question, so feel free to decline to respond." He handed both her and Amon a teacup and settled back into his chair. "What have you promised to earn yourself such a scar?"

Amon prickled, tightening his grip on his teacup. Savara frowned. One hand rested her chopsticks down beside her empty bowl while the other drifted up to her cheek. She'd never considered her soul bond to be an intimate matter. Most people she'd encountered had spoken out freely against hers. The priest she'd met was covered from head to toe in soul bonds, and though he didn't discuss their nature, he also didn't make a point of hiding them either. But then, she'd never given much thought to the personal nature of souls. The more she did now, the more she realised how wrong she was for having bound her own.

"I promised something to someone I shouldn't have, in exchange for the safety of my friends."

"I see…" the king replied, following his words with a melancholy smile. The storm clouds around them quieted. "That speaks volumes of you, my dear. I do not wish to speak for the others when I say this but, perhaps, we were wrong in our judgment of you."

"I'm sorry, I don't quite understand."

"Souls are not solely judged by the acts they commit, but by their motivations. Throughout the years, I have seen people bind their souls, some in acts of stupidity or frivolity, others in agreement of mutually beneficial circumstances." He paused, letting his words sink in. "You don't strike me as either stupid or frivolous, and your bond does not benefit you in the slightest. Whatever terrible thing you have agreed to was not born of your soul, but rather of the need to protect the ones you love. There is darkness in all of us, Savara, but for darkness to exist, so too must there be light. By binding your soul in service of others, you have demonstrated a kindness and a selflessness contrary to what we had assumed of someone of your divination." He sipped his tea slowly before continuing. "It is possible that we in our old age are not quite as learned as we would like to believe, but I am certain you figured this out instantly, Amon."

The Apprentice narrowed his eyes at the old man as a blush covered his cheeks.

The king smiled. "Now, if you will excuse me," he said as he made to stand. "I must prepare for our game. Please, finish at your leisure and take your time in the gardens…" The king strolled over to the ledge, but before taking a final step, he added, "Oh, and be careful with the monkeys. It seems they are energetic this season."

Before either of them could say another word, the king was swept up by the storm clouds and whisked off to a higher level of the palace.

CHAPTER 24

TRUST FALLS

THE GUARDS VANISHED behind the king. The rumbling of the storm clouds returned around them. Aside from the crackling fire near the entrance, they were the only two living things in the room.

"You never cease to amaze me," Amon said as he rested his cup down and made to stand. He unhitched a sigh and let the side of his lips curl upwards as he contemplated her. She could sense a pride rippling from him that she couldn't quite place.

"Are you insulting me again?" Savara growled as she jerked her chair backwards, its legs scratching loudly on the marble floor.

"Not at all," he replied extending a hand out to her. She stared at it impatiently. "I did promise to take you to the gardens. Or have you already changed your mind?"

"No, we're going," she replied, accepting his hand with a smirk that she'd borrowed from him. "I'm not going to let you back out, *Amon*."

"Are you insulting my name?" he mused.

"Just curious as to why you never told me it before."

"You never asked."

Savara relented, letting out an irritable sigh as she took his hand. She'd never known anyone to be as frustrating as him, and she doubted she'd meet anyone comparable anytime soon.

Amon guided her towards the ledge where a violent swirling sea of clouds waited for them. When she'd seen the king depart through similar means, her worries had eased, but now seeing it up close, she remembered she wasn't quite as fond of heights as someone who could practically fly.

Noticing her apprehension, Amon laced her fingers in his and danced his thumb over the back of her hand. "Do you trust me?"

"Do you expect me to jump?" she replied, staring down into the grey abyss.

"If I swore to you I'd never let you fall, would you trust me?"

"I…" She exchanged a timid glance between the clouds and him.

When she looked at him now, she saw someone different—the kind of someone he might have been all along, according to the king. The killer she'd known as The

Apprentice was still there, tucked away like a coat, but she knew the young man she'd been introduced to at the table, Amon, was the one staring back at her. If she'd wanted to, she could've used her powers to search for any traces of malice in his soul, but after everything he'd done for her since freeing her from capture, she'd grown curious about him. It wasn't exactly trust she felt when she was with him, more like hope. Hope that there was a good reason for whatever cruel acts he'd committed in the past. Whoever this version of him was, Savara knew it was the one that had saved her countless times and would continue to do so. The only real question left was which side of him was the façade. For now, at least, what little hope she did have that there was good in him prompted a nod from her.

A sad smile graced his face, as if he'd sensed that it wasn't entirely trust, but he seemed content with her response for now. Amon pulled her in close, wrapping her in the scent of night flowers. Warmth flooded into her body, one that she doubted came from the dying fire.

"Hold on tight," he whispered before stepping off the ledge.

The next thing Savara knew, they were falling. She'd closed her eyes as soon as her feet left the ground. Her muscles clenched as they fell faster and faster. She focused her thoughts and energy into her arms, making sure they clung tightly to him as the rushing wind enveloped them. The last thing she wanted was to fall.

Why did we have to do this right after eating? she thought, clutching tighter to his chest.

"Savara," Amon whispered to her. "Open your eyes."

"I don't love heights," she mumbled. "I'll open when we hit the bottom."

He laughed. "Then open your eyes."

Savara peered through a single squinted eye. The winds still rushed around them, but they had stopped falling.

How is this possible? She opened her eyes and cast her gaze downward. Her stomach gurgled uncomfortably. A constant flow of air, funnelled through a chasm, kept them afloat. It was almost as if they were flying. She gazed up at the ledge which hung in the air a few feet above them. In reality, they hadn't fallen far at all; the winds had only made it seem that way. Still, she didn't love the fact that there was nothing solid supporting them—neither did her stomach.

"That's great, but can we get down now, please?" She tightened her grip on him as her hair whipped around her face. If her nails had been any longer, they might have punched holes in his clothes.

"Are you afraid of heights, princess?"

"No, you ass. I'm afraid of falling."

Amon guided their bodies through the air to another ledge just below them. He seemed entirely at ease gliding through the air. She on the other hand practically kissed the ground as they landed. Once her feet had safely touched solid ground, she'd released him. As she waited for her heart to steady, her eyes fell to her hands.

If he hadn't been born an Izar, he would've surely been a Zerua, she thought. *What made people receive their powers? Was it their personality? Their blood? Or something greater?* It couldn't have been the first time she'd wondered such a thing but, as of yet, she had no answer.

Savara glanced around the landing, spying torches with dancing flames and a spiralling staircase that had been carved into the side of the mountain. It began somewhere above their heads and trailed down and around the ledge.

"Could we have taken the stairs this whole time?" she hissed, turning to face him.

A look of playful guilt streaked across his face. "Yes, but this was more fun."

"You're incorrigible."

"Besides, I was curious as to whether you trusted me or not."

Savara glowered at him. "After a stunt like that, I've changed my mind." She whacked him on the shoulder and stormed ahead, following the stairs to wherever they led.

The air around her was thin, easily making her lightheaded. Each stair had her standing uncomfortably close to the precipice. She took each step with care, knowing there was nothing around to catch her if she slipped, except for him. The staircase itself had been chipped into by the elements and left mostly uncared for. It was clear to her that the inhabitants of this palace had no need for such things.

When the staircase finally curved back in on itself and opened out, Savara found herself standing on a plateau lined with rose bushes and cherry blossoms, babbling brooks and fishponds. Wood and glass windchimes hung from open branches, setting their soft tunes to each gentle breeze, a stark contrast from the rushing roar of the wind on the other side of the mountain. Little wooden footbridges created paths that weaved over the brooks and through the trees. Surrounding the plateau was a misty forest of bamboo.

A smile broke out across her face. "This is incredible," she called out, childish wonder tingeing her voice. Her eyes were wide as they took in the sights.

Savara removed her shoes and strode out onto the grass. It felt wrong somehow to step on it with anything but her bare feet—disrespectful even. Amon copied her, trailing slightly behind as to not influence her movements. She wandered at leisure through the twists and turns of the garden, admiring each colourful flower and vibrant fish that crossed her path. The garden itself felt as though it were welcoming her. It was the same sensation she'd had in the sacred chamber of the Harri, deep within the mountains, but as far as she knew, this place wasn't hidden. She wondered what made some places feel more alive, more magical than others.

"Can you feel this?" she said as she spun around to meet him.

Amon leaned up against the trunk of a tall cherry blossom, the light of the late afternoon sun creating a blue halo around his hair. His eyes glowed a more vibrant shade of indigo as they watched her basking in the garden's power. Savara paused her dancing as her eyes met his. Since the last time she'd truly stopped to take him in, back when they were in Idune, she noticed an olive colouring had returned to his skin, even bronzing at the edges of his jaw and hands. Compared to the last time, when he'd been washed out by whatever darkness The Prince of Shadows had tainted him with, he looked more whole somehow, as though he too were regaining parts of himself lost to the shadows.

What a foolish thought, she mused, but it was true there was something undeniably more substantial and even youthful in him now.

"The force of your gaze?" he asked with a smirk.

"No." Savara dropped her gaze to the ground. She hadn't noticed how long she'd been staring, but clearly, it had been long enough for him to comment on. "The harmony of the place. The way everything fits together. There's an energy around us that feels almost..." But she couldn't quite put her finger on the sensation.

"Electric?" he offered, pushing himself off the tree trunk and stalking towards her. "Vibrant? Alive?" He stopped a mere pace from her, his tendrils of inky black hair curled at his temples, framing the light of his face as he gazed into her eyes.

"Yes," she replied, a crease forming at her brow, curious as to how he was able to pull the descriptions from her mind.

"I've walked these gardens many times and never felt it before but... because of this," he brandished the scar across his palm, "because of you, I'm beginning to feel a lot of things I've never felt before."

She regarded his proximity as a challenge, a test of her courage. More so given the previous night which she'd spent putting up with his teasing. Savara held steady, planting her feet firmly on the ground, rooting herself like the cherry blossom he'd abandoned. "Why do you keep doing that?" she scoffed.

"Doing what?"

"Staring at me that way. I'm not stupid. I might not have noticed when I was mad at you, but I can see it now."

"I'm not allowed to look at you now?" he mused.

She crossed her arms over her chest as she turned back down the path she was walking, moving slowly enough for him to keep in tow. "You don't *just* look, and you know it."

"Fair."

"Then, why?"

"Can I help it if I find you interesting? Besides, I do love the feeling you get when you catch me staring."

"What are you talking about?" She paused her stride, causing him to almost bump into her. Amon circled around her, his face laden with mischief and fixed with a grin. Without saying a word, he simply brandished his scar again. "One of these days I'll chop off that hand," she said with a scowl.

"Testy, princess," he laughed. "Remind me to take away any sharp objects when I'm around you."

"Who said I'd need a sharp object?" she remarked, a grin curling at the sides of her lips. If he could play coy, so could she. Amon swallowed hard as she resumed her curious stroll through the gardens. "Tell me…" she added as she curved around another cherry blossom. "What exactly do you find interesting about me?"

"I have a feeling that if I say your curiosity, you might never speak to me again," he laughed. Savara rolled her eyes at him. "I thought so. What about if I say your spirit?"

"I hope not in the same way that the Prince of Shadows is."

"I can't speak to his reasons, but I can tell you that the more time I spend with you, the more you're growing on me."

"Not just because of that?" she asked as she glanced down at his scar.

"It does help me understand you."

"I don't think it's fair that you have that to tell you how I'm feeling, and I have nothing. You're practically unreadable."

"You have your powers…"

Savara's shoulders drooped. She'd realised as the words fell from his lips that she *did* have the ability, she simply chose not to use it. But for good reason. She wasn't about to lose control and accidentally hurt anyone ever again. He might not have known her reasons for not using her powers, but he seemed to notice the way her mood had turned.

"And you can always try asking," he added.

A soft, sarcastic chuckle escaped her lips. "That has never worked before, and you know it."

"Maybe it will now…" He winked.

Savara bit her lip as she contemplated his words. Whatever game he was playing now had her curious. She wondered what had made him change his mind from needing there to be a game between them to now offering to answer her questions, but she didn't want to miss the opportunity. She leaned up against the trunk of the tree as she thought of questions for him. "Alright… What do you remember most about your childhood?"

Amon leaned up beside her and dipped his head, letting his hair casually fall in front of his face. His usual stiffness disappeared, replaced by a nonchalance that she would have never imagined of him. "I had a rambunctious set of friends that kept me on my toes," he replied, smiling as he lost himself in the memory.

"I bet you were a real troublemaker back then," she mused, thinking of all the trouble he'd gotten her into in the little time she'd known him.

Amon laughed with her. "There was mischief to be had, to be sure…" But as his voice trailed off, she noticed melancholia settle in his eyes where amusement had previously danced. "Piano…" he added almost in whisper.

"Do you play?" she asked softly.

"I used to… Not something I've done in a long time," he said with a sigh. Savara didn't need her powers to sense the shift in his mood. But before she could begin to console him, Amon forced a grin and stared into her eyes. "What about you, princess?" he asked, masking whatever emotion he'd betrayed before. Savara knew better than to press the issue. If he needed to change the subject, she'd play along with his ruse. She smiled, pursing her lips, and mimicking his sealing gesture. "Not fair," he said.

"Absolutely fair. You do it to me all the time. I'm giving you a taste of your own medicine," she replied with a wink.

"Hmm…" He crossed his arms over his torso, puffing it out to seem more intimidating.

"If you must know…" she sighed, relenting to him only in jest. "I don't really remember anything about my time here, but from the other world, turtles. I used to snorkel out into the bay and watch them," she clarified, noticing his confusion.

"Watch them what?"

"Be. They don't do much but watching them was fun. Peaceful. Have you ever seen one?"

"Can't say that I have. I never really had time to 'just be'."

"That's kind of sad."

"Hey, don't turn your pity on me," he said, nudging her shoulder.

Savara let out a soft laugh. She hadn't felt this at ease in a long time. Probably since she'd jumped worlds. Their conversation reminded her of the kinds she used to have with Jasper in Skully's, before destiny came knocking at her door. She twirled a strand of hair around her finger, enjoying their conversation as though they were nothing more than friends sharing in the pleasure of each other's company and not what they actually were: The Apprentice and The Harbinger of Death.

"Alright, next question," she said as a blush crept into her cheeks. "Is there anything you're your past that you regret?"

"There are a few."

"The one you regret the most?"

Guilt flickered in his eyes briefly, but whatever thought he'd had in that moment remained unspoken. Amon thought about the question for a few seconds before replying, "I abandoned my friends with no explanation because I didn't want to hurt them."

Savara shied away from his gaze, feeling a surprising twinge of empathy for him. "Then we're a matching set," she admitted, knowing she'd done the same to Jasper.

Amon nudged her shoulder, trying to bring back the playful smile she'd donned before. She nudged him back, and for a moment, she thought there was more he wished to say, but the words remained on his lips unspoken. Instead, he faced the gardens again and smirked. "I thought you'd have more questions for me."

"I could probably write a book with all the questions I have for you," she said with a laugh.

"I'll let you get one more in. Make it count."

"Hmm…" Savara considered their previous encounters this time, of which there had been many. She wanted to know why he'd been so insistent in standing by her, even as he worked with the very person who might want her dead. It was clear to her there was something between them, now more so than ever, but why? "A while ago you said souls like mine attract the broken," she began. "What did you mean?"

Savara noticed a blush creeping into his cheeks as he turned the question over in his mind. "Something in you makes the rest of us broken souls feel balanced, whole."

"I don't know how true that is. People fear me."

"People fear what they don't know," he replied. "They fear change, and they especially fear healing, because it means they have to confront the fact that they were broken to begin with."

"Do you think if we'd known each other before all this that we would've been friends?"

Amon bit his lip. "Who's to say…" Again, Savara noticed a sparkle of something in his eyes that looked an awful lot like a secret.

She relished the new bond forming between them, the one forged through mutual conversation and not blood, but her enjoyment was short-lived. A small pulse appeared from beneath her clothes, startling her. She pressed her hand to the side of her chest where she'd felt it. *The stone*, she remembered.

"Is everything okay?" he asked.

"Yes, I just…" Her eyes soon fell on a patch of tall bamboo stalks that marked the entrance to a different part of the garden. Guarding this entrance were two large stone lizards with curling tails, forked tongues, and sharp teeth. Her grin faded as she regarded the menacing statues, finding a strange resonance with them. She'd seen them before, and not similar statues, those statues. "What's that?"

"Just another part of the garden."

The path called to her, like a phantom from her past. If what the king said was true and she had been here before, maybe there was a lingering memory of it somewhere in her mind. Maybe if she followed the path, it could be coaxed out.

CHAPTER 25

SOULS IN BLOOM

PRODDED ON BY THE STONE, Savara took a deep breath, readying herself before giving in to the luring calls of her past. She pushed off the tree and began walking towards the statues, a hint of fear rippling through her as she did. The lizard guards looked unfriendly at best, even for statues.

Normally, she would've stayed clear of things marked so clearly to keep people out, but the draw of the path was too strong. Nothing good ever came with that sensation, especially not here in Visanthe, but she knew there was something important for her beyond the bright gardens. Something waiting in the mists.

"Where are you going?" Amon called out to her. He stumbled as he pushed off the tree, but quickly caught up to her. He maintained a steady stride beside her this time, rather than trailing behind.

"Remember when I told you before that I don't recall anything from my childhood here?" Savara began. Amon nodded. "Well, recently, that hasn't been entirely true," she admitted. "I'm now beginning to think I remember this place—or at least parts of it. And something about the king feels familiar too."

They wandered deeper into the forest. As she spoke, the light of the afternoon sun faded, covered by the endless streams of mist streaking through the bamboo. The grounded path turned into one of floating wood beneath their feet the further they got from the entrance. The wind rustling through the chutes provided a melancholy tune over which she recounted her story.

"Do you remember when you rescued me from the cell?" she asked, this time though, she didn't wait for his response. Her mind was fixed on the trail ahead and whatever insights it might offer. "I had a dream about him—or at least I thought I did. It wasn't until I saw him at the table that I realised it wasn't just a dream. It was a memory from my divination. He even admitted to having been there that day."

"Why didn't you say anything before?"

"I was afraid. The king has a lot of power, to the point where even being in his presence set my nerves on edge. It was like…" But she stopped herself, unwilling to call upon the memory of The Prince of Shadows.

"You don't need the kind of powers you have to feel it," Amon remarked. "The king is one of the older souls in Visanthe, and time like that leaves its mark."

Savara considered his words carefully. The other old souls she'd met in Visanthe—Ori and The Prince of Shadows—gave the impression of having wells of power stored within. Their presence alone was suffocating. It even seemed as though time recoiled from them. Savara had the feeling the other leaders wouldn't be any different. She wondered what this meant, whether they were all living unnaturally long lives, or if there was something more to their impressive vitality. Suddenly, the Arima stone pulsed again from within the folds of her clothes. Not a moment later, another person popped into her head, one she'd tried her hardest not to think of since she'd arrived in Visanthe. As she considered him, she realised that he was yet another person who fit that description. Her uncle. He was, after all, a being of this world, just as they were—just as she was. The stone pulsed again. Somehow, she realised, the two were related, and she was determined to understand how and why. But if their extended life came from the stones, how did her uncle benefit from their properties an entire world away?

"I still don't get what we're doing in the stalks…" Amon prodded, harking her back to the present moment. "There are dangerous creatures living here."

"I've been here before," she said, unwilling to acknowledge the thrumming of the stone in her pocket that egged her on. "I know it. I was hoping that following this path would spark my memory."

"You've been doing fine so far. Are you sure you want to remember?" he asked, his voice hinting at genuine concern. He must have noticed her apprehension through whatever connection that scar provided.

"Not really…" she admitted as she came to a halt. "Sometimes I think it's just the morbid curiosity in me." She took a deep breath, trying to process her fears. She didn't know what about him brought on her candour. Perhaps it was the fact that he too was familiar with the shadows and the dark, or perhaps she didn't feel the need to impress him or be anything other than what she was. Worse, perhaps she didn't think that anyone—not even her, with her bloodthirsty powers—could attain the levels of darkness to which she attributed him. Regardless, she admitted her darkest fears as if they were trivialities. "What if, in the past, I wasn't a good person? What if I hurt people and that's why my mind has chosen not to remember?"

"Remember or not, the person you are now is a result of the person you were then. I don't think the you standing before me has it in her to hurt someone intentionally. But even if that were the case, none of us is free from hurting others, nor are we free from their hurt. I told you once before, princess, life is a game, and we are its pawns. What I didn't tell you back then is that, unlike Go or Chess, our pawns aren't black or white, only shades of grey."

A chill brushed over her shoulders beneath the cloak. Savara nodded. "I'm sorry."

"For what?"

"To say something so dark… it sounds like you've been through a lot."

"You have no idea," he mumbled in reply.

They continued down the misty walkway in silence, accompanied by only the echoes of the wind and the synchronised sounds of their steps on the wood. As they walked, Savara knew she had to search for whatever had summoned her into the forest, but her mind kept returning to Amon. The longer she spent with him, the more she began to realise how many dimensions there were to him. He was a killer, a man who worked for the devil, but he was also a scorned son, a mischievous child who played board games with old kings, and not even those summed him up completely. He was infuriating and an incurable flirt, but the interactions she'd witnessed between him and the king were undoubtedly touching. And he always knew what to say when she was in a rut. She thought about his earlier question, about whether she trusted him. Before, she'd said yes so that he'd take her to the gardens. Now, after everything he'd shared, it was possible she was beginning to.

"Why do you play Go with the king?" Savara asked when she grew weary of the silence between them.

"The simplicity of it," Amon replied.

"Those games are notoriously not simple."

"Compared to life? The only pieces that matter are the ones on the board. The only contender is the one before you. The rules of the game are straightforward, there are good moves and bad moves, though even bad beginnings can lead to a good end. And, as I said before, the pieces are black and white."

"You're a bit of a hypocrite."

Amon let out a snort of laughter. "How so?"

"I don't know much about you, and after this little excursion, I realise I know less than I thought, but for someone who lives in grey areas and dances the lines of morality the way you do, it's hard to believe you prefer the straightforward."

He raised his eyebrows in surprise. "Dances the lines of morality?" He took hold of her hand, sending shockwaves of nervous energy thrumming through her body as he twirled her on the shifting planks below them. "How poetic of you, princess," he added, spinning her in close enough for her to hear that echo of a heartbeat in his chest.

"You're an ass," she said, pulling herself from his grip. His antics ground at her nerves. He was charming, the kind of charming that brought only trouble—which, in this world, might just be the death of her. Worse was the grin he put on after rattling her because he could sense the lingering attraction. She'd pray to whatever gods she had to if it meant being rid of him if only so she didn't end up falling for him.

Amon raised a brow at her, and for a second, she questioned once again whether he was privy to her inner thoughts. "I suppose I'm a dreamer," he said. "In a perfect world, maybe I could be just one thing… but perfect worlds don't exist, and I decided long ago that I'd look out for myself, whatever the cost, even if it meant living in grey areas—as you so poetically put it." He shoved his hands in the pockets of his coat and walked on ahead.

Savara contemplated Amon with a frown. She'd been right after all. He'd made it clear before that he didn't have an easy past, but it seemed darker than she'd first assumed. They came to a halt in the centre of the forest, marked by a rotunda at the end of their path that branched off in other directions. The stalks swished around them, dancing to the melancholy tune of the wind. In the centre of the rotunda, a large monkey statue watched over them, balanced on its tail and seated in prayer. Before Savara could ask what had hurt him, he shrugged his shoulders.

"I don't need your sympathy, princess. I'm not broken, the world is, and I made a promise to myself to fix it."

The stone in her pocket pulsed again, calling to something in the dark. By the time she realised this, it was too late. At the sound of Amon's voice, glowing yellow eyes began peeking through the stalks. A low growl rippled through the air around them. Savara spun around quickly but found their path blocked from behind by a large, grumpy-looking primate brandishing a set of sharp fangs. She inched closer to Amon, looking to him for guidance on how to react, but he looked just as surprised as she was. Somehow, the primates had evaded their notice. The rest climbed slowly into view, making menacing chattering noises with their teeth. They were surrounded.

Then, the howling began.

CHAPTER 26

A HIGHER POWER

"DON'T MAKE ANY SUDDEN movements," Amon whispered. "If they feel threatened, they'll rip us limb from limb."

"Good to know. Wasn't planning on it," she gulped, inching back towards the statue.

A chill set in around them. Through the stalks, the monkeys circled them, teeth bared and glimmering yellow eyes fixed in their direction. When the king had warned them about feisty monkeys, Savara had scarcely pictured primates such as these with eyes that gleamed with hatred and nostrils that sniffed out fear. These were wild things, and she and Amon were trespassers.

"What do we do?" Savara asked, sensing the curl of malice around her rising like a sweeping tide.

"I'm working on it," he replied.

Suddenly, Savara noticed a hard jabbing thing at her side. She jumped, realizing too late that it was only the stone statue. The primates began their vicious howl, a cry that signalled to the rest of the clan that blood would fall.

"I'm sorry," she breathed, fearful of their circumstances.

Amon unsheathed a blade from his coat in one hand and harnessed a shield of blue light in the other. "Stay behind me!" he yelled over the screeching.

Savara clung to him, watching as the monkeys jumped from stalk to stalk, picking up speed with each jump. Their movements created a new wind, directing it into a vortex that tugged at their hair and clothes. Savara held tightly; afraid she'd be swept up by the current. Amon readied himself for the attack, but she could sense his nerves. They weren't going to make it out.

The howling grew louder. Savara knew she couldn't wait for them to strike; she had to do something. A curl of power spread across her back and over her shoulders. If she could only harness it the way she had in the alley of Osiir, she might be able to buy them enough time to escape.

"Hold on," she called, reluctantly releasing her grip on him. She shook her hands nervously, attempting to draw out her powers.

"Princess, now is not the time—"

"I got it," Savara stuttered, still trying to coax them out. "I got it…" she repeated, but the powers didn't come. "Please work…" she whispered finally.

"Savara!" Amon yelled.

The stone rattled against her side. A flash of lavender light appeared around them. But it was too late. The monkeys lunged for them on all sides, their sharpened incisors shining from within the shadows. There were too many of them.

Amon dropped his sword and wrapped his free arm around her, raising the hand with the shield over their heads and forcing them both to the floor.

Savara dropped her hands and shut her eyes, expecting the inevitable. It was only a matter of time. She realised the last thing she would hear was the faint beating of his caged heart, and for some reason, she found this comforting. *Whatever happens, you'll be okay…* she thought, waiting for the first signs of pain.

Suddenly the howling died. Silence engulfed them. A familiar scene appeared in her mind…

"He could be a king in his own right," Savara said of the monkey to the king of winds. "He has a good heart, like you." The old monkey sat cross-legged and balanced on his tail, watching the pair of them speak.

"Who is to say he is not?" the king replied. "You have a wonderful way with creatures, my dear."

Savara smiled, bobbing her head to accept the compliment. Back home, compliments were hard to come by, especially since the day Lance disappeared. "It's because I promised to keep his secret."

"And what secret is that, young one?"

Savara beckoned him down to the level of her lips, ready to divulge the truth. "He watches over the land to make sure you remain the king," she whispered.

The king of winds contemplated her with a furrowed brow. His playfulness receded, turning into calculation, like that of her mother. "How would you know that?"

"He told me," Savara replied, tapping the part of her chest that covered her heart.

The seconds ticked by slowly, stretching between each shallow, fearful breath. Another memory had appeared, but what use was it now if she was about to die at the hands of the very creatures she remembered, although, in her memory, they were not vicious at all. Instead of lingering on it, Savara thought of her friends—wherever they may be—and how she'd tell them how much they meant to her if given the chance. She thought of Amon and how she might've liked to get to know him better. She took another breath, and another, waiting for the inevitable.

The next thing she knew, Amon nudged her shoulder.

"Savara," he whispered, her name sounding like a lullaby on his lips. "Open your eyes." When she hesitated, he squeezed her shoulder lightly and added, "It's alright, you did it."

Savara hazarded a peek, but the sight that met her eyes was unlike any she'd imagined.

Her power coiled around them, reaching into the souls of the creatures, turning them docile. Their beady yellow eyes watched on in silence, no fangs bared, no evil howling. They simply sat, waiting. This wasn't the power she'd used in Osiir. None of the creatures struggled for breath or hinted at pain. The malice around them had died, leaving only a sense of calm. Born of fear all the same, this was something different, a power she'd never used before—or if she had, unwittingly so.

"I did this?" she asked, turning her head to find that all the monkeys had come out from their hiding places to watch them.

"I certainly didn't," Amon replied.

"But how?"

Amon gazed deeply into her eyes as he helped her to her feet. "Believe it or not, there's more to those powers of yours than just death and destruction."

A fresh fluster bloomed across her face, noticing the look of awe streaked across his. Respect and longing glinted in his eyes, along with a passion probably brought on by the moment. It was the most of any emotion other than annoyance she had seen in him. Whether it was a newfound appreciation for life after almost dying or a newfound appreciation for her, she couldn't say, but the gentle cupping of his hand over her scarred cheek made her sway more in the direction of the latter. Savara bit her lip, only now realizing how much she yearned for his.

The winds picked up again, but all she could feel was heat; heat on her cheeks, heat on her shoulders, a trail of it running down her spine beneath her coat and corset. Desire drifted in the air around them, and she knew it wasn't only hers. The sound of his uneasy heartbeat filled her ears, and she treasured every shallow breath he took as he inched his face closer to hers. Their noses touched. For a few eternal seconds, they shared breaths, frozen in that frustratingly beautiful moment before a kiss.

But none came.

The chill began to seep back into her bones, the euphoria fading. Amon inched away from her, but this time, she knew it wasn't to torture her. He was torturing himself. If she didn't act soon, the moment would be gone, like the others she'd tried to forget but couldn't.

"Fuck it," she whispered and pulled his head towards her again, pressing her lips to his. The moment their lips touched, she felt their hearts synchronise, his own missing a beat to align with hers. It took him a moment to thaw, but just as Savara was about to retreat, he pulled her body in and deepened the kiss.

The entire bamboo forest disappeared around them. The queues of time went mute. The kiss could've lasted a minute or a lifetime, neither truly knew. The only thing she knew for certain was that he kissed her as if the world was ending. It could've; she wouldn't have noticed.

And then, he pulled away.

Taking a step back, his hand flew instantly to his lips as worry traced the crease above his brow.

"I'm sorry," she whispered, still trying to catch her breath from their strange but welcome moment of passion. Her entire body buzzed with excitement. "I thought you wanted—"

"I did—I do, I thought…" Amon stuttered, trying to get a grip on himself again. "I can't… I'm sorry," he said finally, shaking his head before storming off towards the castle. And then her high came crashing down, the cold taking hold of her once more.

The monkeys had gone, ushered away by the waves of passion that had sucked away the very air they breathed.

Savara reached a hand to her lips, touching the points where the sensation of his lingered. She'd never before received a kiss so unashamedly passionate that it had left her questioning the very occurrence of said kiss. She let him go, knowing better than to follow.

Usually, she worried more about how she was performing than the kiss itself, but not this time. This time, she'd given in. She'd allowed herself to truly feel it, truly enjoy it. The kiss had left her feeling hollow, as though she'd been nothing more than a vessel for these powerful emotions rather than the source, but whole at the same time, connecting her with parts of herself she'd cast down for longer than she cared to admit. Her longing for connection but unwillingness to open up, her guilt for keeping others away to protect herself, her sadness for the losses she could never undo and words that would forever remain unspoken, her fear of the untethered desires she hadn't realised she was harbouring... The kiss had reunited them all. It was something entirely new, yet it felt like home.

For the first time since their lips met, Savara gazed around the rotunda. The forest around her looked to have aged ten years in ten minutes. Mosses had grown beneath her feet and up the stone statue, some even sprouting flowers. Weeds peeked through the gaps in the floating planks of wood. She almost wondered if their passion had caused an explosion of life.

But that would be ridiculous...

As she retraced her steps back to the garden, out of the corner of her eye, she noticed the overgrowth recede. Once again, she was left with more questions.

CHAPTER 27

LESSONS IN GO

"I HAVE NEVER SEEN YOU so ruffled, my boy. Did your time in the garden not prove rejuvenating?" the king said as he debated where to put his piece, smirking from behind his beard.

Amon tapped his foot restlessly as he waited for the clink of the king's eggshell-coloured piece to hit the board. He'd almost tripped over every stone on his way back to the palace. He'd rushed out of the garden in such haste. He cursed himself for having looked so foolish—for having fled—but Iturri only knows what would've happened if he'd stayed. The kiss had left him breathless. Even now as he sat in his favourite armchair by the fire, in a place he'd often come to relax and forget the day's turmoil, he couldn't find the space to breathe.

"You know very well it didn't," he replied as he dropped his slate piece onto the board with less grace and more noise.

"Hmm…" The king stroked his beard and contemplated their board. The game had only just begun and already he was looking for ways to extend it. "Rejuvenating no, perhaps enlightening?" He placed another piece on the board, accompanied by another smirk.

"I have no idea what you're talking about," Amon replied, capturing one of the king's pieces in his next move. He knew the king could see through his lies, but it was easier to keep up the shaky façade than admit to himself what had happened. He was not yet free. He could not yet give in to the things he felt. If any harm came to her because of it, he would never forgive himself.

"Did you see the blossoms? They are beautiful this time of year."

"Yes, Uncle, we saw the blossoms," he assumed. He couldn't remember if he'd seen them. The garden could've been as bare as a forest in winter and he wouldn't have noticed. His eyes had been on her the whole time. The way she'd breezed around the garden, eyes devouring everything in their path, had captivated him. The king took his time with his next move. Frustrated and filled with nervous energy, Amon stood, deciding to dispel it by pacing in front of the fire.

"And the monkeys?"

"Yes, we saw the vicious little things, too."

The king placed his piece, capturing three of Amon's in the process. "They weren't too wild, were they? I did warn you they were quite energetic this season."

Amon placed another piece distractedly and resumed his pacing. "Almost tore us limb from limb," he replied, remembering how, in that final instant, Savara had done something to quell them. He'd felt the energy burst from her body, spiralling outwards and into the hearts of the vicious creatures. Through his scar, he'd felt her fear, but he'd also noticed a loving calm rush over him in that last second. He imagined it was that sensation, that wave of tranquillity and pacifism that ended up staying their rage. He'd known she was powerful, but seeing it with his own eyes, feeling it up close, it left him awestruck.

The king shook his head. "But you are in good health… relatively speaking." The king stared up at him knowingly, his eyes trailing up and down his nervous body. "The young princess wielded her charms, then?"

Amon stopped his pacing abruptly and shot him a dirty look. "What do you mean?"

"She used her charms on the monkeys, did she not?" The king grinned. "I doubt even you could fend off an entire clan unscathed."

"Are you telling me you planned this?" he growled, placing another piece on the board, which the king took easily in his next move.

"Plan? No. I merely suggested a nice stroll through the gardens. My days of planning and scheming are behind me."

Amon rolled his eyes. "*Right* behind."

"You are distracted, my boy…" the king said with a deep sigh as he surveyed the board, ignoring Amon's comment. "Either that or I have truly improved in your absence."

"I doubt that…" Amon replied, capturing another four pieces and turning the tide momentarily in his favour.

The following succession of plays turned the mostly balanced board into a sea of white. "Distractions come at a price, especially in games of such high stakes…" the king commented.

Amon slammed his next piece on the board, rattling the other pieces. "I am not distracted," he growled.

"My prospective win would say otherwise."

"The game is not over yet," Amon remarked, shifting back into the armchair, though his nerves had not yet subsided. He replaced the pacing with the weaving of a stone between his fingers. The game looked admittedly bleak for him, but he couldn't give the king the satisfaction of winning. He bit the inside of his cheeks and tried to focus. If he put his mind to it, he could formulate a strategy. He placed another stone, paving the way to the capture of five—if the king fell into his trap. But his focus was short-lived thanks to the king's next comment.

"She's quite special, isn't she?"

Amon fumbled the stone he'd been playing with between his fingers. "I hadn't noticed." His plan went out of his mind faster than it took for the piece to hit the floor.

The king laughed. "If I remember correctly, my boy, there is little you don't notice."

"Why don't you come out and say what you're thinking? This dancing around the point is tedious, even for you, Uncle."

"Fine. Your heart has changed, but the conditions of your bonds have not. Though it fills me with joy to see you as enamoured as you are…" Amon shot him another dirty look, but the king ignored him as he placed another piece on the board. "I would hate to see you get hurt. Many a time have I told you I consider you a son, even though we share no blood."

"I know, Uncle."

"Then know this: in these many years, I have come to understand you better than you understand yourself. I made a promise to myself not to interfere, even after I discovered your bonds, but I cannot sit idly by while you torture yourself." The king stretched out the kinks in his neck and sighed.

"I am not torturing myself!" Amon furrowed his brow. With a heavy sigh, the king made to stand. "And where are you going?"

"You still have much to learn, I see. I forfeit this game."

Amon glanced incredulously between the board and the king. "Why would you forfeit?" he asked, staring at the majority white-ruled board. "You were about to win!"

"I've grown too accustomed to my losing streak. Besides, not all victories are triumphs, but all losses are lessons." The king smiled. "We shall play again when you are less distracted. Also… I believe someone is waiting for you."

Just as the king was about to depart, weakness rattled through him, causing him to clutch his heart and drop to his knees. A coughing fit erupted from his mouth.

Amon rushed over to him in a frantic panic, eyes widening as he caught a glimpse of the blood in the king's hand.

"Uncle, what is the matter?" he whispered, fear lacing the softness in his voice.

"The king is dying," said Bismuth, who had emerged from the hall. He bowed his head to them as he neared, clutching tight to his staff. He hesitated momentarily before continuing his explanation. "He has not wished to relay the severity of his situation."

"I am fine," the king coughed again, but his skin had grown clammy in Amon's arms.

"Those of us in the inner circle have been worried for quite some time…" Bismuth added.

"Why did you not tell me?" Amon growled at him, violent storms raging in his eyes.

"You lost any privilege at information the day you marred your back with those stones, the day you struck a deal with the devil," Bismuth replied. There was no sympathy in his voice, only sorrow. Bismuth had been one of the first to take a liking to him, even if it was only because of the challenge he posed. But the past was not as easily forgotten as Amon had liked to believe. "You made your choice, without regard for those around you who had shown you kindness, treated you like family."

"I did what I had to!"

"So did we…"

"Forget the squabble," the king said through another bloody cough. "Now is not the time."

Amon hoisted the king up in his arms, cradling the frail body as though it were a babe. He glowered at Bismuth as he marched towards the door. "Get help, get whomever you must." Bismuth must have understood that Amon truly had the king's survival in mind because he bowed his head and launched himself down the hall without any further questions.

Amon traversed the palace halls as quickly as his legs would carry him. His thoughts raced as the man who'd been most like a father to him lay panting in his arms. The king's room lay just ahead. He bit down on the rage that flooded through him. Bismuth would get a healer, and everything would be fine. Until then, he'd stand guard at the king's bedside.

"Hold on, Uncle. Everything will be alright."

CHAPTER 28

AN INSTRUMENT OF DEATH

SAVARA TOOK HER TIME coming in from the gardens. The skies had grown dark by the time she reached the palace's winding mountain maze of stairs. The cold breeze bit into her bones despite the heavy cloak blanketing her shoulders. That brief moment of passionate heat had left her even colder than she'd been before. She hoped to plop herself down in front of a fire with something to warm her stomach. The day had been eventful enough already—the night didn't need to be as well.

She retraced her steps through the airy palace, following the sweet scent of ashes that led to a door left slightly ajar. An inviting strip of flames flickered behind it, their warmth trickling out into the hall and beckoning her forward. When

Savara reached the door, she heard voices in a heated discussion.

Amon and the king.

Savara knew better than to eavesdrop and turned on her heels to seek out another fire when the sound of a harsh thud gave her pause. She turned back and peeked through the slit, watching as Amon paced restlessly in front of the fire. The king's eyes flashed in her direction accompanied by a knowing smile, a subtle invitation to listen in on the conversation. Amon hadn't noticed her, which was strange, considering she knew there was little he didn't notice. She frowned, realizing her kiss must have rattled him more than he let on.

The king mentioned his lack of focus as well. It was hard to believe someone so usually unfazed by the world had been brought low by one kiss. And then she heard something she would never forget.

"Your heart has changed, but the conditions of your bonds have not," said the king. *Conditions of his bonds? So, the king knows...* Savara considered speaking with the king about Amon later, wondering if she could obtain more information from him, when she heard his airy voice again. "Though it fills me with joy to see you as enamoured as you are..." Savara bit down on the smile that grew on her lips. "I cannot sit idly by while you torture yourself."

Her heart sank. *Torture...* Savara turned away from the door, no longer concerned with seeking out warmth. She wandered back through the silent halls, that single word echoing in her head. *Torture.* Somehow, she ended up on a chilly balcony, lit only by a long-stemmed torch that provided little warmth and the stars above. She clutched tight to the cloak around her shoulders. As she perched herself at the edge of the floor, letting her feet dangle and forcing herself to endure the cold a few moments longer, she stared out at the endless stretches of cloud beneath her. *Am I torturing him? Is that why he ran?*

Savara turned her eyes to the spires of marble behind her. Bathed in the light of the stars above and surrounded by the sea of clouds below, the palace radiated magic. It was a vision, something out of one of the fantasy books she'd devoured in the human world, and not nearly as scary as it had been when she'd arrived. If only she could feel the way she did about those fantasy books now.

A gust of wind picked up beside her, signalling the arrival of one of the Zerua. The energy surrounding this individual was unmistakably comforting, so much so that Savara didn't need to turn to know Brass had perched himself at her side. She extended a hand and accepted the steaming mug he'd brought.

"You will catch a cold if you remain here much longer," Brass said, taking a sip of his green tea.

"I needed air," Savara replied, bringing the mug to her lips. Brass always made the best tea. Years of experience, she supposed, and patience.

"You came to the right place, then. These lands are somewhat known for that particular element."

Savara smiled. "I didn't realise you made jokes."

"Occasionally, when merited. Shall I ask why you came searching for the most abundant of all elements on this balcony?" His gaze burned on her neck, prodding her for the truth.

"You know what I am… You've seen what I can do…" she mumbled. "Every time I begin to feel normal—like I am seen as a person and not an outsider, or a weapon, or a threat—life comes crashing back in to remind me that I'm not normal, that I am *other*."

"It is true, you are something the world has not seen for a time." The way he said it made her believe that even he held reservations about her, about what she could be or do. Savara frowned, realizing not even someone as unattached as Brass was capable of withholding judgement. "Griffin believes you to be a saviour," he added, which only made her heart drop further. "The others may not be so grandiose with their thoughts of you, but I know your presence is welcomed." After a moment of silence, he added, "That all means nothing, of course. Only you can decide how your life will be lived and how your powers will be used."

Savara nodded. The thought wasn't exactly comforting, but it reminded her of what the king had said before about everyone having darkness in them. Brass had never shied away from her, nor had Griffin or the others, despite knowing what she was. They may have judged her, but they hadn't left her side, and that had to count for something. And then there was Jasper, whom she'd shared an instant friendship with, one that had stood the test of time—and worlds. She rested her mug on the ledge beside her and hugged her knees in close. She missed him. She missed them all.

A tear carved its path through the stones on her cheek and down her chin as she gazed out over the darkened sea of clouds, wondering where in the world they could be.

"It's nice out here," she sniffled, hoping the view would take her mind off them. "Peaceful."

"A peace earned on the backs of soldiers and many decades of war," Brass remarked.

Savara turned to him, his silvery eyes fixed on the horizon, lost in memories as vivid as the stars above. "Is that why you left?"

Brass took a moment before responding. "Unlike in the Argia lands, blood is not the determinant of rule, though in some cases it may hold influence. Here, force and a strong hand are paramount. The blood of many marks all changes to the throne. They say we are the second most spiritual nation, even above the Izar in some cases, but it is not through an abundance of prayer, as some would believe, but rather because our lands are steeped in blood."

"I had no idea. I've never seen you train—or fight, for that matter. And in Idune, Griffin had you avoid the battle at all costs."

"When I agreed to join Griffin, my one condition was to never have to fight again. I cannot imagine anyone else in his position having agreed to such a thing, but Griffin has never faltered. Not once in all the time I have known him. Not even in moments of need has he gone back on his promise."

"When you say again, what do you mean?"

Brass frowned, burdened by the apparent weight of his story. Savara almost told him to forget it when he let out a sigh. "The king had long primed me to be his successor, even over his own nephew—a dear childhood friend of mine. I was a perfect candidate. I grew up in the monastery, where people are branded with names of metals and taught not only how to be effective killers, but when to put such skills to use. By the time I received my divination, I had a thorough understanding of war tactics and spiritual manifestos, among other scholarly works, and could pin a fly to a tree with a throwing knife from ten feet away, simply by tracking the air currents it generated."

"That sounds terrifying, no offence."

Brass smiled. "So I have been told. I never wished to be king, especially not at the cost of another's life, but as such a perfect candidate, I was the standard to beat. My friend knew he would never become king if I lived…"

"You killed him…" she whispered.

"I was ambushed. A group of seventeen figures in black armour, wearing shrouds over their faces. I slaughtered them all in a fight for my life." Brass gazed up at the stars, as if searching for his history in their all-seeing glares. His eyes were as distant as they were, lost to the tale he'd run from. Savara wanted to spare him the descent into such a gruesome memory, but she knew that Brass never spoke without reason. There was a lesson for her in here somewhere, one he would relive even a nightmare to teach. "It was only after removing the face coverings from each did I realise I had murdered my friend in cold blood." Brass turned back to her with a sad smile. "I am not proud of my actions, but it is because of them that I value the gift of life above all else."

"With such a past, I can see why you left."

"Yes, but no truth can be evaded forever."

"Is that why you came back?"

"No. In my search for you, I encountered other monks who had been gathering information on the aftermath of the war in Idune. They alerted me of the king's current condition, and I knew I had to come at once." Before Savara could muster the courage to ask what he meant by the king's condition, Brass added, "He is dying. The monks who have grown accustomed to his rule have kept his situation from public knowledge, but he is dying, nonetheless. Whether he does so by natural causes or because the news slips from their hands, blood will once again cover the streets. Of this, I am sure."

Savara cupped her hand over her mouth, a gasp escaping her lips. "Does Amon know?"

Brass contemplated her with a furrowed brow. "There is little, I believe, he does not know. You take a curious interest in him," he said, and she was thankful for the surrounding darkness that hid her blush. "He is not to be trusted."

"He's not what you think," Savara replied, frustrated that she couldn't divulge what Amon had told her. It wasn't her place to fix whatever damage was done between them, but she couldn't help coming to his defence. "He's not bad, he's just…" Savara thought back on all their conversations and all the sensations she'd felt rippling off him each time they were together. One word stood out above the rest. "Afraid."

Brass let the pause between her words and his draw out as he considered his response. "It is, in part, as you say. Fear was once his motivator." Brass sighed. "I do not consider him bad, only untrustworthy. His problem is that he has not yet found his limit, the line in the dirt which he would not cross. In the past, he has forsaken friends and family in the name of power. I know not of his current motives, but there is little I believe he would not do for his own advancement."

The more Brass spoke about him, the more Savara questioned which version of Amon was true. His constant insinuations of life being a game might lend to Brass's theory of him looking for power, but only if the end goal was winning. Amon made it clear many times that he considers there to be no winning this game. Maybe he was right. Maybe they were all just pawns painted in shades of grey…

"What will you do?" Savara asked when the silence between them grew stale. Brass raised an eyebrow. "Will you stay on as king? Or will you go back?" she clarified.

The air around him grew cold. "I have pondered this question many times. In honour of my late friend, I swore to never take up the bloodied throne. In my most recent conversation with the king, I told him as much…" Brass gazed up at the moon and smiled. "I owe my new life to Griffin, but I would be foolish to say I had not noticed his suggestions of my return."

"He always has an agenda," she replied, and they shared a laugh. She'd forgotten the richness of his laugh, the one that, despite his general aura of indifference and ease, betrayed his true emotive nature.

"And yourself? Will you take up the mantle of your family?" he asked.

Savara had avoided that very question on many occasions. She couldn't deny that she had once fantasised about being a princess and living in a palace, but they were childish fantasies that did not take into account the hard truths of being a leader. She didn't see herself as capable of making the tough decisions required by one: how to resolve disputes, how to keep the people content, and how to make sure your nation was protected. After hearing Brass's story, she realised she'd underestimated not only what threats could come from beyond its borders, but what dangers lurked within a kingdom, as well.

"When we first went to Osiir, I could tell Griffin was considering having me take up that throne…"

Brass smiled knowingly. "Griffin wants to see good people in places where they can do the most good. That is all. But it will always be a choice, and one you must make alone."

Savara let out a heavy sigh at the insinuation. "Must I?" She hadn't expected an answer, but he gave one regardless.

"No," he said casually. "Nothing but breathing is a must in this life."

She returned his smile. "If it means anything, I think you'd make a great king."

Brass nodded softly in agreement, but before he could respond, he conjured a vortex around them. The force of the wind whipped Savara's hair across her face. She shielded her eyes until the vortex suddenly dissipated. The sound of metal hitting the marble floor surrounded them. When Savara opened her eyes again, she saw Brass already on his feet, hands poised to launch another gust of wind. Something was wrong.

"Reveal yourself," Brass called out into the depths of the swirling clouds below. Savara brushed her hair from her face and glanced at the strange bits of metal that had rained down beside them. Small, bladed weapons were scattered across the floor. *Throwing stars.* They were under attack.

CHAPTER 29

THE POWER OF WIND

"I WILL NOT REPEAT MYSELF," Brass called out into the clouds, his voice commanding and resolute. Despite his exceptional defensive skills, his attacks were ineffective against an enemy hidden within the swirling currents beneath the clouds. Savara watched as Brass flicked his wrist, deftly knocking two more throwing stars off course. "You will not be able to break my defence. It would be best to surrender now before I turn to the offensive."

"Who are they? What do they want?" Savara asked, rising to her feet beside him and scanning the clouds for any sign of their attackers. She felt the winds pick up around them, raising the hairs on her arms. Looking over at Brass she noticed the air of cold fury rippling from him.

"These weapons were designed for soldiers of air."

"Why would people of this nation attack the palace?"

"The king's condition," he replied with a gravity to his voice that sent new shivers down her spine. Savara's heart hammered away in her chest as she recalled what he'd said about there being bloodshed accompanying the change in rule. They could

"They can't mean to kill him!" she pleaded.

The next look from Brass silenced her. "To some, the chance at power speaks louder than loyalty."

"I thought his condition was a secret…"

"As did I. Either way, I cannot allow them to breach the halls. You should head inside for safety," Brass suggested.

The situation brought back memories of the battle in Idune. Ori, the leader of the Harri, had been slain in front of her and she had been powerless to stop it. She wouldn't let that happen again. The king had been good to her, despite knowing what she was. She would not let him die the way Ori had. She wouldn't let the world lose someone like him. Savara steadied her breath and moved towards Brass, ready to assist him in any way she could. She wasn't about to use her powers, but there was still something she could do if given the chance.

Instead of retreating, she cleared her throat. "I have no weapon," she said, casting aside the cloak to free up her range of movement.

Brass said nothing but acknowledged her bravery with a smile. He sliced his palm through the air, creating a sharp gust of wind that severed the stem of a nearby torch. The precise angle of the slice formed a tip at the end of the wood sharp enough to pierce flesh. Brass was truly a creature bred for battle.

Savara hurried over to retrieve it. Though she had received some form of training in staff combat from Sebastian, she had never quite picked up the nuances of it and knew she was no match for this unknown opponent. But it didn't matter if her attacks were slow so long as her defence held, because this wasn't training. This was battle.

She had always underestimated the importance of defensive tactics until she found herself face-to-face with an adversary too powerful for her to defeat, surviving only by sheer luck—if she could even call it that. She hoped for her sake that luck was on her side tonight too.

"Where are the other soldiers?" she called, clutching tight to the makeshift weapon, and shifting her feet until she and Brass were back-to-back.

"I do not know…"

Suddenly, Savara's hand flew up to the stones on her cheek. Her scar burned as if it were a freshly made mark from a white-hot piece of metal. She screamed. A hellish hatred filled the stones. Savara knew only one person that had such an effect on her scar and sufficient hate to make her double over in blinding pain. But how had he managed to catch up with her? Hadn't Amon assured her that he would never find them here? Regardless, they'd made a mistake. It wasn't an attack on the king after all; it was an attack on her.

"Brass," she hissed through the pain, "Big Tog."

Another barrage of throwing stars rained down upon them. Brass flicked each one out of the air easily, but there was no stopping them. "Savara, breathe. This is only the beginning."

Savara took sharp breaths, focusing on the afflicted area. She could almost hear Big Tog's menacing voice calling out to her through the scar. *Still as weak as ever I see, my little duck.* Savara reached over and picked up one of the discarded blades and clenched it between her fingers. She needed to feel a more painful sensation to overcome this one. The metal bit into her skin. She gripped it tighter until the blood trickled down through the gaps in her fingers. The pain didn't subside, but at least she could think clearly enough to get back to her feet. *I am not weak anymore,* she thought, hoping whatever channel of connection they had fed both ways.

Brass acknowledged her rising with a bob of his head. "There are two of them. Be on guard," he said, keeping his eyes fixed on the darkness. As if his words had summoned them, two men clad in black appeared on either side of the landing. Their faces were masked by a thin shroud, just light enough to see the glowing whites of their eyes. They looked determined. There would be blood.

"Big Tog must be hiding somewhere below. He won't be able to attack us though; he needs to be in point-blank range."

"Then let's keep our distance." The winds picked up around them. Savara could sense Brass's patience waning.

"You can try," one of the attackers said.

The other pulled out an extendible staff and sharpened its blade against the floor, sending a screeching sound into the air. The unpleasant noise ground at Savara's nerves, but she held firm to her staff and pointed it in his direction. "This will be easy," he mused in response as he beheld her weak stance and trembling knees.

The attackers lunged at them from both sides. Metal clashed against wood, bone against air. Brass was swift in his movements, keeping to the defence in an act of restraint while Savara struggled to do anything more.

Her attacker whipped the staff around his back, gaining force for his strike. Savara ducked, swinging hers up to stop it. The sharp sound echoed around them. Savara's block had worked this time, but the man's movements were faster than she'd anticipated. Another strike like that one and he might not miss the next time. Savara barely managed to push him off and ready her feet when the next strike came. She held the staff above her head, balanced between her hands. The man's staff slammed into the middle of it, just shy of her brow. She shrugged him off again, but this time, she wasn't quick enough on the rebound. The sharpened tip of the man's staff grazed her ribcage. For the first time since she'd arrived in Haizea, she thanked Amon for having suggested the corset.

"Clever," he growled, "but not clever enough." The attacker spun his staff around again and whipped at her legs, knocking her to the ground. The wind fled from her chest as her back hit the marble. The attacker stalked over to her, dragging the tip of the staff across the floor. "I can't see why he wants you alive… you're a weakling…" He raised his weapon high, the blade catching the light of the moon above. But before he could strike, a vicious gale threw him across the balcony. In the time it took for him to regain his balance, Brass had already closed the distance between them.

Brass moved like the wind itself, his strikes fluid and precise. Both assassins tried to counter his attacks, but he was too fast, too skilled. They found themselves constantly on the defensive, struggling to keep up with his movements. Something had switched in him. The defence he'd been playing at stopped the moment Savara hit the floor. His eyes lost their warmth. His heart grew as cold as the mountains beyond. This wasn't the Brass she'd known; this was the killer he hid within.

One of the assassins tried to strike him from behind, but he sensed the attack coming and dodged to the side, delivering a powerful kick that sent the assassin flying into a nearby wall. The other one charged forward, but Brass created a whirlwind that swept him off his feet. The assassin rolled to avoid hitting the ground too hard, but before he could get back up, Brass was on him, eyes narrowed like the blades of their throwing stars. Savara felt the world still around them.

Brass took a deep breath and closed his eyes for a moment, seemingly gathering his strength. He raised his hands in the direction of the assassins, who suddenly struggled for breath. It took a second for Savara to understand what was happening, but as the assassins writhed on the ground, she realised he was stealing the very breath from their lungs.

"Brass!" she yelled over the swirling rush of the wind around them. "You don't have to do this."

Brass looked from the assassins to her and back again before dropping his hands. The men choked as the air flooded back into their lungs. With lightning-fast strikes, he sent the two men crashing back against the wall, knocking them unconscious. He stood there for a moment catching his breath before he turned back to Savara. The warmth in his gaze returned as he bowed his head towards her. She'd stopped him, saved him from the kill. He'd saved her life yet, somehow, she knew she'd saved his soul.

Savara winced through the pain as she made to stand when, from beneath the sea of clouds, she noticed a glimmer of light. It all happened so fast; she had no time to react.

"Brass!" she yelled again as she watched the lightning strike him from behind.

Brass crumpled to the floor, muscles spasming with the shock, as another man leapt onto the balcony. Electricity danced across his knuckles, pulling at the strands of oily-slick black hair atop his head as he ran his fingers through it.

Savara raced over to Brass's unconscious body, hesitant to touch it until the lingering currents dissipated into the marble beneath him. Terror pooled within her as she stared up at the man, certain she had seen him before, unsure of where or why, but knowing he was no friendly face. "What have you done?" she hissed.

The man fixed his coat and pulled a pair of heavy leather gloves from inside his vest, along with a single cigarette. He brought the thing to his lips and lit it with the sparks from his fingers before slipping the gloves onto his hands. He inhaled deeply before replying through a cloud of smoke, "My job."

Savara pressed her hands to Brass's unconscious chest, hoping to sense a heartbeat. "Please, please, please don't die," she whispered, unaware of the trickling of her blood onto his skin from the wound she'd given herself.

The man across from her took another puff. "And that's why I come at such a hefty price." He extended his palm out beside him as if waiting for something.

Savara looked around, wondering who he'd been talking to, when another figure stepped out of the darkness. Short, gaunt, with two devilish ram-horn-styled red braids laced high on his head with a thread of gold that glinted in the moonlight, along with a matching pair of incisors on full display. He dropped an audible sack of coins into the man's palm and cleared his throat.

"I've been searching for you, my little duck."

CHAPTER 30

BIG TOG RETURNS

"IF YOU'LL EXCUSE ME, I have other matters to attend to," said the man with lightning in his fingers. He flicked away the remains of a half-smoked cigarette, pocketed the satchel of coins, and strode past her into the palace without so much as a passing glance.

Big Tog stalked towards her, murder glinting in his eyes. With her powers, Savara could sense the torture in his soul. She hadn't fulfilled her side of their soul bond and she knew that if she'd been experiencing fevers because of it, so had he. They'd both been on the brink of death, though he looked worse for wear.

"Where is my son?" Big Tog hissed, his voice gravelly and strained. Each footfall of his echoed on the marble floors of the balcony.

"I couldn't find him…" Savara stuttered. "I was captured in Idune before I could find him."

"And the Prince of Shadows?"

"I…" But it didn't matter what she said. They both knew from the beginning that she would never be able to kill the Prince of Shadows. Big Tog had only made this soul bond with her knowing that she'd be bound to his will until she completed both conditions, but it appeared he had underestimated the toll it would take on him as well. "I tried…"

"I should've known you were too weak for such a task," he said through a pained cough. He pulled a knife from the holster at his side, twirling it in front of his face, reflecting the murderous intent in his eyes on its refined surface. "Yet, it is I who seems to suffer more at the hand of this bond. Perhaps that power of yours has protected you?" He drew nearer to where she sat huddled over Brass's unconscious body in protection. "Or else it is protecting itself… No matter, I will take pleasure in freeing myself of this bond, and the world of your wicked magic."

With little time to waste and knowing she could not protect Brass's body otherwise, Savara reached over for her staff and lunged upwards, thrusting it at Big Tog. "Stay away from us," she said, her eyes narrowed in determination though her arms shook with nerves.

"He is of no concern to me," Big Tog replied. "It is your blood I want." He took hold of the wooden staff with one hand and jutted the knife towards her stomach.

Savara slid out of the way just in time. The blade skimmed the side of her metal-laced corset. Twice now it had saved her from injury. If she survived, she'd owe Amon big time. *Come to think of it, where was that pain in the ass?* Now that she could use his help, he was nowhere to be seen. She changed her mind: if she made it out alive, she'd thank him for the stupid corset and curse his very bones for knowing somehow that she'd need it, and that he wouldn't be there to help.

Savara's muscles ached from the previous attack. She realised that, even with all the bruises and beatings, Sebastian had coddled her in training. He'd never gone so far as to break her bones or draw blood. She wasn't prepared for war, and therein lay the danger; it sought her out regardless. Savara didn't know how much longer she'd be able to hold out. The girl she was before Idune might have given up and accepted a quick death, but she'd come a long way since then. *Thanks to a pain in the ass apprentice who had a handle on everything but his own emotions.* She'd be damned if she didn't give whatever strength she had left to walk out of this alive, if only to see the look on his face.

Savara shook off his grip on the staff and rolled her shoulders. The muscles in her calves cramped. Her fingers felt as if they'd fall off if fear had not glued them to the staff. She wasn't strong enough to hold him off in hand-to-hand combat. The lingering illness of the soul bond did little to dampen his strength.

"Do you think you will come out of this unscathed?" he goaded, seeing her stance as a challenge.

"So long as I come out of it alive, I'll be fine."

"Ah… There's that enchanting fire of yours. I knew there was at least one reason I liked you. Shame to be rid of it, but time is wearing thin for the both of us, and between your life and my own, there is no choice." Big Tog charged at her, embedding the knife in the wood of the staff and tossing them both out of reach. He grinned, the shadows filling the hollows of his cheeks and under-eyes, giving a skull-like impression to his face. "I always did work better with my hands."

Savara raised her hands, ready to defend herself. But Big Tog was too fast for her, throwing a punch that landed squarely on her jaw. She stumbled back, pain exploding through her head. The taste of blood flooded over her tongue. It was the first time she'd truly tasted it, her own blood. The thing inside her rattled to life with the hunger of a beast waiting at the edge of its cage. She'd consciously starved it of true power ever since her encounter with the Prince of Shadows. It waited now, as though it knew its time was coming. All she had to do was unlock the door, give in. But she'd made a promise never to use it again. She now fought two enemies instead of one.

Big Tog charged at her again, but this time, she knew to expect it. She ducked and dodged his next few punches, all the while restraining the bloodlust beneath her skin. If she didn't throw a punch soon, she'd be in trouble. She landed a few blows to his stomach, and one to his face that simply made him laugh. She'd put all her might into them, but Big Tog was a formidable opponent, not easily taken down by such paltry attempts at force. Big Tog was relentless, his attacks unyielding. The next punch he threw landed in the soft part of her stomach and sent her flying to the floor. Her head slammed against the marble as she fell, blurring her vision as the pain shot through her skull. A pulse of energy whipped from her body, sending Big Tog back a few steps. The thing inside was building its strength.

Disoriented, Savara twisted her head and found the staff and the knife discarded only a few feet away. She needed a weapon, or else this was the end. She scurried across the floor as best she could in hopes of reaching the staff when she felt something sharp pierce the flesh between her shoulder blades. She dropped to the floor in agony, reaching behind her and ripping one of the discarded throwing stars from her back. It clattered to the ground, sending a splattering of blood across the floor. She bit down on her lip to quell the pain, but it was no use. The thing inside her grew restless, its reach extending through her veins. If she let it out now, she knew there would be no controlling it, no restraining it. Savara feared it would not only stop his heart but tear it still beating from his chest.

Big Tog stalked towards her, licking the blood on his golden incisors. Savara could feel her strength waning with every passing second. He stooped down to meet her gaze and cackled. "You put up a good fight, but your will to survive is not stronger than mine. I told you during our session that those you don't kill have a second chance at killing you. At least in your passing, you will finally understand the truth to my words." He reached for her neck, pinning her in place. The edges of her vision blurred. At points, she saw two of him. Two sets of evil teeth. Two pairs of unrelenting eyes. Four arms strangling her neck.

Savara stretched her hand out as far as she could, but the staff was still a ways away. She knew what she had to do, even if it meant becoming the thing she most despised, even if it meant giving in. She gave the thing inside her reach. Its lavender light extended out past her fingertip, taking hold of the blade instead of the staff. In the next second, she felt the cold metal in her palm. Big Tog had been too distracted to notice her powers at play, and for that, he'd pay with his life. With what little strength remained in her body, Savara plunged it into his chest.

Big Tog stumbled backwards, a look of shock and pain crossing his face. Blood seeped from the wound, spilling onto the ground beneath him. His breathing grew shallow and forced. Fear shot through his eyes as he stared back at her, finally realizing what she'd done. He'd taught her to kill. She'd finally learned her lesson.

"May the world tremble at your feet, Queen of Daemons," he hissed.

As Savara slowly regained her breath, she noticed a trickling sensation on her cheek. She reached her hand up to where the scar had been moments before but found nothing hard marring her skin. She brought her fingers into view. *Blood.* She then realised what she'd done. She'd broken the bond, but not by fulfilling it. Big Tog was dying, his soul was leaving. Soon, there would be nothing left of him to bind her to.

Savara rushed towards him, feverishly pressing her hand to his chest to stop the bleeding, but he pushed back with what little life remained. It was too late.

"I didn't mean to—"

"I don't need your pity," he coughed. "Own your actions, or someone else will." In the end, his time had come. In his final seconds, a look of serenity crossed his face before his heart stopped.

Savara sank to the ground, tears streaming down her face. She made no move to wipe them. She didn't sniffle or sob. Blood covered her hands, and this time, there was no one to blame but herself. She'd done it. She'd become a killer, just like Big Tog said she would—just like Amon said she would. She'd taken the life, not her powers. All her struggling against their bloodlust had been in vain; her powers were not the murderers. She was. She knew she would never be able to forgive herself.

The sea of clouds washed up onto the balcony, pulling in a new chill and a more sinister darkness. And then came the rain. An inoffensive shower that washed the blood from the marble, as if the palace was more concerned about irreversible bloodstains on its tile than the life that had been lost. From a distance, she heard a voice calling her name.

Amon had rushed out onto the balcony, calling out to her as he dropped to her side. When she didn't respond to his request to stand, scooped her up in his arms. Bismuth followed close behind, slinging Brass over his shoulder and darting back inside for cover from the rain.

Time slowed for her. They passed various indistinguishable halls as they made their way through the palace. Her body shivered and he hugged her tighter, but her mind was miles away. "I killed him…" she mumbled finally.

Amon shook his head and replied, "You survived."

CHAPTER 31

A LAKE'S WORTH OF LIQUOR

"GIVE ME TWO BOTTLES of your finest rum," Lucy called to the bartender as she leaned up against the wooden bar, exposing her generous cleavage for maximum attention. She strolled back to Storm, bouncing on the balls of her feet.

Storm cocked her brow. "How much did that cost?"

"A promising night with an interesting bartender," she said as she glanced back at the young man who continued to eye her as she shuffled into the booth.

Storm shook her head and smiled. "You're incorrigible."

"I am a free agent—until that interesting creature in your party with the curly hair and glasses decides to come to his senses," she mused. "Besides, I'm here for a good time, not a long one, and the bartender over there looks like he's promising a *very* good time."

"Good luck with that one," Storm laughed. "And that creature—Jasper—might be a bit out of your reach. He's very much in love with the missing girl of our party."

Lucy uncorked the bottle, and instead of pouring herself a shot, took a long swig. "You sound bitter. Not a friend, I take it?"

Storm looked around the bar but found no one conscious enough to overhear her potentially damning explanations. She sighed and copied Lucy's swig before wiping her mouth to speak. "It's not that." The alcohol went to work, already loosening her tongue. She secretly thanked Iturri that none of the others were around to hear her confessions. "I admire her strength. It takes a lot to do what she did, jumping from one world to another, with no family to speak of and no memories to guide you, but when we first met, I was the only one who could see how dangerous she was. Let's just say I was worried about my friends."

Lucy grinned. "You're a dangerous little sea snake yourself, my friend."

"Yes, but… there's something inside her. I could feel it. A bloodlust that reminded me of my lands."

Lucy's smile faded. "I've heard rumours that your people's history is steeped in blood."

"The history, the land, the people…" Storm looked up at her with apologetic eyes. "Can you blame me for fearing what might happen to my friends with someone like that around? Someone who represented everything I'd…"

Fled, she thought, though she couldn't bring herself to say the word. It was the first and last time she'd truly fled from someone or something. She'd vowed to herself the day she left home that she would be strong enough to never have to run away again.

"I don't blame you, but I do think you hardly gave her a fair chance."

"I—"

"Not everyone is as strong as you and me," Lucy added. She spoke with a clarity that bore little resemblance to alcohol consumption. "And from what I gather, it sounds like this girl needed a friend like you who could teach her how to be strong and not give in to whatever urges lay inside her."

Storm downed a quarter of the bottle in her next go. As much as it pained her to admit it, perhaps Lucy was right. Perhaps she hadn't been as forthcoming as she could've been. Griffin had admitted as much to her the first time they spoke about it in his study. Even if Savara was a danger to them, she could've been there to help guide her in the right direction. But then, those boys had always done the right thing from the beginning. It came easily to them, no second thoughts required.

She swirled the dark liquid around in the bottle as she thought fondly of her friends. Griffin was a strong leader and a true friend, gallant and cunning in every way. She happily served at his side, knowing he always had her back. Brass was another one who'd escaped the blood-marked lands of the Zerua. She'd only heard stories of his prowess, but she imagined that if he'd truly been brought up as one of the legendary monks of the king, all stories of his skills were true as well. And yet not even that blood-stained past could sour the softness in his laugh or wipe the peace from his eyes.

Maybe it was time she took a page from his book. Simon was every bit the quirky little brother she'd never had and always wanted. And Sebastian…

She blushed and took another swig, hoping to mask the fluster behind a wall of intoxication. But Lucy hadn't been fooled.

"Ooh… I've taken enough swigs like that one to know you were thinking about someone special, weren't you?" Lucy laughed, the timbre of her voice ringing throughout the pub, though none of the patrons seemed to take notice.

"I don't know how you managed to weasel all of this out of me in so little time."

"Didn't I tell you? I'm an expert in uncorking bottles. Even ones as tight as the one you've jammed all your feelings into are no match for me," she said with a wink. "Now, tell Lucy about this special someone. It wouldn't happen to be *Mr Tall, Blond, and Handsome* I saw stalking out of your bedroom the other morning looking like he'd lost part of his soul, would it?"

Storm narrowed her eyes at Lucy. "How did you know?"

"I told you earlier, everything on my ship is my business," she said, confidently kicking her feet up on the table and holding the bottle up to the waning chandelier light above. "Though I must admit, I tire of emotional wrecks who can't admit their feelings to the person standing two feet away from them who is also so clearly in love that they practically have the word tattooed across their forehead."

Storm laughed. "Griffin?" she asked, having also noticed the way his nerves tensed at the sight of Lance.

"Obviously."

"Cheers," Storm replied, extending her bottle.

"To the emotional wrecks," Lucy announced to the pub, making sure to brandish a wink of her sparkling blue eye towards the young bartender who would be taking her to bed later. "May they one day find the love so blatantly staring them in the face." The girls clinked bottles and downed another painfully intoxicating gulp of rum before Lucy slumped back into the booth. "So, do tell. Tall, blond, and handsome. What's his story and why does he push you to drink?"

"He's a pain in the ass. Ever since I met him, he's been purposely trying to get under my skin. Making jokes about things that should be taken seriously, mocking me, calling me all sorts of names, and generally looking for every possible way to light a fire under my ass."

"What kind of names?" she asked, a smirk growing across her face.

"Ugh, I can practically hear him now. *Stormy, my dear*," she said, imitating his voice.

"That's kind of cute."

"It's patronizing."

Lucy bit down on a laugh. "I think you mean endearing…"

Storm scrunched up her nose. "He does it to annoy me, makes a big show of being overtly flirtatious because he knows it grinds my bones."

Lucy narrowed her eyes, the drunken haze finally setting in. "And that's a bad thing?"

Storm nodded vividly, the alcohol getting the better of her. It had been years since she'd drunk this much, and longer since she'd felt this good. Lucy was the best kind of bad influence; the kind that healed you. "It is when he has the reputation of a love 'em and leave 'em kind of guy."

"Ugh, they're the worst. Bartender!" Lucy called, waving her hand in the air. "Be a dear and bring two more bottles. My friend is dealing with a lot." The bartender did as she asked and brought over two more bottles without hesitation.

Storm didn't know how much more alcohol she could take without rightfully spewing every last morsel she'd eaten since breakfast, but the liquor was good, and the conversation was better. Restorative even, despite the fact it might hinder her appetite for the next meal or two.

"Okay, I want to get this straight. How do we know about his reputation?" Lucy asked as she uncorked her next bottle.

Storm huffed as she brought her knees to her chest between the booth and the table. "Because he tells me about them!"

"You've added intrigue to my ocean. Do explain," Lucy said as she balanced both hands and her chin over the top of the bottle inquisitively.

"Ever since I've known him, he's always brought up his… *conquests.*"

"Like… in detail?"

"More than I needed, that's for sure."

Lucy beamed. "Describing every delicious detail for you?" She swooned. "Something tells me he knows his way around a body…"

Storm shook her head, trying to remove the images Lucy had conjured of Sebas from her mind. "I wouldn't say that."

"And how often do these conversations take place?"

"More than I'd like."

"What else does he do?" Lucy drew herself in closer, basking in the intimate details of their conversation.

"When we train together—"

"You train together?" Lucy gasped as if she'd heard the gossip of the century. Storm nodded. "At whose request?"

"His, usually. Like I was saying, when we do train together, he's always taunting me, like he wants to get a rise out of me. Many a time have I wished to run him through— if only to wipe that ridiculous smirk from his face."

"I think it's a beautiful smirk," Lucy said before biting her lip. "Is there anything else that irritates you about him?"

"Everything! The way he stares at me behind my back, the way he's always bumping into me—on purpose, I might add—the way he picks fights with me over stupid things and always has us paired up for missions… Actually, before meeting up with you, we were at a gathering in one of the houses of the Harri leaders and Griffin had asked us to do some reconnaissance. Sebas had the bright idea of dragging me onto the dance floor."

"For a dance?"

"Because it would offer a decent vantage point for scoping out suspicious parties."

"But did you dance?"

"Well… yes."

"And was he any good?"

"We know each other well enough to follow movement cues if that's what you mean."

Lucy grinned as though Iturri itself shined down upon her. "I hate to be the bearer of bad news, Anika, my sweet, but that man has been probing you for desire. Brandishing himself like a menu. Begging for you to—"

"You've had too much to drink," Storm laughed, attempting to pull Lucy's bottle from her, but Lucy held to it steadfastly.

"I'm as fresh as the cucumbers we put into brine before embarking on our glorious, seafaring adventures." Storm rolled her eyes, knowing that she meant pirating. "You, my friend, have been so sorely blinded by whatever traumas you have bottled up in that petite frame of yours that you failed to notice this man is completely and utterly in love with you."

"You have no idea what you're talking about." She wished to laugh to prove her point but, for some reason, she couldn't. Sebastian? In love with her? She scoffed, but the thought of him sent goosebumps down her arms even now.

"You forget I keep an incredibly close eye on everything that goes on about my ship. If that man's expression of pure torture upon leaving your empty room alone was anything to go by, I'd say he's absolutely, incurably lovesick. And, judging by the way you're blushing, you might just be as well."

At this, Storm swallowed the lump of emotion growing in her throat. "Drop it, Lucy. It doesn't matter anyway."

"Doesn't matter? You have a god condensed into physical form begging for your affection—affection that is *not* unilateral—and you say it doesn't matter? Do you have something against your own happiness?"

Storm's voice grew silent. She could barely muster more than a whisper. "Actually, yes."

The vibrant cheer faded from Lucy's face, replaced by a grave look of concern. "Anika, you know you're allowed to be happy, right?"

Storm shook her head. "Every time I find the slightest bit of happiness, this world rips it away from me, and makes no small move of it either."

"Care to share?"

Storm sighed. She'd already said more than she'd meant to, but she figured there was nothing worse she could say anymore. "When I was five, my mother died, leaving me with my father. He was an important member of one of the noble houses and had no idea how to talk to anyone under the age of thirty and outside of an official capacity. I used to watch him spar with some of the younger boys in the town and saw how much he enjoyed it, so I'd taken to learning in my free time. When I showed him what I could do, he said it wasn't my place as a little girl to be learning the ways of the sword and barred me from doing anything other than what would further my *marriageability*. My lack of divination lost me any friends I had in childhood, and my skills with the sword lost me any chance of friendship in adolescence. I did find one man who expressed an interest in me." Storm blushed. "We enjoyed each other's company, even made love a few times. He'd wanted to propose…"

"But what happened?"

Storm swirled the dark drink around in the glass, almost picturing him in the reflection of the liquid. "…he died." She'd already thought more about him than she'd allowed herself to in years. Everette. A soul taken too soon. Her guiding light in times of darkness and fear. Her throat grew tight. Warmth poured over her shoulders, reminding her of his all-encompassing hugs. She hadn't thought of him willingly since the day they scattered his ashes. "I vowed I would never attach myself to anyone, ever again." Storm reached a hand to her cheek, wiping away the free-flowing tears that had begun to fall somewhere between the start of her story and now. She'd never cried in public. She hated herself for doing so now, but the damned tears would not stop.

Lucy slid from one booth to the other, pulling her in for a breath-constricting embrace. "Your feelings are valid, but you're also allowed to cry. We don't always have to be strong, especially when we have people around who love us."

Lucy's words, as touching as they were, only made her tears fall faster and heavier. Storm sniffled, hoping to be rid of the emotions before anybody saw her. She'd never opened up to anyone the way she had with Lucy, especially not in such a short time. Something about Lucy's wild and vivacious nature put her at ease, allowed her to be vulnerable where she'd never been able to before. If her crying had gained her anything, it had gained her a friend for life. One that she'd not have to fear losing, because Lucy was as strong as, if not stronger than, she was.

CHAPTER 32

UNCORKED AND UNTEMPERED

LUCY PROMISED TO RETURN, citing the need to free a waterfall as she made haste towards the bathroom. Storm dried her eyes on the sleeve of her jacket. Releasing the emotion had felt better than she'd expected. After having spent so many years hiding away from the troubling feelings, letting them all flow as they needed was liberating. She finally managed to reign in her emotions when the sound of Sebastian's voice behind her made her jump.

"Anika?"

Storm shivered. The way he used her first name when he was concerned or needed to talk about something serious had always rattled her. He was the only person, aside now from Lucy, whom she'd ever let refer to her by her first name, out of respect for his abilities as a fighter—as an equal. It was his worst weapon against her defences. It penetrated every wall she'd built between them. He might have thought she hadn't noticed his particular use of it, or else believed her to be indifferent. But she noticed. Every time. And every time it felt like her inner fortress would fall if she didn't keep a tight enough hold on it.

Whether he knew it or not, he alone had the power to break her.

"What?" she growled, making a conscious effort to hide her face. She couldn't have him see her in such a state, though she found it increasingly hard to maintain control over her emotions. Especially now, as the particularly devilish effects of the liquor were beginning to set in.

Sebastian strolled up to the table, taking in the array of bottles that she and Lucy had somehow finished, and shook his head.

Storm used her strands of brilliant red hair as a shield against his prodding gaze, but she could see the concern in his eyes reflected at her in the glass of the bottles.

"Sebas, save whatever snarky comment you have dancing on the tip of your tongue. I'm not in the mood."

"I wasn't going to comment…" He picked up one of the half-finished bottles and downed the rest of its contents. He slid into the booth in front of her and waited. Storm was sure there had been more noise in the bar when Lucy had been present, but ever since she'd heard him call her name, his voice was the only sound she could hear. "Anika," he repeated her name softly. "Will you look at me?"

"What are you doing here, Sebas?" she hissed, still unable to meet his gaze. The fluster on her cheeks had returned in full force, and the concern in his eyes did nothing to stifle it.

"Griffin asked me to find you and Lucy. He's taking Jasper into Solia. We are to stay on the lookout for trouble coming from outside Iliso."

"Good, you delivered your message. You can leave now."

"I'm not going to leave you here…" he said, his eyes stopping on each of the empty bottles, "…like this."

"Fine." Storm shot to her feet and marched towards the door. It was hard enough to keep her feet moving in a straight line, she didn't need someone to confuse her further. Besides, she figured the harsh cold of the air outside would do her good, or at least better than the alcoholic fumes of the bar. She managed to weave her way through the tables without stumbling, only to prop herself up on the wall just outside the bar. She closed her eyes and breathed in deeply. Her breakfast was beginning its ascent. It was all she could do to keep it down.

Undeterred by her outburst, Sebastian followed her out into the cold. Having noticed her shivers, he snapped his fingers and conjured a small flame in one of his palms. He held it near to her without saying a word. In his other hand, he held a glass of water that he seemed to have no intention of sipping.

"Ugh, what do you want, Sebas?" she practically yelled, bringing her hands to her face.

"To apologise."

"For what?"

"I had no idea what you'd been through."

Storm dropped her hands and gazed upon him with a fury that could have set ice on fire. "You were eavesdropping?"

"I didn't have to," he replied, his voice cold at the insinuation. "You and Lucy were practically yelling across the bar."

"Just how much did you hear?"

"I heard enough…"

"Then? What are you waiting for? We can have a good old laugh at my many misfortunes…"

"You should already know that I would never laugh at misfortune. Least of all yours, Anika."

Storm's skin tensed at the sound of her name. He'd done it again. He'd turned her name into a curse, something to eat away at her nerves. "Sebastian, I beg you. Go away." The sound fell feebly from her lips, more plea than a demand.

"Anika." She winced again. "Look at me," he said. Despite the tears pressing against her waterline, she relented. "I'm not leaving you," he assured her as he gazed into her eyes.

Those eyes of his transported her back to the battlefield. She saw the way they burned, as if he'd rushed over to her mid-fight and carried her to safety all over again. She saw the way he'd looked at her as they danced in the ballroom at Lady Amaia's dinner party, the way he'd searched for her when he was out on the balcony with Griffin. Worse, she saw reflected in his eyes the way she'd fought through flames and smoke to save him the night their camp burned down. She knew that look well. It was a look that, instead of saying *I won't leave you*, said, *we don't leave each other*. And it had her retching up her insides within seconds.

Storm turned around just in time to avoid splashing him. Sebastian stroked her back with a warm hand as she continued to vomit up the generous amount of liquor she'd ingested during her conversation with Lucy. He didn't seem at all put off by it. In the very brief moments of consciousness between retches, she imagined he'd had to endure many scenes such as this one during his notorious nights of Argia debauchery.

When there was nothing left in her insides to bring out and the dry heaving finally stopped, Sebastian handed her the glass of water. She should've figured it had been for her all along. He smiled as he watched her down the glass in seconds, sparing the first sip to rinse the taste from her mouth.

"Out with it," Storm hissed. "Say whatever it is you need to say."

"Can I just take the time to enjoy the fact that, for once, I'm not on the receiving end of a lecture on drinking?"

"Good. You've said your piece. Let's find Lucy and go back to the ship." Storm began walking alongside the wall, avoiding the parts she'd splashed, in search of the entrance to the bar.

Sebastian quickly caught up with her and rested his hand on the wall in front of her, blocking her passage. "Anika."

Storm winced yet again. "Sebastian?" she said with a sigh. She was tired. Her muscles had been worked to the limit with Lucy earlier that day. The alcohol did a number on her stomach. Whatever was left of her had been racked by the release of all her pent-up emotions. She didn't need a lecture.

She didn't need his concern. The only thing she needed now was a nap. "What do you want?"

"I want you to say it."

"Don't speak in tongues, Sebas. I'm not in the mood."

"Admit you love me," he said, his eyes riddled with a mixture of desire and desperation. Storm froze. Whatever illness had riddled her body just moments before had been entirely replaced by fear. He gulped nervously and spoke again. "Admit you love me, Anika. I need to hear it from your mouth." She'd heard him the first time. She'd heard him as though he'd shouted it to the world.

"Sebas, what are you doing?" she asked, her own eyes alert with fear. She was sure the tears had returned as well, but she was too paralyzed by his words to wipe them away.

"I want you to stop fighting me."

Storm noticed his arm trembling beside her. "What do you mean?" she asked.

"Lucy was right…" he began. "Every single word."

"I don't understand…"

"I have loved you, Anika, since the moment I first laid eyes on you. I knew I would never be good enough for you, but I swore I would be the best version of myself that I could be on the off chance you'd fall for an idiot like me." Sebastian bit his lip, struggling with the words. Storm hoped he wasn't waiting for her to speak because he'd taken every word from her tongue and every breath from her chest. "I wasn't even that good with a sword before we met. I'd been so reliant on my powers that I hadn't bothered to pick one up. I so desperately wanted you to notice me, I trained every night in secret, just to be able to train with you during the day and not look like a fool. I told you jokes to try and get a rise out of you, not because I wanted to make you angry, but because I love that sparkle of challenge in your eyes. And when I took it too far, I knew you'd always find creative ways to ground me again. I'd bump into you just to find excuses to be near you. And at Lady Amaia's dinner, I'd wanted nothing more than to dance with you, to pretend we weren't trying to save the world for one night and just dance like two people who could potentially fall in love."

"Sebas, the other night—"

"Lucy was right about that, too. I've never known a sense of peace like the one I felt with you nestled against me. Imagine my surprise when I woke up to find you gone only moments after I'd drifted off." Before she could reply, Sebastian let out a pained laugh. "I can only imagine how broken I must have looked coming out of your room, but it was nothing compared to how I felt. And when you shut me down this morning…" He shook his head and sighed. "I know this feeling is not one-sided, Anika, or else I wouldn't have just bared my soul to you. Especially not standing outside a shanty bar in the cold, somewhere near what I can only assume was your mostly digested breakfast. So, please. Admit you love me and save me from this sickening pit of uncertainty."

For a moment they stood, face to face, each breath a small cloud between them in the freezing air. Then, somehow, those treacherous words crawled up her throat and onto her lips.

"I love you," she whispered. Her confession had been so quiet that, when Sebastian didn't react, she almost convinced herself she hadn't spoken the words aloud at all. She cleared her throat and tried again. "I love—" But the final word caught on her tongue as his lips pressed against hers.

CHAPTER 33

CROSSING THE ISLES

A SUDDEN HEAT RUSHED over them as they crossed into the inner isles. Jasper shed his heavy winter coat, tossing it to the floor of the canoe and causing it to wobble. Griffin shot him a murderous glance. He had to bite down on the smile growing on his lips. He'd forgotten Griffin's weak stomach when it came to the sea. But there was no time for apologies. In front of them, the clouded barrier peeled away as they glided into a crystalline turquoise bay.

The towering arches of Solia welcomed them, a stark contrast to the frigid gates of Iliso. People in passing canoes waved their way, the excitement of their festival permeating everything in sight. It reminded Jasper of the Carnival festivals he used to celebrate back home, as the sounds of calypso music, reminiscent of his grandparent's generation, filled the air. There was a calm to Solia that Iliso didn't have. No soldiers on alert, no spears, no bears, only the gentle rhythms of island life.

As they made their way closer to the shores, Jasper spied low hills and stilt houses built of wood that looked as though they had withstood many a storm—and would endure many more. The white sandy beaches that lined the main isle of Solia provided safe play for the youth of the island and perfect launching grounds for fishermen and their canoes. A network of docks and harbours following the curves of the river delta guided them inland. The scent of salt and coconuts hung in the air, comparatively more inviting than the brine and fish scent of Iliso, but that, Jasper supposed, was because it reminded him of home most of all.

Griffin said nothing and kept his eyes fixed on the front end of the canoe, flinching every time the soldier captaining the canoe rocked it. Though the currents weren't as strong as the ones they'd travelled with Lucy, Jasper knew Griffin was counting down the seconds until his feet touched dry land.

Where ocean turned to river, they found themselves under the cover of a web of mangroves, each one providing refuge for a variety of small fish. Jasper spied what looked to be an octopus and a crab fighting over a carcass, and schools of shimmering silver fish weaving through the roots. Soon, a house appeared at the edge of their mangroved tunnel. A large wooden structure covered in bougainvillaea and bathed in sunlight. The royal house.

As they neared, Griffin's expression grew tense, worry creasing his brow.

"Be careful," he whispered, keeping his voice low to not be overheard by their guide. "We don't know why General Kyara wants the crown, but the fact that she'd go to such lengths to get it signals trouble."

"Have you ever been here before?" Jasper asked, noticing the way Griffin's eyes flicked about their surroundings. Knowing the way Griffin's mind worked, Jasper imagined he was surveying vantage points and alternate routes out in case of an emergency.

"No." The tone of his voice was hard, irritated. Jasper knew how little Griffin liked not having the upper hand in a situation, but he'd never seen him in a position of such doubt. "This place was once dubbed the fantasy isle of the Ur nation, long before this queen took over. One of the previous rulers tucked it away from society, preferring to use it as his own personal playground. No outsider has set foot in here since. I'm out of my depth here, which is why I want you to be on guard. If we get separated, I don't know if I will be able to help you. Did you bring the cane?" Jasper nodded, digging it out from the inner folds of his discarded coat and brandishing it towards him. "Good. Keep it on you… just in case."

Jasper wasn't fond of Griffin's "just in cases." They almost always turned out to be true. Thankfully he'd kept up his training with Storm, though the ship's limited space meant the wide-swinging attacks he'd been used to were no good. Short-range combat had always been a challenge for him. He only hoped he wouldn't have to use it here.

As they pulled up to a final dock, Jasper spied a woman with long white locs tied in large braids that framed the sides of her dark face watching them from one of the grand windows on the second floor of the government house. A silver crown sat atop her head, glinting in the sunlight that filtered through the windows. Her shimmering turquoise eyes reminded him of Lucy's, save for their lack of warmth and vibrance. She stared them down like a hawk in hunt, clutching tight to a fish-hook-shaped staff of ice and silver.

"I take it that's our queen?" Jasper asked, inclining his head in the direction of the window.

Griffin peered upwards just in time to catch her leave. "That's her." As they were about to disembark, one of the soldiers tugged Griffin back, catching his wrist with a thin stream of water.

"General Kyara expects you to keep your promises, Izar," the soldier growled before releasing his hold on Griffin's wrist.

"As do I," Griffin replied.

Jasper and Griffin followed their expectant escort onto the dock and into the main house. Their escort, a young woman with a smile too broad to be real and a white braid that swished behind her like a pendulum, deposited them in a quaint wooden courtyard bathed in sunlight from above and surrounded by koi and lily-filled ponds, and asked for their preference of beverage.

"I'd like a—" Jasper began, but Griffin held a hand up to silence him.

"Whatever Her Majesty's preference is fine with us." When the woman bowed and made off for the kitchens, Griffin turned to him and added, "It's better to come off as gracious in the face of unknown royalty."

"So, water is out of the question?"

Griffin glowered at him. "I wouldn't drink anything until you see the queen drink it as well."

"Oh…" Jasper finally caught on to Griffin's line of reasoning. He was very much out of his depth here, but thankfully, Griffin was experienced in the ways of royalty and manipulation. Jasper knew that, at his side, they would find out who took Savara's memories and why, all while avoiding getting tangled in what looked to be an impending civil war.

"This courtyard has direct access to sunlight," Griffin remarked as he stared up at the various balconies surrounding them. "But those balconies will have direct access to these ponds." Jasper followed his gaze as it shifted from the sky to the depths of the water around them. "And these look like they feed directly into the river, giving them an endless supply of water."

"So, what you're saying is, if they wanted to, they could drown us where we stand."

"Correct."

"Thanks," Jasper grumbled.

"For what?"

"The optimism."

Griffin grinned. "Don't count me out yet. I still have a trick or two up my sleeve."

"Ignoring the fact that those obnoxious muscles of yours can barely fit in your sleeves, I have spent enough time with you to know those wheels in your head are always spinning."

"Whatever you do, Jasper, leave the talking to me, don't speak unless spoken to, and don't answer anything that contains personal information. We are here for answers, not to give them."

Jasper nodded in agreement. "I'll just stand there and look pretty then."

Griffin clapped a heavy hand on his back and replied, "You'll have to try a little harder for that. Just remember to stay on guard, no matter how friendly they seem."

Jasper straightened his shoulders, trying to project a confidence he didn't quite feel. "Whatever. I got it. No guard down, no personal information, and follow your lead."

Griffin nodded. "Keep an eye out for anything suspicious. We don't know what we're dealing with here, and it's better to be safe than sorry."

As they waited for their audience with the queen, Jasper couldn't help but feel a growing sense of unease. The beauty of the courtyard around them was at odds with the tension in the air, and he couldn't shake the feeling that they were walking into a trap. He hoped Griffin's confidence was warranted, but he feared they were in over their heads.

CHAPTER 34

THE QUEEN OF SALT AND SECRETS

THE LAST THING GRIFFIN expected was for him and Jasper to be alone with the queen. That meant she either didn't think them a threat, or she knew that, despite the threat, she alone could manage. Either way, he knew they had to tread carefully.

The queen swept into the courtyard like an evening tide. She exuded power and grace at an almost ethereal level. Even the water in the ponds seemed to rise to greet her. Her dress, from the pearlescent gleam of its fabric to its trumpeting train, gave her the impression of a siren. The spear at her side—a deadly blade of silver and ice with a point shaped like a fishhook—was the only allusion to just how dangerous she might be.

"Your Majesty," Griffin greeted her with a low bow. Jasper mimicked his movement and, as instructed, remained silent.

"Pleased to make your acquaintances, gentlemen. I am Queen Noor of the Isle of Solia." She waved a graceful hand in front of her, forming a dining set of ice before them from the water of the ponds. "What brings you to my domain?" she asked as she took a seat.

The young woman who had escorted them in arrived with a tray of hibiscus tea and biscuits filled with guava jam. The queen, in a show of good faith, poured her guests a cup each and bit into one of the biscuits. Jasper took that as a sign he could eat one as well, but Griffin's appetite had been lost since they'd set foot on that damned boat.

"We wish to ask you about the divination of the Argia princess," he said.

Queen Noor's eyes narrowed. "Curious," she replied in an overly dulcet tone, the accompanying smile too manicured, too composed. "As far as I know, there is no Argia princess. She died many years back."

"With all due respect, Your Majesty, we all know that is—"

"That's a lie!" Jasper interrupted.

Griffin pinched the bridge of his nose, swearing under his breath. He glared at Jasper, hoping he could feel the annoyance in his eyes. Jasper, having realised his mistake, shoved another biscuit in his mouth. Griffin cleared his throat and continued. "You see, Your Majesty, the princess is one of our companions and we were made aware that she lacks all memories of and prior to her divination."

The queen prickled as she sipped on her tea. Griffin noticed she'd tightened her grip on the handle. "What do you mean?"

Griffin glared at Jasper to make sure he didn't jump out of his seat again. "It is not important how, just that you know she has returned to the realm of the living. As such, we believe that in her memories resides information of vital importance to the future of our lands."

"And why is it that you have sought me out then, of all people?"

"It is no secret that your people are manipulators of water, and if the legends have stemmed from any sort of truth, a skilled few of them were able to use said water to manipulate a person's memories." The queen shifted in her chair; her eyebrow raised in challenge. Having not had his claim denied, Griffin continued. "I believe one of yours has manipulated our friend's memories. We would like them back."

"*If* such a thing were possible, why do you assume it would be reversible?" she asked.

Griffin's jaw twitched. He hadn't considered such a possibility. He'd always assumed that what could be done could also be undone. Was there a chance that the damage done to Savara's mind was permanent? And if so, would they ever find out where—

"There is a legend, Your Majesty, a prophecy which foretells the end of Visanthe and involves the uniting of certain magical artefacts," Jasper began, ignoring the shock in Griffin's eyes as he recited the legend. "They say only one can combine them, specifically, '*Only when the end is nigh shall this twilight soul arise*'. This is referring to Savara."

"Jasper," he growled, but Jasper ignored him.

"Let him speak," the queen demanded.

Griffin frowned but allowed Jasper's rant, as per the request of the queen. *Something is wrong…* Jasper would never have disobeyed him so freely. The queen's growing intrigue only confirmed his suspicions, but how had she manipulated him?

"She was born in the land of fire, but her powers come from the land of blood. One symbolises beginnings, and the other symbolises ends, creating a dichotomy that might parallel the twilight hour. The next line in the prophecy states, '*Seven bonds thy keepers make, seven stones must Iturri break*', which has led us—and others—to seek out what we now know as the Seven Stones of Cartha, Cartha being the name of the unified lands before Visanthe."

Griffin stared down at the tea she'd poured and the biscuits before them. Her cup had indeed been sipped on, but Jasper's cup was empty. Griffin thought back on all her responses up until that point. They had all been questions, nothing that would be prohibited by an elixir designed to evoke the truth.

The tea… he realised. The queen might have taken some herself, but she knew how to circumvent its clearly candid properties. Jasper neither knew how nor was strong enough to do so. They'd walked into her trap.

"The part which has us stuck reads, '*Six to broken lands bestowed, a final one soul alone may hold. Lay in that which no blood may currency, uniting stone borne to eternity*'. It suggests that each ruler holds the stone of their land, but the final stone's location is known only to the 'twilight soul'—in this case, Savara. Therein lies the problem; she can't remember anything from before her divination. We believe she must have intuitively known the location of this stone and that's why her memories were wiped."

"Hmm…" The queen took another bite of her biscuit as she contemplated everything Jasper had admitted. She didn't look nearly as surprised as Griffin had thought she might. It looked as though she'd expected this information to arise.

"You already knew this…" Griffin said. The queen pursed her lips but held her tongue. "It was you, wasn't it, Your Highness?" he asked, the pieces of the puzzle finally falling into place. He should have known that only someone in a position of power would have known of the legends, would be capable of such a feat. "You are the witch who took Savara's memories."

A smile curled on her face. "If I were, what would stop me from doing the same to the both of you?"

Griffin hoped to appeal to her better nature—if she had one. "Because you want to protect your people as much as we want to protect our friend. The events to come will affect us all. It would be unwise to think otherwise."

Unable or unwilling to stay the effects of the tea much longer, the queen cleared her throat. "I admit I had my part to play in the events of that day," she replied. "As did we all, though some will know that better than others."

Queen Noor closed her eyes and lifted her palm into the air, closing her fingers with an elegant flourish. Streams of water soared up on her command, swirling overhead before encasing them all in shifting crystalline walls that quickly hardened into ice.

Griffin prickled. It was exactly the situation he'd tried to avoid, the one in which there would be no escape if the conversation went sour.

When the queen opened her eyes again, all pretence of innocence was gone. "This is a conversation that should not be overheard," she said. "What is it you wish to know?"

"Firstly, the rain. It did something to everyone's memory, correct?" Griffin asked. The queen nodded. At least he wasn't wrong in that aspect, but her words from earlier had buried themselves beneath his skin like a pesky little splinter. "Is it reversible?"

"Your lapsus?" She narrowed her eyes at him, searching for something. What? He couldn't begin to imagine. "Possibly… Though, it will come at a price."

There it was. He knew that, at some point, the topic of price would arise. He hadn't lied to Kaito when he'd said he was willing to pay, but he didn't expect the witch in question to be the queen herself. Somehow, he imagined the price would be steep indeed. "As much as I'd like those few minutes of my life back, I am more concerned about hers."

At this, the queen frowned. "Yours was a splice, a portion of your memory was carved out and tucked away. With a little bit of convincing—"

"You mean blood," he corrected her.

She grinned. "Nothing is free in this world. With a little bit of convincing, I can make your body reintegrate the missing time. Her memories, however, were manipulated, altered, like pieces of a puzzle forced into places they didn't fit…" Her gaze fell to her own hands as she recounted her version of events. "I didn't even think it would hold when I made the adjustments."

"Adjustments?" Jasper spat. "She's a person, not a quilt! Her mind is not something you can alter and stitch together as you please. You had no right to—"

"Jasper!" Griffin yelled, the sound echoing off the domed walls of ice. Jasper's wounded eyes stared back at him, lip quivering in earnest. Griffin had been equally as disgusted by her actions, but they couldn't break down now, not when there was still more to learn. He turned back to the queen, who looked slightly put off by Jasper's outburst. "Can you undo it?" he asked politely, returning to the decorum in which he'd been trained for such occasions.

The queen sighed. "Memories are curious things. Their images can be altered through a variety of means: time, inebriation, even suggestion will do. My methods involve a toxic combination of the three, using a desire imbued in blood to alter the composition of the water that comprises them, much in the way the brain naturally suppresses things it wishes to forget. In this sense, a different desire could bring them back. Memories are one thing, but emotions…" She shook her head. "They act like anchors to the truth. Memories with little emotion attached can be altered or suppressed with little effort. You hardly notice their absence. For example, you rightly surmised the tongue-loosening qualities of the tea, which I assume is why yours sits untouched before you. What you failed to realise was that the pot itself was not laced. I added the elixir to your cups after

I took my sip, and then altered both your memories to forget the occurrence."

Griffin blanched as he stared down at the cup. A twinge of fear rippled through him. In part, he was grateful that his seasickness had prevented him from consuming anything, but knowing how close he'd been to being manipulated shattered something inside him. His pride bent. Griffin took this as a sign that there was still weakness in him, one he wouldn't be able to cure.

He knew he'd been dealing with a powerful woman, but he'd never imagined she'd be so outright with her attack. "This was a test," he realised.

"Forgive me if I don't trust newcomers to my domain. The tides have been restless recently. They speak of shadows and warnings. I do not wish to see the peace of my people upended."

"Why tell us this all now? Why not continue to lead us on?" Griffin asked through gritted teeth.

"Because, if what your charming friend here says is true, we are all sailing straight into unforgiving waters. I may not be versed in the tunes of war, but I am no fool when it comes to alliances. As such…" The queen took a breath and made a singular waving motion with her wrist.

The memory reappeared, returned as though it had never been taken to begin with. Griffin saw the exact moment in which she'd performed a similar act, right after streaming liquid from a small vial into their drinks. He swallowed hard. The queen's act had been so unforgettable in nature that seeing how easily he'd forgotten it made him tremble.

This is why she is the one in charge…

"As I said, tucked away is one thing. Altered is quite another."

Griffin swallowed his fear and steadied his breath. Their work was not over. "What were you saying before about emotions? How does that affect Savara?"

"The princess's was a special case, as you can imagine. I had to alter her memories, not just tuck them away, but make her believe that this world and her life here never existed. But life, even one as short as hers at the time, is never free of emotion. Those emotions, if strong enough, could anchor some of the more critical memories. From there, if her mind was strong enough—or else her will—there is a chance she would be able to set things in order, especially given her *particular* breed of power…" The queen stroked one of her long, icy braids as she reflected on her actions. "It was no easy task, I can assure you, for any of the parties involved. I can only imagine the turmoil she must have endured." The queen took another sip of her tea before adding, "I understand why you have come. I'm sorry, but there's nothing I can do for you. If there were a way to return her memories, it would have to come from inside her."

Unwilling to waste the queen's sudden candour, Griffin changed his line of questioning. "Regarding the stones, Your Majesty, your tides were right to have warned you of shadows. There is another on a crusade for these stones, looking to complete the rite. I can only hope the Ur stone is well-guarded."

The queen frowned, but before she could respond, a sharp crash shattered the silence. A spear similar to her own pierced the ice behind her. The noise reverberated across the frozen confines of their dome, intensifying the already tense atmosphere. With a flourish, the queen stood, sweeping her hand above her head, and turning their dome back into streams of water. The spear clattered to the ground.

"What is the meaning of this, sister?" she growled at General Kyara, who stood at the entrance to the courtyard. Guards from Iliso had positioned themselves around the upper mezzanines, weapons drawn at the ready.

Griffin and Jasper exchanged a worried glance. Griffin knew what was coming next. He had to get Jasper out before the fighting began.

"Your time is up, *sister*," General Kyara hissed in reply. "I have come for my throne."

CHAPTER 35

THE DAY THE SKY FROZE OVER

THE AIR SHIFTED AROUND them, matching the hurricane brewing between the two sisters. Griffin summoned the light from above into his fingertips. He didn't want to seem like a threat, but he would do what was necessary to keep Jasper out of harm's way. Jasper's eyes caught his, questioning their next move. Griffin shook his head. They had to be careful. This was not their fight, but that didn't mean he would let them become collateral.

"What spirit has possessed you to march into my home and make such demands?" she yelled. The temperature in the room shifted, dipping with the queen's mood. She thrust her free hand to the side, reverting their table and chairs into pond water, the tea set clattering to the floor around them. With another flick of her wrist, she caught both Griffin and

Jasper in the cascading swell and pressed them against the back wall, far from the coming violence. They flopped from the wall to the ground like fish cast onto the floor of a fishing boat.

"As I said, your time is up."

Griffin quickly regained his composure, running his hand through his hair to rid it of any pond roots. Jasper got up soon after, drenched and shivering beside him. His brown curls hung wet and long in front of his glasses. When General Kyara had asked that they bear witness to the changing of crowns, he never imagined it would happen like this. Thankfully, the queen's actions meant she wasn't about to let them get hurt, but that didn't mean they would be safe if the entire house ended up as rubble. If he had to, he'd step in before the violence spread, and judging by the stares being exchanged between the sisters, violence was underway.

General Kyara gazed upon her sister, murder glinting in her eyes, as though she were nothing more than an adversary primed to fall and not a beloved sibling, let alone a twin. Queen Noor glared back with a mix of sadness and disbelief. She must have known of her sister's ambitions, but judging by her frown, she'd hoped such a challenge would never arise.

"You know I cannot let you take the throne, Kyara," Queen Noor said, taking up a defensive stance. Water from the pond beneath them trailed up her leg on her command, flowing into her free hand and fanning out to become a shield of ice.

General Kyara snorted. "You've always been too soft, Noor. You hide behind Iturri's power as if it will compare to true strength. I know it was you who manipulated Father into passing me up for the throne."

"Do you honestly believe you stood a chance?"

Without warning, General Kyara lunged forward, retrieving her discarded spear from the ground, teeth bared in seething rage. She thrust it towards her sister, that first strike landing with a sharp shattering sound against the icy shield. Noor threw her off, using Kyara's strength against her, but Kyara was undeterred. She continued to press the attack; her movements were graceful, precise. Deadly. Noor struggled to keep up with her sister's pace, but she refused to give up. Over and over, ice met steel in a sharp cacophony that set everyone's nerves on edge. Even if they could, by the looks on their faces, no one dared intervene.

"You see, sister? Not even your fancy water is a match for true strength," General Kyara said as she whipped the spear around her and lashed it out at her sister. The queen barely managed to swerve out of the way as the blade of the spear grazed her arm, drawing out a stream of blood.

Queen Noor winced as she clutched the gash with her hand, releasing the shield of ice back into the pond. "You cannot win all wars with violence, Kyara."

"Nor can you lead a people on well-wishes alone, Noor."

General Kyara charged again, this time piercing the flesh of her sister's leg. Queen Noor let out an ice-shattering scream as she ripped out the spear and sent it clattering to the ground. The pacifism she'd clung to during their conversations dropped as well. Ice lattice grew from beneath her, crawling up the walls and wrapping around the wooden pillars.

Griffin stepped in front of Jasper, whose lips had already gone blue from the frost around them, anticipating the worst. This needed to end soon, or else falling ill from the cold would be the least of their worries.

Queen Noor raised her hands, streaming the water from the ponds upwards. The streams latched onto the feet of the soldiers above, slithering up their legs before finally freezing them in place. She would not have anyone interfere.

"I have been patient with you, Kyara, but I will not tolerate comments against my people or my power. Think what you will, but our father chose my rule of his own free will. He chose me because I am the better leader. You talk to me of strength? I will show you true strength…"

Ignoring the pain she must have felt in her leg, Noor lunged at her sister, spear aimed at her heart. Kyara stood, pinned to the floor by the very ice beneath her feet. She flared her nostrils, readying herself for the lethal blow, but none came.

Noor halted. The fish-hooked tip of the spear hovered over her sister's chest, a small plate of light hovering between the sharpened edge and her sister's heart. Both sisters glowered at each other down the length of the spear before turning to the one person in the room who they knew could manipulate light in such a way.

Griffin held his hand suspended in the direction of the disk as he cast a glance between the two women. If he didn't explain himself soon, they'd kill him for interfering and resume their battle. When he felt the tension against his disk release, he dropped his hand and cleared his throat. "Forgive me, Your Majesty, General, but there will be much bloodshed to come. It is no use eliminating either of the two great warriors of the Ur. Both strengths, physical and mental, will be needed in the war to come." All eyes were on him, staring with a weight to sink a thousand ships. "When such a day comes as that, where we are free of the shadows, please feel free to resume the battle for the throne. You would be doing a great disservice to your people otherwise."

No one so much as breathed for a heartbeat or two.

Just then, a young soldier, clad in the icy warrior robes of Iliso, charged in. His eyes were riddled with urgency as he rushed to General Kyara's side. He dropped to his knees and held out a scroll before her, ignoring the tension of the room he'd just barged into.

Queen Noor parted the spear from her sister's chest and allowed her to stand, curious as to the contents of the strange scroll.

General Kyara's face blanched as she read, passing it off to her sister before confirming the contents aloud. "What the boy says is true, the shadows have returned. They have taken both Queen Anissa of the Argia and Lord Ori of the Harri. As advantageous as this would be under different circumstances, the blood of one king is the blood of us all." She turned to her sister, whose face had grown grave since the announcement. "Should you die, sister, I would hope it be at my hand, or else that of time itself."

"Likewise," Queen Noor replied with a nod. "Remove these soldiers and come with me," she said. "You as well, Izar and friend." Once they were alone, she drove the fish-hooked end of her spear into a gap in the wooden floor and turned it the way one would a key until she heard the satisfying click of tumblers. The water drained from the ponds, revealing a cavernous path beneath them. "We have much to discuss…"

Queen Noor led the way through the dark, twisting tunnels deep beneath the government house. The four of them moved swiftly and silently, each lost in their thoughts. Griffin couldn't help but feel a sense of foreboding the deeper they drew into the tunnel. With Queen Noor in the lead and General Kyara behind them, they were at the mercy of the two strong-headed women of water, neither of which seemed likely to bat so much as an eyelash in the face of murder. They weren't prisoners, but the sensation was surely close.

The darkened tunnel beneath the sea led to a small island in the middle of a sea of mist. A landmass that acted as the final wall of defence between the outside world and Solia. It was a place no other souls dared go, owing to the confusing nature of the mist itself, said to drive all who inhaled it to insanity. The only man-made structure on this tiny landmass was a lighthouse, though it neither provided light nor safety from collisions. It was a fortress of knowledge and secrets. A place, according to Queen Noor, few eyes had been privileged enough to see in centuries. But the times and the tides were changing. If there was ever a time to access such knowledge, it would be now.

CHAPTER 36

A FORTRESS OF SECRETS

QUEEN NOOR HALTED AS she reached the unassuming door at the end of the tunnel. Jasper had clung so close to his side that Griffin had almost tripped on his feet three times since they'd entered. Jasper's fear of the dark was almost as bad as his seasickness. In a small show of comradery, Griffin rested a hand on Jasper's shoulder and guided him the rest of the way. Now, the four of them waited silently for the guardian of the tower, the sound of the waves crashing above signalling they were near the surface once more, though it brought little comfort.

A woman with arms like tree trunks and hair bleached white by the sun met them at the door, immediately clapping her hand over her heart and dropping into a low bow.

"Your Highness, General Kyara." She cocked her head in the direction of Griffin and Jasper, glaring at them sceptically. "Outsiders?"

"Allies. For this moment in time, at least," Queen Noor replied.

The woman assented and allowed them passage into the tower. The fortress itself contained floor after floor of history. Some contained weapons, others books, a few contained gems and gold, maps and ink… One floor alone was entirely dedicated to storing vials of frozen blood from rulers' past. The Ur believed the remnants of their powers were stored in the blood; according to the book, they were right. They passed a level which seemed dedicated to essences and potions—a personal chamber for the queen's most special gift.

As they walked, Queen Noor prodded them, keeping their attention on her. "You claimed they were after the stones, correct?" Her voice hinted at hopeful scepticism.

"Yes, Your Highness," Griffin replied.

She furrowed her brow, a nervous hand sliding down the length of her braided locs. "And you insinuate that my head might be next?"

"Yes."

"Why? Why slaughter members of the ruling houses?"

Despite Griffin's previous warnings against speaking unless spoken to, Jasper answered the next question. "Only the blood of each land's original line can activate these stones."

"If it is only blood they need, why kill?"

Griffin and Jasper shared a grave look between them. "As I'm sure you know, blood is most imbued with the power of a person moments before their death. The stones take advantage of this and act as syphons for the power as the person's life fades," Griffin clarified. "This is what activates the true power of the stones."

No one spoke until they reached the final and most heavily guarded room in the fortress. Griffin could sense power energy emanating from beyond the wall. This room contained no door, only a slit in the stone similar to the one on the floor of the governing house. Whatever lay inside was not meant to be found—or disturbed.

"This is the first time I am setting foot in this room," the queen admitted. "I had always heard of the legend of the stones, though part of me believed it was only a tall tale our father had invented to put us to bed. When he gave me the crown, he mentioned the existence of this very room, and warned me against entering unless our way of life was in danger…"

Griffin's voice was cold as he spoke. "If *they* get their way, Your Highness, the lives of the Ur will not be the only ones in danger."

General Kyara glowered at him. She wasn't interested in the people of other nations, but she would have to bridge any feelings of discord between them. The nations would have to band together if they stood any chance of survival.

"You must swear on your lives that this room and its contents remain a secret, something that you will carry to your graves." Griffin and Jasper nodded, but that wasn't enough for her. The queen turned to her sister who, acknowledging the sign, pulled out a thin dagger concealed within her clothes and handed it over. "Give me your hands. I will not leave a large mark."

Jasper looked at him, his eyes riddled with concern. He feared what would happen when the queen and her sister saw the marks. Griffin bobbed his head, letting him know that it was okay.

The queen took Griffin's hand first, carving a thin slice into the side of his palm. The hairs on his arms stood up as he said, "I vow to keep the secrets of this chamber 'til the end of my days." The droplets of blood burned and sealed into a thin slit of crystals, one that would stay with him for the duration of their bargain. Until the end of his days.

Jasper followed suit, rolling up the cuff of his sleeve. The queen paused as she noticed his blackened veins but refrained from commenting. Trust was a two-way street, and they were being given access to the innermost workings of the Ur nation. It was only right that she kept a secret of theirs, as well.

Satisfied that her secrets were safe, the queen slid her palm over the sharp edge of the blade, letting her blood coat the edge and whispering a small prayer before inserting it into the hole. For a second, nothing happened. Suddenly, the tower began to tremble. The blood trickled through the cracks in the stonework. The wall shifted, rattling the floor beneath them.

Griffin noticed it was more than what the queen had left on the blade, making him believe that the wall was sucking more from her wound. He looked over at Jasper, who bit his lip. He knew he didn't need to remind Jasper of how certain things in this world had minds and desires of their own, or that some of the deadlier things demanded payment for their use. Whatever lay beyond the wall had demanded a high price indeed.

Light filtered in through a stained-glass ceiling, hitting the bejewelled box atop the pedestal at the centre of the room and casting an ethereal glow around the walls. Apart from the ceiling, there were no windows in the chamber, no views to the outside world, or better said, no way for the outside world to catch a glimpse of what lay inside. Undoubtedly the greatest secret of the Ur nation lay hidden away in this tower of shifting and disorienting mists. Not even the woman who had led them to this height seemed to have realised the significance of what she'd been protecting.

Queen Noor strode over to the pedestal, her hand hovering tentatively over the bejewelled surface as if fearing its contents. She hitched a breath as her fingers closed over the clasp.

From what Griffin had known of the stones, he knew she was right to worry.

Something about the room bothered him. Usually, he was able to detect the presence of such powerful objects, even if it was only a slight inkling. The power he felt in this room came from the bloodlust embedded in the walls and not the pedestal. He pursed his lips, his suspicions about the contents of the box growing, though he hoped to be wrong.

Queen Noor flipped open the small gold clasp on the outside of the case and gently lifted the lid. She turned back to them, eyes widened in fear, unable to voice her findings.

"What is it, sister?" General Kyara rushed to her side, only to find herself copying the expression.

Griffin could've recited the very words she spoke before they fell from her lips. He should've known better than to doubt himself. He'd spent enough time around blood-cursed books and other dark artefacts to know what the presence of one felt like, or in this case, the lack thereof. Even as she spoke the words, Griffin found himself wishing he'd been wrong.

"It's gone."

CHAPTER 37

LACK OF A STONE

"HOW CAN IT BE GONE?" General Kyara asked, fuming at the revelation. No stone meant no reserves of power.

Griffin sensed she'd clung to the existence of their stone more than her sister had, despite never actually seeing it. She'd used it as a crutch. He wondered if that were the true reason she'd wanted the crown, to gain access to these reserves of raw power. It didn't matter now. No stone meant trouble. Trouble for them all.

"What do you mean?" Jasper asked, casting glances between the three other members of the party.

General Kyara ignored his question as she turned on her sister. "Where have you hidden it?" she snarled. Griffin's spine prickled, wondering if General Kyara's anger would see them executed on the spot. For now, it seemed she directed it solely at her sister, which, having witnessed their previous battle, still didn't leave out their deaths as a result of collateral damage.

"Me? Sister, I am just as shocked as you are that it is missing," Queen Noor hissed.

"It cannot be missing!" General Kyara yelled, her voice alone rattling the rest of the tower.

Griffin evaded the menacing back and forth between the sisters as he strode over to the pedestal to see for himself. There, in the centre of the box, he spied the faintest imprint of the small orb on the satin cushion that once resided in the case. Unlike the throne in Osiir, there was little—if any—residual energy from the stone, which sadly meant it had been removed a long time ago.

"We must accept for the time being that the stone is no longer in Solia," Griffin began, putting an end to the sibling rivalry once more. "I suggest, Your Majesty, General, that you both remain on the highest alert. Whoever is in possession of the stone may still need the blood of the throne."

"And would that mean any heir's blood would do?" Queen Noor asked, the question falling guiltily from her lips.

"Iturri has the final say, but it would most likely be the strongest kanala in the nation, which in your case—"

"Is not a given," the queen said as she turned to her sister. "Our family has the strongest blood, it is true, however..." she hesitated.

"There is another," Griffin realised.

Queen Noor nodded, maintaining her gaze at Griffin, rather than meeting her sister's murderous eyes. "There was a sister before us, one that was lost to the waves before we were born," she admitted finally. "As a youth, when I was first practising with my powers, I performed a similar truth-revealing trick on my father as I did on you. It was childish, but I asked him which sister he favoured, thinking I would find out whom he wished to see on his throne. To my surprise, the name he gave was neither mine nor my twin's. The name he gave was Aysel."

General Kyara frowned. "How could you keep such a thing from me?"

"For a long time, I'd assumed it was a mistake in the truth serum, but I was too afraid to attempt it again on the off chance that my father had spoken the truth. On the day of my coronation, he told me about the tower and the location of the stone, but by then he'd gone sufficiently senile in his old age that he made the mistake of calling me Aysel. When I asked him about it, he simply stated she was the child they had ten years before us who had gone out to play by the shore when she was explicitly told not to and was accidentally swept up by the sea. They sent out rescue parties all along the coast, but she was nowhere to be found. Solia was closed to the public ever since then. To this day there has never been any record of a corpse. Our father spoke of her great strength and power and of the throne's loss without her at its helm."

"Are you suggesting that there is a chance this sister of yours survived?" Griffin asked. If so—if there was another sister—then there was another contender for the blood payment demanded by the stones. And if she was as strong as the queen claimed, she would most likely be the target of the Prince of Shadows.

Queen Noor sighed. "I don't like to speculate on the subject. Besides, it is more important now that we find the stone before it falls into the hands of the enemy." She turned to Griffin again, worry creasing her forehead. "You said it yourself that they are trying to complete the ritual."

"With all due respect, Your Majesty, it is probably best to consider the stone to already be in the hands of the enemy."

"Even if this Aysel did survive, who is to say that the enemy will find her?" General Kyara asked. "If she has not been seen for over fifty years, who is to say she will be found now?"

"The leader of the Arima is not to be underestimated," Griffin replied. "I have seen firsthand some of the strange powers he and his people possess. He uses creatures made of ash—living shadows that stalk the lands in search of that which he most desires. If your sister is still alive, I doubt she will be for much longer. In any case, we must plan the next course of action."

The sisters exchanged a begrudging look but ultimately agreed with him. "What do you suggest?" Queen Noor asked, seemingly ready to take part once again in events on the global stage.

"We must assume they already have the stones of the Argia, the Harri, and regrettably, that of the Ur. Their next point of attack would logically be the Zerua. One of my companions has informed me that he is already located within those territories. If they make any moves, my companion will alert me."

"And what do you expect us to do, child? Sit on our hands as we wait for someone to potentially come looking for blood?" General Kyara hissed as she paced the length of the room. "No. We will not be caught unawares if I have anything to say about it, and I do."

"My suggestion, General, is that you increase the security both here in Solia and in Iliso. Have your soldiers prepare for a standoff," Griffin replied, his voice steady and unwavering. "Even in the best-case scenario that no one comes to collect on either of your lives, the fighting will not remain outside your borders. You must prepare for the worst."

General Kyara nodded in agreement. "I will round up my best scouts and send them to gather information. We cannot afford to waste any time."

Queen Noor added, "I will send word to our allies in the Zerua and Izar kingdoms. The divides of power will mean nothing if we are all at the mercy of the Blood Daemons. Now more than ever, it is time we banded together."

Griffin nodded, pleased with their responses. As they departed the tower, Griffin chewed on the inside of his cheek, contemplating their next moves. There was no longer any time to waste. The Prince of Shadows surely grew stronger with each passing day, and until now, they had simply been playing catch up. Despite what he'd said to the queen and the general, he was not waiting to hear about a strike on the Zerua. He had to assume they were already in possession of the Zerua stone as well. It was no stretch of the imagination to know that their next target would be the Izar lands.

Though it pained him to even contemplate returning to the land of his power and the people he'd left behind on his journey for morality, Griffin was not about to let yet another stone slip through his fingers. Whatever it took, whatever it cost him, he would not allow them to complete the ritual.

CHAPTER 38

THE EARLY SIGNS OF WAR

"GENERAL ISAAC," said a young foot soldier. "There is a letter for you from General Dhoot."

General Isaac rolled his eyes. *What could that scoundrel possibly want now?* He tore open the small envelope. The letter contained no more than five words, but his usual chestnut complexion blanched at the sight of them. "Are you sure about this?" he asked the soldier.

The boy nodded. "We are to make for the Ur isles."

General Isaac scrunched the letter between his fists. His worst fears were coming to light. He had to warn Griffin—wherever he was—that the old general was about to make good on his promise; the world was going to war. He scribbled a note to his friend, urging him to stay clear of the

Ur isles if he hadn't already made it there, and to get out if he had.

"Send this as fast as you can by courier. It is imperative it gets there before we do."

The young soldier nodded.

General Isaac stared down at the helmet on the table. He'd always dreamed of donning this helmet as his father and grandfather had before him. He was a runt of a child. No one believed he would ever amount to anything. Back then, he didn't have the strength, the skills, or the will to do that which others could not. He'd worked twice as hard as anyone else to get to where he was now, to prove himself worthy, moving up the ranks through discipline and obedience. He wished to be a hero, to be just. To be the man his father had always envisioned him to be.

But these new orders had him questioning his journey.

General Isaac had blood on his hands. No one who'd reached as far as he had didn't. The blood of the past was blood taken in self-defence. No prior warnings, only action in the heat of the moment. Was that justice? He'd once believed so. He'd believed that if an invading force descended upon his lands, it was his duty to protect his people at all costs. He took no pleasure in it. While the rest of his troop celebrated their victories over tall glasses, he would spend the night in the chapel, wishing prayers of peace to the nameless faces lost on the battlefield and their families who would wake up the next morning with one less seat at their dinner tables.

A weak man kills disregarding consequence, were his father's words to him when he joined the army. *A strong man kills accepting consequence. Weak men are little more than animals out for their next meal. We are not animals.*

He'd once believed in the morality of those he served. The late Lord Ori most of all, for he was a man of impeccable moral character. He'd seen too much of the world to act without consequence. But there were new faces on the council. Faces whose morals paled in the dark light of their ambition. General Isaac restrained himself from tearing the note to shreds.

Now, he questioned the morality of those he'd served. More importantly, he questioned General Dhoot. The old general had made it known on more than one occasion that he intended to take control. What price was the general willing to pay? Or if not him, then who?

"My friend, it seems I too have landed myself in trouble," General Isaac said into the emptiness of his quarters. He couldn't disregard the orders from on high. Not now. Not when he had the lives of his soldiers in his hands. General Isaac sighed. Whether he disobeyed the council or followed their orders, his soldiers would pay the price. Not to mention the countless other lives that would be lost in such a fight. "Whether I hold strong or fall in line, the world will go to war…"

CHAPTER 39

A HOLLOW CALYPSO TUNE

THE SOFT SOUNDS OF calypso music mingled with the sea salt on the breeze, the peaceful tunes a stark contrast to the gravity of the situation at hand. Jasper took a last look at the warmer isle and sighed before climbing into the large canoe. As he and Griffin set off for the outer islands of the archipelago, he couldn't help but think of her, Sav.

They'd come to Solia in search of the woman who had taken Savara's memories, in hopes of having them returned to her once they were reunited. Of course, Griffin's motives hadn't been so simple, despite what he'd originally promised. Jasper knew better than to believe anything involving Griffin was simple, but the innocent mortal in him still liked to believe life was not as complex as people made it out to be. That may have once been true in the world he'd left behind

311

in service of a friend. But this world was not that one. It was time he started waking up to the reality of it. This world was changing—and changing him in the process.

There was a war brimming on the horizon, and unlike the one in Idune, this one would see destruction as its end goal. Lives would be lost, nations upturned, and he would fail at the one thing he'd set out to do: protect his best friend. Savara was still nowhere to be found, and that guilt ate at his soul more and more with each passing day.

"You're thinking about her again," Griffin said, bringing his attention back to the present. Griffin sat at the bow of the canoe looking up at him. His face was in the process of shifting as the boat rocked on the unsteady sea. "I know the look you get when you're worried about her."

Jasper sighed and stared down at the dark waters. "We came all this way to try and get her memories back and we are leaving just as empty-handed. I had hoped that if we found something, it would make up for losing her in the first place. But it was all an exercise in futility. She's still gone. We still have no way of getting her memories back. The Ur stone is still missing. And we still have no idea where that seventh stone is."

Griffin considered his dilemma for a moment in silence. "You know, you don't need to prove yourself to her. She already cares deeply for you." Griffin let his words sink in before adding, "And, it should go without saying, you are not the reason she is missing."

Leave it to Griffin to see through me… he thought. The guilt over losing her had cost him many a night's sleep, draining his spirit more than any cursed book ever could. Jasper turned to him and frowned. "Yes, but I didn't turn over every stone to find her."

"If we had stayed in Idune, we would've been tossed into some mountain prison cell and left to rot." There was no sweetness in Griffin's voice as he spoke—no remorse, and no room for alternate interpretation. He wanted to make sure his message landed—which it did.

Jasper knew he was right, but it didn't help that feeling of futility bubbling away inside him. He thought back on the moment they'd first jumped worlds, and how he'd promised he'd go to the ends of the Earth to keep her safe. He'd gone to the end of his world and beyond, and the one thing he'd learned in this exercise was that no one could guarantee safety. He'd been naïve then, and the more he learned only convinced him further of what little he understood still. Safety was a luxury not meant for them, and they all knew it.

"You know, I was about to kill you back there for blabbing on about our plans to the queen…" Griffin added one of his annoyingly charming smiles to the end of the sentence. The one thing he couldn't fault Griffin for was his ability to read a person.

"You can't blame me," Jasper mused, appreciating the attempt at easing his tension. "I saw the look on your face when she returned our memories. You had no idea that tea was spiked."

"Bold accusation," Griffin replied, holding his head higher despite the seasickness. Griffin was nothing if not a proud pain in the ass, but it did give room for playful back and forth that, if nothing else, acted as a welcome distraction. Jasper knew it was to stop him from worrying.

"Accusation, my ass! That's the truth."

"One you will never be able to prove, and I will take to my grave."

Jasper stifled a grin, a small laugh escaping his lips as he spoke. "You're insufferable." He released a bit of the tension in his shoulders.

"Likewise," Griffin laughed.

Griffin might have been the most annoying person that Jasper knew, what with his charm and irritating eloquence, his modestly good looks, and his mind that worked at least half as well as Jasper's own, but he couldn't be entirely written off. Jasper knew from the very beginning that Griffin was trouble, but as much as it pained him to admit, Griffin had kept him sane where he would've otherwise spiralled. He was like an anchor, a point of safety. He brought together all walks of life indiscriminately and made sure they all felt seen.

A curious turn of events it was that they had ended up becoming friends. Neither would admit it, but therein lay the beauty of their friendship. They could argue unfiltered, question each other's actions, take jabs at each other's egos, and none of it would shake the foundation they'd built together on shared goals and—though it hadn't started that way—mutual respect. Though he would never say it aloud, deep down, Jasper admired him.

"Thank you, Griffin," he whispered. "Really."

Griffin bobbed his head in reply and turned back to face the horizon. They were coming up on the wall of clouds that separated Iliso and Solia—and, evidently, Kyara and Noor.

"We have some hard days ahead of us," Griffin said, possibly wishing to change the topic before they admitted their friendship aloud.

"Why do I get the feeling that's an understatement?" Jasper replied, his tone somewhat mocking in nature. But Griffin's banter had since ended. His smile had turned. His eyes had gained distance. He was no longer worried about the past or the present. Jasper realised he was scanning the world beyond the horizon.

Jasper cleared his throat and changed his approach. "Do we have a plan?"

Griffin turned to him with a cold glare. His attempt at masking the worry he felt was in vain. After having spent so much time with him, Jasper had come to realise that the most terrifying expression in Griffin's arsenal was this one. The one that meant they were moving blind.

"We are facing an enemy of untold powers," Griffin began, "whose sole purpose is to destroy the world we know, and he's already got almost all the tools he would need to do so."

"If that was your idea of a pep talk, it needs work."

"I'm not going to give you false hope if that's what you're wanting."

"No…" Jasper sighed.

"Good. I need your eyes open for what's coming next," Griffin said, returning his gaze to the horizon. "Besides, it would be a shame for you to die on me now that I'm finally warming up to you."

Jasper shook his head and clapped a hand on Griffin's shoulder. The movement rocked their boat ever so slightly but had Griffin turning green in a matter of seconds. "Likewise," he replied, biting down on the laugh that tickled his throat.

In truth, Jasper had figured as much about their situation already. He was, after all, the one who'd managed to read the books, who'd given up his blood for the knowledge. The more he thought back on the day he'd discovered the secrets of the book, the more he began to consider that maybe there was such a thing as fate. Only fate could've broken the glass and slit his finger in such a way that the blood dripped onto the page. Only fate could've brought him to the house with Savara the night Griffin appeared. Fate had been responsible for everything that had happened so far—or so he was coming to believe.

Jasper, being a man of science—or at least he was before jumping worlds—hadn't considered things like fate. Occasionally the doubt appeared, more often than not after having too much to drink and somehow ending up at the edge of the water staring up at the stars, but even then, it was something he did in passing and never something he lingered on. As he stared out at the foreign waters, the warm isle of Solia disappearing in the distance and the cold crescent tundra of Iliso appearing on the horizon, he hoped fate had its hands in this exercise. Otherwise, their entire adventure into the Ur nations truly was in vain.

They arrived at the docks within minutes of breaching the cloud barrier, and just in time too. Griffin would not have lasted much longer. Jasper was surprised he didn't immediately drop to the ground and kiss the frosted gravel beneath them. He knew the relief plastered across Griffin's face would only last so long as they made their way through the labyrinth of bridges towards Lucy's ship.

"Do we know where we are headed?" Jasper asked as he spied the masts coming into view over the horizon.

"Yozora," Griffin replied, his tone even now that they were on stable ground.

Jasper furrowed his brow. "Isn't that the home of the Izar?"

"It is."

"What about the Zerua stone? And Sav?"

"I am under no delusions that they don't already have or are close to getting the Zerua stone. It's best we make for the next likely destination. There is a good chance they already have the Arima stone as well, being that it is supposed to be kept within the nation of origin. The last remaining stone is that of the Izar, and I believe I know where to find it. As for Savara, as soon as we board the ship, I'll send for Brass to see if he's found her."

"Do you think it was *them* who took her?"

Griffin paused his confident stride and took his time before responding. Jasper watched him place a still-scarred hand on his chest and stared up at the sky, which was too overcast and bright to provide any access to the stars. Jasper knew the act was of hope alone. "Whether they took her initially or not, I believe they have her now. She is, after all, the final piece to their puzzle."

"Would they have... harmed her?" Jasper asked. It was a question he'd never allowed himself to entertain, fearing what responses his mind would invent. He would never forgive himself if anything happened to her.

"No. Not if they want her to give up that last stone."

"But if she doesn't remember…"

"I know. Which is why we cannot waste any more time."

Griffin strode off ahead, but Jasper stared up at the sky, copying his actions. He wondered what Griffin had seen—if anything at all. Even with the curiously powerful spectacles, all he saw was a field of clouds. Their friends were strong, judging by the markings on their skin made visible by the spectacles and his own experience beside them on the battlefield, they would put up a good fight. But would they be enough? Jasper had only heard of the Prince of Shadows' cruelty, but he didn't sound like the kind of person who backed down from a fight, especially not if he was looking to complete the ritual. Death would be only an afterthought.

Jasper picked up his pace, meeting up with Griffin as he reached the docks. "What you said about the Izar stone…" he asked, trying to catch his breath. Griffin raised a curious eyebrow. "How could you know where to find it?"

Griffin's eyes danced around them, making sure they were out of earshot. "I've seen it," he whispered.

Jasper's eyes widened. "Don't you think that's something you—"

"Keep on a need-to-know basis? Yes, I do," Griffin said, his voice low and serious.

"But how?"

"When I was still in the royal academy, a friend and I stumbled across it while playing in the royal catacombs. We didn't know what it was at the time and, like the curious children we were, we made the mistake of touching it. From my limited knowledge of the stones, I know that a person whose powers align with that of the stone may find them enhanced by contact with the stone. My gift of sight? That power is not common among the Izar. It was a side effect. As it stands, I believe only three people can read the images within the stars: my friend and I, and the leader of the Izar."

"That's how you knew about this before I translated the book," Jasper realised. Griffin nodded. "What happened to your friend?"

"I haven't seen him since." Griffin frowned, ending the line of questioning there.

The pair of them boarded the ship in silence, each one trapped in thought. Jasper contemplated his earlier gripe with fate as his gaze lingered on the lands they would soon leave behind. They had come in search of a witch and a stone, found the first, lost the second, were roped into arbitration of a bid for the crown, nearly ended up corpses at the hands of not one but two violent queens, and somehow possibly saved the nation from civil war. Whatever game fate was playing was a long one, one that spanned both worlds and lifetimes. The idea of surrendering his free will to some higher power still didn't sit right with him, but perhaps there was hope to be had in surrender.

CHAPTER 40

GOODBYE, MY KING

AMON SETTLED SAVARA by the fire in the study and rifled through a large cabinet. Despite his usual emotional composure, Savara had now seen him in an agitated state twice in one day. This time, it was not an act of passion that had him ruffled. She could sense the guilt of not having been there emanating from him in waves—almost as strong as the guilt she felt for her actions. He returned with a soft towel for her to drape over her shoulders. His eyes widened as he gazed upon her back.

"You're bleeding," he said as he stared down at the scored flesh between her shoulder blades. He furrowed his brow, imagining what kind of horrors she must have endured to be so covered in blood.

Savara reached behind her and pressed her fingers to it, wincing as they met the open wound. She pulled her hand back and found it coated red.

"If it weren't for you forcing me to wear the corset, this might not have been the only slice," she confessed, but the confession only worsened his state.

Now out of the rain and harm's way, Savara was able to think clearly. She focused her limited strength on the wound, remembering how it felt to have unbroken flesh. She willed the fibres to stitch themselves back together—the only skill she was grateful to have learned from Big Tog. In the end, he had been right. Whether in self-defence or not, she had become the killer she was always meant to be.

"I should've been there," Amon mumbled as he leaned up against the mantle, arms crossed over his chest. He looked as though he were about to tear someone in half with his bare hands.

"Why weren't you?"

"The king…" he said, but he couldn't bring himself to say more. She knew it was about his condition. Brass had told her the king wasn't doing well. They'd wrongfully assumed Amon had known as well but, judging by the waves of fear and agitation rippling from him, Savara knew it had come as a shock.

"I heard," she replied. Savara turned away from him and gazed into the fire, seeking what little comfort it could provide given the circumstances. The only sound filling the room was the crackling of logs in the fireplace.

"I'm sorry," he said with a heavy sigh.

As much as he wanted to console her, she knew he couldn't. He didn't know how close she'd come to death, how she'd almost let herself give up. He wasn't there when she'd plunged the knife into Big Tog's chest. Not her powers. Her.

"Nothing would've changed."

She saw now the truth in what Brass had told her. Power was neither good nor evil, it was merely a tool. The question lay in the actions of the wielder. But that thought didn't console her in the slightest. In the end, she hadn't used her powers to take another's life. That act came from her own hands, her own heart.

Savara stared at them now—the cold, unforgiving hands that she'd once believed belonged to the thing inside her. She'd been mistaken. They had always been her hands; she just hadn't recognised the full range of their capabilities. If she closed her eyes, she could still see Big Tog's furious face hanging over her own, his blood dripping down her wrist. Amon's words rang through her mind with such clarity that she'd almost thought he'd spoken them aloud. *One day, your hands will be coated in the blood of another…* And then the king's: *There's darkness in all of us…*

Between the damp clothes that clung to her body and the freedom from the tension of the soul bond, she could feel her body breaking down, finally preparing to heal. The cold air around her tickled her nose, prompting a sneeze. A shiver traced her spine. Droplets of blood appeared on her palms. She almost panicked, the sight reminding her of her act, but Amon's voice roused her from the self-deprecating trance.

"Savara," he called. "Put this on," he said, offering her his tunic. Savara blinked at his shirtless, muscled torso. "You'll catch a cold if you stay in those wet clothes." If she couldn't feel the barrage of emotions rippling from him, she would've believed him to be sculpted of marble like the various statues scattered around the palace.

Savara averted her eyes. Memories of their kiss in the garden began creeping in. Under better circumstances, she might have welcomed the thoughts. When she didn't respond, he rested the tunic down on the arm of her chair and knelt before her. He must have believed the guilt rippling from her was from the murder alone.

"You are not at fault for defending yourself," he said, the softness in his voice only deepening the pain in her heart.

Savara took a breath and gazed into his eyes, which were just as fraught with storms as they'd ever been, if not more so. "I didn't have to kill him. I could've pierced his shoulder or his leg…"

"You know you couldn't have," he said, his voice low with concern. Savara shook her head and forced her eyes shut, trying to rid herself of the gory memory, but he insisted on maintaining her gaze. "Savara," he continued, his voice softening as he took her hands in his own. She opened her eyes at his touch, watching as he pressed them to his chest, to his heart. "What do you feel?"

She narrowed her eyes at him. "Your heartbeat."

Amon shook his head. "Go deeper. What do you feel?"

"…Your guilt."

"What else?"

Savara sighed, growing weary of whatever this new game was. "Do I have to do this?"

Amon nodded. "You have those powers for a reason. Use them. What else?"

Savara shifted in her seat, extending the reach of her powers as he'd asked. "Your doubt."

"Deeper."

This time, Savara closed her eyes and focused all her energy on his soul. It was a sad thing to be sure, not small by any means, but caged. All the emotions she'd listed before were there, along with others. Loss, wrath, lust, joy. She searched for one that seemed to encompass them all, the strongest of the emotions trapped within the cage. "Your longing," she replied finally.

"That's why you couldn't go for the shoulder or leg. You can read people's innermost feelings. You knew he was going to kill you. You felt it. It was your life or his." Amon raised his hand to her cheek, gliding over the spot that once held a slit of stones laden with a promise of death, and tucked a stray, wet curl behind her ear. "As far as I'm concerned, you made the only choice you could."

Tears began to fall from her eyes. The stress of the ordeal had finally gotten to her. Savara did her best to ignore them, but Amon locked his eyes on her as if to say she didn't need to be afraid, that she was allowed to cry, that he saw her, and that she'd done enough. His touch made her heart flutter. Part of her wanted him, she'd realised it when they were in the gardens, but she couldn't have him. Whether he wanted her or not, she was his torture. Another wave of guilt rushed over her as his hand grazed her cheek. She shied away from him, feeling as hurt as she had upon overhearing his conversation with the king.

"You're doing it again…" she said. "Please, don't look at me like that."

"Like what?" he asked, finally sweeping away her tears with his thumb. His voice was soft, his gaze prodding. When she refused to look in his direction, he took hold of her hands and guided her to stand. His finger slid gently down her cheek and under her chin, inclining it ever so slightly in his direction. "You can tell me."

Savara shivered under the force of his gaze. The storms in his eyes had quieted for now, revealing his singular focus. "Like you might actually want me," she replied. "Like there might actually be a part of you that cares."

The shadow of a smile appeared on his lips. "Would that be so bad?"

"You ran away…"

Amon pursed his lips. The disappointment in his eyes was almost too much to bear. She tried to pull away from him, but his grip tightened on her shoulder. "What if there was a reason? And not the kind you're expecting?"

Savara shook her head. "I can't do this, Amon."

"Because you don't want to?"

"Of course I want to."

"Then?"

"I can't take the uncertainty," she whispered. "I've had too much of it already."

The seconds ticked by between them with only the sound of the fire crackling to fill the space. Savara could tell he was struggling with words, but there was nothing he could say to change her mind. She'd already heard enough. She wasn't going to be the source of another person's suffering, not again, not anymore. She wanted to pull away, but before she knew what was happening, he'd cupped her face in his hands and brought his lips down upon hers. There was no uncertainty in his act, nor in his heart. It was as if time had stopped ticking all over again.

Suddenly, Bismuth appeared in the doorway. He cleared his throat, the sound of it startling them away from each other. "The king wishes to see you both," he said.

Amon whipped around to face him, his gaze cold and hollow as he spoke. "Is he…?"

Bismuth shook his head. "Whatever final words you wish to share, now is the time."

There was a pain in his eyes that he tried to hide. Savara hadn't noticed it before, but there were bags under his eyes from what looked like long nights of worry and little sleep. As composed as the people of this land—of this palace—wished to seem, Savara could tell they too were plagued with feelings.

Her gaze then fell on Amon, whose body was taught and riddled with fear. A clenched fist shifted at his side. It was only then Savara spied the five evenly spaced gemstoned slits on his back. There was a gap at the base of his spine that indicated there might have been room for another two.

Seven slits.

Seven promises.

Seven bonds of blood and soul.

An eerie glow emanated from the rubies in his skin that beckoned her to reach out and touch them, but Savara restrained herself. Something about them terrified her. Unlike the priest's crystal-ridden body, the gems on Amon's back were laced with malice. The sensation that rippled from them reminded her of the energy that surrounded The Prince of Shadows.

Before she could spiral further into those thoughts, Bismuth brandished a dress that he'd slung over his forearm. "I suggest changing out of those wet clothes, princess. You will catch a cold." With his eyes fixed on her, Savara could now see the whites of his eyes had been stained red by tears that must have recently fallen in private.

"Thank you," Savara replied, wanting to wish him well but knowing that he, like Amon, needed to maintain some semblance of the exterior strength they'd grown accustomed to.

Bismuth bobbed his head. He left the dress perched on a vase near the door and disappeared, leaving them to finish their moment.

Amon swiftly retrieved his tunic and slid it over his muscled torso. If he'd realised that she'd been staring at his scars, he made no mention of it. He stopped in front of her before she could collect the dress and bent down so that his lips were level with her ear. "One day, princess, you will no longer question my intentions."

The chamber was quiet, the wind little more than a whisper accompanying the king in his final hours of suffering. Flames flickered in the sconces on the wall, their shadows stretching across the room in a caging embrace. The white of his eyes had all but consumed his irises, two stars shining in the dim of the room, though their glow seemed to belong now more to death. His breath was soft and low, a spell to ease the pain as he waited patiently and unhurried for his final appointment.

"One at a time, children," he wheezed, hearing their light feet and whispers, feeling their forms in the breeze, knowing they were there despite his fading sight.

"You go first," Savara said. "In case…" Neither of them wished for her to finish the sentence, though they both knew what she meant. *In case there isn't time,* she thought, and the more she thought about it, the more she realised how little time any of them truly had.

Amon slipped into the room and closed the door behind him.

Savara toyed at the sleeves of the dry dress given to her by Bismuth before wrapping her arms around her corseted waist, conscious of the stone nestled within. For now, it lay dormant. Perhaps it too was waiting for the eventuality of death beyond the door. The thought sent a shiver down her spine.

Instead of lingering on the bitter thought, she wondered what the king could have to say to her. Whatever it was couldn't be good if she needed to be alone to hear it. Despite only fifteen minutes passing between Amon's entry and her own, she'd already imagined a lifetime's worth of scenarios.

When he re-emerged from the room, Savara noticed his eyes were bloodshot from holding back tears. He gazed at her, allowing her to see every bit of the sorrow he held within, unabashedly unfiltered. She reached a hand up to cup his face, letting it hover tentatively at the side of his cheek. Amon exhaled deeply as he took hold of it and pressed it against his skin, closing his eyes to better focus on the feeling of her touch. She wished to linger there, trapped in the moment like when their lips had met for the first time, but the creak of the door behind her meant that it was time to go.

"I'm sorry," she whispered as she dropped her hand, knowing the defeated look in his eyes would haunt her long past the moment the door clicked closed.

The room was quiet, save for the echo of the king's fading heartbeat in the emptiness of the room. Savara tiptoed towards the dying king, holding her breath as she neared for fear a stray wind would take him. She stood at the foot of his elegant four-poster bed, fixated on the white of the king's eyes, the grey of life losing its battle against the haziness of death. Still, they shone with what little life remained.

"How are you feeling, Your Highness?" Savara asked, bowing her head respectfully.

The king struggled a smile. "Do you know, when a man is as close to death as I, the titles all sound utterly ridiculous," he said, trailing his words with a cough that might have been a laugh under better circumstances.

Savara frowned. "Shall I fetch some water?"

"No," he coughed. "No, I am fine. I wish to tell you…" he took a shallow breath, filling his lungs as much as they would go, "not to fear it."

"Fear what?"

The king lifted a shrivelled finger towards her, beckoning her close. She knelt at his side so he wouldn't have to raise his voice. "The end," he whispered. "It is in death we learn who we truly are, and what we are made of."

Savara knew where this was going. The king would fight no more; these were his last goodbyes. Tears welled in her eyes. She knew it was time and that he was choosing to let go, but the tears appeared nonetheless. She nodded, maintaining her silence, believing that the last sounds of the final resting place of the king of storms should be those of his voice.

"But you must know this already," he added with a soft smile. "Harbinger of Death, she who walks with broken souls…" She found guilt and insult in the words. She was about to apologise when the king spoke again. "You are not the monster we envisioned. I see now the error of our ways." His sigh deepened. "I know it is no longer my place to make decisions for this world, perhaps it never was. But you, child… The winds speak of you more frequently of late. Of lessons to be learned and choices to be made."

Savara hardly knew when the tears had finally begun to fall, only that they fell—warm and sorrowful—in streams down her cheeks. They pooled at her chin before dripping to the marble floor below. She reached over and took hold of the king's frail hand, unsure of what had possessed her to do so but knowing she'd made the right choice when she spied the smile spreading across his face.

"It is curious… In your presence, fear and regret do not haunt me as they once did." He took a deep breath, filling his lungs as though he'd never taken a full breath before. "You must feel when it is near, as though it were a shadow in the back of the room. I see it now. Yes… Now, I understand." He coughed once more as his eyelids slowly lowered.

The king was right. She could feel Death lingering. He was somewhere near, waiting for the king. The first time she'd noticed the presence of Death, she'd feared it was only paranoia. But it was more than that. Death had been there, a companion in the shadows she'd chosen to ignore. He'd stalked the grounds after the fires in Camp Saar, he'd waited for her in the cell in Idune, he'd leered at her when she was in the heat of battle with Big Tog. And now, he was here. Waiting.

"I never knew."

"That which you are… That which you feel…" She felt his soul pulsing, softening, fading. "Gifts we never imagined." The king's eyes flickered over to the door, behind which Amon paced the floor. "But he did." His voice was as light as a feather now. "He knew. I believe he has always known." His eyelids drooped shut as he whispered his last words, "Take care of him, guide him back to the light…"

For a moment, all was quiet. No sooner did she whisper the words "I will" did a howling gale rush from his body. It tore through the room with all the force of a tornado, extinguishing every sconce from there to the far end of the hall, and lifting curtains and sheets like phantoms readying for a dance. They swirled once, twice, and finally, with a cry that could be heard from the other end of the city, the wind burst through the windows.

The stillness of the night settled around her once more. Savara waited until the last sheet drifted to the floor before wiping her eyes. A final smile graced his face, a look of plain serenity. It was official…

The king was gone.

CHAPTER 41

LEGEND OF THE STONES

AMON ENTERED THE ROOM shortly after the winds died down. "It's time," he whispered, his voice ripe with tension as he extended a hand towards her. He'd just lost the closest friend he'd had. Savara wondered how he was even able to stand.

She sighed and took hold, allowing him to help her to her feet. She had no idea what possessed her to do so, but she wrapped her arms around his waist and squeezed as tightly as she could, vowing not to let go. She could feel every nerve in his body fighting a losing battle. She wanted him to know that it was okay, that the king had gone in peace, and that, with his last breath, he'd wished him well. Just as fate had brought these two unlikely friends together, it had consented to one last game of Go before ripping them apart. At least he'd been gifted that.

It took a moment for him to understand what she was doing—so long in fact that Savara wondered if he'd ever been hugged before. But, soon enough, he wrapped one arm after the other over her spine, letting her sink into the contours of his chest, draped in his signature black tunic that always glittered like wet ink. And night flowers. Her favourite scent spilt from him even now, even through his pain. Suddenly, she felt his lips press against her forehead as if to kiss her, but mouthing the words *thank you* instead. There was a part of her that wished to remain in that moment of vulnerability, but they had other matters to attend to, other wars on the horizon.

Savara followed Amon through the noticeably empty halls as he made his way semi-unconsciously to the throne room, the loftiness of it allowed for each footfall, each breath, each heartbeat to echo as though being shouted into a cave. He stared up at the throne, paying his respects to his dearly departed friend who seemed to have been more like family to him than anyone else she'd encountered.

"Amon," she began, wishing to tell him the king's final words, when a low growl came from the other end of the room.

"That took way too long for my liking." The man appeared from behind the throne, a look of mild impatience lining the creases in his brow as he nonchalantly slumped into the seat. He toyed with a small, ethereal white orb between two leather-gloved fingers. Savara recognised him instantly as the man who'd attacked Brass, the one who held lightning in the palms of his hands. And now that she caught him under better lighting, she realised he was also the one who'd come looking for her in Idune. "I do hate being late…"

"Alexei," Amon growled, anger rising in his voice.

"Cousin," he replied with a curt bob of his head.

Savara wondered why she hadn't noticed it before, the thin sliver of family resemblance. Both men were tall with sharp, midnight blue eyes that every so often glinted with the colour of lightning. Strong noses and high cheekbones, all framed by onyx waves of hair. Where Amon's physique was slightly fuller, his muscles more rounded and even, Alexei leaned into a lankier frame, tight cords of muscle trailing over bone. His chin was not as pronounced, but the hollows in his cheeks gave him a slightly more ethereal impression. Another kind of devilish handsome not easily overlooked, and judging by his arrogance, it was a handsome of which he was very much aware.

Alexei stole a glance between them, a mischievous grin reminiscent of a wolf readying an attack growing on his face. "Have you finished playing house?" Amon stepped in front of her. "Oh, cousin, you are pathetic." Alexei pocketed the stone and removed a single glove. Streaks of blue lightning weaved through his fingertips and over his knuckles. He gazed upon them fondly before turning his eyes on Amon. Alexei pointed a finger at him and winked, releasing a single, sharp bolt towards his shoulder.

Amon held his hand up, allowing the lightning to strike his palm, wincing through the pain, but ultimately dropping an unburned hand. The move had been so quick, Savara hadn't had time to gasp. Somehow, he'd interiorised the attack. She sensed it prickling around the contours of his soul, prodding dangerously near to his heart. The energy was searching, either for a way into his vitals or out of his body, but Amon held it there, his strength being consumed by the act.

"Tsk, tsk, cousin. You know better than to hold it in." Alexei struck again and again, each time aiming for a different appendage.

Amon caught each blow, pulling the unstable energy into his body. Savara had no idea how much of it he could take, but she sensed his strength was wearing thin. The energy needed to be released. The mere act of sustaining it would kill him.

Alexei seemed to notice this as well and ceased his fire. "Those morals of yours…" He replaced the glove and ran his fingers through his greasy black hair, the static creating a floating effect to it that made it seem as though he were underwater. "As much as I'd love to stay and play, cousin, we are not children anymore, and I have a job to do."

"Spare me the false sense of familial attachment and leave before I kill you where you stand."

"Oh… Testy. Have you forgotten your old motto? *Life is a game…*" Alexei mocked with a flamboyant wave of his hand. "Or something or another. Or…" He placed his two hands beneath his chin, feigning interest. "Do you no longer subscribe to the very notion that helped us survive childhood?" Amon glowered at him as he held his tongue. "That's alright, cousin, don't answer. I tire of you anyway." Alexei's eyes turned hungrily to Savara. She narrowed her own in response, but he seemed to take pleasure in her caution. "Princess Savara, heir to the Argia throne, first and only divined Arima in 775 years, presumed dead for an additional six…" Alexei clapped his hands together in anticipation before leaping to his feet and executing a graciously low bow. "It is truly an honour."

"Alexei, leave. I will not ask again," Amon hissed, his body taut from restraining the lightning still coursing through his veins.

"Bark as much as you'd like, cousin, you still won't be able to move. I've stuffed you with enough lightning to stop an elephant's heart." He stalked towards them. "I mean… you could let it out, but there would be no guarantee as to what or whom it might strike. And if you continue to hold it in, well, we won't have to wonder whose heart will stop, now, will we?" Alexei's voice might have hinted at amusement, but Savara could see concern highlighting the bags under his narrowed eyes. He patted Amon's cheek in a way that was too heavy to be playful before turning his full attention to her.

"Alexei, don't you dare touch her," Amon said as Alexei weaved his way between them. Savara retreated a step, afraid of being the target of his next bolt of lightning.

"Relax, cousin. You know I don't kill unless paid. Besides, I want a closer look at your plaything is all. I wish to better understand the reason I was hired to fix your mistakes."

Savara looked from him to Amon. "What is he talking about?"

"You mean you don't know? Cousin, you haven't told her?"

"Alexei…"

"Let me guess, those soul bonds of yours, still intact?" Alexei's eyes glittered, ripe with intrigue as they beheld her, waiting for a response that wouldn't come. "I see… You know what? I do have time for just one more game, and seeing how she gazes upon you, cousin, as if you could do no wrong, this will be a fun one indeed."

"Amon?" Savara stuttered.

Alexei shook his head. "No reason to fear, princess. I have no intention of hurting you. My job is to collect you. It's all I was paid to do. Anything more would cost extra."

"What do you mean, *paid to do*?" she asked, adding further distance between them.

"And so it begins," he smirked. "Cousin, would you like to answer this one?" Alexei asked, but Amon was silent. "Didn't think so. Soul bonds are tough things to break. But fret not, princess, I am an unbound man. I can tell you everything you wish to know… For instance, do you know whose hand it was that robbed you of everything you held dear?"

"Stop," Amon hissed, but Alexei's grin only grew. His eyes glowed, charged with the pleasure from the pain he caused.

"Whose hand slit your mother's throat?" he continued.

"No…" The word was more wish than demand as she grappled with the full force of what Alexei was insinuating. There was no way. He was surely trying to get a rise out of her, and if so, he would not succeed.

"Or impaled that human woman? Or that decrepit, imprisoned Visanthian prince?"

Savara's feet led her in a circle, coming to a halt in front of Amon, whose eyes now avoided her own. "You're lying…" she whispered, though Amon's refusal to look at her sent an angry fluster blooming across her cheeks.

Alexei inserted himself between them and stared her down, his features twisted by a harsh and stoic sense of pride. "I have one rule, princess, one rule alone. I have no qualms with torture or murder, I don't subscribe to any altruistic morals like my cousin or his pathetic friend, but make no mistake, I do not lie."

Savara gazed past Alexei, rage building in the pit of her stomach like a volcano poised to erupt. She couldn't believe what she was hearing. "Please tell me it wasn't you," she begged. "Amon, please tell me you didn't murder my family." But Amon said nothing. Her lungs began to repel the air, letting only shallow breaths through. The pounding of her heart in her ears drowned out Alexei's smirk in the background. Betrayal—his betrayal—was suffocating her. She waited for his response, but still, none came.

"He can't," Alexei mocked. "Those soul bonds on his back prevent him from saying anything related to our dark prince's crusade. Which is why, dear princess, he can't tell you how he offered his body to the Prince of Shadows in exchange for some of the darkest secrets Visanthe has to offer. Or, how he, upon learning them, willingly offered to help collect the seven stones for our dark prince, binding himself even further to those twisted morals of his."

"Amon," she whispered, desperation creeping into her voice. Savara's eyes stung as she willed him to look in her direction. She needed to see it, see the words confirmed in his eyes. Only then would she truly believe it.

Amon remained silent, his gaze fixed on the ground, his body still straining against the lightning and, as Alexei so eagerly pointed out, the soul bonds.

The pain in Savara's heart grew stronger, her eyes filling with tears. She couldn't believe it. There was no way the man who had saved her life on countless occasions—the man who'd brought her back from the edge of despair, the man she had begun to trust with her heart and soul—could have done such terrible things.

"Look at me," Savara demanded, her voice racked with hurt and desperation.

Amon finally relented, a murderous cold burning in his eyes as, for a moment, silence consumed the air around them. Savara felt as if she had been punched in the stomach. She stumbled back, trying to distance herself from the man she no longer recognised. Alexei's words echoed in her head, and she couldn't stop the tears from falling.

"How could you?" she whispered, looking up at Amon with disbelief.

"It's not like that," Amon said, but Alexei interrupted him.

"Possessed or not, cousin, *you* chose to give up control over your body. It was *your* hand holding the knife."

"I trusted you!" Savara yelled, and she could see the pain in his eyes. She knew that he was struggling with his soul bonds, that he wanted to tell her his side of the story but couldn't.

"I'm sorry," he whispered, his voice barely audible. "I never wanted to hurt you, Savara."

Savara shook her head, numb with anger and betrayal. She couldn't process what was happening. She'd once promised—no, sworn on her ancestors that she would kill the person that robbed her of her family, but she had never expected it to be him. Her heart felt as though it had ruptured.

"Why are you doing this, Alexei?" Amon asked through gritted teeth.

"Aside from the fact that I love proving to you why morals are a waste of time? I know that there's no way our little friend here will want to be anywhere near you after this. You see, cousin, because I so readily put a price on everything, nothing comes at the cost of my freedom, ergo, free agent. You on the other hand, because of those morals, soul bond or not will always be bound to something or someone. Shame too, following those stars of yours, thinking you were out to right some cosmic wrong. I bet those stars didn't tell you you'd end up falling in love with the one person who would bring an end to everything. Though, I doubt she'll feel the same any time soon."

For the first time since they'd locked gazes, Amon averted his eyes. Savara's heart broke further. She knew there was truth in his words, she'd noticed the threads of longing weaving themselves between herself and Amon each time they were together. The idea that they might even be feelings of love on his part shocked her. But she had her own truth to grapple with. Amon killed her family. She didn't know how she'd ever be able to stand the sight of him again.

"That's what happens when you spend too much time focusing on the gods in the sky rather than the demons on the ground," Alexei concluded.

"I don't understand…" Savara stuttered.

"My patience is growing thin, princess. This is the last bone I throw. My darling cousin over there, in his so-called divine search for knowledge, abandoned his two closest friends and struck a deal with the devil, wishing to break a curse placed on the land by his own mother, the charming—and occasionally terrifying—Princess of Light herself."

"But that would make him—"

"The heir to the Izar throne? Correct. I see his secrecy knows no bounds. As I was saying, seven bonds for seven stones, and with each bond fulfilled, he would gain new insights and eventually new extents to his power, but he'd temporarily have to give up some of his faculties first. Fair trade? Let's see… After the first stone, that of fire, his willpower was returned to him. Ironic, though, that he should meet you after only just regaining it, as if you were to become his guiding light, his reason to live. Fate is a cruel and wicked mistress," he said as he raised an eyebrow.

"Stop," Amon pleaded, but Alexei only smiled.

"The second stone, that of earth, returned autonomy of his body, ridding himself as well of the part of the Prince of Shadows that resided in him for lack of a body of his own. Somehow, though, I get the feeling that something gave him a sliver of control before then… The third stone, that of water, our dark prince is in the process of collecting and should return Amon's full range of emotions—so, don't worry, cousin. When we go, you should be able to cry once more. The fourth, that of air, I have in my pocket and will return his voice—though I can't imagine there will be much more to say.

"The fifth, that of light, is where this problem began, and is the reason my dear cousin was able to commune with the stars in the first place. If I'm not mistaken, it is still buried in the palace catacombs where you hid it, and once handed over, should offer you a greater insight into those celestial messages. The sixth, belonging originally to those who have become synonymous with nightmares and blood, would return to him his heart—if he hadn't already given it away." Alexei winked at her knowingly.

Amon's fists clenched at his sides. Savara knew he wasn't going to last much longer.

"And that, my dear princess, leaves one final stone. One that, as of yet, not even the Prince of Shadows himself has been able to find. Only one person, a chosen one, if you will, can encounter and wield said stone. A person unbound by Iturri, meaning their powers appeared before their divination. Considering the curious nature of these powers, in that they don't belong to the usual spectrum of elements, this chosen child might not have even realised that they possessed any power before their divination at all. In legend, this child is referred to as—"

"The Harbinger of Death…" she said, the realization hitting her like a bolt of lightning to the chest. "…me."

"Ding, ding, ding. We have a winner, folks! Wasn't that an enjoyable game?" Alexei announced, basking in his twisted sense of self-righteousness.

Savara frowned. The tears had stopped, along with her anger. Both had been replaced by an all-consuming feeling of defeat. So, she really did have no control over her destiny. Everything had been preordained by a set of sadistic stars from the beginning, from before she was born. But why? What purpose did she truly serve to the world?

She remembered Alexei saying she was the first and only Arima divined in 775 years. That couldn't be a coincidence. Something must have happened to set this chain of events into motion. Whether the men before her knew it or not, she knew there was more to the story, her story. And she wasn't going to stop until she got to the bottom of this mystery.

"And now, princess, we really must get going," Alexei said impatiently as he extended a hand towards her. "I don't think my cousin will last much longer."

"Savara, don't," Amon called to her, his throat tight with worry.

Savara met his eyes one last time. Maybe it hadn't been entirely his fault. Maybe he didn't have control of his body when he was committing those murders. But she wasn't yet ready to forgive him. Before this conversation, she might have even believed herself to be falling in love with him. Now, she realised that love and hate were truly two sides to the same coin, and, though difficult, it was not impossible to feel both at the same time.

Part of her still felt indebted to him for saving her life. For that part, the part of her that loved him back, she would help restore his soul, even if it meant handing herself and the rest of the stones over to the Prince of Shadows. She owed him that much. But the other part of her couldn't stand to be near him. Not now. Not for a while. Not until she understood why he'd agreed to such a terrible mission in the first place.

She didn't know which of these reasons propelled her to take Alexei's hand. She'd feared and hated him from the moment they first met, from the moment he tried to kidnap her in Idune. But at that point, she knew the only person with any real answers was waiting for her beyond these halls, at whatever destination he had in mind. Alexei was simply a means to an end.

"Well, cousin, this has been an immensely entertaining reunion. Sucks that this is how you find out just how heartbreaking it is to be abandoned by those closest to you. The Prince wished to remind you of your deal, you'll still have three bonds to contend with. Don't worry about this one, I'll take good care of her," Alexei smirked. "Oh, and I do hope you survive that little spark, cousin, because I can promise you that the next family reunion is going to be a blast."

Before Savara knew it, Alexei had pulled her in close and showered them in travelling dust. She didn't even have time to react to the lightning that erupted from him, bursting out into the night sky and across the sea of clouds in a roar that could've brought the palace down. The depths of Amon's anguish reached out for her in her last moments, but it was already too late. As the world warped and bent around them, the only sound that filled her ears was that of him crying out her name. He may have broken her heart, but she'd just broken his soul.

Savara closed her eyes and gave in, allowing herself to fully feel the pain of being torn apart, knowing that on the other side of the jump, she'd finally be made whole.

CHAPTER 42

A NEW PLAN OF ATTACK

NOT LONG AFTER THEY boarded the ship, Lucy summoned them both to her quarters. She'd sent one of the crew members to fetch them, which Jasper took as the first warning flag.

"Come in," she called to them from behind her desk, her voice tantalizingly sweet in sound—the second warning flag had been raised. She hadn't yet spared them a glance, but Jasper could tell by the stillness in the air around them that something was amiss. Lucy was not the kind to keep a quiet composure. This quiet conversation she'd requested had him hiding a step behind Griffin, who was not so easily scared.

"Out with it, Lucinda," Griffin said.

"Griffin, darling, bane of my existence," she began, twisting in her chair and stalking towards them, her bangles jingling with each step. "How did your excursion go?" She gave him the once over before turning to Jasper, her true prize it seemed.

Jasper recoiled slightly, confused by her strange attitude. "Is everything okay?" he whispered to her.

She tapped his cheek lightly and replied, "Oh yes, everything's fine, sweetness." She ran her fingers along his sleeves flirtatiously.

"Not as fruitful as I'd hoped," Griffin said dryly as he watched her movements with a furrowed brow.

"Oh?" Lucy said, feigning curiosity.

"We are going to Yozora," he added.

"Big talk for someone like you who hates the water," she mocked. "It must be urgent."

"It is."

"Well, then…" She looked up at Jasper and bit her lip. "I'll expect something in return."

"Ten bottles of sea grape wine from the royal stores," Griffin replied without hesitation.

She grinned at him, her hands still sliding down Jasper's arms. "I'd expect nothing less."

"Are we done?"

"Not quite." Jasper hadn't time to recoil as she drew a knife from up her sleeve and sliced open his tunic, exposing the network of blackened veins from his wrist to his collarbone. "Just as I thought."

"Lucy, what is this?" Griffin growled.

"Funny, I wanted to ask you the same thing," she said as she made her way back to the desk and dropped a heavy tome on its surface. "Seven stones of Cartha," she read. "Sounds interesting. Legendary stones of power that control the essential elements of our land. What I found even more interesting was the fact that, if you listen carefully, the book whispers to you. Asks to be fed as you read its pages. That is, only after the blasted thing gave me a paper cut and swallowed the drop of my blood. So, shall we try this again?"

"You went snooping," Griffin hissed.

"You brought a dangerous relic of the old world onto my ship!" she yelled. "The time for secrets has ended, Griffin. If you expect my help, you will explain your plans."

"Is everything alright?" called another voice from behind them. Lance had poked his head through the door, followed by Sebastian and Storm, who looked like they'd had some sort of altercation before racing over to the captain's quarters at the sound of her yelling. They all glanced from Griffin to Lucy before their eyes inevitably landed on him and his web of blackened veins.

"As we're all here…" Griffin rolled his eyes and ushered them all inside. He closed the door behind them and latched it, making sure no one else would enter for his explanation.

Griffin proceeded to tell them about the legend he and Jasper had discovered hidden within the book, how the leader of the Arima was out to destroy Visanthe by way of combining these seven stones of otherworldly power, and how he already had at least four of those stones. He explained how they were going to Yozora to protect the stone of the final land and that, no matter what, the Arima could not succeed.

Most shocking of all Griffin's revelations was that of the true identity of Lance, the man who'd been taken hostage by the Arima and liberated in Idune. All eyes turned on him with a mixture of shock and awe, some wondering why they hadn't realised sooner, Jasper at why there hadn't been more family resemblance. The young man with the princely brow and regal stare was none other than the bastard heir to the Argia throne, and Savara's older brother.

"How is this possible?" Jasper asked the question that was on everyone's mind.

Lance stepped into the centre of their conversation, turning as he spoke so that all may meet his eyes throughout the story. "I was kidnapped one night after sneaking out of the palace. They took me to the Red Desert, the harshest lands in the Argia kingdom, and stripped me bare of everything—including my memories. For a few weeks, I was a husk of a child, living as I could from scraps, and eventually thievery. One day, as fate would have it, I tried to steal from the wrong person; a man whose hair curled into horns atop his head, making him the picture of sinister. I might've ended up a piece of charcoal had he not taken pity on me. He took me in, trained me, treated me like family, even going so far as to call me his son—something I now know to be a cleverly concealed truth. For years I lived that way, kept just far enough out of range from the royal house to never be recognised, doing the bidding of the man who ruled the darkest parts of the city of light. But it wasn't until the shadows came and the ashes flooded our streets that I understood true darkness…"

As Lance recounted his story, Sebastian tensed. Little flames sprouted at his knuckles as his eyes narrowed into slits. "Was it you?" he growled, startling everyone. "Was it you who killed my family?"

"Sebastian," Griffin cautioned.

"My family was murdered in cold blood by the mafia," Sebastian continued, ignoring him.

"I couldn't say. I am no innocent, however. Many corpses have been charred as a result of my actions," Lance replied, his voice steady and unwavering in his conviction. He held his squared jaw higher in the face of wrath and punishment. "If it will bring you peace, I beg of you, take your anger out on me. A king is nothing if he cannot be held accountable."

Jasper took a step back, sensing the lid on Sebastian's anger about to burst. As he glanced around the room, he noticed Lucy clutched readily to the knife she'd used to rip his tunic, and Griffin's hands twitched, ready to conjure his power at a moment's notice.

"Sebas," Storm said as she inserted herself between them. She laced her fingers through his with one hand and placed the other on his cheek, unafraid of the flames licking his person.

The world held still a second. Jasper had no doubt that if Storm had not taken Sebastian's hand, ignoring the flames as they burned her skin, the whole ship might have gone up in flames.

Sebastian lowered his flames at the scent of Storm's charring skin and the sight of the tears pooling in her eyes from the pain. He pulled her in close and whispered an apology before directing his gaze once more at Lance. "When this is over and we have won, you will take up the crown, and I will personally escort you around Osiir to make amends for your crimes, though little will heal the wounds of loss you have inflicted on countless citizens. You will restore Osiir to its former glory, and dismantle the same organizations you worked for that have held us all hostage for years. If you refuse, my face will be the last you see as your body writhes in the flames of vengeance. I will leave you lingering until your skin and bones meld together and you beg for the sweet release of death, and not even that will be punishment enough."

"I would expect nothing less," Lance replied.

Sebastian let go of the tension in his shoulders. Everyone else lowered their weapons. Jasper unhitched a breath. He'd seen just how deadly Sebastian could be on the wide streets of Idune. Any exchange of fire here would've sunk the ship.

"With that settled," Griffin began, but Lucy quickly interrupted.

"That's only six." She held up her fingers as she counted off the regions of Visanthe. "Argia, Harri, Ur, Zerua, Izar, Arima. Six. But the book clearly states seven."

Griffin and Jasper shared a knowing glance between them. Jasper cleared his throat. "The seventh stone can only be found by a soul untethered to Iturri, one that could use their powers outside of their divination. We have reason to believe that Savara is this soul."

"My sister?" Lance interjected. "She's alive?"

Griffin nodded. "We have reason to believe that she was divined Arima, but that she was able to use their powers long before her divination." Lance furrowed his brow, but before he could argue the point, Griffin added, "You've seen it.

Growing up she had this way with creatures that was almost supernatural."

"Yes, but that doesn't mean—"

"You used to tell me she would talk to herself in the palace. What if she wasn't talking to herself, but rather the spirit of the place itself?"

Lance bit his lip as he considered this momentarily, but what Griffin said must have struck a chord with him. He nodded.

"That's why you brought her back knowing she was dangerous?" Storm asked. Judging by her expression, Jasper could tell any ill will she'd harboured towards Savara vanished in that moment.

"For years I had seen her face in the stars. Believing her to be dead, I saw no use in the vision. Not until I received word of her containment in the land of the others. I knew I had to retrieve her. If *they* had found her first, we might not be having this conversation," Griffin replied.

At that moment, Jasper finally understood what the others had been telling him since the day he and Savara arrived at the camp. Griffin was many things—proud, secretive, calculating, and condescending, but everything he did was in service of others. Every move he made, every thought he had, all with someone else in mind. There was something admirable about his conviction to be a saviour, but then, Jasper also noticed the wounded side of him that Lucy mentioned when they first met. That fire in his eyes no longer looked like know-it-all righteousness but rather fear that, even in doing everything perfectly, he will never be good enough.

Jasper could see it now, clear as day, and seeing that it was a sentiment they shared he wondered how he could've missed it. He wished to tell Griffin that he was already enough, but if the looks of faith and love in his friends' eyes weren't enough to convince him, words would do little. Whatever approval he was seeking had to come from within. Jasper recognised this now, both in Griffin and himself. No wonder they had become friends; they were nurturing the same wounds.

"I am waiting for Brass to send news of her location," he continued. "For now, we must console ourselves with the fact that she cannot remember anything of her past, which means that, if she did know where this stone was, they would be unable to get this information from her. We are not out of the water yet, however. I have consulted the stars many times on this matter, but they continue to show me death and destruction…"

Jasper thought back to his earlier qualms with fate—the thing that had somehow led him here, to the place of magic that needed a human as ignorant as him to feed blood to a book and uncover a legend. If it could traverse worlds in his case, and lifetimes in Savara's, he figured there was little it couldn't do. Like it or not, there was something bigger at play. Something he knew he could never hope to understand. He hoped for all their sakes that fate—or whatever it was— was on their side.

"We have a daunting task ahead of us." Griffin paused, letting his words sink in. His eyes scanned the room, taking in the faces of each of his friends. "I know that this journey has not been easy. We have already lost countless loved ones, and I am sorry to say that we may continue to lose more. This is the reality of our situation. I will not pretend victory is easy or within our grasp. The truth of the matter is all signs look bleak. But we cannot give up. We were brought together by fate but have stayed together by choice. We are family, we are all each other has left, and I will fight for my family with every fibre of my being."

Griffin turned to Jasper as he spoke those final words, and Jasper understood that his definition included not only himself but Savara as well. He knew they would find her. He knew they would make things right. Even though Griffin wasn't convinced, he knew there would yet come a day after the battles and bloodshed when things would be okay.

"Sebastian, you once asked me why we fight," Griffin said. "Why we don't leave it to others or let the world burn. Do you remember my answer?"

Sebastian nodded, and as he spoke, he looked only at Storm. "It's because we care."

"Times will get harder, but we must persevere. We must be strong, and we must be brave. This world is not perfect, but it is our home, and it is the only one we have. We must fight for what is right, for the future of our people, because, if nothing else, we care enough to hope for better days."

By the time the explanation had ended, Lucy had changed her tune. An understanding frown graced her usually ecstatic face. She realised, as they all had, that no one, no matter how far they believed themselves to be removed from the world's problems, would escape what was coming.

"If we leave immediately, we can be in Yozora in just under a week, but we will have to cross through the open waters along Middle Isle," Lucy said, directing the comment towards Griffin and his temperamental stomach.

"Weigh anchor, captain," Griffin replied.

Lucy smirked as she said, "Best batten down the hatches. We have a rough few days ahead."

The rest of them began to shuffle out of the room in preparation for their journey.

"Not you, scarface," Lucy added as she rested a hand on Griffin's shoulder and held up a small piece of parchment. "You received a letter."

Jasper lingered in the doorway, hoping to see if it was news of Savara, but judging by the look on Griffin's face, the news was neither expected nor welcome.

Griffin frowned as he turned it over in hand. "You opened it."

"You should know better than to think I wouldn't." She clapped a hand on his back and strode back over to her desk. "As for you, brown eyes," she called to Jasper and tossed the large book in his direction. "If I were you, I'd burn that book and send its ashes back to the demon they came from."

Jasper caught the book with ease, feeling its weight in his hands. He looked down at the leather cover, contemplating the intricate designs etched into the surface. For a moment, he considered Lucy's words. Maybe she was right. Maybe it would be safer to destroy the book and never think about it again.

But then he remembered the stories it held, the secrets it revealed, the power it could bring. Jasper knew that burning it would be a waste of knowledge, a waste of history, a waste of the truth. He tucked it under his arm, feeling a sense of responsibility and excitement in equal measure. This book held the key to their success, the key to defeating the Arima and saving Visanthe.

"Thanks, Lucy," he said, and shut the door behind him.

CHAPTER 43

THE FINAL FRONTIER

GRIFFIN EXAMINED THE NOTE once more, his fingers tracing the lines of the carefully crafted handwriting. It was longer than any message his "friend" had ever sent him, and the words seemed to dance off the page. Despite the familiarity of the handwriting, Griffin couldn't help but question the sudden appearance of this letter. Why had his anonymous pen pal finally wished to reveal themselves now, after all this time? The ink and parchment matched those of the previous letters, leaving no doubt as to the author, but the timing of this message left Griffin feeling unsettled.

He reread it for what must have been the tenth time since Lucy had given it to him. The insinuations it made were nothing short of deadly.

In seeking the sun, I found only its shadow. In walking in darkness, I see that starlight makes for a poor guide. I have failed you, my friend. I have failed us all. The time for war has come, the winds have died, the skeletons will sleep with no candle tonight. Words that once fell on deaf ears now ring out with sour notes, and time has cursed us all. Your presence is requested at the final frontier.

 ~ a friend

If the contents of the letter were to be believed, the Zerua king was dead and the Arima were in possession of their stone. A growing sense of unease washed over him with each reread of the cryptic message. His "friend" had not yet been wrong, not about the massacre in Osiir, or the battle in Idune, and he was damned sure he wasn't wrong about this. And as for the final frontier? Griffin knew he'd been right in his initial assumptions. The Izar stone, the stone of light, was their next target.

The week at sea did nothing for his stomach. Not even the strongest of the tonics he took to quell nausea made even so much as a dent in his lack of appetite. The second they'd arrived in Yozora and Griffin's feet touched dry land, his heart leapt from his chest. His feet carried him automatically through the winding granite streets of Yozora towards the chink in the wall that served the best potato and egg sandwiches in all Visanthe. He hated how much he'd missed them.

Sandwich in hand, Griffin wandered the streets of the place he, for a time, called home. It had been years since he'd returned, yet the memories of the vendors, the streets, the sounds, and the smells came flooding back to him as if he'd never left. How young he'd been then, how innocent.

It pained him to remember how, despite once being the celebrated Captain of the Royal Izarian Guard, he'd never felt less at home. This place hummed with memories of the person he once tried to be, the person he thought his father could eventually love—or at least be proud of. His time with the guard had taught him strength, cunning, and most importantly, to abide by the rules—no matter the cost. But celebrated or not, respected or not, he knew there was more good to be done elsewhere. Weary of following orders that were only designed to keep others submissive and maintain a broken status quo, he left and never looked back. Not until now.

He strolled beside the main river until he came to a small, dimly lit bridge. A faint smile crossed his face as he remembered a time when he once skipped stones from that very same bridge with other troubled youths. Clouds overhead cleared the path for the moon, and soon the bridge was alight. Little crystals embedded in the stone of the bridge floor twinkled under the moonlight. For someone who couldn't interpret the signs in the sky, it might have looked like a blessing. To him, it was a warning.

That's when he appeared.

Whatever lightness Griffin had felt moments before evaporated, replaced by a cold rage at the sight of the man before him, a man whom he'd once trusted more than any other, with his life even. Now, all he felt was contempt.

Aside from an obvious growth spurt, he hadn't changed in the slightest. His casual, nonchalant gait still accompanied him. His inky black locks still looked as unkempt and lovely as they had when they were boys, waiting for the crown his birth had promised him but that he'd refused. That wild thirst for knowledge still sparkled in his eyes; though, judging by the shadows that lined them, he'd already learned more than he'd previously thought possible. His old friend stood before him almost entirely unchanged on the outside, but inside he was a stranger.

"I should kill you where you stand, Amon," Griffin said, contempt punctuating his words.

"If only you had done that sooner," Amon replied with some amusement. "But you were always too good for that, Griffin."

Griffin wasn't fooled. He once knew the young princeling better than even his mother. Though he walked with some semblance of indifference, his shoulders were drawn taut, his smile forced. The amusement in his tone was a façade, and behind it, worry glinted in his eyes.

The pair of them were so similar all but a lifetime ago when fate had brought them together. People used to refer to them as the sun and moon because of their looks and the fact that they were the two brightest stars in the royal academy. Griffin still remembered a time when they were inseparable, back when they were still running through academy halls and exploring the secret passages of the palace. Back then there had been three of them: Griffin with his kind heart and soft-spoken shyness, Amon with his carefree magnetism, and Alexei, who had always been a bit volatile. But when Amon left, there was nothing to hold Griffin and

Alexei's friendship together. Amon was the bridge between worlds, but he burned all bridges the day he disappeared.

"Why have you come back?" Griffin asked, irritated by his old friend's reappearance, the bitterness of abandonment adding bite to his words.

Amon's eyes were dark and troubled, teeming with worry and reflecting the moonlight as he spoke. "You are the only person I trust."

"Why should I ever listen to another word out of your mouth?" Griffin spat.

"Because we were friends once…" Amon took a tentative step towards him, but Griffin summoned the light to his fingers, the bright blue glow illuminating his sharp features and the violent claw-marked scar tracing his jawline. He held his ground, ready for any attack that might come his way.

"Once," Griffin agreed. "You abandoned us. Friends do not abandon each other, Amon."

"I am still your friend, Griffin. I have been looking out for you, as I promised I always would. You did receive my letters, did you not?"

The moon cast a pale glow over the two figures on the bridge, highlighting the tension in the air. The soothing sound of the river flowing below was overshadowed by the heavy silence that hung between them.

After a long moment of contemplation, Griffin finally frowned. "I should've guessed by the riddles that they'd come from you…" He lowered his light and crossed his arms over his chest. "That still doesn't explain what you're doing here now."

Amon sighed and leaned against the side of the bridge, staring out at the river. The moonlight played across his face, highlighting the deep lines of worry etched there. "Remember that day in the academy, when we escaped from Master Young's class to eat sweet buns by the river?" Amon asked, his voice laden with melancholy. "Remember how I told you I'd seen something in the stars?"

Griffin shook his head disappointedly. "Amon, what did you do?"

"I needed to know if it was true… if there was a curse placed on the lands to temper Iturri's power…"

"Amon, please tell me you didn't break the seal on the Arima lands to find out," Griffin said, but he knew his old friend was capable of anything, even breaking the cardinal rules laid out by the leader of the Izar herself if his desire for knowledge was great enough. Perhaps having her as a mother was what spawned such a dangerous act of rebellion. Griffin shook his head and sighed, mimicking his once-friend's act of leaning over the rail.

"I met a spirit at the edge of the lands who promised to enlighten me, offer me power beyond my wildest dreams, even more than my mother's. He freely confirmed what the stars had been telling me all along, that there was a barrier placed on the lands to limit Iturri's power—limit our power—and that it was placed there by my mother."

"Whatever she did must not have been without just cause."

"My mother destroys anything that might be seen as a threat to her reign. You know this, Griffin. You've seen it."

"She has kept the world safe for hundreds of years."

"She has kept herself safe!" Amon pounded the railing with his fist. Bats that had been roosting beneath the bridge flew out from under them and off into the night sky. "At the cost of everyone else's power, at the cost of balance to the world, all because she was afraid." He sighed, releasing the tension in his shoulders. "I promised I would always keep you safe. I couldn't tell you sooner because I gave my voice, and other things, as collateral."

"You gave parts of your soul as collateral for whatever bond you struck?" Griffin asked incredulously. Amon nodded. "You know how dangerous that is!"

"No need for lectures or hysterics, Griffin. Not even you with your perfect moral compass can change the past."

"What did you give?"

"I wasn't thinking when I agreed to bind my soul. I only wanted to see the other side of this world… one in which there was no divination or abuse of power."

"What did you give?" Griffin prodded, knowing that whatever Amon had given had to be serious to have him dancing around the issue.

Amon bit his lip. "Willpower for the stone of fire, bones for the stone of earth, emotions for the stone of water, a voice for the stone of air, clarity for the stone of light, a heart for the stone of the spirits, and freedom for the seventh stone."

"But that's your body? Your soul? You gave everything…"

"I know…"

"And what of your bonds?"

"Three remain. The Izar, the Arima, and the seventh… So far."

Griffin narrowed his eyes. "Why do they not have their stone?"

A hint of that childish mischief glimmered in his eyes. "My mother, terrible person that she is, must have stolen it when she locked them away and sent it to a place no one would ever find it."

"But, of course, you found it… Why not hand it over? Be rid of the bond sooner?"

"Because that would've been the end," he said with a frown. "But it won't be long now. It's with her… and she's…" He bit down on his lip, almost ready to draw blood.

"Calm down, Amon. If all that is true then, what you said in the letter… the Zerua king is dead?"

Amon shifted restlessly under the soft moonlight, turning to face Griffin. As he did, Griffin noticed the tell-tale stains of tears in his once-friend's eyes. The warmth in Amon's voice faded away as he spoke, leaving behind a cold, hard truth. "Yes."

Griffin's heart sank at the news. He remembered how much the Zerua king had meant to Amon, the way he had always been a father figure to the boy. Despite the distance between them, Griffin felt a pang of sympathy for Amon. But he couldn't forget the terrible things that Amon had done in service to the bonds, things that were surely inexcusable. And worse still was the fact that he'd been right about the Zerua stone. In no time, the Arima would have everything they needed to go through with the ritual, and it was all his fault.

"Did you know back then what was going to happen?" Griffin asked, his anger beginning to simmer beneath the surface.

Amon stared down at his hand, grazing his fingers over the jagged, star-shaped scar that ran across his palm. "No," he whispered, his voice heavy with regret.

"Did you know how many would have to die?" Griffin growled.

"If I had, do you think I would've gone through with it?" Amon replied, glowering at him, the harshness in his tone a signal that Griffin's words had struck a nerve. "The Prince of Shadows turned me into a vessel for hatred, fuelled by his anger at the ones who'd imprisoned him and syphoned away his power. I spent most of those years trapped in a cage that only resembled my body, Griffin."

"But you chose the darkness, Amon," Griffin reminded him, his voice as cold as the night falling around them.

"I know!" He let the echo of his outburst die and welcomed the silence that filled its place. After a long pause, he unhitched a breath. "I made a mistake. I let my ego, my thirst for knowledge and power, get the better of me. I made a mistake, but now I need to fix it. Please, Griffin, I have no one else."

Griffin scowled. "You don't get to come back, much less ask for my help… Not like this. Especially not after everything you've done."

Amon rested his back against the railing, letting the moonlight hit the back of his head, creating a halo across his crown where one of metal should've rested. Shadows streaked across his face, cast by the waves of onyx hair that hovered in the breeze. His eyes were fixed on a point well beyond whatever was illuminated by the light-reflecting streets. "I never meant to hurt you," he confessed. "I wanted to tell you, but I knew you'd be safer in the dark."

Griffin lowered his head, realizing whom he'd learned that particularly frustrating trait from. He also realised how awful it felt to be on the receiving end of such secrecy despite it being in the name of protection. "Why did you come here, Amon? Because I know it wasn't only for a trip down memory lane."

"I thought I could stop it from happening. I thought if I'd only been there, I could've changed fate…"

Griffin reached out to steady Amon, but hesitated at the last moment, pulling his hand back. "Amon, you're not making any sense," he said. "I've never seen you like this."

Amon sighed heavily. "You asked before why the Arima don't have their stone? Well, I gave it to her. I needed to make sure she was safe. I thought if she had it, she'd finally understand her powers and be able to use them to defend herself. But not even that…"

Griffin's confusion deepened. "I don't understand. Whom are you talking about?"

Amon's face crumpled, tears streaming down his cheeks. "He's got her," he said, his voice barely above a whisper. "He sent Alexei after her, knowing I couldn't be trusted because of what I was starting to feel. I should've known better than to think I had any private thoughts at all…"

"Who?" Griffin asked urgently, a name appearing in his mind that he wished above all else not to hear from Amon's mouth. But of course, he was never wrong…

L. M. SANGUINETTE

"Savara."

EPILOGUE

ELIAS WAS PLAYING TOO CLOSE to the edge of the frozen shore, again. His mother had always warned against it, afraid any manner of creature would come and snap him up for an afternoon snack since he was too little to be anything but. This didn't worry Elias though. He had wandered the coast with his late father many times and he'd never seen such a creature as the ones his mother described. He hadn't seen anything larger than a seal in a long, long time, and though these seals were big, he knew they were nothing to fear.

Elias had a tentative agreement with the king of the seals—or at least, in his mind he did. He would be allowed to lounge between their many hides, so long as he brought them a fish from the village, and for the past few weeks, this innocent deal between a seven-year-old boy and a seven-thousand-year-old seal king remained intact.

Today was no different. Elias had stolen his mother's freshly caught salmon and presented it to the king, as per usual. The king bowed, and with a bark that echoed through the icy valleys, permitted him to once again play amongst the seal pups and snow pits. This time, however, instead of remaining with the herd, Elias followed one of the seal pups—the feisty child of the king—to the edge of the shore.

"You shouldn't stray so far," he said to the young seal pup, imitating his mother's chastising voice. The seal pup squeaked and danced around in a circle. Elias copied him with an innocent laugh until he realised the seal was dancing around something shiny. "What did you find?" He stooped down to get a better look at the strange object embedded in the snow. With his small mittened hand, Elias dusted the flakes from atop the glowing blue orb. It was the size of a large marble, fitting snugly into the centre of his little mittens. "What is it?" Elias asked the seal pup, but when he turned to the poor creature, he found it cowering behind a mound of snow.

"Hello little one," said a voice Elias had never heard before. He turned to find a man dressed in a crisp black suit too fresh for the weather standing before him. Elias thought he looked like the shadows under the ice. "What do you have there?"

Elias frowned and looked up at the man with eyes as blue as the sea and as wide as the ocean. "Mama Aysel says I shouldn't talk to strangers."

"Your Mama Aysel is very smart."

Elias nodded and pursed his lips, realizing that in answering the man, he had spoken to a stranger.

"How about we introduce ourselves, so we become acquaintances instead of strangers?" the shadowy man said.

Elias furrowed his brow, working out the logistics of whether or not that would break his mother's rule, before finally nodding again.

"I, young one, am Adrius, Prince of Shadows," the man said with an illustrious bow.

"My name is Elias. And this is my friend…" he said, inclining his head towards the seal pup. "He's a prince too." The seal pup hid himself further behind the mound.

The shadow man bowed. "A pleasure, Elias and prince pup. Now that we are no longer strangers, would you like to tell me what that is you have found?"

"It's a ball," Elias replied as he held up the orb with both hands, as though a prized possession.

The shadow man smiled. "Are you sure, child? Why don't you look a little closer?"

"I—"

But Elias's thought was cut short, just as his neck was. There was not even time to scream. The blood dripped from the glittering black blade into the pristine white snow as a heavy storm picked up around them. Part of the red shower fell onto the orb, which the Prince of Shadows plucked from Elias's still, mittened hands. The orb began to glow a bright tropical blue, more vibrant than all the seas and all the oceans of all the world.

The Prince of Shadows smiled as he turned it over in his hand. "Four down, three to go," he said, letting his words carry on the wind. And in the blink of an eye, he was gone.

The seal pup nudged at Elias's corpse with his snout, pleading for the young boy to wake. When it finally realised its friend would budge no longer, it let out a wail of sorrow loud enough for the rest of the herd to hear. One by one they too chimed in, elders and young alike. Even the king of seals howled, for he had recognised the young boy for what he was: the rightful heir to the nation of the Ur. Blood stained the white snow like a target for all the world to see, red as the dawn skies of a sailor's nightmare.

Enjoyed this book? Here's a teaser of the first chapter of the third book, **Visanthe Rising**, coming soon to eBook, paperback, and hardcover!

PROLOGUE

General Isaac tugged at the iron chains binding his wrists and ankles to the stone wall behind him. The cold of the granite soothed the welts on his back from the lashing he'd gotten for his dissidence. The dark of the night and the cool mountain air that filtered through a grate in the ceiling came as a blessing. He knew the soldiers who had beaten him had sympathized with his plight, but they couldn't disobey their orders lest they find themselves in a similar position.

He'd lost track of the days since his capture. The routine of his punishment—lashings during the day, nightmares through the night—caused them all to blend into one, though the biting cold would not see him alive much longer if his situation did not improve soon.

On occasion, someone would sneak in to apply salve to his wounds and spoon-feed him a tepid soup. But this was no great mercy. Merely postponement. Someone, it seemed, wanted him alive, but for what purpose, he knew not.

Tonight, however, brought variance to the routine. The sound of heavier footsteps echoed through the cavernous halls beyond his cell. General Isaac raised his head, curious as to who the new, incautious visitor might be. As expected, a different figure strode confidently into the dungeon, the torch in his hand burning a sickly green which matched the emotions he provoked. A sinister grin curled on his face as he admired the torture written across General Isaac's bare skin.

"I must say, Isaac, there is a small part of me that pities the sorry sight you have become," said Councilman Dhoot.

General Isaac kept his mouth shut as he glared defiantly at his superior. The newly appointed councilman had taken too quickly to his position, in his opinion. His eyes lacked their previously characteristic dark circles, now that he was in a position to sleep in more luxurious quarters, with people to wait on him hand and foot.

Councilman Dhoot let out a hissing laugh as he contemplated General Isaac in the shifting green firelight. "Not in the mood to talk at all, I see. Perhaps the guards were not hard enough on you. I thought that the sight of your own blood on the floor beneath you might have had an effect. Clearly, the rope was too soft. Maybe a stoning is in order..."

Still, General Isaac said nothing. He was not going to fall for the goading, knowing all too well that it would only mean additional punishment.

Councilman Dhoot sighed. "I tire of you, Isaac. A boulder would offer better conversation. And here, I thought I might make you an offer at escape from this dungeon…"

"I will not help you in your tyrannical quest for power if that's what you're asking."

"You mistake my motives. I was offering you a chance at glory. I see promise in you, Isaac, but if I am to allow you a place in my new regime, you will need to learn to take orders."

"There is nothing glorious about what you are doing," General Isaac said, attempting to keep the rage building within from shining through his tone.

"Bringing fruitful lands under our domain to offer better lives to our people is not glorious?"

"You only plan to enrich yourself. The impoverished of our lands will see none of it. And that says nothing of the casualties the Ur will surely face."

Councilman Dhoot raised an eyebrow; his brow bone being highlighted by the glow of the flames. "And here, it sounds as if you are more indebted to a people not your own. Tsk, tsk, tsk. More reason you should be hanged… but I am yet merciful."

"You can't believe me to be so dense…" General Isaac scoffed through laboured breaths. "You're keeping me alive to use as a scapegoat in the event that your plans do not pan out as expected."

"Well…" Councilman Dhoot brandished another wicked grin, licking his pointed incisors as he prided himself on the perfection of his plan. "It seems that blockish head of yours is filled with something other than your pathetic ideas of morality and justice after all. Little good it will do you. I do not intend to let you out of this cell unless otherwise necessary. Either you will be tried and hanged, or your corpse will rot here indefinitely."

Councilman Dhoot turned confidently on his heels, leaving General Isaac the way he'd found him. General Isaac waited until the echo of the councilman's footfall faded into nothingness. Only then did he unhitch a laboured breath. He smiled into the darkness.

So… I was right all along…

General Isaac bit down on the laugh that was forming in his throat. The councilman was just as dense as he'd imagined. His ego had somehow landed itself in the clouds since the promotion. This, General Isaac knew, he could use to his advantage.

Above him, what little moonlight filtered through previously had faded. Clouds blotted out the rest of the lights in the sky. General Isaac cast his gaze upwards, the hairs on his neck and arms rising with a further drop in temperature. His smile widened. The sweet scent of rain quickly followed, along with a rhythmic clap of thunder.

It seems Iturri is on my side, after all, he thought.

The soldiers who had chained him to the dungeon walls had forgotten to chain his feet. An oversight on their part that General Isaac had been waiting to exploit, but not before finding out who was behind the troubles of his land. The incompetent councilman had ousted himself. Under the guise of the storm, Iturri was allowing him to work unheard and unseen. This was the only chance he was going to get at an escape. He would not waste it.

* * *

An invitation arrived unceremoniously on the doorsteps of each of the ruling houses of Visanthe. This invitation was not only unexpected but very much unwelcome by all. The messengers alone struck fear in the hearts of all those who witnessed them. Even the skies seemed to take a turn for the worse with the arrival of the strange roll of parchment.

Shadows swept through the streets, following the path from each nation's gate to its palace. Upon arrival, the shadows pulled themselves together into eerie, person-like forms—featureless save for beady, red eyes. These figures waited patiently, hands outstretched, holding a single piece of dusty, rolled parchment. They stood through shifts in weather and climates, unmoved and unaffected by the world around them. Not even the various palace guards, with their exceptional training and prowess, could shake the stance of these creatures.

Queen Noor regarded the outstretched hand of the shadow before her with narrowed eyes. Initially thinking it was a living creature, she'd tried freezing its internal organs, but there were none to be found. The shadow was nothing more than a dust shifting in the breeze. Her guards had attempted slashing through it as well, but the figure's body simply dissipated at the point of impact before reforming unscathed. She quickly realized there would be little use in any further attacks on it. Instead, she ordered away her guards and the stragglers of her court and sat a small distance away from it, arms interlaced over her chest, staring into the glowing red of its eyes in challenge.

Various hours passed by, unnoticed and void of action, save for the growing potential for trouble. Queen Noor anticipated dangerous whisperings throughout her kingdom of the arrival of such a creature on their shores, but there was little that could be done to quell the anxieties of her people after the shadow's audacious entrance. Both she and it remained unfazed by the slow traversal of the sun across the sky. Her own shadow followed the shifting light, creeping up to the edges of the intruder in tune with the setting sun. Still, she waited.

The moon climbed higher and higher into the sky. She could feel the strength of it in the swelling tides around her—strength she would need in the event that this shadow came prepared for a fight. The shadow remained still, statuesque, hand outstretched, holding the roll of parchment. Once night finally descended, and the rest of the shifting shadows of daylight disappeared, Queen Noor rose from her seat.

She drew closer to it, never once breaking eye contact with the creature. Slowly but surely, she reached out for the scroll. Her hand closed gently around the parchment which, unlike the shadow, was entirely stiff and tangible. Then, noticing release, its eyes disappeared. Startled, Queen Noor took a sudden step backwards as the shadow, having now completed its task, dissipated into nothing.

* * *

"I have told you once before, Bismuth, and I will say it again. I will not be king," he said as he stared at the shadowy creature and its outstretched hand.

This same conversation had haunted their interactions ever since the funeral, always in the background, lingering like a sour aftertaste on his tongue. But the appearance of the creature brought the topic front and centre. From his bed in the hospital wing, he'd seen its ominous arrival, watching as the clouds darkened and parted as its shadowy dust swept through the streets of Haizea before pulling itself into the singular, almost human form.

Bismuth shook his head in dismay and stepped towards the shadow. He made a show of attempting to take the roll of parchment from its hand, but the dust comprising the creature flooded over the scroll, making it just as intangible as the creature itself.

"It watches you and you alone," Bismuth said, turning back to him with a frown. "Ever since its arrival, its eyes have been on you, as if knowing—"

"I have sworn to our late king, to Iturri even, that I shall not be king. Have someone else handle this situation," he said, holding firm to the oath sworn to the friend he'd accidentally killed in his youth to never take up the bloodied throne.

"We have had all our guards attempt to vanquish the creature. All with the same results as I." Finally, noticing reason would not sway him, Bismuth signalled for him to step towards the creature and attempt to take the scroll himself.

He let out a heavy sigh, relenting to the old guard's prodding. He hobbled towards it, still lending part of his weight to a cane given to him in his recovery. The beast of a man who had scorched his back with lightning had left him with significant damage to his internals. He was doing his best to keep up his strength, but his nerves still had a ways to go before he would be back in fighting condition. Part of him wondered why he had survived at all, and he knew better than to attribute his continued life to Bismuth's healings alone. Such an attack should have left no room for healing, let alone survival. But he, like Bismuth, had begun to believe in what, for him, was the worst possible outcome—divine intervention.

Brass came face to face with the creature, staring into the glow of its beady red eyes, and finding a part of himself knowing what was about to happen. Before the shadow vanished into thin air, before his fingers closed around the scroll, before he'd even raised his hand... staring into the creature's eyes, he knew what the outcome would be.

Thunder rolled through the sea of clouds above them as a gentle shower began to fall. For him, the rain had always been a symbol of renewal, revival, of better times ahead. But this rain, gentle as it was, felt heavy as it seeped through his robes. A new beginning waited on the horizon, tangling itself with the scent of water on weathered stone... but a soft voice in the back of his mind wondered if it wasn't the beginning of the end.

Brass turned back to Bismuth, scroll in hand, unable to hide the frown that had settled on his face. They exchanged a single, knowing glance; their suspicions having been confirmed at that moment.

"It seems, my king," said Bismuth, "the choice is no longer yours. Iturri has chosen for you."

If you enjoyed this book, please feel free to leave a review of it on your favourite sites. These reviews help small-time authors like me reach new audiences and are much appreciated!

Stay up to date on L. M. Sanguinette's new releases and giveaways by signing up for her mailing list or following her on social media. Find all the links on the page below:

https://linktr.ee/lmsanguinette

Be on the lookout for **VISANTHE RISING,** book 3 of the Legend of the Stones series, coming in 2024!

ACKNOWLEDGMENTS

When I first had the idea for *Welcome to Visanthe,* the story looked vastly different from what it has become. First of all, there weren't supposed to be three books. The original story was entirely self-contained. There were fewer characters, and the ones that were there in the first iteration weren't nearly as dynamic and fleshed out as they have become. Upon speaking with my editor, Cara Flannery, way back in 2020, she helped me to realize that there was so much more to the story that needed to be told. A big thank you to you, Cara, and your team at FlukyFiction for all the hard work and support. This series would not be what it is now without you.

Secondly, I'd like to acknowledge the extraordinary work done on both the hardcover and paperback editions by the brilliant cover artists at MiblArt. Tania, Nadia, and the team knew exactly how to take the loose ideas in my head and turn them into a cohesive series that looks spectacular on the shelf. Every time I see these covers a smile grows on my face, knowing not only that the ideas in my head were given life, but that others around the world enjoy them as much as I do, if not more. I'd also like to thank my incredible cartographer for the wonderful depiction of Visanthe.

Next, I want to say thank you to my friends in the bookstagram community, Sonia, Fiona, Roxy, Fae, Assia, Marcia, Jasmine, Kiera, Britt, and Jenn, whose support throughout this publishing process gave me the strength to push forward, even when my impostor syndrome wanted to hold me back, and the drive to keep improving both my writing and storytelling abilities. This one is for you girls. Thank you all from the bottom of my heart.

Also in the bookstagram community, I'd like to thank those at Storygram Tours and MTMC Tours for helping to push my books out to a broader audience, and for their support of indie authors around the globe. They were a pleasure to work with and made the digital tour process both easy and exciting.

This next one is a bit of a strange one, but I thought I'd bring it up here too, especially after the mention of indie authorship. The other day, when I was cleaning out an inbox I hadn't touched in over a decade (side note, did you know cleaning out email is actually good for the environment? Saves space on servers across the globe which means less resource consumption, etc. Sorry, tech rant over), I came across one of the first rejection letters I'd ever received for a book I don't even remember writing back when I was thirteen. Clearly, I had always wanted to be a writer. This rejection letter, which explained how surprised they were to see the quality of writing and storytelling that thirteen-year-old me was capable of (which wasn't great but with work could be) is now framed and hanging on my wall as a constant reminder of how far I have come and how much you can achieve when you put your mind to something. Thank you for the rejections that made me what I am today.

Moving on to someone who has no idea they are getting a mention but will appreciate it while reading this on his vacation, I'd like to thank my day job manager, Tom, for being the first one to purchase a copy of my first book and sitting through the "whiny, angsty, main character and lack of violence." Don't worry, Tom, message received, loud and clear. I hope this book had more enjoyable action.

I'd also like to say a special thank you to my life companions, Jade, Rachele, Sara, Megan, Tiffany, and Emma, who have all had to sit through readings of scenes at odd hours because my emotions were running high, and I needed someone to share them with. They have probably already heard the best parts of this book many times over, but still share in my happiness each time I read to them. They have been a great source of motivation and I am extremely grateful to have friends like them. Love you girls!

Speaking of emotions running high, there were many times when, for one reason or another, I didn't feel I could write due to the weight of certain feelings. During these times, I had a special guiding light that led me to the end of the tunnel, so to speak. Thank you to my partner, Michael, for making sure I got the words from my head to the page and for never letting me sink. This book may very well have never been written without him.

Finally, I would be nothing without the love and support of my family. This first thank you goes out to my parents, for letting me be the quirky little witch with too many fairy tales in her head, and for pushing me to be the best version of myself in whatever I choose to do. Thank you for always supporting my passions, even when you didn't understand them. And, of course, thank you to my siblings, for reminding me not to take life so seriously, and for being the reason I want to do better, I love you guys.

OTHER WORKS

Also available in hardcover!

POETRY COLLECTIONS

COMING SOON…

Of Arrows And Roses (A Visanthian Novel)

ABOUT THE AUTHOR

L. M. Sanguinette was born on a small island in the Caribbean, where the palm trees watched over her like giants and the sea crept up to her feet to say hello. Ever since she was little, she surrounded herself with tales of fantasy and magic, hoping that one day, she too would be involved in a story like the ones that captured her imagination.

Years—and many rewatching's of Avatar the Last Airbender—later, she is happily living in the worlds that her mind created, filling her bookshelves with more books than she will ever read, and practising her own version of magic.

When she's not sitting at the computer, she can be found snorkelling near forgotten shores, twisting from silks that hang from the ceilings, or in one of the many hidden coffee shops of Madrid, conversing with the spirits of the old city and dreaming up new adventures.